VENGEANCE IS MINE

VENGEANCE IS MINE

WALTER GOFF II
CAPT USN, (RET)

FRANKLIN GREEN
PUBLISHING
www.franklingreenpublishing.com

ISBN 978-1-936487-370

Library of Congress Cataloging-in-Publication Data has been applied for.

Cover and Interior Design: Bill Kersey, www.kerseygraphics.com

Dedication

This book is dedicated to my beautiful wife, Sandra E. Goff. She is the mother of our children and a true Proverbs 31 woman.

ACKNOWLEDGMENTS

My wife, Sandra, is always my helpmate. Her professional skill, her exceptional guidance, and her keen insight into my thoughts have ensured that the storyline moves forward at a rapid pace. Her precise sense of detail guarantees the accuracy of the characters, the portrayal of the locations, and a thousand other details. There are insufficient words of praise for her assistance, her commentary, her criticism, and her love.

This is my second novel with the leading characters Dr. William Chandler and his wife Holly. My first book, *Chain of Command*, published by Word Publishing, came out eighteen years ago and was recently rereleased in paperback and electronic media by Franklin Green Publishing, LLC. Both stories are in print thanks to the efforts of Lee Gessner. Lee is not only a consummate professional but is also a true friend. His presence at a crucial time in our lives will never be forgotten. My gratitude also goes to Mary Sanford for her editing skills and Bill Kersey for his wonderful artistic talents in design and layout. Major G. Allen Kruse III USMC (RET), my son-in-law, has been an invaluable asset for critique and technical information. These people are all gifts given to me by the One to whom I give the highest praise, my Savior the Lord Jesus Christ. HE has given me the talent for all I have accomplished in life, including writing this novel.

PROLOGUE

The Ferrari's low rumble resonated against the trees and disturbed the quiet night. A man in his late forties and a much younger woman sat motionless in the bucket seats. Sedated by drugs placed in their drinks earlier in the evening, they had been driven to this lonely location. Their deaths, from an ice pick-like blade skillfully inserted at the base of the skull, came quickly.

The assassin positioned the man's hands on the steering wheel. A block of ice pushed the foot pedal to the floor; the RPMs pushed dangerously near the red line. The engine screamed a murderous rhapsody as the transmission engaged. The red convertible shot forward, sheared off the guardrail, and launched into the air three hundred feet above the Pacific Ocean. Crashing waves muffled the impact's sound. In the quiet moments as the foaming cold surf retreated from the shore, a seagull's razor-sharp screech lamented the death and destruction that lay in the shallow water.

Silently, a dark automobile drifted to a lazy stop near the edge of the cliff. Slowly the back door opened and a short, slightly built figure stepped from the car and walked noiselessly to the rail. Stepping past the broken guardrail, he surveyed the wreckage in the pale gray light of the predawn morning. He stood, hands behind his back, and swayed slightly forward on his toes. Several minutes passed. He wanted to remember all that lay before him. Quietly, he walked back to the car and got into the backseat.

"Cloth!" It was an order, not a request.

"Yes, sir," the driver replied with a respectful subservience mixed with fear.

As he took the cloth, Koto methodically wiped the dust from his highly polished leather shoes and then looked at the figure seated next to him. His eyes narrowed; the dark black evil of his soul showed through. The distinctly Asian features of his face appeared twisted and grotesque. "You do very nice work," he paused, "for a—" he stopped abruptly.

"For a woman," she murmured, a voice hardened with bitterness.

"Ah, I am not used to such efficiency and elegance by so beautiful a woman in dispatching a problem from my life."

"I believe there is the matter of the remainder of my fee," she stated.

The only sound that broke the silence within the car was the distant surf. The two dead bodies, three hundred feet below, were forgotten.

"Yes, the price; in the beauty of the act, I'd forgotten there is money involved," Koto said as he picked up his cell phone and pushed one of the buttons.

"This is Han," came the answer on the other end of the line.

"You may make the transfer now," Koto replied, pushed the button, and broke the connection.

"Drive on!" he ordered the chauffer.

Obediently, the driver pulled onto the highway and headed for San Francisco. For the next thirty minutes, no other cars met or passed them, which gave credence to the loneliness of that part of California's northern coast. The man and the woman sat in silence and watched the passing trees as a new day dawned.

A short time later, a pager chirped three short beeps. She opened it and read the message displayed on the LED. "The fund transfer is complete," she announced. "I have a car in the next town. I'll get out there."

As they entered the town, she pointed to a parking lot, where a single car sat next to a deserted restaurant. "Let me out there."

The limousine drifted to a stop ten yards from the car. The door locks released automatically. Her gloved hand took hold of the door's handle.

Koto, intrigued by the black leather gloves, thought, *A womanly, if not sensual, touch.*

"If you should need anything in the future, you may contact me in the same manner as before," she said.

"I would like to entertain you at my estate some weekend." He always liked Western women for a tryst.

"No, you wouldn't," she said.

"Oh, why is that?" he questioned.

"I don't think you are into pain," she replied as she exited the limousine and walked toward her parked car. The sway of her hips accentuated her tight, fitted black jumpsuit, and her stiletto heels exaggerated her height.

How can a beautiful creature like that kill so efficiently? he thought to himself.

"Take me to the office," Koto commanded.

As they continued toward San Francisco, Koto reflected on the events that had precipitated this action.

The door opened and Han (his butler and bodyguard) entered the room; he stood quietly.

Lee Koto looked up. He motioned Han forward with a wave of his hand.

"I apologize for the interruption, but Ned Litten of Litten Industries asked to speak to you on the telephone," Han explained.

"Did he say what he wanted to talk to me about?" Koto inquired.

"No, he would not tell me, but he said it was very important," Han answered.

Koto nodded his head yes.

Han hurried from the room to transfer the call.

Seconds later, his phone rang. "Hello," Koto said.

"Mr. Koto, this is Ned Litten from Litten Industries." The man's voice hesitated as he spoke.

"What may I do for you, Mr. Litten?" Koto replied.

"Well . . ." he stammered and paused.

"Please tell me," Koto coaxed. "I'm certain it is important, or you would not have called at this hour."

"I can't give you any more codes and airplane information. This has to stop, and you can't use the three I gave you." Ned hoped he sounded forceful, but his voice cracked slightly.

"Mr. Litten, I believe you owe me a great deal of money for services rendered at one of my casinos. Is that not true?"

"Yes," Ned replied.

"Are you in the position to pay it back with the interest which has accrued?"

Silence dominated as Ned held the phone to his ear. Then, with conviction in his voice, he said, "Mr. Koto, what we are doing is wrong. It's immoral; it's criminal. I am prepared to go to court to fight any charges which may be leveled at me. Are you?"

Calmly, Lee Koto answered, "Mr. Litten, I'm sure that if we sit down together, we can come to an agreement. I will come to the United States next Monday. Why don't we meet at my office?"

"Okay, I'll wait until then before I contact the authorities. However, I don't want to meet at your office any more than you want to meet at mine. I propose we meet at the Coastal View Inn in Mendocino County."

"The Coastal View Inn? Where is that located?" Koto questioned.

"It's about a three-hour drive north of San Francisco. They have private cottages on a large estate with complete privacy and security. No one will bother us, and I can assure you they provide complete secrecy." Ned was sweating, but authority had returned to his voice.

"That will be agreeable," Koto answered. "Will you make the reservations?"

"I'd like that. This will be just you and me. Correct? I mean, none of your—"

"Ned, I am a businessman, not an American gangster," Koto replied.

"Next Monday then. I'll let you know the time. And, Mr. Koto," Ned said.

"Yes?" Koto answered.

"I know we can reach a satisfactory conclusion," Ned reiterated.

"Yes, Mr. Litten. I am certain this can be settled quickly." Koto ended the call. "HAN!" Koto uncharacteristically shouted.

Running into the room, Han answered, "Yes, Mr. Koto."

"I want someone with very special talents, preferably an American. Mr. Litten must have an accident, and it must be soon," Lee Koto stated in a normal voice.

"Yes, Koto," Han replied.

The next day, Han brought Koto the name of an assassin who would fulfill Koto's contract.

As the black limousine continued its journey toward the Golden Gate Bridge, Koto concentrated on the evil committed against his mother that fateful day, August 6, 1945, in Hiroshima, Japan. Koto whispered to the spirit of his dead mother, "It won't be long now, Mother." Lee Koto's desire for vengeance weaved like a thread of steel throughout his body, mind, and soul. The Chinese had named 2003 the Black Sheep Year. Lee Koto liked that. This would be a good year.

1

WILLIAM CHANDLER–POTOMAC, MARYLAND

Spring 2003

"Bill! Answer the phone!" Holly shouted down the stairs.

He ran through the foyer toward the kitchen phone. "Hello!" he answered. A dial tone was the reward for his expended effort. Bill threw the paper, still in its wet plastic cover, onto the counter.

"Who was it?" Holly asked as she turned the corner from the bottom of the stairway.

"Don't know, didn't make it in time," he answered.

"Ugh, you're wet," she said as she rubbed her hand through his wet hair and slicked it back like one of the new hairstyles in a men's magazine.

"It's raining out there. Leave the locks alone!" he protested playfully as he took her in his arms and kissed her tenderly.

"Good morning, Dr. Chandler," she teased.

"Good morning to you, Mrs. Chandler," he said and smiled at her.

Holly pulled from his grasp and busied herself with the cappuccino machine.

Bill watched her for several seconds and then slid the paper carefully from its wet plastic wrapper. The gurgling of the milk's steam signaled him to start the microwave.

They were halfway through the morning breakfast of coffee and bagels when the phone rang again.

"Hello," he said.

"Dr. Chandler?" the voice asked.

"Yes."

"Dr. William Chandler?"

"Who wants to know?" He was suspicious. Several years earlier, he had been drawn into a nightmare experience with a group of renegade ex-CIA agents. Since then he had received more than his share of nuisance calls.

"This is the sheriff of Sonoma County, California."

"I'm Bill Chandler, what can I do for you, Sheriff?" Bill asked.

"Do you know a Theodore Litten?" the sheriff asked.

"Ned Litten?"

"We have identification of Theodore M. Litten from San Francisco."

"Yes, I know him. I always call him Ned, a nickname from childhood."

"I'm afraid I have some bad news. He's been killed in an accident."

"Killed? It can't be; I talked to him just a few days ago. When? Where? How?"

"I can't go into all of that now, but you were listed in his billfold as the person to contact in case of emergency." He paused. "Are you related?"

"Related?" Bill's mind moved into that state where reality and the past begin to merge in ways that don't always make sense. "Uh no, not by blood, I mean, we aren't really relatives, but we grew up together kind of like brothers."

"Well, I am very sorry, Mr. Chandler, to have to let you know like this. Do you know how I can get in touch with any of his relatives? We haven't been able to locate any yet."

"He doesn't have any close relatives alive that I know of," Bill stated and stared off into space.

Holly sat on a kitchen stool and anxiously watched Bill as she tried to piece together the conversation.

"Do you know who I would contact for the arrangements?" the sheriff questioned.

"Sorry, Sheriff, I didn't hear what you said; I was thinking," Bill said.

"Well, Mr. Chandler, do you know who would make the arrangements for him, that is, for his funeral?" the sheriff asked again.

"I suppose I would," Bill replied.

"If you could let me know the arrangements as soon as possible, I'd appreciate it," the sheriff said.

"Okay, Sheriff, I'll make arrangements and get there as soon as I can." Bill started to hang up the phone but paused and said, "Say, Sheriff, where are you located again?"

The sheriff gave Bill the contact information.

He quickly wrote down the address and phone number. "Can you suggest a hotel in the vicinity?"

"Sonoma county is just north of San Francisco," the sheriff answered.

"Well, if it's close to San Francisco, maybe we'll stay there."

"It's almost a two-hour drive north," the sheriff replied.

"Oh, not quite close enough. We'll find a hotel closer. I know this must be a tough part of your job and, well, thanks." He hung up the phone.

"Bill, what happened?" Holly asked.

"Ned was killed in an accident yesterday morning."

"Ned?" she questioned.

"Ned Litten; I've told you about him. We grew up together," he replied.

"Where, how?" Holly asked.

"He didn't want to give me all the details on the phone, but apparently he had a car wreck yesterday morning north of San Francisco."

Holly got up, put her arms around his shoulders, and laid her head against his. "Bill, I'm so sorry, he must have been a very close friend."

Bill spent the rest of the day rearranging meetings and reassigning projects at his company, Chandler Electronics, which developed Tel-Ray and manufactured other security products.

Holly made reservations for the flight, for a motel, and for a rental car. By the time Bill returned home, she had them packed and ready to go.

"Our flight is early; we have to be at National by six thirty in the morning, but it gets us in at about ten," Holly said.

"Thanks," Bill replied. "I think I have everything taken care of at the office. I really don't know how long this will take. I certainly don't look forward to another funeral." He stared off into space.

"I know, I'm really sorry you have to do this."

The next morning, they flew to San Francisco and picked up the rental car.

"Let's drive to the sheriff's office before we check in," Bill said.

"That's fine; I guaranteed the room for late arrival; I thought you'd probably want to go there first."

"You're always one step ahead of me, aren't you?" Bill said appreciatively.

"Just call me a mind reader," Holly quipped.

The warm sun and clear skies provided a perfect day as they drove the convertible across the Golden Gate Bridge and headed for Healdsburg, California.

2

KOTO INTERNATIONAL—SAN FRANCISCO

"Mr. Koto, please forgive the interruption, but there are some visitors to see you," said Han.

"Thank you, Han. Make them wait ten minutes and then show them in," Lee Koto instructed.

He was still basking in the pleasure and satisfaction of the vengeance he had experienced yesterday. The death of Ned Litten would also allow him to enlarge his international holdings by acquiring Litten Industries. With that procurement, his illegal profits would also increase. Personally, he needed only a few of the codes for his own use. The rest he could sell at a tremendous profit. *This morning's meeting with the American representative of the shadowy Mr. Smith will provide me with a significant sum—all tax free,* he thought.

Han bowed respectfully as he took two steps backward before turning and striding out the door.

Koto International owned the thirty-story building. Decorated by a Japanese decorator, Koto's office occupied the entire thirtieth floor and overlooked the San Francisco Bay. A large modern desk and a chair sat near the window. In the middle of the room sat a couch and a chair. A simple table and a beautiful bonsai plant sat between them. An oriental rug adorned this sitting area. On the far wall, an ancient Samurai sword sat on the credenza. Though in a scabbard, its blade retained the sharpness the original master sword-maker had painstakingly created. Behind a retractable oriental screen, a narrow passageway led to a room filled with incredible electronic communications equipment. Facing the monitors, a single chair served as Koto's throne. From his seat of power, Lee Koto could review his empire throughout the world. Only a few of his most trusted employees ever saw beyond the retractable panel in his office.

The door quietly opened as Koto gazed at the graceful line of the suspension cables in the distance. Ironically, Bill and Holly Chandler were in the middle of the bridge's span at that very moment.

"Mr. Emmet Adkins," Han announced.

"Mr. Koto, great to see you again!" The tall American strode quickly across the room with his hand outstretched. His cowboy boots accentuated the significant difference in height between the compact Asian and the tall American.

Lee Koto bowed respectfully and ignored the handshake. Smiling, but still ignoring the outstretched hand, he said, "Mr. Adkins, how very nice to see you again."

This immediately created a feeling of awkwardness for Emmet. Finally, he let his hand drop to his side and unsuccessfully suppressed his embarrassment and his anger.

"Would you be so kind as to sit down? Can I offer you some tea?" Koto questioned as he registered Emmet's emotions.

"Tea, uh, no—could use a cup of coffee, if you have any," Emmet replied.

"Han, please bring our guest a cup of coffee," Koto said to his aid. Koto kept his eyes fixed on the tall American. He escorted Emmet to the sofa and sat across from him on the tall straight-backed chair. The sofa, unusually low, made the oversized American uncomfortable. The chair Koto sat in gave him a height advantage he didn't have when they stood.

"Now tell me, Mr. Adkins," Koto started to say.

"Emmet, call me Emmet," he said.

"Emmet, how can I, your humble servant, be of assistance to you?"

"Cut the bull, Koto. You know why I'm here. Now that Litten's out of the way, let's do some business."

"Oh, has something happened to Mr. Litten?" Koto asked with feigned Asian kindness in his voice.

"Yeah, I read in the paper he had a car wreck up the coast. He had some bimbo with him. Must not have been keeping his eyes on the road, you know what I mean? It sounds like he drove off the cliff into the ocean." He laughed with a deep horselaugh that was more of a mockery of the man's death than the sick joke he tried to make.

Koto ignored the crass remark, which added more unspoken tension to the room.

Han arrived with a tray that held two cups and a sterling silver coffee urn. Steam emanated from its spout. He poured a cup of the hot black liquid into an antique blue and white china cup and bowed as he handed it to the American. He then gave Koto a cup of the pale green liquid and set it down quietly before he withdrew with another bow.

"Now, Mr. Adkins, I believe you wanted to see me about some business?"

"You bet your sweet ass." Emmet paused; his language and manners had started to make him feel ill at ease. *I hate dealing with these people!* Emmet thought to himself. *We kicked their butts in World War II, and we should never have let our foot off their necks!* "Mr. Smith wants to buy five more of the codes today and is prepared to give you the price you requested. Half now, and the other half after the first code is used and operates as you advertised."

"Now, I can only offer you the two items that Mr. Smith and I previously negotiated. I cannot give you any more until I own Litten Industries," Lee Koto said. "Until we determine if Mr. Litten had any living relatives, I don't have access to any more codes. However, I am certain I will soon own Litten Industries and all of his assets." He paused and looked at Emmet.

"Okay, I'm ready to make the transfer of funds for the two that you and Mr. Smith previously negotiated. Just tell me when and where. Remember, Mr. Smith also wants at least five more codes as quickly as possible."

Koto pushed a button and Han appeared. "Give Mr. Adkins the information."

Han walked to Emmet, bowed, and handed him a document folder. He said nothing and then withdrew.

"You and Mr. Smith previously agreed that you'll get half now and half when the first plane is tested." Emmet took his cell phone and tapped a speed dial number. "I'll make the money transfer now," he said as he looked at Koto. "Hello," Emmet said. "I have the codes; you may complete the transfer." He listened and then answered, "Yes, Mr. Smith; I'll call you later." Emmet Adkins broke the connection and carefully placed the document in his briefcase.

Koto stood.

"As for any new work that Litten Industries might do, Mr. Smith promises to be a good customer." Emmet extended his hand again and looked Koto in the eyes with a look that dared him not to take it.

Koto, a shrewd businessman, quickly took the large white hand in his delicate almond-colored hand and shook it in the most Western manner he knew.

"Ya never know when ya might want to be sure which plane you get on, if ya know what I mean," Emmet said and laughed. "I think that's all we have to talk about, so I am out of here. I got a lot to do today. Ain't every day I add a whole new prospective to our business." Emmet, without being asked, started for the door.

"Mr. Adkins," Koto said.

"Yeah?"

"It's always nice to do business with you." He bowed deeply as Emmet turned on his heel and left the room.

Emmet left Koto's office and strode to the bank of elevators. Two other Americans stood by the open elevator door and followed Emmet into the six-by-six-foot box. The door closed quietly, and the elevator began its descent to the parking garage. Mirrors, polished brass, and walnut adorned the elevator walls and told of the money that moved daily through the office suite. Emmet and the other Americans did not know that video cameras, placed behind the mirrors, and sensitive microphones, embedded in the surrounding walls, picked up the most closely guarded conversations.

"So, how'd it go, Emmet?" the shorter of the associates asked.

"Not a hitch. We got what we came for."

"What about that guy Koto?" the other asked.

"He's useful for what he's useful for," Emmet answered.

"That guy, Han, gives me the willies," the shorter man stated.

"Yeah, well, I wish we never had to do business with any of them, but business is business," Emmet answered.

The elevator reached the parking garage and slowed to a gentle stop. The three men disembarked and walked into the nearly deserted garage.

"So where's the car?" Emmet asked.

"I parked it right here!" the aid protested.

Roaring like a lion announcing its arrival, an engine rumbled to life. The three men stopped and looked at each other, then squinted into the darkness. As the tires screeched and accelerated toward them, both aids pulled nine-millimeter semiautomatic pistols from shoulder holsters and crouched into firing positions. The darkened windows of the Suburban completely obscured the driver and any occupants. Adrenalin surged through all three men's veins, accelerated their pulses, and made their mouths dry. As the brakes were suddenly applied, the vehicle slid sideways toward the trio, then stopped.

Cautiously, the shorter man grabbed the front door handle with his left hand, still holding the pistol in his right hand. He jerked the door open and aimed into the interior.

"Hi, Uncle!" a grinning teenager said from behind the wheel. "Need a lift?"

"What the hell are you doing here?" Emmet demanded. "You coulda gotten yourself killed with a stunt like that!"

"Ah, I thought it was funny."

"Like I asked, what are you doing here?" Emmet questioned.

"Your secretary told me you had a meeting here. I was on the train when I called her. She said I could try to catch up with you here and get a ride home. When I saw your car, I decided to hot wire it and surprise you. Bet you were really surprised."

Emmet climbed into the front seat, and with one of his massive hands, ruffled his nephew's hair. "I was surprised all right, but you could have gotten yourself killed. Now take us home. Get in, guys."

Koto, fumed by the meeting, worried that these Americans might become a problem. *They have enough information about the aircraft; they think they can demand anything they want. It will soon be time to rid myself of Mr. Adkins and Mr. Smith,* he thought.

3

SONOMA COUNTY, CALIFORNIA

The sheriff's office, located in the municipal building, faced the Healdsburg town square. Several black and white squad cars sat in front.

Bill pulled into an empty space across the street and stopped the engine. He turned to look at Holly and then surveyed where they would go next. "I guess that's the place," he said.

"Yes, must be, at least that's where the patrol cars like to hang out," she quipped.

Bill exited the car and walked around it. He leaned on the door before opening it for Holly. "Are all of the days out here as beautiful as this?" he asked, since he knew she had been raised in California.

"No, some of them are better," she answered.

They walked hand in hand across the street, up the steps, and entered through old glass and brass doors probably set in place before the turn of the nineteenth century. It was cool and a little dark in the hallway, but a sign clearly announced the sheriff's office. A bar stood in the reception area and gave the room the appearance of an old west saloon. Behind the desk, a young woman sat on a barstool and talked on the phone.

"Yes, Sally, I'll be sure and tell him just as soon as he gets back, but it will be late, since he went clear to Edmonton." She hung up the phone and turned to greet the visitors.

"May I help you?"

"I'm Bill Chandler; I'd like to see Sheriff Sparks."

"Oh, Mr. Chandler, the sheriff said you'd be coming today. He had to go to the doctor's office for a few minutes; he should be right back. Would you like to have a seat?"

"We've been sitting in planes and cars all day. I think we'll go for a short walk around the square. How's that sound, Holly?" Bill asked.

"You won't get any argument from me," she responded. "Isn't this a beautiful little town?" Holly asked.

They crossed the street to the park and angled toward a pharmacy on the far corner. As they passed the park's bandstand, Bill heard someone call him.

"Dr. Chandler! Dr. Chandler! Wait!"

They turned and saw a man in uniform and a cowboy hat run toward them.

Bill and Holly waited at the bandstand for the person to catch up.

"Dr. Chandler, I'm Sheriff Sparks, Sonoma County Sheriff," he said as he held out his hand.

Bill took his hand and shook it with a firm grip; each man gazed intently at the other. "Glad to meet you; this is my wife, Holly," Bill said as he motioned toward her with his head.

"Nice to meet you, ma'am," the sheriff said as he touched the brim of his hat.

"Do you want to come back to my office or talk here?"

"Can we sit here? It's such a beautiful day," Holly said.

They sat on separate benches.

The sheriff took off his hat, laid it down, and absentmindedly ran his finger along the brim as he stared at the two strangers.

Bill and Holly waited in silence.

"Well, there isn't much to tell. According to the coroner's report, it looks like your friend, Theodore Litten, and his girlfriend, were doing some heavy drugs and fell asleep at the wheel. The toxicology screen is not finished, but from the pills found in the glove box, I suspect they were high. Missed a T intersection over by the ocean and drove off a three-hundred-foot cliff onto the rocks below," Sheriff Sparks commented in a very professional and nonemotional way.

Holly held Bill's arm with both hands. Bill sat rigid as he listened to the story.

"Is there anything you can add that would help the investigation? Had he been into the drug scene, or did he have a history of usage?" the sheriff asked.

As the oak trees swayed in the wind, Bill stared at them for several seconds before he answered. "Ned and I grew up together. We were as close as brothers until I went to college. We still talked occasionally and wrote a few letters, but honestly, until about three weeks ago, I hadn't heard from him in several years. I called him when Holly and I were married, but he couldn't come to the wedding. Said his business was at a critical stage in negotiations with some international firm for something immense and important. I told him good luck; he wished us the best," Bill said.

"You said he called you three weeks ago?" the sheriff queried.

"Yes, just out of the blue. I took the call; Bill wasn't home," Holly answered.

"Did he say anything that might tie into any of this?"

"No, just asked if Bill could call when he got in," she replied. "I told him it might be better to call him at work. So I gave him the number."

Bill continued, "He called and I talked with him for about an hour, mostly catching up on small talk and reminiscing about old times. He said he wished we could have the old times back."

"Does that mean anything to you in light of what happened?" the sheriff asked.

"Not really, but one thing was unusual: he insisted that I sign some papers he was going to send me. He said it had to do with his company, and that I was the only one he would trust with it."

"Did you?"

"Pardon?"

"Did you receive and sign some papers for him?"

"Yes, they arrived the next morning. I signed them and sent them back the same day."

"What were they?"

"He made me the executor of his estate," Bill murmured.

The sheriff sat in silence and eyed Bill and Holly. "And now he turns up dead three weeks later. Kind of ironic . . ." The words hung in the air not blown away by the afternoon breeze.

"Now wait a minute!" Bill snapped.

"Don't get me wrong, Dr. Chandler, I didn't mean anything by that; it's just sort of ironic. I mean, the timing and all."

The questions from the sheriff ended abruptly.

After ascertaining the name and location of the local funeral home, Bill asked for directions to the site where the accident had occurred.

"Why do ya want to go there?" the sheriff asked, suspicion creeping into his voice.

"I don't know, maybe morbid curiosity. I want to see where he left this earth—just feel like I want to," Bill replied.

"By the way, where are you staying in case I need to get in touch with you?" the sheriff asked.

"Tonight, we'll be at the Wine Country Inn in Santa Rosa. After the funeral, we'll go back to San Francisco. I'll call and let you know where we're staying down there, if that's okay," Bill replied.

"Not a problem. Just keep in touch in case something comes up."

"Are you expecting something to come up?" Holly asked defensively.

"No," the sheriff said, "but in my line of work you never know."

Bill and Holly went to the funeral home and made arrangements for a service and cremation. Then they turned south to Santa Rosa. After arriving, Bill called Litten Industries. He talked with Larry Cotting, the head legal counsel, and passed along the plans for the funeral. He and Cotting discussed Bill's arrival at the company. Bill detected uneasiness in Cotting's voice. Since Bill had never met him, he assumed the uneasiness was due to the sudden death of the company's head and the uncertainty for the businesses and his own future. Cotting assured him that a representative group from the company would be at the funeral. When the call was finished, Bill and Holly collapsed into bed at the motel. It had been a long day, both physically and emotionally, for Bill, and he was asleep in record time.

Holly lay beside him, stared at the ceiling, and pondered the terrible waste the drug scene caused. She was in the twilight of early sleep when she heard a scratching sound on the door to their room. "Bill!" she whispered and shook his arm.

He moaned softly and turned away from her.

The sound occurred again. "Bill!" she said more insistently this time.

"Uh," he said.

"I hear something at the door!" she whispered.

"Yeah, go to sleep," he said lazily.

"Bill! There it is again," she whispered.

He rolled over and looked up just in time to see a fleeting shadow pass quickly by the curtained window.

"What did you hear?" he asked.

"It sounded like someone was trying to get in the door," Holly replied.

"Maybe they just had the wrong room," Bill said.

"Sure. Just the *wrong room*," she mocked.

"All right, all right, I'll take a look, but it'll cost you," he teased.

"As fast as you went to sleep, I'm not worried," she quipped.

Bill got out of bed and went to the door.

"Be careful!" Holly whispered.

He put his eye to the small peephole and tried to adjust his focus. A piece of white paper lay just in front of the door. Cautiously, he opened the door, snatched the paper, and then shut and locked the door as quickly as he could.

"What's that?" Holly asked.

Bill turned on the light and opened the paper. It read:

Need to see you
Tomorrow 3 p.m.
Nells in Cazadero
IMPORTANT

Bill read the message to Holly and then said, "It's printed, probably from a computer, judging by the script and the bold lettering of the word *important*. Maybe this came from the sheriff; he's the only one in California who knows where we are staying. And where in the world is Cazadero?"

Holly got out of bed and found the map they had purchased earlier in the day. She opened it and laid it on the small round table; they both searched for Cazadero. Finally, they found it. "Looks like it's on the way to the place Ned died," Holly said.

"Well, the funeral is at nine, so we should have plenty of time afterward to get there and find Nells, whatever Nells is," Bill replied.

4

NED LITTEN AND BILL CHANDLER—MARYLAND, THREE WEEKS PRIOR

Bill was concentrating intently on a particular relay design that operated too slowly for the new Tel-Ray transmitter when the buzzer on his intercom interrupted his concentration. "Yes," he said less than enthusiastically.

"I'm sorry to bother you, Dr. Chandler, but you have a call from a Mr. Theodore Litten in San Francisco."

"Litten . . . did you say Ned Litten?"

"Yes, sir, that's what he said his name was, and I'm sorry, but he was quite insistent," the secretary apologized.

"Not a problem, put him through," Bill answered.

After a momentary hesitation, Bill asked, "Ned, is that you?"

"Hey, Bill! Long time no talk," Ned responded.

"Ned, I can't believe it after . . . I don't know, how many years has it been?"

"Too many; I don't think we've talked since that great TV show you directed, produced, and starred in a few years ago," Ned responded.

"So, to what do I owe the honor of this call?"

"Well, I wanted to hear a friendly voice again." The pause was a little too long. "Anyway, I was sitting here and thought, now, who haven't I talked with lately, and you came right to mind. Actually, that's not quite the truth. I know we never ended up like we said we would. You know, starting our own company and making millions together, but I hear through the grapevine that you're doing well. And I just wanted to let you know that things have also turned around for me."

"Ned, that's great. Are you still with the upholstery company over in Berkeley?" Bill asked.

"No, I'm not with the upholstery company, I *am* the upholstery company," Ned responded.

"You what?" Bill questioned.

"I had an opportunity and a little spare change lying around and guess what? I bought out the owner, so I own it lock, stock, and plastic barrel! Now, it's more than an upholstery company. It's called Litten Industries; we repair and restore furniture, and we also do refits of airliners. I've expanded it to include electrical, mechanical, and interior restoration. Bill, I can paint a jumbo jet with pink polka dots if someone wants. So I guess you could say I'm in both the upholstery and the renovation business."

"Ned, that's terrific."

"Well, that also prompted my call. You know, since Mom died and I could never find a girl that would put up with me for more than a few days, I'm kind of alone. Hell, I don't even have someone to be the executor of my estate or handle things if I suddenly dropped."

"Ned, why are you talking like this? Do you have a health problem?" Bill asked with concern in his voice.

"Hey, don't get me wrong, I'm not sick, other than sick of the lawyers," Ned joked.

"The lawyers?" Bill queried.

"Yeah, the lawyers. They said I have to name an executor and have all this legal stuff signed. Well, Bill, you're my best friend and certainly the only one I can really trust, so would you do that for me? This is on the level," Ned said.

"Ned, you know I'll do whatever you ask, but don't figure on putting me to work doing that anytime soon."

"Not a problem. I'll over-night some routine papers to you tomorrow. If you could sign them, keep a copy, and then send them back, I'd sure appreciate it." Ned paused again. "And you know, Bill, I really wish someday we could get into business together. It'd be great to work with someone I know like a brother and can trust."

"Yeah, Ned, but you're on the wrong coast."

"Maybe we could go international! Hey, give my best to your new wife. I'll talk to you later," Ned said and hung up the phone.

Bill slowly put the phone back in the cradle and sat back in his chair. As strange as the call from his old friend had seemed, it was also perfectly normal. That was the way their relationship had been since they were children. Bill's thoughts drifted back to their first meeting.

1970

"Mom! Mom, there's a truck next door!" Bill shouted excitedly.

"Why, so there is," she answered.

"Do ya suppose there'll be any kids?" he asked as he looked out the window at the moving truck.

"Well, after the truck leaves, why don't you go over and knock on the door? It would be the neighborly thing to do," his mother said. "I'll give you a plate of cookies to take along."

Bill wanted to, but he held back until his mother agreed to accompany him, so together they carried the plate of cookies to the new neighbors. He met Theodore Litten for the first time. Bill was a year older than Ned, but with another boy on the block to play with, it made no difference. They were inseparable throughout the rest of the summer. A friendship began that lasted until Bill left for college. Many friendships start to drift in adulthood, and theirs did also, with only an occasional meeting at the holidays.

Then unexpectedly, just as Bill started graduate school and married Sandy, his first wife, Ned showed up at their door. Bill could see him standing at the door as if it was yesterday.

"Bill, can you get the door?" Sandy shouted.

"Got it!" he called.

Bill walked to the door and opened it. Ned stood there soaked to the skin, unshaven, coughing, and dirty. He leaned on the door as it opened. He fell forward. Bill caught him before he collapsed onto the floor.

"Ned?"

Looking up with a grin that was formed from pain and relief, he mumbled, "Bill, I made it, help me in, quick . . ." With that, he went limp and lost consciousness.

Bill carried him to the couch and laid him down.

"Who was it?" Sandy asked as she came though the bedroom door. As she saw Ned lying on the couch like a dead man, she gasped, "Is he dead?"

Bill checked Ned's pulse and respiration. "No, but he doesn't look too good. Call an ambulance."

The ambulance took him to the University Hospital emergency room, where the emergency room doctor admitted him.

Several hours later, as Bill and Sandy sat in the waiting area at the end of the corridor, a young intern walked up to them.

"You the folks that brought Mr. Litten in?" he asked.

"Yes, we are. How is he?"

"We got him stabilized, and he's starting to come around. Can you give me any history on what happened?"

"I wish I could; he rang our bell and fell into the apartment," Bill replied.

"Do you know him?"

"Yes, we grew up together through high school. I've only seen him occasionally since then."

"Does he live around here?" the intern asked.

"As far as I knew, he lived in California," Bill answered.

"Well, we're a long way from California," the intern replied.

"Can we see him?" Sandy asked.

"He probably shouldn't have any visitors until morning. Sleep, assuming he can get some here, will help him the most."

"All right, we'll come back in the morning," Bill said.

As they got up and started to walk away, the intern said, "Whoever worked him over was a real professional."

"Worked him over?"

"Yeah, I've seen some guys really beaten up, but your friend, wow, whoever did that must have been a real professional. Otherwise, he would have been dead."

Bill and Sandy walked toward the elevator. As her heels clicked on the tile floor, they heard a beeper go off in the waiting area and a weary, "Oh . . ." muttered by the intern.

The next morning, Sandy went to work. Bill's first class wasn't until ten o'clock, so he went to the hospital early. Slipping past the nurses' station unnoticed, he went straight to Ned's room.

Ned, awake and alert, said, "Morning, Bill."

"Hi, friend," Bill said.

Ned gave a weak grin. He looked like a raccoon, with deep blue-black circles under both eyes. A bandage surrounded his head and a cast encircled his left arm.

Bill wasn't sure Ned looked any better now than he had when he'd stumbled through the door the night before, except now he was clean, dry, and under white hospital linens.

"Hey, Buddy, how do you feel this morning?" Bill asked.

"Like I've been shot at and missed and shi—"

"Yeah, well you don't look any better than that either. Ned, what happened? When did you get to Boston, and who beat the crap out of you?"

"Bill, no questions right now, please, as a friend, no questions," Ned answered.

"Okay, Ned, no questions for now, but you owe me one someday. Deal? By the way, your clothes were destroyed, so I brought in some stuff you can wear when you get out. I'll put them in the closet for now."

"Sure, some day over a brew I'll tell ya all about it. By the way, who all knows I'm here? I mean, did you tell anyone?" Ned looked genuinely concerned as he asked.

"No, Ned. No one knows you came to our place or were brought here except for the ambulance crew."

"I came in by ambulance?" Ned paused and then said, "Bill, ya have to get me out of here! Now!"

"Ned, I don't think you're in any shape to go anywhere. This is the best place for you. Anyway, you're in a hospital; this should be one of the safest locations in the world," Bill consoled. "Look, I have to get to the university. I'll be back after my classes, and I think Sandy will be here as soon as she is off work. Just rest until then. As soon as you're able, come and stay with us so you can get back on your feet."

Ned was quiet as he watched his friend leave. Then he said to himself, "Well, let's see what works." With a great deal of pain, he sat up and put his legs over the side of the bed. Nothing appeared to be broken, though he wasn't sure if his legs would hold him. *I have to take this slowly, but I don't know if I have a lot of time,* he thought. With tremendous pain and a lot of difficulty, he slowly stood and walked around the bed. He still had an intravenous needle in his left hand. He took off the tape, removed the needle, and used the tape to stop the bleeding. Then he made his way to the closet and opened it. The clothes he had worn the night before looked like rags, but beside them hung the clean clothes Bill had brought.

When the nurse came in with the next dose of medication twenty minutes later, she was startled to see the empty bed. After a thorough search of the hospital, his chart was signed off AMA, Against Medical Advice, by the same tired intern who had admitted him the night before.

As he recalled the incident, Bill wondered about the explanation Ned had provided.

The next time Ned had contacted Bill was several years later. "Hey, Bill, been awhile." Ned's voice was as cheery and easygoing as if they'd talked just last week.

"Ned? Is that really you?" Bill asked, astounded to hear from his friend.

"Yeah, it's me. Been a while, huh?"

"You sort of left me hanging the last time. I never knew if you were dead or alive." Bill sounded irritated. "Sandy showed up at the hospital and discovered you had signed out AMA."

"You're not pissed, are ya?" Ned questioned.

"Ned, if it was anybody else, I'd hang up on you right now!"

"Okay, Bill, I acknowledge I sort of ran out without saying thanks, but if ya got time for that brew, I'll tell you all about it. I'm in between planes and have about four hours."

"So where are you?" Bill's tone softened.

"I'm out at Dulles. I have a flight to Rome at six tonight. Do ya have time? I'd really love to see ya."

"Sure, Ned, I can be there in about forty minutes if I don't get hung up in traffic. Let's meet at the bar in the International Terminal. Is that okay?"

"Looking forward to it, and I promise I'll tell you what happened in Boston," Ned said.

When Bill arrived, he saw Ned seated at a table next to the window. Winter in Northern Virginia on a cloudy day is best described as dreary. This day produced gray drizzle and wind. The standing water on the runway and tarmac alternated between ice and liquid. The trees in the distance appeared dead against the bleak sky.

Ned stared out into the dismal scene and didn't hear Bill's approach. When Bill spoke, Ned was startled, and for an instant, Bill thought he could detect fear in his eyes.

"Ned!"

"Bill!" Ned jumped up from the chair and gave Bill a long-lost brother bear hug. "Bill, great to see ya! Sit down, let me get you a brew."

Ned walked over to the bar and returned with a beer and a new basket of popcorn. He set the beer in front of Bill and sat down.

"Okay, friend, I think you have a few things to explain. Do you realize I haven't heard from you since that day in the hospital up north? Sent you a Christmas card and it came back address unknown and then out of the blue, you call years later and say, 'Hey, I'm in town, how about a beer?' I know we're good friends, but sometimes, Ned, you push the limits." Bill's eyes punctuated the questions.

"You're right, I'm a screw-up, but hey, you knew that from the first day we met. That doesn't mean I don't love you like a brother. And Bill, I wouldn't hurt you for anything." He took a long swallow of his beer and then slowly pulled a cigarette out, played with it for a few seconds, and finally put it between his lips. "I know I said I'd tell you what happened, and I will, but first, how is everything with you and Sandy?"

"Great. I finished my PhD and took a job here in Washington that I've been at since graduation, so I guess you can say it's going well. Actually, it's a good thing you called this week. Sandy and I are going to London next week. We'll be gone for two weeks. We haven't had a vacation for quite a while. She's so excited; she can't wait."

"Any kids yet?" Ned asked.

"No, but it's not because we haven't been trying. Just hasn't worked out yet. By the way, I had no clue where you were; how did you know where I was and how to get ahold of me?" Bill queried.

"Well, I have contacts from a previous business," Ned said.

"Oh, and just what business are you in?" Bill questioned.

"I used to work for a plastics and security company years ago," Ned answered, "but now I work for an upholstery firm called Airline Refit Incorporated."

"Now that's a weird combination. Plastics and security—just what do they have to do with each other?" Bill asked.

"It's not as strange as you might think. Not all security involves using burglar alarms and watchdogs. Remember, any place that wants to be protected from bullets needs plastic. We make bulletproof glass, though most of it is plastic, like the canopy of a jet fighter. We make shielding for banks, planes, or anything that needs that kind of protection. See, it all makes sense when you think of it like that," Ned explained.

"Tell me about this airline upholstery company," Bill said.

"Airline Refit is a company that overhauls the interior of aging airliners. It grew out of an upholstery company in San Francisco," Ned replied.

"Okay, I understand, but you owe me an explanation about the incident at the hospital years ago," Bill demanded.

"It was really quite simple. I wanted to surprise you. The mistake I made was walking that night instead of taking a cab to your apartment. The desk clerk at my hotel told me to cut through the park, that it would only take about fifteen minutes to get to your place. Anyway, I was almost through the park when these guys came up and asked for a match. It was obvious they were going to rob me. I decided to give them my wallet, but one of them must have thought I might be going for a gun when I reached into my coat. He hit me before I could say anything and knocked me down. They punched and kicked me until I passed out. When I came to, all I could think of was getting to your place. You know the rest." He took a long drag from his cigarette, exhaled slowly, and watched the pale blue cloud drift toward the center of the room.

"That sounds plausible, but why check out AMA and why no word from you for years?"

"I checked out AMA and left town because there was a cop standing about ten feet away from these fellows when they rolled me. He did nothing but watch the whole thing. I was afraid that if that policeman came to the hospital and knew that I was still alive and could identify him . . ." He took a drink of beer and signaled the bartender for another round. "Most cops are okay, but this one," he took another drink of his beer, "I figured he was on the take. If I said anything I was afraid I'd be killed. When I got back to California and recovered, things began to happen fast with the business, and honestly, I've been working my butt off. Am I forgiven?" His boyish grin spread across his face. When Ned was little, people often said that he could charm the skin off a snake with his grin.

Bill rolled his eyes and smiled. "Sure, Ned, you know we've been friends too long to let a little thing like that come between us." He thought, *Who knows what the truth really is?* "By the way, what's with the trip to Rome? Business or pleasure?"

"Primarily business, but I hope to have a little pleasure too," Ned said.

Bill thought, *That was 1996. Now here it is almost seven years later and I've just became the executor for Ned's estate.*

5

THEODORE LITTEN—CALIFORNIA

Ned, born in a small-town high in the Sierra Nevada Mountains, was the apple of his mother's eye; his blond hair, his ruddy complexion, and his smile that never seemed to cease captivated her. When he learned to talk, it was soon evident that he was not born with a silver spoon but with a silver tongue. Ned could talk his way into and out of almost any situation. He was average in stature, with a slim build. Ned was no stranger to violence; it seemed to be a part of his life from the beginning, but when he was eight, Theodore Litten's life took a radical turn.

"I hate you!" she screamed just as a large hand slapped her and left its impression on her pale white skin. "Help!" Sherry yelled as she fell to the floor. Blood trickled down her chin from the split in her lip. She covered her face and head from the next blow and felt the bone in her hand break as her attacker swung a piece of broken chair on her.

He staggered back against the gate-legged table and knocked it over. The objects on it fell to the floor. "You worthless piece of trash!" he snarled through his clenched teeth. "I'll teach you a lesson. Go out and get a handout from the neighbor because we're too poor. Make me look . . ." He lost the rest of his thought as he tripped over the table's legs and crashed to the floor. His head grazed the corner of the stove and opened a gash an inch above his right eye. His vision blurred.

Sherry struggled to get away from his grasp as he tried to crawl toward her.

The commotion and screams woke Ned from a deep sleep. At first, he laid still and listened to the shouts, threats, and oaths as his parents fought another fight, but this argument seemed louder and more violent than most. He knew that usually after a few minutes, one of them, usually his father, would stomp out the door and drive off. By morning, everything would be quiet again, and no mention would ever be made of the activities the night before. This time was different. The sound of his mother's screams and the thud of her body as it hit the floor brought Ned out of bed. Cautiously he opened his bedroom door and peered through the crack. He saw his father, whose face was distorted with rage and blood, try to crawl over the broken table toward his mother. He saw his mother frantically attempt to get to her feet and put distance between herself and his father.

"Come here, you . . . I'll show you what you're good for!" He struggled forward and slipped on the broken dishes that held the spilled leftovers from dinner. He got to his feet and was still bent over when Sherry grabbed the black iron skillet filled with pork chops and grease. Some of the gelatinous grease sprayed around the room as she swung the pan. The sound of his jaw braking was like a pistol shot. He staggered wildly as he tripped on the soiled floor and fell with his right leg under him. His two hundred–plus pounds came down on his right knee, snapped his ligaments, and fractured the top of his tibia. He howled in pain. Blood spewed from his mouth. He looked up just as the black pan, held in a death grip by his wife, struck his head again. Everything was quiet, except for his wife's sobs and her heavy breaths, as she watched his last convulsive jerks.

Ned stood paralyzed as he held the door knob. His heart beat rapidly and his stomach churned audibly. The acid taste in his mouth made him feel like vomiting. His gaze swept the battlefield and finally rested on his mother. She stood like a statue, legs apart, and feet squarely planted, as tears streamed down her cheeks. Her dress was ripped and her bra was stained with the blood that had dripped from her mouth. Ned wanted to run to her, but he was scared. His legs shook and his teeth chattered uncontrollably.

His mother looked up and saw him standing in the darkened doorway. "It's okay, Ned. Come here," she said gently as she stifled the cry in her throat. "He won't hurt either one of us anymore." She held out her arms to him after she laid the skillet back on the stove.

Ned ran to her and avoided the crumpled figure of his father, who lay on the kitchen floor.

His mother held him for several minutes. "Now, Ned, we have to call the police. When they come, they will probably want to talk to you. Just tell them what you heard and saw." She squeezed him. "Oh, Precious, I wish you hadn't seen all this." Tears ran down her face. Slowly she released him. "Now let's go call the police." They didn't have a phone, so they walked about a half mile to the general store.

"Mr. Miller!" Sherry shouted as she knocked on the door. "Mr. Miller, oh please be here, Mr. Miller!"

"What's all the racket out there? I'm closed; don't ya know what time a night it is?"

"Mr. Miller, it's Sherry Litten. Please, I have to use the phone!" she pleaded.

"Art, who is it?" a female voice called out.

"Sherry Litten," Miller answered.

"Well land sakes, let her in. Don't make the poor child stand out in the night air."

Art Miller unlocked the door. "Come on in. What? Ya have the boy with ya this time a night?" he exclaimed.

"Mr. Miller, please call the police; there's been some trouble," Sherry murmured softly.

Clara Miller, who wore a nightgown and a housecoat, shuffled in wearing large pink fuzzy slippers that were severely matted down. When the light came on, she saw the blood and the streaked makeup on Sherry's face and exclaimed, "Why, child, oh my goodness, what happened? Come in here and sit down."

Sherry's adrenaline had kept her hyped to this point. However, it began to fail and she suddenly knew she was going to faint. Her eyes suddenly went black and her body went limp.

Art Miller caught her before she hit the floor and slowly lowered her onto the couch.

Ned, who had been standing by the door until this time, rushed to his mother's side and looked up at the Millers. "She isn't going to die too, is she?"

Mrs. Miller bent down and felt for Sherry's pulse. It was strong and her skin was warm. "Art! Get me a cold washcloth and a blanket from the hall!" She barked the order, and Mr. Miller dutifully turned and left the room. "Ned, your mother's going to be okay. Are you all right?" Clara Miller asked.

"Yes, ma'am. I'm okay," Ned responded.

"What did you mean when you asked if she was going to die too?" Clara Miller questioned.

"My daddy's dead. There was a big fight and he's dead," Ned stated flatly.

"Art," Clara hollered.

"I'm coming, I'm coming," he replied.

"Art, I think I know why Sherry wanted to call the police," Clara said.

6

THE FUNERAL AND A THREAT

The funeral was strange; Bill and Holly were the only people there who were actually friends of the deceased. The other mourners were representatives of each major division of the company or from the sheriff's office. Many of the company employees acted as if they'd never known Ned. Bill assumed Cotting had arranged a "rent-a-crowd" for appearances' sake. Holly contacted a minister from one of the local churches who tried to say some comforting words about going to heaven, but since he didn't really know Bill, Holly, or Ned, he was on shaky ground about Ned's salvation and Ned's assurance of eternity in heaven. Ned's body was then taken to the crematorium, and guarantees were given that his ashes would be scattered over the ocean. It was 9:40 when the service was over and Bill and Holly left the funeral home. They were quiet and pensive.

Larry Cotting

Larry Cotting held the position of chief legal officer for Litten Industries, a position he had obtained after Ned Litten became the owner. With a law degree and a master's in business, Cotting knew he fit the corporation like a glove, and his salary enabled him to enjoy his latent hedonistic lifestyle. When Ned died, Larry worried Dr. Bill Chandler might liquidate the company and take the profits or use his own lawyers from his Maryland company, Chandler Electronics. His first meeting with Bill Chandler occurred at the funeral for Ned Litten, and it did little to settle these questions in his mind.

"I'm Larry Cotting," he said and offered his hand.

"Bill Chandler, and my wife Holly," Bill answered. The men shook hands. "I'd like to talk to you after the service."

When the funeral was over, Cotting waited for Bill on the steps of the funeral home.

"Mr. Cotting, what is the next step?"

"You need to come to San Francisco so I can read the will and go over the other documents that appoint you as head of Litten Industries," he answered.

"You are the legal counsel for Litten, correct?" Bill questioned.

"Yes," Larry answered slowly.

"Do I need my own lawyers in on this?"

"The answer to that depends on what you intend to do with the company."

"Suppose I wanted to sell it?" Bill asked.

Larry's face brightened. "There is an interested party," he said too quickly.

"Oh, and who might that be?"

Larry took a step back. "Well, when I say an interested party, I mean a conglomerate from outside the country. Its owner used our services for his airplane and became attracted to the operation. I think he and Mr. Litten had a personal relationship, and I'm certain he would be very interested in talking to you."

"I see," Bill said as Holly walked up to the men.

"Mrs. Chandler," Cotting said and then smiled at her.

"Mr. Cotting, I wish we had met under other circumstances," Holly said and offered him her hand.

Bill said, "I'm going to take a hard look at Ned's company. We were boyhood friends, and if he was building something, I'm not just going to dump it on the market. Do you know this person who is interested in Litten?"

"I have seen his proposal, and we were casually introduced once, but honestly, I don't know anything about the man. I could arrange a meeting with him if you wanted. I'm certain we could reach a deal quickly," Larry said eagerly.

"No, that won't be necessary. I want to thoroughly look at what Ned built. Who knows? Maybe I'll like airplanes. There is no hurry. We'll meet you in San Francisco the day after tomorrow at Litten Industries' headquarters. In the meantime, I'll talk to my lawyers in Washington. I'm sorry, but we have to be somewhere. I'll see you the day after tomorrow." Bill turned, took Holly's arm, and walked away.

On the drive back, Larry worried. *Will Chandler take over the company and bring in his own people? Will I be out on the street? I have a good job and I don't want to lose it; however, if someone else owned Litten, I might move up.* These thoughts festered in his mind until he determined to do whatever was necessary to get Chandler to sell. *I have a fiduciary relationship with Litten Industries, but I also have a fiduciary relationship with myself.* When he returned to San Francisco, he placed a call to Lee Koto.

Later that day, Koto returned his call. "Mr. Cotting, this is Lee Koto. You wish to talk to me?"

"Yes, sir. I attended the funeral for Ned Litten today, and I met Dr. Chandler, who will take over the company when he arrives here," Cotting said.

"And when is that?" Koto questioned.

"He told me he to expect him the day after tomorrow. I mentioned a party was interested in buying Litten Industries."

"Did you tell him my name?" Koto asked.

"No, sir, I did not," Cotting replied.

"Good. And thank you for the information." Koto broke the connection.

Bill and Holly

"Bill, I didn't know Ned, but I'm so sorry you lost your friend," Holly said as they sat in the car.

"Yeah, you know," he paused to look at the sky and hills laid out with vineyards, "Ned was a strange kind of friend, but I liked him. I guess I really loved him like a brother because I never had one. We were always going to go into business and make our millions together. I think you would've liked him. But . . . he did have a wild side."

"A wild side?" Holly asked.

"Yeah, in the old days they called a guy like him, a rounder. Ned was always trying to work an angle or he was just on this side of trouble," Bill answered.

Bill put the convertible top down for the drive to Cazadero. It was a warm, sunny day, and puffy clouds hung over the coastal mountains as they headed west. The two-lane road twisted through the mountains that separated the coast from the inland valley. They passed very few cars on the drive over the hills.

Built in 1910, Nells Café had passed its prime years ago. The door didn't close completely and the wooden floor listed toward the barstools in front of the counter. Booths with torn faux leather seats lined the walls. Cracked red Formica covered the counters. The café smelled of grease, baked apple pie, and coffee. Bill followed Holly through the door and guided her to a booth. As Holly slid into the booth, the side of her skirt rode up her thigh and she caught Bill's admiring glance.

"You had your chance last night," she said playfully as her eyes met his.

"I thought we did," he countered.

"Men," she said, trying to act disgusted, "there's only one thing you ever have on your mind."

"Oh, and what would that be?" he asked.

"You were looking at it," she joked.

"Women." Bill smiled and continued, "You'd be depressed if we didn't."

"Hi, what'll it be?" the waitress asked.

"Just coffee for me," Holly said.

"Make it two, please," Bill answered.

A large man, dressed in denim shirt and khaki slacks, sat at the counter and nursed a cup of coffee. Keenly interested in Bill and Holly, he glanced sideways to study them closely. They matched the description he had been given, but he needed to be sure. He slowly spun around on the antique barstool and then placed his feet on the floor. As he looked out the door, he saw the convertible parked in the dusty parking lot. The top was down; he knew he needed to see the registration, but Holly had a full view of the car and it would be too obvious if he went poking around in it.

"So, Bill, where's the mystery man?" Holly asked.

"I don't have a clue where he is," Bill answered turning around to see if anyone was coming in the door. The waitress served the coffee in large white glazed clay mugs. Bill watched the steam curl from the top of Holly's cup as she stirred it. Her hand was smooth and graceful as she absentmindedly twirled the spoon in the cup. *This is a great little place for coffee, but what are we doing here and how is it going to make any difference in solving the mystery of Ned's death?* he thought.

Bill and Holly paid no attention to the large man as he stood and walked toward the door. He ignored them. At that moment, a large six-wheeled county road truck pulled into the dirt and gravel parking lot. Dust blew in small swirls as the truck stopped next to the convertible and blocked Holly's view of their car. The large man left as the county crew came in for a late morning coffee break.

The large man quickly walked around the county truck and behind Bill's rented convertible. He rapidly opened the passenger door and slipped into the front seat. Opening the glove compartment, he pulled out the rental agreement that read, William Chandler. "Right," he said out loud.

Bill and Holly sat in the booth for forty-five more minutes.

"This is a waste. We have things to do and we need to get back to San Francisco," Bill said.

"Maybe we should wait just a little longer," Holly replied.

"I don't think anyone's coming. This is some kind of trick by someone who has a sick mind. Come on, let's go." Bill walked toward the cash register.

"I'm going to the ladies' room," Holly said.

"I'll meet you in the car," he replied.

Bill paid for the coffee and walked back to put down a tip before he headed out the door. Since the county truck had left about ten minutes earlier, the convertible was now the only car in the parking lot. He walked up and put his hand on the door handle. Lying on the seat was an envelope.

Holly walked up beside him.

"Now that's interesting!" he said. Carefully he reached in and picked it up. It was a standard white envelope, sealed and taped. The outside revealed no writing. He held it up toward the sun to look through it.

"Where did that come from?" she asked.

"You didn't leave any letters in the car, did you?" Bill questioned.

"No." She paused. "So are you going to stare at it or open it?"

"I don't know; it might be Pandora's box," he replied.

"You know you're going to open it, so just do it."

Bill tapped the end of the envelope on the door of the car and tore one end off. He carefully turned the envelope upright in his hand and dumped the contents out. A piece of white paper fell out. He opened the paper. It read:

I need to talk to you about Ned.
I'll be on the beach at the end of this road.
Please come.

"What now, Sherlock?" Holly teased.

"Looks like the printing on the first note we received. Want to walk on the beach?" Bill asked.

"Thought you'd never ask; seriously, Bill, what's all the mystery? I mean, how or why is this connected to Ned's accident? And why should you and I be involved in it anyway?"

"As usual, my dear," he teased, "you ask too many questions for me to ever try to answer, or for that matter, to seek to remember, but seriously, I don't have the foggiest idea." They stared at each other for several seconds.

Holly broke the silence and said, "Well, let's go for a walk on the beach."

Bill drove the car west along the county road toward the ocean. The drive was spectacular as they descended the coastal mountain range toward the blue Pacific.

The road came to a T intersection at the Pacific Coast Highway. As Bill slowed the car to a stop at the intersection, they saw an entrance to a state beach. Bill and Holly looked at each other, shrugged their shoulders, and then simultaneously said together, "Must be the place." They laughed. Bill pulled across the highway and onto the road that led to the ocean. There were no other cars visible in any direction as the car coasted to a stop on the sand.

Bill stepped from the car, walked around the car, and opened the door for Holly. The moderate breeze caused the sound of the surf to echo above the dune. A few puffy white clouds floated lazily across the pure blue sky. The small sand dune blocked the view of the water's edge. They walked toward the sound of the surf and crossed the top of the dune. At the summit, Bill and Holly stopped and looked up and down the beach. To the south, there was nothing but an expanse of sand and water as far as they could see. To the north, there was a large tree stump about a quarter mile away. Beside it was a Jeep with a lone figure sitting in it.

"I guess we can assume that's our mysterious writer," Bill said.

"Do you really think this is a good idea?" Holly asked worriedly.

"Why don't you go back to the car? If I'm not back in twenty minutes, you go for help," Bill said.

"Not on your life. We're a team, remember? Anyway, when I leave you alone, you seem to get into the most trouble. So I think I'll go along," she said as she followed him down the hill.

During the five minutes it took to walk to the tree stump and the Jeep, the only distractions on the beach were the waves and the birds. Bill repeatedly glanced over his shoulder to be certain they were not followed, though he conceded to himself that they could be being followed by an army on the other side of the dunes—not a comforting thought. They slowed their pace slightly as they neared the Jeep. The occupant never moved. He just sat and watched them.

Bill stayed in front of Holly as they approached the rendezvous. "Good afternoon," Bill said.

"Howdy," came the reply.

"Didn't I see you at Nells Café about an hour ago?" Bill asked.

"Maybe." The stranger did not seem to be long-winded.

Bill studied the man who sat in the Jeep; he appeared to be tall and solidly built and had sandy-colored hair that was somewhat long and slightly unkempt. His full mustache and beard looked darker than his hair and contained a moderate amount of gray. He wore sunglasses, a green T-shirt, and blue jeans. With his foot propped on the side of the Jeep, his reptile-skinned cowboy boots spoke of money. The rest of his clothes appeared average.

"I'm Bill Chandler; this is my wife, Holly. And you are?"

"Emmet." He gave a one-word answer.

"Nice to meet you, Emmet," Bill said as he extended his hand.

They shook hands.

Holly made no move to be friendly; instead, she stayed behind Bill.

"Emmet, did you send me a couple of notes? Or am I talking to the wrong person?"

"You mean a letter like this?" He handed Bill a piece of computer paper with the identical note they had received at the motel.

"Yes, that's one of them," Bill answered.

Emmet turned his attention away from Bill and looked out to sea. A fishing boat moved south parallel to the beach about a half mile off shore. He watched it for several seconds and then said, "You're that friend of Ned Litten, right?"

"Ned and I were friends most of our lives. What's that to you?" Bill felt both defensive and threatened by the question.

"He was murdered; you do know that, don't you?" Emmet asked.

"Murdered? No, he was killed in a car crash while under the influence. I've seen the coroner's report at the sheriff's office and the lab tests from the hospital," Bill replied. "Is there a reason I should be standing here talking to you? If you know that, why haven't you told the sheriff? Why tell me?"

"Because now that I've said it, I won't live long, and now that you've heard it, you probably won't either." His eyes fixated on the boat as it made a slow turn toward the shore and then reversed direction to begin its move north up the beach.

"I think you read too many novels, or else you're crazy," Bill replied.

"Bill," Holly whispered as she pointed toward the Jeep. "What's that?"

Bill saw a small red dot on the Jeep just below the windshield and knew instantly what it was.

"RUN, Holly—behind the dune!" he shouted. Then he reached forward and grabbed Emmet by the shirt and pulled him out of the Jeep. Emmet did not expect the action and fell out onto the sand. "Come ON!" Bill shouted as he began to drag him to his feet.

Holly reached the crest of the dune, then stopped to look back. Bill and Emmet had taken about ten long strides away from the Jeep when Holly shouted, "BILL, DOWN!"

A white puff of smoke signaled the launch as the handheld guided rocket left the boat and sped on its deadly mission toward the Jeep. They buried their faces in the hot sand when the missile impacted the Jeep. The vehicle erupted into a fireball of burning gasoline and molten metal.

The intense heat warmed their backs as small and large fragments of metal rocketed over their heads.

Bill grabbed Emmet by the arm and again shouted,"GO!" They made it to the top of the sand dune as a hail of bullets sprayed the ground behind them from a gun mounted on the stern of the boat.

"Let's get to the car and hope they don't have any friends on the shore!" Bill shouted.

All three ran to the car, which seemed to be an eternity away.

The sound of the boat's engine escalated above the noise of the surf as it set a course toward the shore.

"They're going to have fun in about two minutes," Emmet said as he glanced back over his shoulder and they ran between sand dunes.

"Why's that?" Bill asked and wished he didn't have to waste his breath talking.

"There's a reef between us and them; I used to surf here when I was a kid. Got some great rights from it," he said and chuckled.

At that moment, the sound of the boat's engine raced to a high-pitched whine as it approached the red line. The boat began to heel to the right as the pilot laid the rudder as hard over as possible. He quickly reversed the starboard engine and saved the craft from impaling itself on the reef. Smoke drifted from the exhaust as the rings on the engine gave their life to the emergency reverse maneuver. The boat went dead in the water; the occupants lifted themselves from the deck, where they had been thrown when the vessel suddenly changed course. This delay gave the trio time to reach Bill's car and start the engine.

Still hidden from view by the sand dune, Bill swung the convertible around and accelerated across the sand parking lot toward the road. In the loose sand, the muscle car lost traction. This caused the man aiming the rocket launcher to overestimate the vehicle's speed. The next missile took the park's sign out just yards ahead of the car. The tires finally left the sand and found grip on the blacktop of the entrance road. When Bill felt the increased momentum, he pressed the accelerator to the firewall.

The V-8 responded with all 485 horses and launched the car with its occupants across the PCH and up the county road.

"Incoming!" Emmet yelled.

Holly and Emmet ducked down, but Bill fought the car for control and could not duck. An explosion rocked the air and caused dirt and gravel to rain down on the car, but the convertible continued its mad dash. The speedometer passed 115 miles per hour and climbed toward the 150 mark. The RPMs hovered at the redline as the engine screamed. Bill crested the top of the hill seconds later and let off the accelerator; this did little to slow the forward motion. Curves appeared on the horizon. He jammed his foot on the brakes; the antilock feature took hold as the vehicle began to decelerate. Holly and Emmet pitched forward and only quick reactions saved Holly from a collision with the dash.

"Ladies and gentlemen, please fasten your seat belts as there may be some rough air during the rest of the flight," Bill quipped as he tried to relieve his tension. "Is everyone in one piece? Holly, are you all right?"

She rubbed her wrist. They all had dirt in their hair and Emmet bled from a small scratch on his face. Holly handed him a Kleenex and he began to dab at the wound.

"I believe, when we talked on the beach, you said I was crazy," Emmet said with an 'I told you so' intonation.

"Well, maybe you're not crazy," Bill replied. He turned around and extended his hand. "Let's start over. I'm Bill Chandler; this is my wife Holly. I think you had something you wanted to tell us."

Emmet took his hand and said, "Emmet Adkins; yeah, I do have something to say to you, but not in the middle of the highway. About four miles up ahead is a road to the left; take it. I don't like it out in the open right now, how about you?"

7

NORTHERN PACIFIC AIRWAYS FLIGHT 303TN—LOS ANGELES

At seven thirty in the evening, the massive airliner sat at the gate ready to leave Los Angeles International Airport bound for Narita International Airport in Tokyo with continued service to Kuala Lumpur. People filled the waiting room and spoke Malaysian, Thai, Japanese, and English. Babies cried, children ran back and forth, parents minded their young, and businessmen wished children weren't allowed on the overseas flight. The gate personnel made last-minute seat changes. Outside on the tarmac, the ground crew busied themselves as they loaded cargo and luggage into the plane's holds. With diligent work by all concerned, Northern Pacific Airways 303TN, fully loaded and ready, pushed back from the gate at eight in the evening, only a half hour late.

"Should be a great flight; she just came out of refit and everything's new," the captain said to his first officer.

"Yeah, even smells new, you know, that new car smell."

"I bought a bottle of spray and sprayed it in here just for you!" one of the flight attendants said laughingly.

"Northern Pacific Airways Flight 303TN, this is Los Angeles ground control. You are cleared for pushback; taxi to 24L via sierra-echo-victor taxiways, hold short at 24L, over," the air traffic controller said.

"Los Angeles Tower, this is Northern Pacific Airways 303TN; WILCO, will hold short at runway 24 Left, over."

The massive airliner taxied from the terminal area. As graceful as it looked in the air, it lumbered like an overgrown cow on the ground. The flight crew continued their preflight preparations. After a brief pause at the end of the runway, permission came for takeoff. The airliner rolled down the runway, left the ground, and climbed steeply over the Pacific Ocean. The passengers watched from their windows as the lights of the Los Angeles basin began to fade. The plane headed north-northwest and took the great circle route to Tokyo.

When the airliner left the runway, a nondescript man in a gray business suit who wore latex gloves pulled out his cell phone and touched memory 5; small beeps emanated from the phone as it dialed the preset number.

"Hello."

"Lift off at eight seventeen." The line went dead. He then took the battery out and dropped it into a trash can. It was a burn phone, but since he wanted no one to trace it, he would soon dispose of the rest of the phone in the ocean when he reached San Diego. He wondered why he had been paid so much money in cash to watch a plane depart and make a phone call, but in his line of work, the fewer questions asked, the better.

At 1:37 a.m. Los Angeles time, a cargo transport pilot reported a bright light that resembled an explosion near the horizon west and south of Kodiak Island, Alaska. One of the Air Force's surveillance satellites also recorded an explosion in the same location. When contact with Northern Pacific Airways Flight 303TN failed, a search and rescue signal went to the US Coast Guard on Kodiak and to all US Naval vessels in that part of the world. The wreckage spread over several thousand square miles due to a storm at sea. Any pieces too heavy to float sank six thousand feet. The cause of the plane's loss would lead to enormous speculation over the next few weeks.

8

IN THE WOODS—SONOMA COUNTY, CALIFORNIA

Bill, Holly, and Emmet turned off the highway onto a dirt road. Erosion had cut deep ruts into the ground. The car wound its way through the dense forest and up the mountain. After ten minutes, they emerged at a clearing. A log cabin sat nestled in the forest. A barn stood to the left of the cabin; its roof drooped like a sway-backed horse. An ugly propane tank stood beside the barn, and a large satellite dish sat perched on the barn's roof.

"Pull the car around back; the forest is thick enough to cover it there," Emmet instructed.

Bill followed Emmet's command. He then turned off the engine and said to Emmet, "Okay, we're not in the middle of the road and we're not on the beach under attack—let's talk."

Emmet leaped over the side of the car and headed toward the back door of the cabin. "Nah, let's go inside and get something to drink."

Holly and Bill looked at each other, shook their heads, and then followed.

Deer heads mounted on the walls greeted them as they entered the cabin. In front of a massive stone fireplace sat heavy rough-hewn furniture with moose motif upholstery.

Holly focused on the kitchen. Amazed that this rustic cabin came with granite counter tops, she walked over to look at the appliances.

At first glance, Bill's attention was drawn to the extensive computer equipment set up in one corner.

"So, Emmet, you have quite a system; it must be quiet up here so you can play a lot of solitaire," Bill said as he motioned to the computer.

"We'll get to that later. How about something to drink?" Emmet questioned.

"It's a little early for me, but if you have a diet soda, I'll have one," Holly replied.

Emmet and Bill each twisted the top off a bottle of beer, walked to the sofa, and sat down near the fireplace.

"Bill, what do you know about Ned's life and his work for the last five or so years?"

"Not too much. In fact, I hadn't talked to him for some time until a few months ago, but that wasn't unusual with Ned. You just never knew when he would show up," Bill said.

"You mean, like the time he fell into your apartment and then disappeared a day later?" Emmet asked.

"How did you know about that?" Bill questioned.

"Never mind, it's not really important; what is important . . ." Emmet paused and then continued, "is that you now control his companies, his fortunes, and his problems."

"Wait a minute; you seem to know a lot about Ned and his financial arrangements. What is your connection to this whole thing?"

"I represent a man who is interested in buying Litten Industries. He is willing to pay fair market value." He took a long swig of his beer, sat it on the coffee table, and watched the droplets of water run down the side of the bottle. He fidgeted with the bottle and scraped off part of the label.

Bill grew impatient as he watched. "And . . ."

"And?" Emmet answered with a question.

"You said he wants to buy the company for a fair market value and you never finished the offer." Bill's irritation showed.

"And, if you cooperate, you and your lovely wife won't be hurt," he added quietly.

Holly's back straightened and her stomach tightened with fear.

Bill's steel blue eyes glared across the coffee table at Emmet. Bill's muscles coiled and his jaw tightened. "Why do you think we would be hurt? Or is that something you had in mind? I suppose those rockets on the beach were for us, not you?"

"Ya know, that thing on the beach really bothers me, because I figured it was for you, but they targeted my Jeep. I guess they figured on taking out both of us." He took another long drink of beer.

"Well, Emmet, I do appreciate this little talk, but I think it's time for us to leave." Bill motioned with his head to Holly to go toward the door.

Holly immediately got up and walked toward the door.

"Maybe I'm interested in selling, maybe I'm not, but not if the offer is accompanied with threats. So why don't you tell them to come and bargain in good faith without any strong-arm tactics and we'll see." Bill rose from the chair, moved toward the door, and continued to stare at Emmet.

"You folks can go ahead and leave, but first, I'd like you to talk with the interested party. Could you grant me that much time?" Emmet walked over to the computer and turned it on. He moved the mouse and brought up a video communication link. An older gentleman appeared on the screen; the camera was at a focal distance to obscure the background, but his face, neck, and upper torso filled the screen.

"Good afternoon, Mr. Smith," Emmet said.

"Good afternoon, Emmet," Smith replied.

Holly and Bill were at the door ready to walk out. Bill stopped and looked at the screen. There was something familiar about the man. Bill hesitated, then slowly walked back across the room. The computer's camera, mounted above the monitor, adjusted to the changing focal distance as Bill approached.

"Ah, Dr. Chandler, it's a pleasure to finally meet you. I have followed your career from a distance in the news media for some time," Mr. Smith said.

"You have the advantage, sir; you seem to know who I am. I would like to say we've met before, but I can't," Bill answered.

Mr. Smith was in his late sixties or early seventies. His face was thin, his hair was light gray, almost white, and his eyes were a deep penetrating green. His accent was foreign, probably either British or Australian.

"No, Dr. Chandler, we have never met. I will confirm that the offer Emmet made for Litten Industries is a most generous and very credible offer. In a matter of a few days or weeks, you could return to your life in Maryland with no problems and you could be a great deal richer."

"Well, I'll have to say, an unknown face on a computer monitor does not carry a lot of trustworthiness. You could be anyone. No offense intended," Bill replied.

"I can understand your skepticism. However, I can assure you that when you have looked at the books, you will find the company today is worth about two hundred twenty-five million dollars. I am prepared to offer you two hundred million dollars on the spot, fifty million in cash, the rest in payments over the next ten years. The money can be paid in the US or to an offshore account of your choice."

Two hundred million dollars, fifty million up front in cash, with no personal investment—this is unreal! Bill thought. "Well, to be quite honest, I haven't looked at any of the books yet, and before I accept any kind of a deal, I will need to look things over. I owe that to my friend Ned." Bill knew he was stalling for time because something did not feel right.

Holly, who stood at the door, opened it slightly.

"I can understand your hesitancy, and I agree, this is a bit unusual," Mr. Smith said. "I assure you the deal is legitimate. You will find there are other interested parties. I would be much easier to deal with."

"Mr. Smith, give me a number. I'll get back to you one way or the other," Bill responded.

The face on the screen became decidedly less friendly as his piercing eyes looked out from under his bushy eyebrows. "Before his . . . accident, we did some profitable business with Mr. Litten. His work enabled us to buy two units at a very profitable margin. Additionally, we talked about a sale of the company. I'd like to continue that negotiation with you. Our offer is fair. You won't get many offers like this, or many opportunities to respond to them." The screen went blank.

"Ya really shouldn't piss him off," Emmet said as he started to walk toward Bill and Holly. "I'm supposed to impress on you that the offer is a good one. It would be real uncomfortable for you both not to give it favorable consideration." He clenched his fists at his side as he stopped a few feet in front of Bill.

"So, are you going to hold us hostage or beat me up to make that point?" Bill asked and stared coldly at Emmet.

"Something like that," Emmet threateningly replied.

Holly opened the door and stepped through it onto the porch.

As Bill blocked the doorway, he turned to face Emmet. They stood, glaring at each other like two wild dogs. Which one would blink first?

Holly broke their stand-off when she ran toward the car.

Emmet lunged to get past Bill and stop her. Bill bent low and drove his shoulder into Emmet's midsection. Emmet let out a grunt as Bill's blow forced the air out of his lungs. The collision threw Bill onto his back; he landed on the porch. Emmet stood bent over and tried to catch his breath as Bill struggled to get up.

Bill heard the deep rumble of the engine when Holly started the car. Gravel and twigs flew as she spun the tires in reverse and headed toward the house.

"Bill, get in!" she shouted.

Bill stumbled down the few steps onto the dirt and fell to one knee.

Meanwhile, Emmet, who had finally regained control of his breathing, shot out the door and headed straight for Bill. Emmet grabbed Bill by the shirt as Bill tried to regain his balance. Emmet easily lifted him and pitched him through the air.

Bill landed on the trunk of the car just as Holly skidded to a stop. Bill wedged his leg against the spoiler, pushed himself over the trunk into the backseat, and dove headlong toward the floor. "Drive!" Bill shouted.

Holly slammed the gear shifter into drive and floored the accelerator. With so much power and so little traction, the big racing tires momentarily spun in the soft dirt. As they found traction, the car shot forward as Emmet reached for Bill's leg. The car threw dirt and leaves at Emmet as it sped across the open pasture toward the road back to civilization. Bill righted himself in the back seat and said, "Might want to slow down some before you bury this thing in the forest."

They retraced their path to the main road and turned east; they hoped it would lead them back to town.

That evening, the sheriff, Holly, and Bill drove to the beach, where Bill tried to explain what had happened there.

As the sheriff retraced the path of their escape across the sand, he said, "Now, folks, I really don't see any evidence of bullets, much less rockets fired around here. Are you sure you have the right place?"

"You don't believe us?" Holly asked incredulously.

"Well, this is the West and all, and you folks being from the East, are you sure this really happened? You said the sign was hit, but as we drove in, it looked okay to me. I don't know what to tell ya."

"It's no use wasting any more of the sheriff's time, Holly. Obviously, either we are at the wrong beach or no one ever fired rockets at us," Bill scowled. "Thank you very much for coming with us and checking this out. I think we'll head back to San Francisco tonight."

"Well now, you folks have a nice trip back down the coast. And if ya get a chance to visit up this way again, stop in and say hi." He smiled as Holly and Bill walked away. "Well, that's a crazy story, but who knows,?" he said to himself, puzzled.

After the video conference with Bill Chandler, Mr. Smith turned to Useph, a former Mossad agent, and said, "Useph, I don't think Dr. Chandler is going to be as malleable as Ned Litten. We may need to use other means of persuasion. Go to San Francisco. I don't want to buy codes anymore. I want to make them. We need Litten Industries!"

9

PACIFIC OCEANIC SERVICES AIR TRAFFIC CONTROL

"Frank, Frank! Get over here!" the controller called to his supervisor.

"Yeah, what's up?"

"I lost Northern Pacific Airways flight 303TN," he answered.

"Lost? What do you mean you lost 303TN?" the shift supervisor asked.

"I mean, they were right here." He pointed to the screen that displayed all the trans-Pacific flights in the northern Pacific airspace.

"Did you have any communication with them?"

"Not yet. After they cleared Seattle control, they were handed off to me, and I had just tried to contact them when their signal disappeared. I thought maybe their transponder was on the blink."

"Well, try them again," the supervisor said.

"Northern Pacific Airways 303TN, Northern Pacific Airways 303TN, this is Central Pacific Control, over."

Static crackled on the microphone; no answer.

"Northern Pacific Airways 303TN, this is Central Pacific Control, over." New urgency permeated his voice.

"Keep trying to contact them," the supervisor ordered as he hurried off to send an alert that a fully loaded jumbo jet had disappeared from their sight.

10

THE CHANDLERS—SAN FRANCISCO

Bill gazed from their hotel window. The view from the fourteenth floor was breath-taking. In the distance, partially shrouded in fog, loomed the towers of the Golden Gate Bridge. Beyond the bridge, the mountains of Marin County cast a stark contrast to the fading light in the western sky. He then noticed a lonely ferry as it plowed its way through the dark water toward the ferry landing. He wondered about the people on the approaching boat. Who were they? What was the purpose for their trip? Were they coming to the city for dinner? Did they work on the other side and were they on their way home? In his engineer's mind, he liked to put everything in its own compartment and to wire the different compartments together to make something logical from them; however, this trip did not form a coherent picture for him. The events were too discordant, too different. He was troubled. He stood there lost in his own thoughts when he felt Holly's hands begin to massage his shoulders.

"Hum," he murmured.

"What's 'hum' mean?" she asked.

"It means you must be thinking the same thing I'm thinking."

"Then pull the draperies and put your thoughts into action," she said.

Later, Bill remarked, "That was incredible. I could stay here all night."

"I could too, but now I'm hungry," Holly said.

"Right, what do you want?"

"Let's go to Sausalito, find a quaint restaurant along the water, and have a memorable night," she replied. "It's only a block or so to the ferry; we can take it across and never have to bother with the car."

"Sounds good to me," Bill replied.

He went into the bathroom for a quick shower.

Holly turned on the television. The cable news was broadcasting continual coverage of the Northern Pacific Airways disaster.

"We can now bring you aerial footage of wreckage over the Pacific Ocean near Kodiak Island." The image on the screen revealed debris that floated on the water below as the plane circled overhead. "There appears to be a large debris field drifting in this desolate area of the world. It will be difficult to recover much of the wreckage in these choppy waters, and it will be some time before any rescue ships will be in the vicinity. Our thoughts and prayers are with the passengers, the crew, and their families."

"That's terrible," Holly said.

"What's terrible?" Bill asked, emerging from the bathroom.

"The plane wreck; it sounds like an airliner went down somewhere over the northern Pacific in the middle of nowhere."

"Oh, what caused it?" Bill asked.

"They don't seem to know at this point. It certainly is too bad. There are no apparent survivors, and they doubt that they will find much of the plane since the water is so deep."

Bill held the hotel room door open for Holly; then he securely closed it, leaving the Do Not Disturb sign visible. He took her arm as they walked to the glass elevator, which was stopped at their floor. As most people do, Bill and Holly walked to the back of the elevator to gaze at the mosaic pattern of the tiled floor below. They stood hand in hand as the elevator started its silent descent. Neither noticed the interest paid to them by a tall thin man and a beautiful woman who stood on the mezzanine balcony below.

In the past, Charlene Dominic had usually worked alone, but when Han approached her for a new assignment, she knew she would need help. She contacted Jim McKay, who she had heard was reliable.

The blue sport coat, the grey slacks, and the wingtip loafers that McKay wore gave him the appearance of an executive in his midthirties. His closely cut blond hair emphasized his chiseled face. Charlene Dominic's long-sleeved black dress accentuated her figure. The only thing about her appearance that was somewhat unusual was the fact that she wore shoes with one-inch heels and rubber soles. Her black hair, pulled back and draped over her shoulders, was held in place with a pearl hair clip. For all appearances, they could easily pass as a professional couple out for the evening; however, she carried a nine-millimeter semiautomatic and a silencer in her black purse. He carried the same type of weapon in a shoulder holster under his left arm. Charlene turned to Jim and said, "It's show time."

When the elevator reached the lobby, Bill and Holly exited.

Jim and Charlene took the escalator from the mezzanine to the lobby.

A sunny day had warmed the pavement and the buildings, but a breeze from the bay brought a promise of a chill in the evening air as Bill and Holly walked hand in hand from the hotel and turned the corner toward the ferry landing.

"Do you think I should have brought a coat instead of a sweater?" she asked.

"No, you have me to keep you warm," he said and smiled.

"Like I said, do you think I should have brought a coat instead of a sweater?" she asked.

Bill made a mock gesture of hitting her on the arm. They both laughed. Neither noticed the couple who crossed the street with them and then stood behind them in line for the ferry tickets.

As the boat left the dock toward Sausalito, seagulls circled closely behind and waited for pieces of popcorn or hot dog bun to be thrown by the children on the ferry. Bill and Holly stood by the rail and watched the birds swoop and dive to catch the crumbs of food in midair.

"Bill, are you going to talk to the sheriff again?" Holly asked with a more serious tone in her voice.

"Without some substantial evidence, I don't think there's any point in trying to convince him that anything happened. However, I believe that Ned did not die in an accident caused by drugs. Ned had his faults, but he was not into the drug scene. Another thing bothers me. The woman who was killed with him—who was she?" While they stood on the upper deck, the wind blew harder as the ferry neared the middle of the bay. Bill noticed Holly shiver, so he slipped his sport coat off and draped it around her shoulders. He then took Holly by the arm and they walked forward to see the approaching shoreline. Bill and Holly watched the lights of Sausalito spread along the shoreline like tiny stars in the night sky. "It's kind of windy up here," Bill said as he led Holly toward the stairway to the enclosed deck below. "I've been thinking about Ned and his businesses. Tomorrow morning, let's go see his lawyer and see what we've been drawn into."

"There certainly are quite a few unanswered questions," Holly replied. "Well, my beloved husband, that's tomorrow; tonight, I want to have a most memorable night. This is our first trip to Sausalito." She stopped, pulled him toward her, and kissed him passionately. "But I'm cold, so let's go inside."

When they walked into the passenger lounge, Bill noticed the couple from the line at the ticket office. He thought, *They seem very interested in us; maybe it's our good looks, but somehow, I doubt it.* His grip tightened on Holly's arm as he walked her toward the stairs that led to the bottom level where the cars were parked. "I need something out of the car," he said.

"But we don't—" Holly's sentence was interrupted by Bill's increased pressure on her arm.

As soon as they were through the door, he broke into a sprint and pulled her with him. "Come on, quick!" he hoarsely whispered. They crossed the auto deck. None of the cars had their occupants in them. The drivers were topside on the second deck for coffee or a comfortable seat during the thirty-five-minute ride. Bill pulled Holly behind a dark blue Nissan on the far side of the boat. They cautiously peered above the edge of the car toward the door they had just exited. Silence pervaded the eerie dimness of the car deck.

"Bill, I don't see anyone or anything," Holly whispered.

"I may be paranoid, but let's give it just a few more seconds."

The door slowly opened. At first, no one appeared. Then, cautiously and carefully, the man in the blue blazer peered around the corner. When he was certain no one was in sight, he stepped through. The woman in the black dress followed closely behind. They were obviously looking for someone, and Bill knew instinctively it was for them. The man put his right hand inside his jacket and withdrew a semiautomatic. He quietly slid the slide mechanism and released the safety. They watched as he removed a silencer from his pocket and affixed it to the gun. The woman opened her purse, withdrew a pistol, and did the same. They turned left and began to make their way toward the front of the boat as they checked each of the empty cars. Bill and Holly watched as they rounded the front car and started down the second row. It was a very systematic search.

"We can't stay here much longer," Bill whispered.

Nearby, a watertight hatch led down to the engine room. Holly and Bill crept to it in a crouched position. It was not bolted. They cautiously opened it and stepped through. The smell of oil, grease, and diesel fuel almost overpowered them, and the noise from the thundering diesel engines almost deafened them. They quickly descended the stairs to the engine room. No one was in sight in the engine room. Bill hoped to go toward the back of the ferry and come up behind the people looking for them. The ferry had two diesel engines, one on each side of the boat with a narrow passageway between. The ceiling was low, and Bill had to walk hunched over or risk hitting his head on the steel supports of the auto deck. The engines were controlled from the wheelhouse, so no crewmen were present. They crossed to the port side of the boat and looked for a stairway up. They found one, which led to a closed door, but its six watertight latches were sealed. Bill tried to move the first one;

it quietly and smoothly rotated. The other five also cooperated. Holly looked hopefully at Bill and wondered if they would soon be out of the noisy room. Bill then spun the locking wheel in the center of the door; it swung open, but did so with a loud crash, knocking over three paint cans piled in front of the door on the other side. The cans began to roll across the car deck between the automobiles. Bill and Holly sprinted through the door.

An earsplitting ping echoed and sparks flew when a bullet glanced off the bulkhead just behind Bill's head. They ran toward the back of the ferry. Several more bullets ricocheted off the metal walls as they ran for their lives. Terror surged through Holly and Bill as they crouched behind one of the cars and surveyed their situation.

The female assassin stealthily moved down the starboard side as the male assassin crept along the port side of the car deck. They would have their quarry trapped in a crossfire in a matter of seconds.

Bill pulled Holly up and ran to the last car in the line. The ferry was not full. The last car, a white sedan, sat about twenty-five feet from the end of the boat. "Get *in*!" he yelled as he pulled open the door.

Holly quickly entered the driver's seat and climbed over the gear shift; Bill got in behind her. The keys dangled from the ignition; his heart raced as Bill started the engine.

"Hang on and roll down your window!" Bill shouted as the engine roared to life. The window behind Holly exploded and showered them with tiny fragments of glass. Another round crashed dangerously close. She screamed and ducked lower in the seat. Another bullet hit the chrome molding just above the front window and reflected harmlessly upward. Bill pushed in the clutch and shifted into reverse; he popped the clutch; the car shot backward and gained momentum as the tires smoked from spinning on the slippery deck. The only safety feature at the rear of the ferry was a chain, which the Volvo broke through as if it didn't exist. For a split second, they were airborne as the car arched toward the cold water of San Francisco Bay. The back of the car entered the water with a spine-jarring crash. The impact triggered the airbags that held Bill and Holly in place. Water spilled over the edge of the open windows and began to fill the vehicle with frigid seawater. The car started to sink rapidly.

"Get out now!" Bill yelled. They both squeezed through their respective side windows and pushed away from the sinking car.

In the distance, the ferry continued toward Sausalito while they floated alone and helpless in the cold water. Bill and Holly could see the silhouettes of the assassins who had tried to kill them.

Bill swam to Holly. "Well, I think you said something about a memorable night."

"Shut up and swim," she countered.

They began to swim toward the lights of Sausalito. Unfortunately the current flowed away from the shore. The three-knot current carried them toward the Golden Gate Bridge. The cold water quickly sapped their strength.

"I can't go much longer," Holly said.

"Come on, Honey, it's not too much farther," Bill encouraged. He looked back and saw boat lights that headed toward the position where the Volvo left the ferry, but he knew there was little chance of them being spotted in the dark water. *Maybe a bullet would have been better,* he thought as he looked at his wife who struggled a few feet away.

"I just want to close my eyes and rest, just for a couple minutes," she said panting.

"Holly!" Bill shouted, "That's hypothermia—you close your eyes now and you may never open them." He swam closer to her and slapped her on the shoulder.

"Hey," she retorted, "I'm okay."

In the distance, Bill heard the faint sound of a motor. "Come on, Holly, you can do it. I hear an engine!" A wave lifted them slightly and he could see the running lights of a small boat headed directly toward them. "Holly, this way, and start making noise!" Bill shouted.

The vessel closed in on them; they began to tread water and wave their arms. Its bow was practically on a collision course with them, and Holly wondered if they might be run down in the dark water.

Sam Barkley felt disgusted; he had fished all day and had very little to show for his efforts, not even enough fish to pay for his diesel fuel out and back. It was great weather, but the fishing wasn't like it was in years past. *All the damn people and pollution,* he thought. He still considered the weather warm, so the windows and doors to the wheelhouse of his dilapidated fishing boat were open. He enjoyed the salt air on his face. He fixed his attention on the compass for several seconds when he thought he heard something. It sounded like a faint human voice. He knew he had the radio off, but he turned and looked at the front of it anyway. No, the face plate was black. There it was again, "Sam, you're hearing things. Sounded like a woman's voice, maybe one of Ulysses's sirens . . . or a mermaid," he said laughingly. There it was again, only closer, and perhaps a man's voice too. He grabbed the throttle and brought the pulsating engine to an idle. "I gotta be crazy." He frequently talked to himself out loud because he lived alone, fished alone, and except for the waitress at the tavern near his shack, he slept alone. He reached for the key and switched the engine off. The night became very quiet, except for the slap of the waves against the wooden hull as he drifted through the water.

"HELP! OVER HERE!"

There it was, two voices in the middle of San Francisco Bay, not far from the bridge. He grabbed a spotlight and switched it on. The sound was close; he swept the beam over the water's surface in the direction of the voices. His boat drifted toward them. Suddenly his light focused on Holly's blonde hair about twenty yards from his port side. *What the hell are two people doing swimming out here?* he thought. "I see ya!" he shouted. Sam grabbed a life ring from the side of the wheelhouse, held the line in his left hand, and threw it as far as he could toward Holly.

They both swam toward it and grabbed on.

Sam began to drag them through the water to the boat. When they were alongside, he reached over the side and put a large leathered hand down as far as he could reach. As Bill treaded water he lifted Holly by the waist. Sam grabbed her wrists. Sam was a burly man with a quantity of fat around his waist but solid muscle in his arms and shoulders. He hoisted her onto the deck of the *Samantha* as quickly as he would land a small fish. Bill was another matter. It took both hands and Bill's help to bring him in over the railing.

"What the hell ya guys doing out here?" he asked incredulously.

Bill and Holly looked at each other. "Uh, we fell off the ferry?" Bill said it more as a question than a statement.

"Thank God you heard us," Holly said as she reached up and kissed his cheek.

Sam put his hand to his face where she had kissed him. "When I first heard ya, I thought ya was a mermaid. Ya sure ya ain't?"

Holly smiled a genuine smile, but she started to shiver violently.

"Let's git you folks warmed up a bit," Sam said as he ushered them into the wheelhouse. He disappeared down a small ladder into the boat and returned with two blankets; he wrapped one carefully around Holly, and without looking at him, handed the other to Bill.

There was a stool in the corner; Holly moved to it, sank back against the bulkhead, and closed her eyes.

Sam disappeared again down the ladder and returned with a bottle of bourbon. He unscrewed the cap, wiped the top of the bottle on his sleeve, and held it out to Holly. "Here, take a big gulp of this. It'll warm ya up," Sam said.

Holly took a small drink; the liquid burned her throat and set off a spasm of coughing. She handed the bottle to Bill.

He took a longer drink, anticipated the sensation, and could swallow quietly.

Sam smiled approvingly at Bill. He'd passed at least one macho test.

Bill handed the bottle to Sam, who took a long drink as if it were bottled water.

"Ah . . ." he exhaled.

"My name's Bill Chandler, and this is my wife, Holly," Bill said and extended his hand.

"Sam, Sam Barkley," he replied and clamped Bill's in a viselike grip. The two men looked intently into each other's eyes like two male animals sizing each other up. Bill saw a rugged individualist, an old man of the sea, probably an alcoholic, but also fundamentally honest and hard-working.

"Ya know, there's a lot of boats searching over yonder, reckon they're lookin' fer you?" Sam asked.

"Most likely," Bill replied.

"Want me ta' take ya over there?" he asked.

"Not really," Bill answered.

"I didn't think so. Any objection if we head in? I been out all day. I'm tired and there ain't no fish in the hold. So, if it's all right with you, I'd just as soon head fer port." He turned the key and the engine sprang to life. Engaging the gear, he pushed the throttle forward. The air rushed through the open windows. Bill and Holly shook again. "Go ahead an' close the windows. It'll git warm pretty quick in here." Sam guided the boat clear of the searching vessels as they angled toward the San Francisco side of the bay. "Hope ya don't have any objection to the place we put in. I need to git home. Which way was the ferry headed when ya fell off?"

"Toward Sausalito," Holly answered quickly. Then she added, "That sounds pretty dumb, doesn't it?"

"Whatever ya say is fine with me," Sam replied.

They motored in silence for several minutes as they watched the lights of San Francisco enlarge on the horizon. Bill could now make out their hotel and the thought of warm and dry clothes occupied his mind.

"Ya know, it ain't none of my business, but you two ain't really dressed for swimmin' the bay, and even if ya wanted to try, night ain't the time. Is there anything I can help ya with?" Sam asked.

"Well, we didn't exactly fall off the ferry," Bill replied. "We sort of . . ." he hesitated.

"We drove off," Holly chimed in with a whimsical musical quality in her voice.

Sam looked at them like they were nuts.

11

ON THE FERRY—SAN FRANCISCO BAY

A crewman stood on the ferry's upper deck and saw the Volvo crash through the chain and disappear into the water. He called the captain, who put the ferry into neutral, turned on searchlights, and then radioed the Coast Guard. Everyone on the ferry rushed to the fantail to look for the car. Rescue boats set out from the Sausalito pier. A Coast Guard helicopter launched and repeatedly swept the area with its intense searchlight, but no trace of the car or any occupants were found. When the ferry docked, the two assassins walked off with the rest of the passengers. The assailants then strolled down the street to a bayside restaurant.

A hefty tip procured Charlene and Jim a table that faced the bay, where they watched the boats search the area. They both dined on lobster and shared a bottle of white wine.

Charlene placed a call from a pay phone in the restaurant lobby. It was answered on the second ring. "The party is over, and all of the packages were unwrapped," she said.

"That's excellent," Koto answered. "The money transfer is activated."

She was always sexually aroused after a hit. Tonight was no exception. She had no emotional entanglements. She'd never worked with Jim before, but she liked the way he performed. He was strong, quiet, and handsome. Earlier at dinner, they'd made small talk; however, he had brushed her leg with his under the table. She'd slipped her foot out of her shoe and caressed his calf. They both knew what was coming later, and while acting nonchalant, they hungered for each other throughout the meal.

Later they took the last ferry back to San Francisco. As they passed the spot where the Chandlers car had driven off the ferry, Charlene and Jim looked at each other and smiled.

As they disembarked, Jim put his arm around Charlene and whispered, "Let's go up to my room for a nightcap."

12

NED LITTEN—DESERT WELLS, CALIFORNIA

Five Years Earlier

He waved Ned into the inner office with a hand that held a smoldering cigarette. "Ned, come in and grab a seat," said Westlake, the founder and owner of the company.

"How ya doing, Charlie?" Ned asked as he sat down.

"Piss poor," Charlie answered.

"Bad day at the office?" Ned asked.

"Bad day for Charlie; I just got back from the doctor. I had my physical," he answered.

"Ugh, had the old finger wave, eh." It was more of a statement than a question.

"Yeah, that wasn't so bad; I've taken it in the behind in business deals so often I guess I'm used to it. No, Ned, it's more than that." He sat silently for several minutes and looked depressed.

Ned didn't want to disturb him, but he and Charlie were close. He could tell Charlie wanted to talk. "Hey, Charlie, we've been through a lot together. There isn't much we can't work out. What's the problem?"

Charlie got up from his desk, walked to the credenza, and opened the cover. He took out two glasses and filled them with a double shot of fine Kentucky bourbon, then added one ice cube to each. He walked back to Ned and handed him one. "To your new business," he said as he held up the glass in a salute to Ned.

"Charlie, just what the hell's going on?" Ned asked before drinking.

"I got cancer, Ned."

"Cancer? No way," Ned exclaimed.

Charlie stubbed out the cigarette he had just lighted. The smoke curled lazily from the glowing embers of the burning tobacco. "Yeah, Doc showed me on the X-ray, and then they put me in one of those CAT machines. That was a trip; a real wild ride. Put stuff in my vein, made me hot all over, kinda like that time in St. Louis with what's-her-name?"

"You mean Charlotte?" They both laughed for a moment. It helped break the tension in the room.

"Yeah, like Charlotte," Charlie said. "Anyway, I got this big thing in there, the cancer, probably from my smoking."

"Well, just get the doc to cut it out and throw it away. I know a lot of guys that have had a lung out and do just fine," Ned answered.

"Ned, don't ya hear what I'm saying? The doc says no dice. It's already gone too far. I got maybe six months left. Some of that isn't going to be too pretty. So anyway, here's the deal. You have been with me since we moved from that shop in San Francisco to this airport setup. That's what? Probably twelve years?" He turned to gaze out the window at the large hangar nearby. "I don't have any kin, and you're like a son to me. Hell, Ned, this company wouldn't be anything more than that two-bit upholstery shop if it wasn't for you. I'm going to give you the chance to have it. I want two hundred fifty thousand, and I'll sell you my share. That will give you one hundred percent of the business." He paused. "Now, how does that sound?"

"Sure, Charlie, but let's not talk about that now. Let's go get stinking drunk," Ned said.

Six months later, Charlie was dead and Ned was the new owner of Airline Refit Incorporated He promptly renamed it Litten Refit and worked tirelessly to expand the business. Several years later he became involved with Liz, a slightly too young blonde in the billing section of the company. She had an insatiable appetite for the fast life. He spent thousands of dollars on jewels, cars, and entertainment for their pleasure. An extended weekend in Las Vegas was one of their favorite activities. For Ned and Liz, the excitement and entertainment of the gambling capital of the world fulfilled all their hedonistic pleasures.

"Ned, are we really going to go to Vegas again?" Liz squealed with delight.

"Come here and tell me how much you want to go there," he replied.

She walked around his desk as he spun his chair toward her. Liz sat down on his lap and made sure a generous portion of her thigh was visible. She then threw her arms around his neck, kissed him, and forced her tongue into his mouth. "You know how much I like it there," she said with an alluring smile on her face.

That trip to Las Vegas forever changed the lives of Ned, Bill, and Holly. It started as innocently as any other trip. Ned and Liz drove to Las Vegas in his convertible. It was springtime, and the desert furnace was on low. A green hue spread across the bleak horizon, courtesy of the winter rains. An abundant number of cars filled the highway as people from San Diego to San Francisco flocked toward the vast wasteland. Some wanted to see the desert flowers in spring, while others wanted to gamble in Vegas. Ned and Liz had no ambition to leave the Interstate for the trivia of smelling the flowers. They set themselves on a course that would eventually lead to destruction. The velvet harpoon of pleasurable sin lay in wait.

"Oh, Ned," Liz exclaimed, "this room is just fabulous!" She rushed to the window to survey the scene. Looking out from the forty-second floor of the High Desert Casino Hotel, she could see the entire city of Las Vegas, as well as the distant purple mountains. The suite had a living room with a stocked bar, a bathroom with a whirlpool tub large enough for four, and an extravagant bedroom. "This is going to be the best trip ever!" she said as she put her arms around Ned and pressed her body tightly against his.

"Is there anything else I may do for you, sir?" the bellhop said after placing their bags in the bedroom closet.

Ned handed him ten dollars and said, "No thanks, I think that will do it."

"Thank you, sir," he replied as he pocketed the tip and walked out the door. *Welcome to Las Vegas!* he thought as he walked down the plush carpeted hall toward the elevators.

Ned and Liz went to the casino. They stopped at the teller, where Ned traded five hundred dollars into silver for Liz, who ran off happily to the slot machines and started feeding in the coins. She jumped from machine to machine, rarely staying with one for more than five dollars, convinced that the next machine would be the winner. The free drinks came often to anyone feeding hundreds of dollars into the little one-armed bandits. Within a few hours, Liz was completely inebriated and unable to function.

Ned, on the other hand, started at the blackjack table and won the first few hands. He was ahead about five hundred dollars when the game became somewhat boring and he left to find new excitement.

"Sir," a polite security man said as he approached Ned.

"Yes, can I help you?" Ned asked.

"We have a young lady who says she is with you and needs your assistance," he answered. "Could you please come with me?" It was more of a statement than a request as the security man walked away from the blackjack tables toward the slots.

Ned trailed along. Then he saw Liz in the distance. She sat on a high barstool. A woman in a cocktail uniform supported her.

"Sir," the security man said, "this lady claims she knows you."

"Whoa, Liz baby, looks like you got into the sauce a little heavy," Ned said as he walked up and put his arm around her. She smelled like the hops room of a brewery, and her head lolled over to the side as if she were a rag doll. "Yes, I know her. I'll take her up to the room. Come on, I think you've had enough for tonight."

"No! I want to play; I like to play!" she slurred.

"I believe that you've had enough for this evening," Ned said as he lifted her off the barstool. She tried to walk, but he fully supported her and almost dragged her to the bank of elevators. Ned punched the number forty-two on the panel and leaned Liz against the back rail of the elevator for the ride up.

"I think I'm going to be sick!" she said.

"Not in here, I hope," Ned answered.

He helped her into their room and she ran to the bathroom. He could hear her vomit as he walked into the bedroom. *Great way to start the trip,* he thought. *I'm sorry you came along.*

Ned looked into the bathroom; Liz was on her knees with her head in the toilet. A stench hung in the air. He turned on his heel and left the suite without a word. *She can sober up by herself!* he thought as he quietly closed the door and padded down the hallway to resume gaming. "I hope she didn't cause me to lose lady luck," he said to no one but himself.

Lust is a powerful motivator. When a man's eyes see something inviting, he wants it. When a man's nose smells a fragrant scent, he wants it. Las Vegas can fill all the senses with wanton lust twenty-four hours a day. Ned looked out the elevator's glass wall at the controlled chaos below. The sounds drifted up like an old friend calling to him. The noise crescendoed as the elevator descended into the gaiety and the gaudiness of the casino. He felt the thrill of the chase, he felt the stimulation of the chance, and he felt the exhilaration of the challenge. Ned Litten thought with his emotion, not with his head; he would soon pay dearly for that mistake.

Roulette is the ultimate game of chance for a man's wealth. The metal ball, rolling around the spinning wheel, mimics the life of a man who wanders aimlessly on the earth with no direction. Ned watched the ball devour a thousand dollars, then ten thousand dollars and more. Mesmerized by the spinning wheel, he fervently believed he would soon win and recover all that he had lost, but by three thirty in the morning, Ned knew it was hopeless. Drunk, he stumbled into the elevator and didn't bother to look out at the merriment of the casino. The luster of Las Vegas had dimmed. He now noticed the elevator carpet didn't seem so plush because spilled drinks matted it. He now saw a torn piece of wallpaper that hung from the ceiling. He now spotted a gouge on a wall. Reality set in as he stumbled down the hall. It was difficult to get the electronic key into the door properly. An annoying red light continued to appear as he tried the key first one way, then the other. Finally, the door opened.

Ned dropped his coat on the floor, staggered into the bedroom, fell into bed, and went to sleep. The sun was past the noonday high when it broke through the window and disturbed his slumber. He sat on the side of the bed. His head felt like a ripe watermelon about to explode. The taste in his mouth could have only come from licking ashtrays or eating the sawdust from a mill floor. He held his throbbing head as he made his way into the bathroom and ran some water in the sink. He took a deep breath and looked into the mirror. He looked like hell.

"Better get up!" he called to Liz.

No answer.

"Hey! It's morning. Better get up. Hell, it may be evening for all I know," he said.

Still, there was no response.

Ned walked toward the bed and thought, *Since I lost a small fortune last night, I might as well have some good sex before we leave.* It was a sure bet, in his mind, that she would be gone by tomorrow morning. Liz was a lot of fun, but she was not one to stick around when things turned south. He approached the bed; she laid with her back to him. He took hold of her bare shoulder and rolled her onto her back. Her right arm flopped lifelessly against his thigh. He looked down and saw her eyes. The pupils were large and dilated. He jumped back in horror. A scarf was tightly tied around her neck; her face still held a slight bluish cast from suffocation. Ned started to scream.

Just then there was a knock on the door. He was horrified. *What have I done? NO! I haven't done anything. I was too drunk last night when I came in to do anything.* The knock was louder and more persistent. "Calm, you have to be calm," Ned told himself. He went to the suite's door after he closed the bedroom door. He opened it with the safety chain still on and peeked through the crack. "Uh, yes?"

"House security—had a report of a disturbance here. Are you all right?"

"Uh, sure—sure, I'm fine. Just woke up late," Ned stuttered.

Holding up an identification badge, he asked, "Can I come in?"

"Uh, what for?"

"I need to check it out. Had a report, you know," the security officer said.

"Just a minute," Ned answered as he closed the door and removed the safety chain.

The security agent entered the room and looked around. "My name's Gregg Newman." He again showed his identification. It was a laminated card with his picture on one side of a leather case and a large silver and gold badge on the other with Hotel Security stamped into it. He motioned toward the bedroom door. "Let's go in there."

"Uh, my girlfriend's sleeping. Do we have to disturb her?" Ned paused. "She was sick last night; I wanted her to get as much rest as she could."

"Well, let me talk to her; I can get the hotel doctor up here. Maybe she needs the doctor." He walked toward the door.

Ned tried to stop him, but the man was larger than him, and Ned was in no condition to stop anyone. He opened the door and saw Liz lying on the bed. "Got a little rough last night, Mr. Litten?"

Ned sat down slowly on the couch, buried his face in his hands, and whispered, "I don't know."

"What?"

"I DON'T KNOW! I don't remember anything. I couldn't have done anything like this without knowing. I DIDN'T DO IT!" he shouted.

"Now calm down; just take it easy. Try and tell me what you remember about last night," the security agent said soothingly.

"I lost a lot of money, drank a lot of booze, and fell asleep," Ned replied. "Oh God, what am I going to do?" he wailed.

"Mr. Litten, just calm down. You know, you were seen taking the lady out of the casino last night. We had a report you were manhandling her. I found out when I read the report by the evening crew that she had drunk enough to float a battleship and you weren't pleased." He looked at Ned. "Do you think you might have gotten a bit rough with her when you got back to the room?"

"No, no way. When I left the room, she was on her knees in the bathroom throwing up in the toilet. I never looked at her or touched her after that until five minutes ago. I couldn't have killed her."

Gregg Newman looked down at Ned with an 'I'm going to take you to jail now' look. "Well, I guess I better call the police," he said.

"NO!" Ned shouted. "I didn't do this. You have to believe me. You have to help me," he pleaded.

"I'm afraid there's not too much I can do for you," he paused, "however . . ."

"However what?" Ned demanded.

"You say she was your girlfriend, not your wife?" he asked.

"Yes, why?" Ned answered.

"Well there are some people who can probably make it look like an accident that happened somewhere else. Then you'd have a good alibi that you never left the hotel. It would put you in the clear. And from what you say, it probably was an accident. You know, rough sex or whatever."

"Do you know these people?"

"Yeah, but it'll cost you."

"I lost a lot of my money last night. . . ." Dejection settled over Ned.

"Do you have any collateral?" the agent asked.

"I have a company near San Francisco." Ned was now on autopilot and was no longer thinking. He just wanted out of the situation.

"Stay here. Don't go out, and don't let anyone in until I get back. You understand?" Gregg Newman ordered.

"Yes. Do you think you really can help me?" Ned looked up hopefully.

Ned passed the morning in the suite pacing the floor and trying to reconstruct the events of the evening before. At this point, he did not know anything for certain, even the amount of money he had lost. He knew he had signed several markers, but he wasn't sure how many.

The first knock at the door was the maid. Ned told her to come back later, that he wasn't feeling well. That, at least, was the truth. The second knock was the security agent. He had another man with him.

"This is Mr. Litten," Gregg Newman said without mentioning the other person's name. They nodded at each other.

"I understand you have a situation you would like handled."

"Yes, did ... did he," motioning to the security agent, "did he explain?" Ned asked.

"I understand." Silence prevailed in the room as the men looked at each other.

"And?" Ned asked.

"Anything can be handled for a price," the man said.

Ned knew that was coming. He looked at the man, about average height, maybe a little overweight, with an olive complexion, probably from the Mediterranean area, maybe Italy. *Yeah,* Ned thought, *the mob. Well, it won't be the first time I've done business with them.*

"So, what are we talking?"

"Two hundred fifty thousand, cash, today," he said flatly.

"TWO HUNDRED FIFTY THOUSAND!" Ned exclaimed. "That's unreal. How do you expect me to lay my hands on that kind of money today? It's already past noon."

The man looked at Gregg. "I thought you told me he wanted help. Might as well go ahead and call the police." He turned and walked toward the door.

Ned watched in horror as the man took hold of the doorknob.

Then the man hesitated. "I know that kind of money might be hard to get on short notice. I have a contact who would spring for the money up front." He looked back at Ned.

Ned took a deep breath and looked at the closed bedroom door. Liz had now been dead probably eight to ten hours, and he knew he had to get her out of there. "All right, let me talk to your source."

The man turned from the door and walked back to Ned. "I'm authorized to conduct the transaction." He held out his hand toward Ned.

Ned looked puzzled, then took his hand and shook it. "Uh, what's the interest rate, payment method? You know, the business side of it," he asked.

"You will be contacted in the future; just cooperate with whoever comes to you and says it's time to make your payments. Interest will be discussed later."

Ned knew in his heart that it was too good to be true, but he was in no position to bargain for better terms. The only other alternative available would be fifteen to twenty-five in the State Prison as some baboon's boyfriend. He softly replied, "You got a deal."

The man looked at Ned. "You can go for a walk down the strip. Take a couple hours and play some cards at the other casinos, maybe your luck will be better than last night, huh? I'll have my housekeeping crew take care of the room." He then turned and walked into the hall without another word.

"It will be okay now, Mr. Litten," Gregg Newman said.

When Ned returned to the suite, it was dark. He turned on a light and went straight to the bedroom. It was as clean and neat as if no one had ever been a guest there. Ned breathed a sigh of relief, though the little voice in the back of his mind questioned the deal he had made.

13

THE CHANDLERS—SAN FRANCISCO

Sam expertly maneuvered the fishing boat between two other similar boats that were in slightly better repair. It was like parallel parking a car, but he made it look easy.

Okay, folks, here we are, back at the dock safe and sound. Now I'd recommend if ya want to go to Sausalito again, ya take the bridge. You might have a better chance of making it." He laughed. "Are ya goin' to go to the police an tell them about driving off the ferry?" He looked out the window at the pier. "Reason I ask is," he put his hand on his beard and pulled at his chin, "I really wouldn't like them, the police I mean, nosin' around. I ain't got nothin' to hide, mind ya. Jest' don't really have much use for police or Coast Guard."

"Sam," Bill said, "we have no intention of calling the police, but I might want to go fishing while I'm in San Francisco, and if I do, I'd like to know that you and your boat are available. I'd like to have you on kind of a retainer. You know, sort of like a lawyer. I'd pay you something to be available. Nothing illegal, mind you."

"Well, I've never been on . . ." he looked puzzled, "a retainer. But if that's what you need, we can probably git together."

Bill took three hundred soggy dollars from his billfold and handed them to Sam. "Here's a down payment. Sam, thanks for being out there tonight and pulling us from the drink."

They shook hands.

Holly stepped over and again kissed Sam on the cheek. "Thanks," she said.

Sam put his hand up to his unshaven face, lightly touched his cheek, and smiled at Holly.

Bill and Holly left the boat and walked down the darkened pier toward their hotel. Their clothes were relatively dry by the time they arrived. The lobby was not busy, so no one noticed the unkempt couple slip into the elevator and ascend to their room.

As Holly jumped into the shower, Bill unpacked his encrypted satellite phone and punched in a Washington, DC, area code.

Holly walked out of the bathroom, her body wrapped in a large fluffy white bath towel, as Bill hung up the phone. "Who did you call?" she asked.

"Just called home to get some supplies." He smiled. "Just in case."

The next morning Holly and Bill checked out and went to the Litten Industries' headquarters. They took the elevator to the twenty-eighth floor and exited the elevator. Bill pushed through a set of glass doors marked Litten Industries. The reception desk sat just inside.

"May I help you?" an attractive brunette, who sat at the reception desk, asked.

"We're Dr. and Mrs. Chandler. We have an appointment with the legal officer this morning."

Blushing, she stood up. "I'm sorry, I didn't recognize you, Dr. Chandler. We had a call earlier canceling your appointment. I don't know who cancelled it. Please forgive me," she stammered. She stepped around the desk and led them toward a set of solid walnut doors. The nine-feet-high doors were highlighted with gold lettering that read, Litten Industries, Theodore Litten, President.

Holly exclaimed, "Wow, what a view!" She walked to the windows and looked at the San Francisco Bay.

A large desk and leather executive chair occupied a strategic position that took advantage of the view. A set of leather couches, with a large copper coffee table between them, provided a seating area. A tropical saltwater fish tank noiselessly bubbled in the corner.

Bill whistled. "Now this is an office."

Holly agreed. "This certainly puts your office to shame."

"What's the matter, lady, you have something against the second-hand store furniture I have back home?" he joked.

"Please have a seat; Mr. Cotting will be with you shortly," the receptionist said as she turned to leave the room. "Would you like some coffee?"

"Thanks, that would be nice," Bill said. He watched her sway as she walked toward the door.

Holly scowled at him. "Dirty old man," she said.

"Can't help it, I'm a guy. What can I say?" He smiled at Holly and let his eyes linger on her shapely legs a few extra seconds.

She smiled at him.

The door opened; Larry Cotting, dressed in a navy-blue suit, white shirt, and blue and white striped tie, walked in. He held out his hand before he was halfway across the room. "Good to see you again, Dr. Chandler, Mrs. Chandler." He tilted his head toward Holly. Cotting's smile was too broad and too forced to be friendly. "The funeral was nice." His comment fell flat.

They sat down on the opposing couches.

The receptionist arrived with coffee and rolls. Silence hung uncomfortably over the room as she poured the coffee. She then quietly withdrew.

"I'm sorry I wasn't out front to meet you. We had a call earlier this morning saying you wouldn't be coming. Obviously, that was in error," Cotting said.

"Obviously," Bill agreed.

"Well," Cotting was ill at ease, "I suppose you want to go over the will and your duties as the executor?"

"That'd be a good place to start," Bill replied.

14

KOTO INTERNATIONAL—US DIVISION HEADQUARTERS, SAN FRANCISCO

"Koto!" The young Japanese man bowed respectfully as he hurried into the room. He stood still, bent at the waist, and waited until Koto recognized him.

"Yes," Koto replied without looking up.

"I just had a call from Litten Industries. Dr. Chandler just arrived there to begin his duties as the executor." He was afraid to look Koto in the face as he relayed the news. He knew Koto believed the Chandlers were dead.

Koto looked up from the paper he was reading and said, "That is very interesting. I thought we had a call last night stating that they had had a tragic accident and had drowned in the Bay."

"Yes," was the reply.

"Thank you." Koto dismissed Han with a wave of his hand and never really looked at him. Koto then walked to the wall and pressed a button. The wood paneling moved and revealed the second room. A desk and chair faced multiple computer screens. Koto sat down and pushed a button on the control panel in front of him, which electronically dialed a number. The phone rang three times before it switched to a satellite connection in Tokyo.

"Aye," Long said.

"Dr. and Mrs. Chandler are not dead," Koto stated flatly.

"I will see what happened," Kim Long replied.

Koto hung up his phone. He sat back and looked at a strategically placed bonsai. It had perfect form and beauty. The pruned branches and needles, proportional to the main trunk, displayed perfect symmetry. A small volcanic rock lay near the base of the trunk and gave balance and serenity to the composition. This little arrangement mirrored the one place on earth he found tranquility. He thought of his home near Tokyo. He remembered the terraced garden and the beautiful koi in a pool below it. He loved to sit on the rock above the pool and meditate. He liked to listen to the sound of the wind in the trees and the occasional bird that flew by. He longed to be back in Japan.

Koto was not fond of the Western culture, except for its women. His mind drifted to Charlene, the tall, slender woman who had dispatched Mr. Litten with such grace and elegance. *What caused her to handle the Chandler job so badly? I will invite her to my house and ask her. I paid the money; she will make good on the contract,* he thought.

"Han!" Koto commanded.

The young man appeared almost instantaneously. "Sir."

"I would like to have an appointment with Dr. Chandler. Call that lawyer, Mr. Cotting," Koto said.

"Yes, sir."

"And, Han, I'd like the lady who worked for us on the Litten matter to come to my house tonight."

"What should I tell her?" Han asked.

"Tell her the party is not over and the packages are still wrapped."

"Yes, sir," Han said as he backed out of the room bent at the waist.

15

ORLY INTERNATIONAL AIRPORT—PARIS, FRANCE

"Daddy! Is that the plane we are going to go on?" the little girl asked as she pulled her father toward the window.

"Yes, it is," he replied. "There's the pilot and copilot performing their preflight checks." He pointed toward the cockpit windows of the jumbo jet.

"Tomorrow morning, we'll be in New York with your mother. Now that your school is out, we have the whole month together."

"Can I go to the Statue of Liberty and Coney Island?" She bubbled with excitement.

"We'll go to a lot of places, including the Statue of Liberty and Coney Island," he responded.

The gate crew boarded the 390 passengers in an orderly fashion. Then the massive plane lumbered onto the taxiway for an on time take-off at six thirty in the evening.

The pilot announced, "Flight attendants, please take your seats. We've been cleared for departure."

The airliner began the roll down the concrete runway blackened with the rubber from thousands of airplane tires. Though heavily loaded, the powerful jet turbines quickly lifted the mammoth airliner. After departing from Paris air traffic control, the plane turned north for the circular polar route toward New York City.

The phones rang simultaneously at the Paris embassies for the countries of Israel and the United States.

"Hello," the Paris operator for the Israeli Embassy said.

"Listen carefully, this will be repeated only once," the computer-generated voice announced.

"Who do you want to speak to?" the operator asked. She stalled for time; she had already pushed the red button beside her phone to alert the security forces there was a probable threat on the line.

The message began:

France International Airline flight number 607-UF has just departed from Orly Field on its way to New York City. There is a bomb on board. If the seven innocent Palestinians who were illegally kidnapped from Palestine and taken to Israel last Monday are not released within six hours, the plane will be destroyed. If the aircraft is recalled or sent to any other airport, it will be destroyed immediately. We have electronic and radar tracking and will know if the plane deviates from its filed flight plan. The released innocent Palestinians must be taken to the airport in Hebron. You now have five hours and fifty-nine minutes. If you do not believe we can destroy the plane, ask the Americans what happened to Northern Pacific Airways Flight 303TN. Remember, if the aircraft deviates from its flight path, it will be destroyed.

The line went dead.

"Did you get a trace?" the American Embassy head of security asked.

"No, it was too short and the routing was too convoluted."

He picked up the phone and pressed a button. "Get me the ambassador ASAP!" Several seconds passed. His office was deep in the third sub-basement of the embassy. Normally it was quite cool, but now he began to sweat. He knew this had disastrous potential for the people on the airliner and for the nations of the United States and Israel, and it was a potential disaster for him personally—his wife and daughter were on that plane heading for New York to attend his mother-in-law's seventieth birthday party. *Where is HE?* His mind screamed as the phone's earpiece remained silent.

"Hello," the American ambassador responded.

The man's southern drawl brought him back to the present. "Mr. Ambassador, we have a situation."

After listening to the message, the American ambassador placed a call to the President at the White House.

Across Paris, the Israeli embassy played a similar scene.

The Israeli ambassador immediately contacted the prime minister of Israel in Tel Aviv, who listened to the message. Then the ambassador asked, "Would you like it repeated?"

"No, I don't. You know what to do. Let me know as soon as you have anything." He sat back in his chair and thought, *no prime minister of Israel ever negotiated with terrorists.* However, he felt certain that this was exactly what France and the United States would pressure him to do. Their leaders did not like the hard stance he took in response to a recent terrorist bombing in Tel Aviv. "I don't care what it takes; find these people *now*!" He hung up the phone and wiped his sweaty and trembling hand on his trousers.

16

FLIGHT 607-UF— NEAR THE ARCTIC CIRCLE

"This is France International Airline Flight 607-UF; go ahead, Orly," the copilot said.

"Flight 607-UF, we have information that you have a bomb on board. Do not, I repeat, DO NOT deviate from your flight plan. Do you understand? Over."

"Yes, Orly, we understand. Anything you can give us about the bomb? Over."

"Not at this time. Over."

The pilot and copilot looked at each other.

"William, take the chief steward and begin to search the plane," the pilot said to his copilot.

"Right, Captain. I'll start with the galley and the food carts. I doubt if one of the passengers carried it on; they were screened. I'll let you know. That bomb on the Pan Am flight over Lockerbie was probably inside a radio. I don't have a good feeling that I can find it."

"William, I know, but until we get more information that's all we can do."

In the reality of this moment, Captain St. James knew that every pilot's fear had now become his.

17

LITTEN INDUSTRIES, SAME DAY—SAN FRANCISCO

The satellite phone in Bill's briefcase began to ring. He opened it and lifted the phone from its cradle. "Excuse me, please," he said to Cotting. Then he replied, "Chandler here."

Fred Thorpe, Bill's vice president at Chandler Electronics, said, "Bill, Homeland Security called the office. They want me to forward this call on the secure line. Do you want me to stay on the line?"

"Yes, stay on the line," Bill replied and then pushed the encryption button on the cradle. "It's secure now," Bill said.

"Dr. Chandler, my name is David," the Homeland Security agent said.

"I'm Bill Chandler; what can I do for you?" Bill asked.

"We need some help with a very delicate situation; I was told your company has a prototype electronic device that might be very useful to us."

"What exactly do you need?" Bill asked.

"A commercial airliner reportedly has a bomb on board. The detonation will come as an electronic signal. We need to know where the transmission signal will come from so we can block it as quickly as possible before it activates the explosive.

"Where is the plane located?" Bill asked.

"Right now, it is one hour out of Paris, and it is headed for New York City."

"Shi—excuse me, sir." Bill's face flushed.

"Don't worry, that was my first reaction too, Dr. Chandler," he replied.

Bill thought, *If we shut down all incoming communication to the plane, then at the appointed time, the only signal to deal with would be the signal to blow the bomb. . . it might work, but oh God, if it doesn't!*

"Can it be done, Dr. Chandler?"

"Maybe, but it would be very, very iffy. If we block the wrong signal, the device will explode. I can't guarantee anything. Isn't there any way to get the plane down and the people off?"

"Not that we know of. The terrorists said that all communication is monitored, and that the plane is tracked by radar every second, so if the plane deviates from its original flight path, they will blow it immediately," he answered.

"How much time do we have?" Bill asked.

"Now, less than four hours, forty-five minutes."

"Can you give me fifteen minutes and call back on the same number?"

"Yes, but can I ask why? There is not a lot of time."

"I have an idea I want to run by someone. Also, can you have another duplicate plane which could have the transponder set to match the one already in the air?"

"Most likely, but why?"

"Please, just call back in fifteen minutes." Bill pushed the button to terminate the call.

Holly arose from the couch and walked toward Bill. "Problems?"

"Uh, yes." He looked at Cotting. "I have kind of an emergency; can we break for thirty minutes? I need to make some calls." They were both statements of fact and a notice for Cotting to leave.

Cotting assured Bill that he would be available at any time to resume reading the legal documents. "Please feel free to use any of the phones here. Just so you know, you are the only beneficiary of Mr. Litten's will. It all belongs to you, Dr. Chandler." Without looking back, he quietly walked out the door.

Bill and Holly looked at each other with astonishment.

"What's the problem?" Holly asked.

"Apparently there's a bomb on a plane over France," Bill said.

"Like the plane yesterday that disappeared over the Pacific?" Holly asked.

Bill stopped in the middle of dialing, raised his eyebrows, and said, "Now that's something to think about." Then he continued dialing. "Hello, Fred, we need to do something and do it quickly."

"Okay," Fred said. "I heard the conversation."

"Good. Here's what I want to do . . ."

Fifteen minutes later, the encrypted phone rang again. "Chandler here," Bill said.

"Well, Dr. Chandler, what do you have for us?" David from Homeland Security asked.

"How soon can you have a second plane in the air?" Bill questioned.

"Consider it on the end of the runway," he answered.

"Be sure the transponder is set exactly as flight—what did you say the flight number was?"

"France International Airline 607-UF," he answered.

"Right; call the first plane B for bomb and call the second plane F for fake," Bill said. "Now, make sure the transponder is set on plane F to match plane B. Only don't turn it on—just get it in the air. What is the maximum time from right now that we have to get plane B on the ground safely?"

"Four hours, twelve minutes. That will give us ten minutes to get everyone off."

"That's cutting it close, but here goes. In three hours, I want plane F completely blacked out five thousand feet above and one mile behind plane B. From my office in Maryland, I will send a cloaking signal by satellite, which will make plane B disappear from radar and will interrupt all communications. No signal will go in or go out for thirty seconds. Plane B must dive for the deck and plane F must move in and turn on its transponder. I will continue to block the transponder on plane B, but I cannot maintain complete cloaking on that plane for more than a few minutes. Then, if that works, get plane B on the ground and unload it quickly. If they trigger the device, it may go off." Bill paused, then he continued, "You know, they might do that when the plane goes black."

"It's a chance we'll have to take. So far, you have the only possible solution," the agent said.

"Could you let the Palestinian prisoners go?" Bill asked.

"No, we can't. Three of the prisoners were killed trying to escape last night. So even if the Israeli prime minister wanted to, he couldn't," he replied slowly. "Can you really do all of this electronically?" David asked.

"If I can't, you'll have the second jumbo jet blown up in two days, won't you?"

"How did you know the plane over the Pacific blew up? That was in the terrorist's statement, which hasn't been released yet."

"I didn't; my wife put it together," Bill answered.

"If she ever wants to work in security, tell her to give me a call," David said.

"Fred, my vice president, is an engineer. He will handle the communications, and he is on this line—"

"Impossible!" David said. "I have the highest encryption; no one but you and I are on this line." He was indignant.

"Fred, let the man know you're there."

"Hello, David," Fred answered.

"Now, sir," Bill continued, "Fred will handle the necessary arrangements, so do exactly as he tells you. Are there any questions?" Bill waited; the line was silent. "Then, Fred, you take it from here and do as we discussed. Let me know how it goes." Bill hung up the phone.

18

ORLY FIELD—PARIS, FRANCE

A France International Airline jumbo jet sat, with engines idling, at the end of the runway. The pilot, the copilot, and the flight engineer were all volunteers; they were the only occupants. They dimmed the instrument panel lights and intentionally did not turn on the interior or the exterior lights.

"Jack, do you understand what we're doing?" the flight engineer asked.

"Trying to save flight 607-UF, I guess."

"How do they know what the plan is?" the copilot asked.

"You're never going to believe this," the pilot answered.

"Yeah, tonight I might believe anything," the copilot replied.

"Morse code," the pilot said.

"What?"

"Morse code—you remember, dots and dashes."

"Whose idiotic idea was that? Sounds like something left over from World War II."

"The guy that came up with this whole scheme is some electronic wizard in the United States."

"If he's a damn electronic genius, why is he using Morse code? Why not use some of his electronic tricks?"

"The terrorists said they were monitoring all communication, so they were afraid to try the usual channels. He hopes the terrorists will think it is static or that they can't read Morse code."

"France International Airline Flight F, you are cleared for takeoff. Good luck and God bless you," the air traffic controller said.

The captain placed his hand on the throttles and began to advance them forward. The race to get to the appointed place on time and execute the moves exactly was foremost on his mind. The empty airliner rumbled down the runway, leaped into the air, climbed rapidly, and raced toward its rendezvous over the Arctic Circle.

France International Airline Flight 607-UF

Calm under pressure, and considered one of the best pilots in the world, Captain Andre St. Paul felt the weight bear down on his shoulders. His hands were sweaty, his stomach churned, and his muscles tightened. A repetitive beep in his headset interrupted his thoughts. *Dot, dash, dot, dot*—a distant memory from the past struck a chord and released a flood of recollections. *Dot, dash, dot, dot. A call sign! Morse code!* His brain recalled a skill long buried. The sounds brought back scenes of pilots flying propeller-driven airplanes that required star sightings and a sextant to navigate.

"Dot, Dash . . ."

"If you read this, key your mike one long."

Captain St. Paul complied.

The sender, using Morse code, sent the following message: *Good. This will be repeated only one more time in thirty-five minutes. At twenty-three hundred, all communications will be blacked out; dive to five thousand feet and proceed directly to Keflavik International Airport as rapidly as possible and evacuate on landing. Do not discuss this verbally.*

Andre wrote the message in longhand and handed it to the copilot when he returned to the cockpit after his search.

"We've found nothing that might be a bomb," the copilot stated while he read the note.

"Keep searching," Andre replied.

Israeli Embassy, Paris, France

The ambassador of the United States, the minister of defense for France, and the ambassador of Israel met at the Israeli Embassy. They sat in a secure room and discussed the terrorist threat.

"Do you think Dr. Chandler's plan will work?" the American ambassador asked.

"We transmitted the instructions, and so far, the plane has not exploded. We can now conclude that they did not monitor the Morse code transmission, or if they did, they didn't understand it," the French minister of defense said.

"How long will it be until the planes switch?" the Israeli ambassador questioned.

"Less than an hour," the American answered.

"How will Dr. Chandler block out the airliner's communication and make the airliner disappear from radar?" the minister from France inquired.

"Those problems are handled by a company in the United States that uses one of America's satellites," the United States ambassador answered as he looked at his Israeli counterpart.

Arctic Circle—Thirty Thousand Feet

Stars shown like millions of tiny sparkling diamonds set in perfect settings as France International Airline Flight 607-UF sliced its way toward the Arctic Circle. Below, in the vast darkness, lay thousands of square miles of ice. The blasting wind roared across the frozen ocean and created razor sharp hills and valleys.

The captain and first officer watched the digital clock recessed in the instrument panel. It was 2252. Captain Andre St. Paul reached for the microphone, switched on the internal system, and said, "This is Captain St. Paul; I'm sorry to disturb your sleep, but we have been advised of some rough weather ahead, so I am going to turn the seatbelt sign on and ask that all passengers and crew return to their seats immediately. I'm sorry for any inconvenience. Thank you." He closed the mike. They continued to stare at the clock. At 2258, he paged the head cabin attendant. "Lisa."

"Yes, Captain," she answered.

"Is everyone tucked in? The weather disturbance is closing in on us."

"Yes, Captain; I'm the last, and I'm just sitting down."

"Thanks, Lisa." He looked over at his copilot. "I hope this ride's not too rough."

The clock clicked over to 2300 hours exactly. The next few minutes would make a high-speed roller coaster feel like a tame ride.

Captain St. Paul pushed the yoke forward and committed the gigantic airliner to a dive toward earth. His radio went dead along with the radar and all other communication gear on-board. Except for the red glow from the instrument panel, the cockpit was a surreal experience.

One mile away and five thousand feet above, the pilot of the jumbo jet designated plane F started a rapid, but by no means diving, descent to plane B's cruise altitude and turned on the transponder.

Simultaneously, in the hot Lebanon desert near the Israeli border, a thirty-second disruption of the monitoring signal from the transponder of France International Airline Flight 607-UF occurred.

"What's the matter?" the leader asked the technician, who began to twist the knobs on his monitors.

"I don't know; we seem to have lost the signal . . . maybe some electrical disturbance in the atmosphere, maybe it's this god-awful heat out here. I DON'T KNOW!" he shouted. Then, as suddenly as it went blank, the screen lighted again, and communications resumed.

"New York Control, this is France International Airline 607-UF, requesting an update on the weather conditions over Newfoundland. Over."

"See, everything's all right," the technician replied. "The transponder signal is as strong as ever. And their communication is normal."

In San Francisco, Bill looked at his watch. *It's zero hour; I wonder what's happening,* he thought.

He wanted to solve the problem, but he knew he was in the wrong place to handle the situation. The key lay in the equipment at the Maryland office and Fred, his assistant, had to do the job.

Larry Cotting finished reading the corporate document to Bill and asked, "Are there any questions about this last section?"

Bill answered a little too crisply, "No. I'm hungry; let's break for lunch."

Holly, Larry Cotting, and Bill walked from the Litten building a few short blocks to a Greek restaurant. The salad and gyros were good, but now they needed to return to Litten Industries and continue reading Theodore Litten's last will and testament.

Holly could see the tension in Bill's face.

Meanwhile, Captain St. Paul shouted to his copilot to be heard. The violent maneuver they had executed triggered every warning horn in the cockpit. He watched the altimeter count off the feet as they screamed toward the frozen ground below. He began to pull the shuddering plane out of the dive to level off at exactly five thousand feet. Slowly, the giant airliner flattened out at five thousand feet and the warning horns ceased. He pushed the throttles forward to bring the RPM's dangerously near the red line.

He handed his copilot a note that read: "Set a course to Iceland and give us the maximum speed and the shortest distance!"

They barreled toward Keflavik and turned the plane south. He keyed the intercom, "Lisa, please bring me a cup of coffee," he calmly stated.

"Captain?" She answered with a definite quiver in her voice.

"How are the passengers?" the copilot questioned.

"A lot of screaming went on, but they're quieting down now," she replied. "I don't think anyone was hurt. What happened?"

"Lisa, please bring me a cup of coffee," the pilot repeated.

When she arrived with his coffee, he handed her a notepad with the following message:

"I can't talk now, our voices in the cockpit may be monitored. Please quietly prepare the passengers for an emergency evacuation as soon as this plane stops; you have about forty minutes or so to get them ready. We have to be off this plane as soon as it is on the runway!"

Lisa nodded her head in the affirmative.

Forty-five minutes later, the Keflavik airport lights were in sight. Captain St. Paul saw a single green light in the control tower that indicated he could have a straight in approach. He observed vehicles with flashing emergency lights at the end of the runway. As soon as the wheels touched down, he reversed the thrusters and applied the brakes. Lisa and the crew had previously briefed the passengers on the evacuation procedures. They opened the doors and the exit windows before the plane finished its rollout. Emergency vehicles and emergency personnel stood by as the passengers slid down the evacuation slides and quickly ushered the passengers away. Captain St. Paul and his copilot were the last to leave; they jumped onto the slide at 2357. As they hit the ground, a truck waited for them. They dove into the truck bed; it roared away to the hastily erected command post. The truck skidded to a stop. They climbed out of the truck and stared at the empty jumbo jet that sat on the runway.

Israeli Embassy—Paris, France

The phone rang at zero zero three hours. "Hello, Embassy of Israel."

"We did not get the call. You can say good-bye to the plane." The line went dead.

"Did it work?" the French minister asked.

A man walked into the room and whispered to the Israeli ambassador; he nodded and waved him away with the back of his hand. "Gentlemen, a bomb just destroyed France International Airline Flight 607-UF."

The ambassador from the United States and the French minister both clenched their jaws and slowly let their gazes drift toward the floor.

"However, the airliner was on the runway in Keflavik, and all passengers and crew were off the plane and at a safe distance!" He was almost shouting by the end of his announcement. "Now, gentlemen, this operation is top secret. We averted the tragedy, but it must be kept absolutely quiet."

19

TADAO KOTO—OKINAWA, JAPAN, 1933

"Koto, Koto!" the young Chinese woman ran after the stately Japanese man who slowly walked down the narrow path that led toward the house. In the distance, the azure blue Pacific Ocean appeared as calm and peaceful as its name. A gentle breeze rustled the leaves and the grass along the path. "Koto! Koto! Please wait!" she called over and over. The man continued his rhythmic plodding as he descended from the Giant Buddha. He never looked back or acknowledged her. Soaring magnificently overhead on a thermal, a hawk turned in graceful circles. The updraft, created by the Pacific's cool ocean breeze and the volcanic rock's warm stone surface, provided the energy for its effortless flight. Tadao Koto reached the front door and removed his shoes as the young woman caught up with him.

"Koto, what am I to do?" she asked.

"It is time for a young bird to fly. You cannot stay on this mountain forever."

Koto thought, *The chest pain is getting worse, but the gods must allow me to live long enough . . .* He had started coughing blood when his illness began a year ago; now at fifty years old, he could feel the sickness devouring his life.

"Why, Koto, why?" she asked with pleading in her voice and in her eyes.

"The gods have deemed that you are to sire a great man. I have seen it in a vision," Koto replied.

"But, Koto, I am Chinese. No one on this island will have anything to do with me. When I go to the market, they make fun of me; when I am not looking, they throw things at me. If it were not for you, Koto," she grabbed his hand and began to kiss it, "I would probably be killed." She held his hand to her cheek.

He could feel the wetness of her tears flow over the back of his hand. "My dear Sinshee, the gods will protect you. They will keep you safe, and they will assure that your path will be of their choosing." In the house, Koto sat down on a pillow at his small table. His legs were still nimble enough to cross easily under the table; he folded his hands and closed his eyes to meditate.

Sinshee removed her shoes and quietly went to the small kitchen; the water was still hot on the stove. She placed some tea leaves in a cup and poured the scalding water over them. Her feet moved quickly in small running steps as she brought Koto his afternoon tea. With great ceremony, she wiped the table in front of him, then wiped the cup and with gentle but exaggerated movements of her hand, she set the tea in from of him.

Tadao Koto reached for the drink without opening his eyes and brought the cup to his lips. The warm liquid flowed smoothly over his tongue and down his throat. *It is a very beautiful life to have this young Chinese woman wait on me,* he thought. *Alas, the gods have spoken. After tonight, she must leave; however, she will not leave alone.* He smiled at the thought.

Sinshee sat on her knees, folded her hands in her lap, and bowed her head in submission to Koto while he finished his tea.

Later, as he sat in the bath, she poured hot water over him. "Sinshee," he said.

This startled her, as he rarely used her given name. She heard it so infrequently after arriving on Okinawa that she almost forgot how to answer to it.

"Yes, Koto," she replied with her head bowed.

"How long have you been here?" he asked.

"Almost four years, Koto," she replied.

"And how did you come to be here?"

"I was taken by pirates one day while I was fishing, Koto." She had told this story to him many times. "They sailed to this island, and I was sold as a slave in the market, Koto." She took a deep breath and added, "But the gods were kind. It was you, Koto, who bought me. You treat me like one of your own, not as one of your possessions. You are very good to me, Koto." She poured more water on him.

After the ocean swallowed the sun, millions of stars appeared in the cloudless sky.

A noise awakened Sinshee from a deep sleep. Neither she nor Koto ever ventured off their mats until daybreak, so the house always remained quiet at night; however, tonight someone moved across the entry to her room. A shadow appeared on the rice paper door as the door silently glided open.

She lay under the light blanket and began to shiver, even though the summer air was warm. Sinshee closed her eyes and hoped she was dreaming, but she knew it was not a dream. She could hear breathing; she could feel her blanket being lifted. Hands took hold of her sleeping garment and opened it. She wanted to cry out, but fear restrained her. She wanted to open her eyes, but apprehension prevented it. She lay very still as if she were dead. She was now naked; the warm summer breeze gently blew from the ocean and enveloped her body.

The man stood over her and opened his kimono.

She bit her lip. She stifled a cry in her throat . . .

Later, Koto left the room.

In the morning, she made no mention of the night, though the ache between her legs told her it had not been a dream.

Tadao Koto walked with her to the dock at Naha, where her passage to China was secured on a merchant ship. Sinshee's small silk bag held enough money to ensure her travel back to her village once she reached China.

Koto placed his hand on her head and said, "The gods will be with you."

She looked up at him. The tears in her eyes glistened from the sun. She repeatedly blinked to keep them from overflowing onto her cheeks.

"Here is a box. You are to open this only when you have a male offspring who is old enough to understand. You must promise me." His tone was emphatic.

"Koto, I promise." She bowed her head.

"And always remember, I will be with you," he added. With that, he turned and slowly walked from the dock up the dusty road toward his mountain home. Sinshee did not see him repeatedly blink as he tried to prevent the tears from streaming down his cheeks. It was late evening when he finished the climb up the mountain to his home. He left his shoes at the front door and went to his bed. Tadao Koto lay back on the soft mattress, closed his eyes, and died.

Lee Koto was born nine months later in Beihai, China, near the Viet Nam border.

20

LITTEN INDUSTRIES—SAN FRANCISCO

It took fifteen minutes of nonstop reading for the lawyer to read aloud the will. "Do you have any questions, Dr. or Mrs. Chandler?" he asked.

"There seemed to be a lot of legal verbiage in there, but let me see if I can sum it up. Stop me if I'm wrong," Bill replied. He then continued, "Ned was the major stockholder in Litten Industries. He has left all his stock and all his personal possessions to me. Additionally, there was a vote by the board of Litten Industries that if anything happened to Ned within the five years from the date of that election, I was to be named CEO of the organization." Bill sat back in his chair and stared at Larry Cotting.

"Well, it's a little more complicated than that, but I think you caught the idea." Cotting smiled a manufactured smile to prove he was a yes man.

"I'll have my company lawyer from Maryland contact you and your department to go over the exact details, but in the meantime, I guess we better look at the operation. We don't want it to become rudderless, do we, Mr. Cotting?" Bill asked.

"Larry, please call me Larry," he responded. "No, we don't want that to happen. The only thing on the plate you might consider major is an informal talk with a Japanese conglomerate that is interested in buying Litten Industries." Cotting took a deep breath and thought, *There, at least I got it out on the table. Koto will have to like that.*

The phone buzzed; Cotting answered. "Hello." He paused, he listened, and then he said, "Certainly, Phyllis, I'll tell him." He hung up and then realized he occupied the boss' chair. "Uh, Dr. Chandler," he stammered, stood up, and stepped away from the plush leather high-backed executive chair, "I think we should trade sides of the desk, sir." He folded the will and placed the original documents into the leather binder. "I will file this today to get the process started; if you give me the phone number for your lawyer, I'll also contact him." He started out of the room.

"Larry?" Holly asked.

"Uh, yes, Mrs. Chandler?"

"What was the phone call?" she asked and smiled at him.

"The phone call?" he asked.

"Yes, the phone call you just took. You said, you'd 'tell him.'" Holly paused and continued, "Don't you think you should before you leave?"

"Oh, my, yes! I'm sorry; Mr. Lee Koto, from that Japanese firm that wants to buy Litten, is waiting to see you."

He left the room by the side door.

Holly thought Cotting's exit was too hurried. "I don't think I trust him," she said to Bill.

"Don't start making any lawyer jokes; I think he was caught a little off guard with the sudden change in ownership and management."

Bill stood and walked to the window; he felt out of his element. A large percentage of his electronics business in Maryland came from the bloated appetite of the government. He knew the players in the Washington, DC, area and he was aware of their expectations. San Francisco was an entirely different environment. Litten Industries definitely projected an international profile. Bill felt like a fish out of water.

Holly could sense his uneasiness; she walked up behind him, put her arms around his chest, and laid her cheek on his back. For several prolonged seconds, she just held him; then she said, "Hey, this isn't any worse than trying to get off Carolina Beach with Jarvis after us; you'll do fine."

"Keep reminding me of that as we get deeper into Litten Industries," he responded.

"Now, Dr. Chandler, you have someone waiting to see you. Remember, I used to be a secretary, so I still know how to order a boss around." Holly laughed.

"You can order me around any day," he said as he turned around and kissed her.

Bill started to press the intercom button, then stopped. Instead, he walked across the expansive office and opened the door to the reception area. "Did you say I have a visitor?" he asked the secretary.

She was caught off guard. "Yes, Mr., I mean, Dr. Chandler."

Bill strode to the elderly Asian man who sat on one of the chrome and leather side chairs that faced the secretary's desk. He stopped about three feet from him and bowed slightly at the waist. "I'm Bill Chandler; I'm sorry, but if you came to see Mr. Litten, he is dead. Is there anything I can do to help you?"

The man stood and bowed at Bill. "Dr. Chandler, I am Lee Koto. I had an appointment with Mr. Litten, which I had made some time ago, to discuss some business matters. Unfortunately, I was not informed of his passing. Was it sudden?"

"Yes, there was a car accident," Bill responded.

As the two men talked, Holly stood outside the door to the office and observed them. She noticed several things. First, she noticed that as Koto talked, his eyes were everywhere except on Bill, as if he were looking for someone in particular. Second, she noticed that his name did not appear in the secretary's appointment book on the desk. Third, Holly noticed that Ned had spared no expense on the decorating of his offices, so she assumed his secretary must be a very well-paid executive secretary.

As such, she would certainly have contacted Koto when Ned was killed to postpone the appointment until a new CEO was in the office. Her suspicion was that the appointment was made yesterday or today and that she and Koto knew each other.

"Please, come in. Maybe I can help you, though I'll admit, this is my first day on the job. I offer my apology in advance if it is a waste of your time," Bill said.

"Thank you very much, Dr. Chandler. I would very much like to talk to you, if just for a few minutes. Do you mind if my aide joins us?" he asked as he pointed to a young Asian man who stood by the wall.

"Sure, no problem," Bill answered. He felt very awkward as they had not shaken hands, but he was trying not to blow his first international conference on a protocol problem. *Where's Holly? I need her to work her people magic and make this come off okay,* he thought.

"Mr. Koto, I'm Holly Chandler," she said as she walked past Bill and took the gentleman by the arm to lead him into the office.

"You must be the esteemed doctor's wife; however, from an old man's eyes, you look like his daughter."

She laughed on cue, turned her head, and gave Bill an "I told you so" look as she whisked Koto toward one of the leather couches.

"Dr. Chandler, I am sure this is not the right time for such an offer, but I am interested in acquiring Litten Industries. Mr. Litten and I had begun negotiating before his unfortunate accident. Your lawyer, Mr. Cotting, has most of the details of those meetings. Koto sat back in silence.

"Would you like some tea, Mr. Koto?" Holly asked.

"That would be very nice," he responded.

Holly went to the door and talked quietly to Phyllis. This pause gave Bill time to collect his thoughts as to how he would answer. The tea appeared moments later and was placed on the coffee table between them. Holly poured each one a cup and then sat down next to Bill.

"Well, I appreciate the fact that you and Ned had started negotiations. I can assume, since it was mentioned only in passing to me, that the talks are still preliminary?" Bill asked.

"Well, yes and no," Koto replied. "I believed Mr. Litten and I had reached a meeting of the minds; however, no official papers had been drawn up." He felt the tension build in spite of the manners everyone displayed.

"Obviously you have me at a disadvantage since I haven't been briefed on this and I just took over the organization this morning. I hope it won't be too much of an imposition to schedule another meeting after I have reviewed the situation with Mr. Cotting and looked at the proposition." It was a statement; Bill was not asking permission.

When the meeting was over and Lee Koto had left, Bill and Holly weren't sure why it had taken place at all. Koto talked much but said little.

Bill was sure he was noncommittal about his own position. He recalled that Koto's aid was never introduced, never spoke, and never even sat down with them. Bill assumed he was a bodyguard. They were about to leave the office when the phone rang.

Holly picked it up on the second ring. "Dr. Chandler's office, may I help you?" She sat on his desk with her skirt pulled to mid-thigh and smiled at Bill. "Who is calling, please?" There was a pause, "David? Is that a first or last name?" she asked.

Bill took the phone from her. "Bill Chandler," he said with a strained voice.

"Dr. Chandler, David here. Just wanted to let you know the device did detonate."

Bill tightened his jaw and took a deep breath. He could see hundreds of men, women, and children blown to pieces at forty thousand feet when the airliner came apart.

"But it was on the ground and empty!" David enthusiastically stated.

"Did you say empty?" Bill asked.

Holly looked at him with an inquisitive expression.

"Yes, Dr. Chandler. Your plan worked perfectly. I would like to meet with you as soon as possible—at your convenience of course—and find out exactly what you did."

"Well, David, damn, it looks like we hit a home run. Score one for the good guys." Bill, now relaxed and elated, continued, "Sure, I'm kind of tied up in California right now, but I'd love to meet you sometime. You obviously have my number, so give me a call."

"Dr. Chandler, Israel, France, and the United States owe you a debt we cannot pay. Unfortunately, we can't tell anyone about it either. You do understand, don't you?" David asked.

"Hey, not a problem, I wasn't real busy today anyway," Bill joked. He hung up the phone, grabbed Holly, and swung her around as if they were dancing.

"I assume, Super Doc, that you saved the airplane and humanity from another calamity," she said teasingly.

It brought his ego back from the ceiling at the same time. "The answer is yes, but thanks for the reminder that I'm just an ordinary guy," Bill humbly replied.

"Well, you're not too ordinary, or I wouldn't have married you, so why not take me dancing to celebrate? It was kind of a big day. You just increased your industrial base, though I don't think you qualify as a robber baron yet, and you did help that plane."

"Don't we need a place to stay first?" Bill asked. "I don't think going back to the old hotel is a good idea."

"You have the keys; why don't we stay at our new West Coast house?" Holly asked.

21

LEE KOTO—BEIHAI, CHINA

1933

Sinshee moved into a small shack and lived as an outcast behind her parents' home. The homecoming was not an Asian version of the Prodigal Son. Her father did not think that she put up enough struggle at her capture; thus, she brought shame on the family name. Things deteriorated further as her pregnancy progressed. The baby was obviously fathered by the hated Japanese. Sinshee was a pariah in her home and in her village. Her existence, after Lee's birth, was insufferable. Her subsistence came from scrubbing floors for the village mayor's wife and from begging food, but Sinshee endured in silence.

The Japanese had invaded China several years earlier; however, the small village of Beihai had no strategic significance and had remained unaffected for those years.

Sinshee sat in her little shack and held Lee on her lap. "I heard a man talking in the market today, Little One," Sinshee said to Lee. "He said the Japanese were moving out of Viet Nam and heading this way." She set him down on the floor to play.

"Everyone is scared because they say the Japanese will do bad things to us; but Little One, you are part Japanese." She picked up Lee and pushed back the fabric covering the door to their house. "No, Little One,

I am not worried. I like the Japanese. They didn't treat me any worse than my own family, and some of them treated me better."

The Japanese invaded their village three weeks later. The entire community was summoned to the center of the village, and the elders were called. Reluctantly, the mayor and several of the older men of the village stepped forward. Then their wives were called. They too came forward. With no reason given or a trial held, they were placed against a wall and machine-gunned to death.

"Now, people of Beihai, that is to show you that to resist us is futile. We will not harm any more of you if you cooperate with the occupational forces! Are there any questions?"

The villagers were quiet; the weeping had even ceased when the Japanese commander began to speak. He stood on the back of a truck and talked to the people. The wind whispered down the street through the crowd. The smell of cordite was pungent as the blue smoke slowly dissipated from the machine guns. "Well, are there any questions?" he demanded.

Slowly and timidly, Sinshee stepped from the crowd. She wore a tattered dress and carried a two-year-old baby on her hip. The crowd immediately began to put as much distance between themselves and her as possible. Her mother and her father were among the elders who had been executed. "Commander," Sinshee said with her head obediently bowed toward the earth. "Your humble servant would like to ask a question."

"So, only one small girl with a baby has enough courage to speak?" he asked and looked down at her. "What do you want, girl?"

"Commander, do any of your men come from Okinawa?" she asked in perfect Japanese.

"How did you learn to speak Japanese in this wretched village?" he asked as he wiped the sweat from his face.

"I was a slave to a wonderful Japanese man on Okinawa for four years, Commander. I would like to know what has happened to my master since I have been gone."

"Bring the girl and her baby. I will have my headquarters in the mayor's house." With that, he climbed down from the truck and walked up the street.

A soldier walked over to Sinshee and Lee, took her by the arm, led her down the road, and followed his commander.

During the occupation, Sinshee met Heri Okoy, a sergeant in the company stationed in Beihai. He provided food for her and Lee and treated them with kindness. His presence shielded them from the hatred of the rest of their village.

Sinshee and Lee moved into her parents' house after their death.

The occupying army used the better houses in town as quarters for their soldiers. Sergeant Okoy was billeted at her house.

Sinshee stood five feet one inch tall and weighed one hundred pounds. Several generations earlier, a European had intermarried into her family. This gave her facial features a mixture of European and southern Chinese. Her long straight jet-black hair draped around her face. Her dark eyes sat closer together than the average Chinese. Her nose and lips were prominent. In the proper setting, she could easily pass for someone of Mediterranean origin.

Sergeant Okoy stood taller than the average Japanese and had broad shoulders and a narrow waist.

Sinshee thought he looked quite handsome.

"I'm going to live here for a while," he announced as he stood in the doorway to her house.

"Please come in," she responded. Sinshee gave the sergeant her parents' room. She and Lee moved into the smaller space. Lee enjoyed the sergeant's presence, as he often played with him. For several days, the conversations were only at mealtime and were very limited in scope. The sergeant was not from Okinawa, but he had a private in his platoon who was, so he enquired about Tadao Koto. The private did not know Tadao Koto, since the private was from Hedo Point on the most northern end of the island.

A tropical depression moved into the South China Sea; the temperature and humidity became unusually oppressive. Sergeant Okoy finished his work at the headquarters and slowly walked up the dirt street toward Sinshee's house. All he could think about was cooling off. He was from Hiroshima, a city in the southern part of Japan, but it was certainly never this hot! When he entered the house, he immediately took off his shirt and sat down on one of the floor cushions. The sky began to darken and thunder could be heard in the distance. A breeze blew through the doorway, which only brought more heat. "A damn miserable place!" he said.

"Why is that?" Sinshee asked.

"There can't be any place hotter on the face of the earth. This must be where the gods send people when they have died and have led a bad life!" he mumbled.

"I don't think our village is so terrible," Sinshee timidly said.

He looked up at her. She stood with her back to the open door, her silhouette outlined by the fading light through the single wrap of white cotton she wore. The lines of her body could clearly be seen through the fabric. "Sinshee! You're beautiful!" he exclaimed.

"Oh, Sergeant Okoy, I think the heat of our village went to your brain or maybe to your eyes," she said and blushed.

As she served him dinner, he continued to stare at her. The storm increased in intensity. The small house almost shook with the deafening thunder and the torrential rain. After dinner, she put Lee to bed in her room and returned to the living room. Okoy held out his hand. Sinshee knelt on the floor in front of him.

"You are very beautiful," he said as he took her face in his hands, brought it up to his, and kissed her. She resisted slightly at first, then relaxed in his grip. "I want you," he whispered.

"Do you want me because you want me, or because you miss someone back in Japan?" she queried quietly.

"There's no one in Japan. A soldier moves too many times to have a girl back home."

"Then you have had lots of girls all over China?" she asked.

"No, Sinshee, I haven't had any girls anywhere in China." He kissed her again; this time, he pulled her closer to him.

Sinshee took his hand and pressed it to her breast. He felt the softness under his fingertips and began to gently caress it. They kissed more passionately, and she felt him respond. "Come," she said as she led him into the bedroom. "Lie down here." She motioned him toward the futon. She undressed him and brought a pan of cool rain water that she had collected from the torrents that flowed from the roof. Lightning flashed and gave a strobe light effect as she stood at the foot of his bed and let her dress fall to the ground. In the flashes of light, she appeared as a statue standing before him. She then knelt beside him and began to wash him with the cool rain water.

Sinshee was devoted to Sergeant Okoy. She felt as if she were married, even though they had had no ceremony. When he arrived home in the evening, she had his dinner prepared and was ready to serve him. He and Lee played continually until it was time to put Lee to bed. Then he turned his attention to Sinshee. Her dreams and her desires were fully fulfilled with this soldier from the occupying army. She knew she was hated by her neighbors, but that was nothing new; it had been that way since she'd returned from captivity and given birth to Lee. Sergeant Okoy wrote his parents and told them of his new love, promising to bring her to Japan as soon as possible. Their life was one of bliss for five months.

Then one evening, he told Sinshee that his unit had received orders to move northward. He arranged passage for Sinshee and Lee to mainland Japan and sent her to Hiroshima to live with his parents. Sinshee knew there was no future for her, or for her son Lee, in Beihai. She knew she would do whatever was necessary for Lee Koto to fulfill the destiny hinted at by Tadao Koto that night on Okinawa.

Okoy's family took her in, treated her as a daughter, and treated Lee as their grandson.

22

SAN FRANCISCO—PRESENT DAY

Bill and Holly prepared to leave Litten Industries at the end of the day. They agreed to drive to Ned's house and stay there. As he closed the office door, the phone rang. Bill grabbed it at the secretary's desk and punched three different buttons before he got the correct line.

Holly rolled her eyes and shook her head. "You can design space systems yet can't figure out how to answer the phone?" she whispered.

"Bill Chandler, here," he said. "Right . . . good; I'm glad you got here that quickly. For now, find some warehouse space and just sit tight. Keep one man with the gear, and keep your phone handy. I'll let you know if and when I need you. And, John, thanks for the support and the service." He hung up the phone.

"I presume you got the toys you wanted, right?" Holly asked.

"You betcha." He took her hand and started for the elevator. "Now let's go find that house."

The elevator carried them to the lobby, where they signed out with the evening guard. Bill and Holly then walked toward the street corner. Earlier in the day, they had parked their car in a public garage across the street. Bill took Holly's hand as they stood at the corner and waited for a walk light. The traffic moved at the usual "it's past five o'clock and I'm going home" pace. The stoplight turned; they had just stepped off the curb when Holly yelled, "Bill! Look out!" She pulled her hand from his and ran back to the edge of the sidewalk. He looked up and saw a car bearing down on him. He didn't have time to think, just to react. He jumped onto the bumper of the car, then dove onto its hood. Bill landed on his shoulder and rolled off onto the sidewalk. Holly, safely behind the stoplight pole, stared in disbelief. The car bounced against the curb and skidded sideways down the street before regaining control. Incredibly, no cars were struck.

"Bill!" Holly screamed when she regained her balance. "Bill, are you all right?" She looked about frantically. "BILL!"

He pulled himself up using the door handle of a parked car next to him. "Holly! I'm over here. You okay?" He hobbled down the sidewalk to Holly; his pant leg was torn at the knee and his suit coat was torn at the shoulder. Evening rush hour traffic sped by without anyone stopping. He leaned on Holly as he surveyed the damage to his knee. There were no serious wounds, just an abrasion that needed a wash and a bandage. "What was that about?" he asked.

"Maybe the same ones from the boat last night?" Holly asked as she surveyed the damage to his suit. "That's the second suit in two days. San Francisco is hard on the wardrobe." She put her arms around him and held him tightly. "Seriously, Bill, someone really wants us out of the way. Don't you think we need to get the police involved?"

"Well, remember we tried to get the sheriff involved. There was no evidence of the attack. Do we want to tell them that we stole a car and drove off the ferry last night? Oh, by the way, did you see the piece in the paper this morning on that?" he asked.

"No, I looked. It certainly wasn't on page one," Holly replied.

"No, I found it while I was in the head—"

"I get the idea," she responded.

"Anyway, it was a small article near the classified section. It said a car accidentally rolled off the ferry last night. Blamed the driver for leaving it in gear with the engine running. I'll bet their insurance company loves that one. Hope they don't get stuck with the search and rescue bill."

He lowered his voice. "Come on," he said as he took her by the arm and started briskly across the street when the light turned. "Let's get under cover; I feel pretty exposed out here." Bill limped as they hurried to their car.

Ned Litten's San Francisco mansion sat high on a hill in the Pacific Heights area. Built of stone after the 1906 earthquake, it came complete with an old carriage house that now served as a garage. Holly drove the car to the garage door; Bill got out and used the code that Larry Cotting had provided to open it. Holly then pulled the car in beside Ned's collection of restored vintage automobiles and motorcycles.

"Wow!" Bill let out a long whistle as he surveyed the machines. "This is incredible; I had no idea Ned was into cars. I love it!" he shouted, as his engineering nature led him from one vehicle to another. The collection included a 1960 black Triumph, a 1950 red Ford, a 1957 turquoise Chevrolet, and on the end, a 1963 green Jaguar XKE convertible. Additionally, several Harley-Davidson and Triumph motorcycles rested in the far corner.

"I'll never get you out of here," Holly bemoaned.

"It'll take a lot," Bill countered.

"Cookin' won't do it, but I'll bet I know what will!" she said with a gleam in her eye. "But for now, I'm starved." She left the garage and headed toward the house.

Earlier on the drive to the house, they had picked up Chinese food. They sat in the kitchen and ate from the white containers.

"Bill, does it seem to you there is a lot of violence connected to Litten Industries?" Holly asked.

Bill was quiet for a prolonged time. He laid down his fork and looked at Holly. "Yes there seems to be, which isn't logical. Everything that has happened since Ned's death, combined with your observations, points to something deep and sinister, but I have no idea what."

After dinner, Holly and Bill toured the house. An open stairway led to the second floor. Three bedrooms, each with a private bath, took most of the north end of the second floor. A movie theater and an entertainment center took most of the south end. The master bedroom suite occupied the entire third floor. A sitting room, with a leather couch and a large federalist desk, dominated the north end of the chamber. A four-poster king-sized bed and two marble-topped end tables graced the back wall. On the largest wall, a tapestry of a hunting scene hung from the ceiling's molding. The lighting was dim in the bedroom; the walls held substantial sconces with large candles. The marble bath contained a large walk-in shower and an iron ball-and-claw foot tub. The interior decorating of the master suite revealed no sign that a woman ever lived there on a permanent basis.

"Well, it has a man's look," Holly murmured.

"Gee, I kind of like it," Bill retorted.

"You would."

Bill carried their things in from the car, checked the locks on the doors, and then joined Holly for the night.

23

KOTO'S HOUSE—SAN FRANCISCO

The doorbell rang; Han let Charlene in and escorted her to the library. The house, situated on the crest of one of the eastern mountains, faced the bay area and commanded a view of Treasure Island, the Oakland Bay Bridge, and the downtown skyline of San Francisco.

"Koto will be with you soon," Han said as he backed out of the room and quietly closed the door.

She walked to the window and concentrated on settling her nerves. Charlene never missed on a contract. As she repeatedly reviewed the entire sequence in her mind, she did not understand how Chandler and his wife could possibly be alive. Even if they had missed when they'd fired at the airborne car, there was no way to swim from the middle of San Francisco Bay at that time of night. She decided they must have been picked up by someone in a boat. That was the only answer. She remembered watching the car sink; there were no lights from other boats except one in the distance toward the mouth of the bay. "Just what are the odds?" she said aloud to the empty room. "Well, whatever the odds are, Chandler and his wife must have hit the jackpot that night!"

Her thoughts were interrupted by the door opening. "Ah . . . I don't seem to remember your last name," Koto said.

"I don't believe I told you my last name. My full name is Charlene Dominic, but you may call me Charlene, if you like," she answered.

"Charlene, that's a beautiful name; I will call you that, though I wonder if it is your real name," Koto responded.

"Real names are like perceptions. Whatever the perception is, that is reality. The same with names," she answered.

"Well, Charlene, my perception is that Dr. Chandler and his wife are still alive. Is that perception reality?" Koto asked.

"Yes, it would seem so," she answered flatly.

"Then I assume the contract has not been fulfilled," Koto angrily said.

"That's true." The words stuck in her throat; she hated failure in herself. But the truth was the Chandlers were still alive.

"What do you see as a solution to our dilemma?" Koto asked.

"The obvious answer is to complete the contract," she said. "Or do you have something else in mind?"

"A recent turn of events precludes immediate completion of the contract. In fact, it may be fortuitous that they are still alive. What I do want from you are two things. First, I want you to become friends with Mrs. Chandler. Then, should we need your services to detain them either temporarily or permanently, you will be in a perfect position so that there will be no more failures." He let the word *failures* hang, like a dead leaf on a tree in winter, as he walked toward her. "It is a beautiful view, isn't it?" He placed his hand on the small of her back. He felt her stiffen under his touch. *There is a woman under there, and not just the frigid, cold-blooded killer she likes to portray,* he thought.

"You said there were two things. Getting to Mrs. Chandler is one. What is the other?" she asked coldly.

"Let's call it some recompense for not making good on the contract the first time."

"And what do you have in mind?"

He let his hand slide down the small of her back, felt the firmness of her hips and the top of her thigh. "Han will show you where you can change into something more suitable for the rest of our conversation." He looked at her with lust in his eyes; tonight, he would use the body of this cold-blooded assassin for his own entertainment.

Charlene knew she must pay a price for failure. If satisfying an old Japanese businessman was the only price, she would comply. Taking the initiative, she turned to him, kissed him on the mouth, and thrust her tongue into his mouth while she sensuously rubbed her body against his. Then she turned abruptly and followed Han out of the room.

"You will find everything you need in here," Han said as he held a door open.

Charlene walked into the bedroom and saw a thin negligee lying on the bed. She walked over, picked it up nervously, and fingered the fabric. *Oh well, I must pay the price for a messed-up job,* she thought. She walked to the mirror and held it up. In the mirror, she could see the door on the opposite wall open. Out of the shadows stepped an Asian female. She was slim, wore a kimono, and was probably about forty years old.

"I'm Toki; why don't you slip that on and join us in the other room?"

24

NED LITTEN AND KOTO—DESERT WELLS, CALIFORNIA

Lee Koto had established his business practices from his study of world history, not from Japanese history. He recognized that the outcome of World War II proved that Japan had no concept of the Western world. To him, the men who started and conducted the war suffered from traditional Japanese values of ancestor worship and the Samurai code. He reasoned that to win in the international marketplace, he must use Western strategies and out-maneuver them. To do this, he traveled widely in North America and in Europe and studied their business practices. He also realized that honesty was not always the best policy and that, if challenged, he must stand ready to shift any blame onto his adversary. To him it was obvious: he would exploit their weakness for his gain.

During the fifties and the sixties, Lee Koto built his power base with the determination and the focus of a man on a divine mission. He began to build his empire at the age of twenty-five by leveraging the property he had inherited in downtown Tokyo. He used these proceeds to invest in a struggling automobile manufacturing company. This business enterprise then led to an aftermarket parts company that produced parts for European and American cars and trucks. Soon, he had acquired a fleet of ships that carried his goods, and other Asian manufacturers' goods, throughout the world. Through shrewd investing, his real-estate holdings extended from the United States and Europe through Japan and Malaysia. By the late eighties, the world recognized Lee Koto as a world industrial leader and entrepreneur.

Although Koto's public life demonstrated philanthropy, his private life plotted revenge against his hated enemy, the United States of America, for killing his mother. *Vengeance is mine* became his mantra.

Lee Koto's involvement with Ned Litten occurred by accident. In 1998, his corporation owned a fleet of small corporate jets. None were large enough to carry more than ten or fifteen people. One evening, an executive from an airline company and Lee sat in a bath at one of the Tokyo clubs. As they relaxed in the hot water, Lee learned of the impending sale of a medium-size airliner. He inquired about the condition of the plane.

"It needs work, but the airliner is structurally sound. I know a company in the United States that performs complete overhauls; we have used them on several airliners. The company is Litten Industries. They perform excellent electronic and mechanical services, and they can customize the inside to any specification," the executive told him.

Lee calculated that the airplane would be as good as new at a fraction of the cost of a new plane. He made the deal that night.

The next morning, he phoned Litten Industries and talked to Ned Litten.

Lee Koto's newly acquired airplane landed at Litten Industries' Desert Wells facility one month later. Following a six-week restoration, Koto flew to America with his crew to inspect his new plane. They arrived at Los Angeles International Airport.

Ned provided a beautiful young bilingual Japanese-American woman to meet Koto at the airport and dispatched his personal Lear Jet to fly him to Litten Industries at Desert Wells. It was a short thirty-five-minute flight. Koto alighted from the plane and was greeted by the blistering sun of the Mojave Desert.

Ned's limousine coasted to a stop beside the aircraft as the engines spun down. Ned Litten stepped out. "Mr. Koto, welcome to Litten Industries," Ned said as he bowed at the waist.

"Ah, Mr. Litten, I have been anxious to meet you," Koto replied and returned the gesture.

Ned ushered him into the car. The air-conditioned air inside the car contrasted starkly with the heat that emanated from the tarmac. They drove to the hangar; the door opened slightly to allow the vehicle inside and then closed behind them.

"We can't keep it cold in here, but it is bearable if we leave the door shut," Ned said as they alighted from the car.

Koto stepped from the limousine. His refurbished airplane sat in the dim interior of the massive hangar. The silver metal of the fuselage shown even in the muted light.

A spotlight was turned on, and it illuminated the company logo of Koto International painted on the tail. Lee smiled with pride.

"Hey, Mr. Koto. If you think that looks good, come on in and see the inside," Ned said enthusiastically as he escorted him up the ramp parked against the forward cabin door.

Inside, four compartments divided the interior of the airliner. The first held thirty seats, two on each side. Reversible backs allowed two seats to face each other with a table between. The second compartment contained the galley and the lavatory. The third compartment housed large leather chairs, a bar, and a dining area. The fourth compartment comprised Koto's bedroom. Windows with automated shades formed the ceiling over the bed. If Koto flew at night, he could lie on the bed and see the moon and the stars.

"I hope this meets your approval," Ned said as they walked into the bedroom area.

"The workmanship is excellent, but I never thought it would be otherwise. If my pilots and mechanics are satisfied with the work performed on the engines, then I'd say it is more than satisfactory."

"If you have time to stay overnight, I'd like to have dinner with you. We have accommodations here," Ned said.

Earlier, Ned had flown in a chef from Los Angeles to cook a gourmet Japanese meal. That evening at dinner, Ned and Lee talked about the work necessary to makeover a used airplane. This fostered a friendship between the men, at least from Ned's point of view.

Koto was an exceptional listener. Sinshee, his mother, had taught him that most people, if not all, will open up if someone is willing to listen. Koto coupled this with his creed that knowledge is power. As he listened patiently to Ned, he acquired the knowledge he needed. Lee Koto sipped brandy on the patio and looked at the expanse of the desert sky; there, he formulated his plan to carry out the next phase of his vengeance. His plan would involve Litten Industries. He would assign his best agent, Kim Long, to find Ned Litten's Achilles' heel.

Kim Long and Ned Litten

Kim Long followed Ned Litten for several months and looked for Ned's weaknesses.

"Mr. Koto," Kim Long said into the phone, "I have an idea I'd like to explore with your permission."

"You know, Kim, I want control of Litten Industries. For the present, though, I just want control of Mr. Litten. If you have something in mind that will work toward that goal, please proceed." He encouraged his agents to use their own initiative.

"Yes, sir, I understand. I believe I can deliver control of Mr. Litten to you within two years, or possibly less," Kim replied.

"I am a patient man; I will trust you to do your best," Koto responded.

For the next six months, Kim Long continued to shadow Ned. He became thoroughly familiar with Ned's moods, Ned's preferences, and Ned's vices. He concluded that the fruit lay in Ned's vices.

Long knew Koto owned the High Desert Casino Hotel in Las Vegas, Nevada. This venue provided the perfect location to spring the trap.

By use of an alias, *Jin Choi,* Kim Long developed a cover as a vendor to Litten Industries and cultivated a friendship with Ned. After a year and a half, he concluded it was time to put the plan into action.

Ned welcomed Jin Choi into his office. "Great to see you again, Jin."

"Good to see you too, Mr. Litten. Our company has a new valve I want to show you. I think you'll be interested in using it, but first," he reached into his briefcase and withdrew an envelope, "this is a token of my appreciation for your company's business over the past year." He handed the envelope to Ned. "Litten Industries' use of our products has greatly increased my sales this year." He smiled.

Ned opened the envelope and took out a certificate for a free long weekend's stay at the High Desert Casino Hotel in Las Vegas, Nevada. Ned grinned and said, "Hey, Jin, this is great."

"The certificate is good for a suite. When would you like to go?" Jin asked. "I'll make certain it is reserved."

Ned looked at his day planner. "The first weekend of next month would be perfect," he replied.

Jin said, "I'll make all the arrangements."

After he left Litten Industries, Kim Long called Gregg Newman, the head of security for Koto's casino, and instructed Newman to make the reservation for the suite. As they talked, Kim Long laid out the rest of the plan.

After ensnaring Ned Litten, Kim Long placed a call to Lee Koto, who was not immediately available. As Kim waited for Koto's call, he recalled the beauty of his plan ...

The air was cool that spring morning when Kim Long followed Ned and Liz from the Litten Industries Headquarters at Desert Wells, California, to Las Vegas.

Kim Long and Gregg Newman put their plan into motion after Ned left a drunk Liz asleep in the hotel suite. When Ned sat down at the poker table, Gregg instructed the bartender to increase the amount of alcohol in his drinks. Simultaneously, the surveillance cameras in the corridor on Ned and Liz's floor began to play a loop that had been recorded earlier. Only the date and time stamp kept recording. Nothing was actively filmed for the next thirty minutes.

Kim Long took the elevator for his rendezvous with Liz.

Upon exiting the elevator, Long slipped on white latex gloves. He opened the door with a passkey and stepped into the suite.

"That you, honey?" a slurred and drunken voice called from the bedroom.

Quietly he glided across the plush carpet to the bedroom door. He peered in.

Liz lay on the bed. Her hair fell in tangles across the pillow and her arms were sprawled out to each side. Her eyes remained closed as Kim Long approached the edge of her bed. She lay under a satin sheet, with only her shoulders and her head exposed. In her drunk and drug-induced stupor, she saw shadows and wavy lines. Her mind tried to sort out the difference between reality and dreams, and the dreams won.

Kim Long sat on the edge of the bed. Liz's scarf lay on the nightstand next to the bed. He took it, slipped it around her neck, and began to tighten it. She awoke enough to sense the danger and tried to resist but could not. In a matter of seconds, she was unconscious. He continued to hold the scarf tightly until he was certain she was dead. Then he rolled her on her side and pulled the sheet over her shoulders so it looked like she was asleep. He left the scarf tightly wound around her neck. He then quietly left the room.

Kim walked down an empty corridor to the elevator. As he entered the elevator, he slipped an express card into the elevator control panel. He then removed his white latex gloves, slipped them into his pocket, and took an uninterrupted ride to the casino floor. He passed Gregg Newman and stopped ten feet away. Kim pulled a package of cigarettes from his pocket, took one out, and put it between his lips. This signaled to Gregg that the job was finished. The rest was easy. Ned Litten would be theirs in a matter of hours.

Kim Long then returned to his hotel room across town and waited for Koto's call. He knew Koto would reward him for a job well done.

"Mr. Long," Koto said, "I'm sorry I missed your call earlier."

"You should know that Mr. Litten is now obligated to you as we planned," Kim Long answered.

Koto swelled with pride. His long-term plan went into motion.

Koto, always a patient man, waited several months before contacting Ned Litten. During that time, he used his influence in Asian economic circles to divert more business to Litten Industries, thus ensuring the prosperity of Ned's enterprise.

"Litten Industries, Mr. Litten's office," Phyllis, Ned's secretary, said into the phone.

"Mr. Koto of Koto International calling for Mr. Litten," Koto's secretary said.

"I'm sorry, Mr. Litten is in a meeting. If you would like to leave a message, I'm sure he'll get back to you later today." She always handled the overseas calls very carefully. Ned had made it clear to her that a lot of their work came from abroad, and she should treat any call from an Asian country with special respect.

"Mr. Koto is very interested in speaking to Mr. Litten as soon as possible," she replied.

"Yes, I'll have him call Mr. Koto back as soon as possible," Phyllis replied.

Ned returned the call just after the sales meeting and placed the call to Japan. "Mr. Koto, great to hear from you again. What can I do for you?" Ned asked.

"Mr. Litten, I have an associate on his way to the United States, and I would like you to meet with him. He has a business proposal from me. I'd like you to give it strong consideration."

Ned knew Koto had been instrumental in sending a significant number of contracts for airliner overhauls to Litten Industries from companies as well as governments in the Asian community. He eagerly listened to him. "Well, thank you, Mr. Koto. I'll look forward to meeting with him. What was his name again, please?"

"Long, Kim Long; he has worked for me for many years. I trust you will consider his proposition very carefully. He will arrive in the States tomorrow. I hope you can see him at your office next Monday, if that is convenient for you?" Though phrased as a question, it was a command, and Ned understood he was to change his plans if necessary.

"Hey, Mr. Koto. Not a problem. I'll look forward to seeing him. Be sure and tell him that if there's anything he needs while he's here in the States, just let me know." Ned sat back in his chair with his feet propped up on the desk as he looked out the window. "And, Mr. Koto, you know it's always a pleasure doing business with you," Ned said as he hung up the phone. "Funny, I know most of Koto's front office personnel, but I don't know that name," Ned said to himself with a puzzled expression on his face. *Well, Ned ol' boy, you've really arrived!* He thought smugly as he gazed around his office at his trophies. *You started as a low-life salesman, and now some of the most powerful men on the planet are calling you to do business. Yeah, you've really arrived.*

As Lee Koto hung up the phone, he smiled a sarcastic smile to himself. *Litten, you're like the rest of the world. You are only interested in your own lust, but what you don't realize is that I will use your lust against your precious United States.* With that thought, he laughed out loud for one of the few times in his life.

25

NED LITTEN— DESERT WELLS, CALIFORNIA,

The Year 2000

After his experience in Las Vegas, Ned decided to concentrate on business. Ned focused his attention on his company as if it were his family. He quit drinking, gambling, and carousing. His contract with the United States government to renovate a fleet of transport and executive planes, both military and nonmilitary, crowned his accomplishments that year.

The old US Air Force base at the edge of the Mojave Desert, closed by the BRAC Commission, once again bustled with activity. Airliners filled the hangars; other planes sat on the tarmac and waited their turn. Ned took the old commanding officer's building for the company headquarters and reopened the officers' club as a company restaurant and bar. He sponsored local music groups, and on Friday and Saturday nights, the club opened for dinner and dancing.

The once-faded town of Desert Wells rose like a Phoenix. Many locals found work at Litten Industries, and new people moved into the area. This spawned a building boom. Overnight, Ned's company transformed this small isolated corner of the Mojave Desert.

Competitive business practices and shrewd investments allowed Litten Industries to acquire other companies. Acquisition of Rogers and Bailey Import Export Inc. provided an essential element for Litten Industries; however, unknown to Ned, it also provided an essential element for Lee Koto. With that purchase, Ned moved his corporate headquarters to downtown San Francisco. Born into poverty, he now controlled a conglomerate with a net worth of more than two hundred million dollars.

Rogers and Bailey Import Export began as a fabric importer. After Ned bought the company, he expanded their imports to include heavy equipment parts.

The day started like most. Ned ate his usual breakfast of coffee and a bagel, and then he drove his favorite car, the '57 Chevy, to work.

"Good morning, Mr. Litten," Phyllis said as he walked past her toward his office.

"Morning, Phyllis. What's on the agenda today?" She followed him into his office; therefore, he did not stop at her desk or even look back.

"Mr. Hansen from Rogers and Bailey at nine o'clock, Mr. Cotting at nine forty-five, and a Mr. Kim Long at ten thirty," Phyllis answered.

"Kim Long? Oh, yes, a representative from Koto in Japan," Ned said.

"Mr. Long's secretary made the appointment. She told me Mr. Long represented a far-eastern oil company. I just assumed they had a plane or planes they wanted overhauled," Phyllis said.

"Okay, thanks. Say, would you get me a cappo this morning? Thanks." He didn't wait for an answer.

The morning proceeded very routinely until Mr. Long arrived.

"Mr. Litten, Mr. Kim Long is here," Phyllis said into the intercom.

"Fine, I'll be right out," Ned replied. He personally greeted and escorted potential clients to his office. He felt it gave him an edge and demonstrated the type of customer service Litten Industries provided.

"Mr. Long," Ned said as he bowed. He then looked up with shock as he recognized a man he knew as Jin Choi. Ned stammered, "Uh . . ."

Kim Long stood up, brushed past Ned, and entered Ned's office. Dressed as a business executive, he wore a Western business suit. Ned did not notice the bulge under Long's left arm from the holster for his Glock nine-millimeter pistol.

Ned followed Kim Long into his office and shut the door. They walked over to the couches and sat down.

"What the hell's going on?" Ned asked.

"I do appreciate your secretary's promptness in scheduling this appointment." He spoke condescendingly with a pronounced British accent.

Probably Oxford educated, Ned thought.

"Certainly, Mr. Long—or is it Mr. Choi? How can Litten Industries be of service?" Ned replied patronizingly after he regained his composure.

Long ignored the question. "My employer sent me to settle an account," he replied.

"Does your company owe Litten Industries a payment for services?" Ned questioned.

"No, Mr. Litten. You owe my employer for housekeeping," Kim Long responded.

"Housekeeping?" Ned responded completely confused. "If there is a problem with a housekeeping contract, couldn't you get it handled via the usual channels?" Ned had no idea about the direction of this conversation. "I'm sure if you will give me the details, we can solve the problem in no time."

"It seems a year ago, my employer arranged housekeeping services for your hotel room in Las Vegas." He paused to let the silence drive home the point, then continued, "It's payback time!"

Ned gasped audibly. His mind raced back to Liz, lovely Liz, drunk Liz, dead Liz. "I don't know what the hell you're talking about!" Ned said as he jumped up from his seat, stood, and glared at Kim Long.

Long sat relaxed with his arm casually draped on the back of the couch.

Ned thought, *You little . . . you can't come in here and do this!*

Kim set his briefcase on the couch beside him. Carefully, he opened it and took out a manila folder marked Executive Correspondence. He handed it to Ned. "Please, Mr. Litten, if you would be so kind as to look at the paperwork I have brought with me." His voice was silky in its sweetness. "I believe you will find everything in order," he paused, "and we can get down to the method of payment."

"I see," Ned's voice cracked. Ned took the envelope; his hand shook as he opened it. The envelope contained a series of photographs, all with time and date stamps. The first photo documented the arrival of Liz and him at the casino. Other photos showed him fighting with her at the slot machines, him dragging her down the hall, and her throwing up in the bathroom. It showed him looking at her dead body. As Ned went from photo to photo, his bravado faded and he developed an attitude of resignation. "Okay, Long. What's the scam?" Ned asked in a subdued tone. He could imagine his whole organization taken from him. He envisioned his entire life crumbled in that moment. Ned sat down and faced Long, but stared at the floor.

"Then you are familiar with the debt?" Kim Long asked mockingly.

"Yes," Ned whispered. Suddenly his shirt was wringing wet and there was visible perspiration on his forehead. He stood up and walked to the wet bar. His hand shook as he poured himself some water from a carafe. Finally, his hand stopped shaking, and he returned to the couch. "So, what, may I ask, is the balance on the bill?"

"It's very simple. Occasionally, certain airplanes brought into your facility for maintenance and overhaul will be designated Special Projects. When these planes arrive, a specific crew, which I select, will be assigned. These people already work for you—we placed them at your organization over the last two years—so nothing will look out of the ordinary. Also, a division of your company handles imports; I believe the name of the company is . . ." he hesitated.

"Rogers and Bailey," Ned supplied.

"Ah, yes. Rogers and Bailey. There is a Mr. Hansen who works there. He will receive an occasional delivery which must go directly to your desert facility. This will *NOT*," he paused for emphasis, "go through the usual channels, and the shipping crates will *NOT* be opened."

"Are you talking drugs?" Ned asked. "I want nothing to do with drugs!" He tried to sound emphatic and authoritarian.

"First, Mr. Litten," Kim Long said in a quiet whisper, "you have no basis to say what you will do and will not do for my employer, but to answer that question, no drugs are involved. These aircraft have a specific purpose for a later date. Details on each Special Project airplane will be retained by you personally and will not be given to anyone until my employer needs it. Second, you will get a handsome bonus for each Special Project that is processed at your facility. The money will not come from the party that owns the aircraft. The payments will be in cash and untraceable. You will not report this income on your personal income tax." He opened his leather briefcase and took out a computer disk. "Here is all of the information you will need. It gives the names of the crew members who will do the work and it contains contact information if any problems develop." Long handed the disk to Ned, watched him look at it, and wondered if Ned could see Liz's face reflected in the disk. *The woman gave her life for the most perfect extortion scheme ever devised,* he thought. "Upon completion of the aircraft renovation, the overseer of the crew will provide you with specific information. You will have the only copy of that information. When that information is needed, you and you alone, will be contacted." Kim paused. "If you understand everything, that concludes our business today. Do you have any questions?" Kim Long asked.

Ned sat in silence and stared at the disk in his hand. Then he looked at Kim Long and answered, "No questions."

Long stood up and walked to the door. "I'll be in touch with you." He then opened the door and left.

Ned's mind replayed the night in Las Vegas over and over. The sudden buzzing of his phone interrupted his thoughts. Slowly he stood up, walked to the desk, and answered it. "Yeah," he mumbled.

"Are you all right, Mr. Litten?" Phyllis asked.

"Uh, yes," he said as he regained his composure. "What do you want?"

"I have the strangest caller who insists on talking only to you, but, Mr. Litten—he won't give his name or anything. Just said to tell you he is from security at a casino in Las Vegas. What should I do with him?" she asked.

Ned's mouth was dry and he could not speak.

Several seconds passed. "Mr. Litten, are you there?" Phyllis asked again.

"Yes, Phyllis." Ned took a deep breath. "Go ahead and put him through." He looked at the phone in his hand. It shook almost uncontrollably.

"Hello, Mr. Litten?" the voice asked on the other end of the phone.

"Yes, this is Litten. Who's this?" Ned demanded.

"Ah, Mr. Litten, you know names ain't necessary. For the record, though, my name is Hank Zellar. You might remember, we met in your hotel room some time ago. I helped you with a situation. Remember?" He paused.

"Yeah, I remember, what do you want?" Ned demanded again.

"Hey now, Mr. Litten, don't go and get all bent outta shape at me. Like everyone else, I just work for a living. Know what I mean?" he said. "Hey, not a problem. I suspect this ain't been one of the best days you've had for a while, huh?" He paused, but Ned didn't reply, so he went on. "My boss said I was to call you and ask two things. One, if you remembered the situation? I think you do."

Ned now responded, "And the second thing?"

"Well, she said if I were to ask real nice, you would offer me a job at your desert plant, the one that works on airplanes. She told me you would make me chief of security."

"Is that so? Did your boss tell you what I'd pay you for your services?"

"Ah hell, Mr. Litten, she said you'd be fair. I trust you. Do you trust me?"

"Do I have a choice?" Ned asked as he looked down at the pictures and videotape on his desk.

"No, not really," Hank said matter-of-factly. "It'll be real nice to see you again and nice to work for you. I'll call back in a couple days to make the arrangements for my new employment."

The line went dead in Ned's ear. However, he knew payback had arrived.

Over the next two years, the Desert Wells facility received fifteen planes from Kim Long designated as Special Projects. They were mostly commercial, but a few were government-owned. One was a plane in the US presidential fleet. Ned assigned the correct work crew to each plane's renovation. His plant manager at the facility thought it unusual that Mr. Big was so eager to participate in the assignment of crews.

"Hey, what's the deal on this project that you're all over it? Did I do something wrong?" the plant manager asked when the first one arrived.

"No, I have a special relationship with the owner, and he asked me for a favor," Ned replied.

"What favor?"

"He wants me to oversee this one. Anyway, it'll make your life easier for a few weeks," Ned explained.

26

LEE KOTO—HIROSHIMA, JAPAN

Sinshee awakened early the morning of August 6, 1945, even though today began her assignment to the second shift at a ball-bearing plant. Officially, victory over the United States was imminent by the triumphant Japanese forces, but the rumors told of one disastrous campaign after another. She looked at Lee's picture. Her son would soon be a man. Sinshee thought, *This war must end before he is old enough to also be claimed by it.* Grief had come to their house eight months earlier when they had been informed that Sergeant Heri Okoy had died in battle in China. She left the house by the back door and walked up a small rise into their garden. This plot of land helped supply the meager rations they all shared. As she looked up at the sunny sky, the sounds of the city floated past her on the breeze. Again, Sinshee thought about her son; suddenly, there was a flash of light as bright as the sun. Sinshee felt the intense heat. Her clothes burst into flame; her skin was burned; her hair and her eyebrows were singed off; she was in severe pain. She tried to scream, but her scream vanished into the eternity of the universe and was forever lost by the explosive blast that literally blew her burning body into a million pieces.

Lee and his grandfather escaped the blast of Hiroshima on August 6, 1945. The week before, he and his grandfather had traveled to Lee's uncle's house in a small mountain town three days' journey away by foot. They left for home on August 4. The road twisted around and over several mountains and threaded its way through lush green forests. An occasional cloud punctuated the blue morning sky when suddenly a brilliant flash lighted the sky before them and grayish black smoke ascended toward heaven. It appeared as if the fires of hell had burned through the earth's crust. A thunderous boom echoed across Japan and around the world.

"Grandfather, what is that?" Lee asked as he pointed toward the sky.

"I don't know; it sounded as if the gods were angry."

As they approached the last hill before Hiroshima, they found the way clogged by masses of people fleeing the city. Lee's grandfather stopped a man. The man hurriedly told him about the explosion.

"Grandfather, why are there so many people on the road?" Lee asked.

"The man said a bomb dropped, but what he said can't be true . . ." His grandfather's voice dropped to a whisper. "They are saying it was as bright as the sun and hotter than a thousand furnaces; that many people have died and they say the city is ... is gone." He pulled Lee from the road. "We can't get there on the road. There are too many people." He hurried through the trees. At the top of the mountain, he stopped. Lee caught up to him; together they gazed down at the ruins of their beautiful city by the ocean. It was gone; tangles of buildings marked the landscape. Fires burned to the south, north, west, and east to the ocean. Smoke drifted toward the mountains. "We must find your mother and grandmother," his grandfather said. He grabbed Lee's arm and started down into the hell on earth that remained after the first atomic bomb.

When they reached their home, they found it standing. A larger building stood beside it and provided protection. They found Lee's grandmother in her bedroom. The motionlessness of her body announced her death. Her blanket covered her body to her neck, but a large mass of concrete, torn from the adjacent building, covered her head. They never found a trace of Sinshee.

With the loss of his wife, Lee's grandfather sank into despair. He ate very little and within two months became a cachectic shell and died.

Alone, Lee knew he must deal with his grandfather's body. He found a small cart and placed his grandfather's body on it. With tears streaming down his face, he pulled the cart through the wasteland to the mass grave west of the city. No one helped him unload the body and lay it beside many others deposited that day. He wanted to say a prayer, but he did not know how, so he cried. On his way home, he passed the skeleton of his school. Lee's fifth grade year had ended with a party two months previously. Now the twisted and fused poles of the swings stood as a headstone to his schoolmates, now dead. Arriving home, he lay on his mat for two days before hunger drove him out of the ruins of his house. He went to the countryside, scrounged for food, and often ate from garbage cans. Lee Koto, small of frame but strong of spirit, spent his days alone with the stench of death, rotting food, and decaying corpses as his only companions. These early days of survival simulated a blacksmith's furnace and anvil which forged into his soul a single truth. The United States of America ripped his mother, his grandmother, and his grandfather from him. For Lee Koto, vengeance became his only reason to live.

Lee woke one morning with the impulse to clean up the remains of his house. He began to remove debris from his grandparents' bedroom. A gaping hole in the floor beckoned him. Lee laid down on the floor and peered under the house. There was a crawl space large enough for him to explore. He found a candle, lit it, and slipped through the splintered opening. Cobwebs sizzled when the flame of the candle touched them, but he saw nothing else. He was about to return to the opening when a gleam of light sparkled to his left. He quickly moved toward it. There he found a box; the top was ornately carved, and there were small brass rings on each end for handles. He tried to lift it, but the box was heavy and he needed both hands, so he blew out the candle. The darkness closed in on him like a black curtain. Without the light, he felt fear wash over him and wondered if he would be trapped under the house forever. He had no more matches. Panic surged through his body like a typhoon.

He looked toward the hole; an old Japanese man held a lantern through the hole in the floor; the light flooded the dark space and illuminated the pathway out. Immediately, he crawled and dragged the box toward the old man. By the time he reached the hole, there was no man visible; puzzlement filled his mind and a chill ran down his back. Lee scrambled through the opening with the box. He was glad to be out of the darkness. He took the box to his room and dusted it off. The tooled brass latch began to shine as he rubbed it with a cloth.

Lee Koto opened the lid. Several tightly rolled scrolls lay on the top. Anxious to see what the box contained, he took out the scrolls and saw a wooden tray. Carefully, he lifted the tray and looked underneath. First, he saw gold coins; he eagerly counted them—twenty-five in all. Next, he saw a small gold statue of a Buddha. He was ecstatic. He now had money and possibly something to trade. Food would be easier to find. Years later, Lee learned that one of the scrolls was his greatest treasure. He held in his hands a deed to a significant piece of property in downtown Tokyo. The land was a gift; it had come from the Japanese emperor to the man his mother had told him about, his own father, Tadao Koto of Okinawa. All taxes and fees were exempted for the life of the empire. He remembered that his mother had told him about the box and that she had said she would give it to him "when it was time."

A short time later, the occupation troops arrived and brought with them food and assistance. Many of the survivors were hesitant to take anything from the conquering army; however, Lee recognized that knowledge was power, so he immediately worked his way into good standing with the Americans. He did not speak English, but he found it easy to learn. He was bright and energetic and found favor with one of the bureaucrats sent to rebuild the infrastructure of the southern mainland. As soon as a rudimentary school was established, he enrolled. With some mastery of the English language, he quickly found work as a translator for the occupying forces. With the money he made, he began to rebuild his grandfather's house.

A family moved in next to him; the father worked in a plant that built trucks during the war. With this man's knowledge and with some money supplied by Lee, they opened a small vehicle repair shop. Then an opportunity arose to buy a struggling automotive manufacturing plant. It later grew into a major manufacturer of cars, trucks, and heavy equipment that further expanded Lee Koto's fortune.

Lee was thirty years old when he found his first catalyst for vengeance. He visited the small city of Kamakura on business and felt called to visit some of the famous shrines in the area. He took a trolley inland to a small neighborhood. Partway up the mountain, a giant Buddha statue gazed at the azure ocean. It was a warm day; a few white clouds drifted lazily over the rugged mountain tops. As he neared the shrine, he saw a sign that marked the maximum height of a devastating tidal wave in the late 1880s. He stopped and turned toward the sea; the ocean lay several hundred feet below. Lee tried to imagine the size and the force of a wave that tall. He tried to imagine the panic that the people in its path felt. *That's nothing like the power I will exert on my enemies and the panic it will cause,* he thought. Looking east toward the United States, he felt the hatred burn. A commotion occurred near the statue. A small group of demonstrators was exchanging angry words with police. The tenor of the crowd grew louder. Pushing and shoving ensued. Lee stood in a group of tourists and watched the developments until a shot rang out. There was a scream and one of the policemen fell to the ground. A growing lake of blood flowed from the policeman's chest. The tourists ran in panic in all directions and took any cover they could find. Several bumped into Lee as he stood motionless and watched the police, who charged the demonstrators with their batons.

The once-peaceful demonstration descended into pandemonium and panic. A young girl ran toward Lee; a policeman followed closely behind her. The officer grabbed her by her long black hair and dragged her to her knees. He raised his baton to strike her. Lee, without thinking, seized the club from the policeman's hand, spun him around, ripped off his riot helmet, cracked him on the front of his skull, and knocked him unconscious. He lifted the girl by the arm and quietly escorted her away from the melee.

They didn't speak until they were in his hotel room. "We should be safe here," he said.

"Thank you very much," she said. "Now I must go."

"I think it would be best for you to wait a while until the police capture all of the people they want. Someone might recognize you on the street right now."

"Are you worried about my welfare, or do you expect something from me for the rescue?" she asked.

"I expect nothing. Your virtue, if you still have it, is safe in this room," Lee stated flatly. "What I would like to know is what you and your friends demonstrated against today."

"We angrily protest the capitalistic policies of the central government. They are just a puppet for the despicable policies of the dogs in the United States. The only ones with the real concern for the people of Japan are we, the Japanese Communists," she said with defiance in her eyes and with a fervent belief in her cause. "We are ready to die for the people of Japan!" she announced.

He had no use for the Japanese Communist Party, but it occurred to him that perhaps they could be useful.

"Who is your leader?" he asked.

"Are you a security policeman?" she asked.

"No, of course not, silly girl. Would I have hit that policeman to save your neck if I were?" he asked her.

"No, I guess not."

"Of course not! Now, tell me who your leader is."

"I won't tell you, but I will arrange a meeting if you really want to meet him," she said.

Lee took a piece of rice paper from the hotel desk drawer and wrote his address on it. He then took out enough yen for two train tickets to Tokyo and handed them to the girl. "Don't tell me who he is. Just bring him to that address on the thirteenth of October. That's a month from now." He looked at her; she had quite a beautiful face. She was small framed and had long black hair that hung straight and fell below her shoulders. *Another time I might be interested,* he thought. "Now, I believe that it's safe for you to leave. Please go out the back door so no one sees you."

27

THE CHANDLERS—DESERT WELLS, CALIFORNIA

Bill and Holly spent the next morning in briefings at Litten Industries. Presentations by the accounting, production, and sales departments took nearly three hours. Ned had developed an efficient and forward-thinking organization. They reviewed the company's vision and mission statements and then were shown the company's organizational charts, which included all of the divisions' charts. Bill absorbed as much as he wanted, then decided he needed a diversion.

"I'd like to go to the production facilities at Desert Wells," he announced to Larry Cotting.

"Well, sir," Larry stammered, "we actually hadn't set up for that yet. There's still a lot more paperwork to deal with."

"What's the fastest way to get there?" Bill asked.

"Uh . . ." Larry appeared to be searching desperately for a delaying action.

"Phyllis, when Mr. Litten wanted to go to the production facilities, how did he do it?" Holly asked Bill's secretary.

"Ma'am, the company helicopter took him to the airport, and he flew down in the company Lear jet," she replied without hesitation.

"Phyllis, please have the helicopter and the jet ready at once," Holly said. "Dr. Chandler and I will be going to Desert Wells this afternoon. Please let them know of our arrival."

Larry looked stressed, a fact that was not lost on Holly.

Thirty minutes later, Holly and Bill boarded the helicopter at the heliport atop the Litten building, which took them to the airport. Fifteen minutes after that, they entered a Lear jet for the ride to the production facility at Desert Wells. The plane flew southeast through the San Joaquin Valley to Bakersfield, and there it turned due east to the Mojave Desert.

"It's so bleak—it's beautiful!" Holly exclaimed as the Lear dropped below ten thousand feet. "There's really nothing as far as you can see, is there?" Then she gleefully added, "Wait! I see the airport."

The long runway extended over two miles from the southwest to the northeast and was quite capable of landing a plane of any size. Adjacent to the tarmac, the mammoth hangars loomed high into the air. Next to one of the hangars sat a jumbo jet.

The pilot requested permission for a low pass over the field and over the facilities to give the new "bosses" a bird's-eye view. The Lear then banked for final approach and landing. As it rolled to a stop on the tarmac, a black limousine drove up. Holly and Bill descended the plane's short ladder and were met by Joe Turnball, the facility manager, and Hank Zellar, the chief of security.

Joe wore khaki slacks and an open-necked shirt, sunglasses, and a straw hat. "Glad ya didn't pick too hot a day for your first visit," he said as he thrust his hand toward Bill. With his other hand, he tipped his hat and said, "Ma'am."

"Hi, I'm Bill Chandler, and this is my wife, Holly," Bill said as he shook Joe's hand. He noticed Joe's hand was rough and calloused. *He must still participate in some of the actual work. I like that,* Bill thought.

Joe introduced Hank Zellar, escorted them to the waiting car, and opened the car door. Holly stepped in, followed by Bill; Joe slipped in, took a fold-down seat, and faced them. Hank Zellar headed to a security vehicle parked nearby.

"Well, Dr. Chandler, what is it that you want to see?" Joe asked.

"Since we've taken over the controls of Litten Industries, I'd like to have the five-dollar tour, not the two-bits tour," Bill said and grinned.

"All right then. To do it justice, it'll take about a full day. We can start now, and if you can stay over, we can finish in the morning." Joe seemed to know what they wanted. "We took the old Air Force VIP quarters, remodeled them, and now they are the executive quarters for company personnel. I think you'll be comfortable there."

They toured the headquarters, the control tower, and the recreational facilities.

Turnball's secretary hastily organized a casual dinner. She invited the division heads and their spouses; most attended even though it was short notice. Everyone worked hard to impress the new boss and his wife.

After dinner, Holly heard music coming from the bar. "Bill! Let's go in and dance!" Holly said. "That sounds like great country music."

"I have to get started early in the morning, so if you don't mind, I'll pass," Joe said.

"Sure, that's fine. We can walk back to the quarters. Thanks to you and all of your people for the great reception you gave us today on such short notice," Bill replied. He and Holly then entered the bar and found a table. After Bill ordered a beer, they danced several dances.

"I'll be back," Holly said. "I have to powder my nose." She walked down the hallway to the ladies' room. Holly stood at the mirror and retouched her makeup; a young woman walked up beside her.

Holly smiled a greeting.

"You're the new boss man's wife, ain't ya?" the young woman, about twenty years old, said with an accent that was a cross between illiterate and Southern drawl.

"Yes, I'm Holly Chandler," she said as she offered her hand.

At first, the woman was unsure of what to do; then she took Holly's hand and shook it almost as a man would shake another man's hand. "The odds are against him, ya know that, don't ya?" she asked.

"Odds? Against him? I'm not sure what you mean," Holly answered.

"Of livin'," the woman stated rather matter-of-factly.

"Living?" Holly parroted.

"Lady, you livin' in some kinda hole er somethin'? There's talk all 'round that yer husband's gonna be killed real soon. Probably just like poor Mr. Litten." She fluffed her mass of curled blonde hair with a long-toothed comb.

"Just who is going to kill my husband?" Holly asked.

"Ah come on, yer not fer real. How'd some poor ol' gal that works the line goin' to know who would do somethin' like that? But that's what the talk is." She quit playing with her hair and walked toward the door, and then she stopped and turned back. "I'll bet it has somethin' to do with those planes they don't let most of us work on." Before Holly could respond, the woman slipped out the door.

Holly rushed after her but lost her on the crowded dance floor.

Holly stood at the edge of the floor and tried to find the girl as the music reached a crescendo in both volume and rhythm. The dancers crowded the floor, moving faster. Multicolored strobe lights flashed about the room. After drinking the beer, the inundation of her senses made Holly feel dizzy and faint. As she was about to collapse, a strong arm encircled her and held her up.

"You okay, little lady?" a deep voice asked.

"Yes, I think so. I guess it got a little warm in here for me. Could you help me to my table?" she asked.

"Sure enough, just point me in the right direction," he said.

Holly and the stranger made it through the throng just as the music ended. He helped her into her chair.

A surprised Bill looked at her. "You all right?"

"She looked like she was a going to pass out, so I grabbed onto her. Hope that's okay."

"Thank you very much. Please sit down," Bill said. He looked again at Holly. "Are you sure you're all right? You don't feel sick or anything, do you?"

"No; really, I'm fine. I just got too hot or something. The noise and the lights seemed to get to me."

Turning to the stranger, Bill said, "Again thank you, Mr.—uh—I'm sorry, I didn't get your name."

"Slick Jones," he said with a smile as he shoved his hand forward. Like most of the other men in the room, he looked like a cowboy.

Bill took his hand and shook it warmly. "Slick, that's an unusual name."

"Well, partner, it's not my real name, but it's the one everyone around here knows me by. So, if someone was looking for me, they'd ask for Slick. If you tried to find me by my real name, you'd never find me." He continued to grin a broad smile. "I need to get back to Ginny, otherwise she might end up heading out of here with some other cowpoke tonight. Wouldn't want that to happen, ya know what I mean?" He stood up, nodded at Holly, and then left.

"Bill, let's get out of here. I'd like to go lie down. I still feel a little queasy."

When they hit the cool night desert air, Holly immediately started to feel better, and the block and a half walk to the executive quarters revived her. The clear night sky revealed millions of stars that twinkled brightly in the heavens; a new moon added to its splendor. "It's so magnificent; let's sit down for a while," Holly said.

"Sure you feel good enough?" Bill asked.

A bench, made from a tree trunk, sat by the walk. A cactus garden separated them from the entrance to the quarters. "Bill, something happened in the ladies' room that may have precipitated my fainting," she said.

"Oh, what was that?" Bill questioned.

She told him about the entire conversation with the blonde. Afterward, they both sat in silence for several minutes. "So it would appear, my darling husband, you may be a marked man," she said.

"Hum . . ." he replied.

"No offense, Bill, but that's a heck of an answer," she said sarcastically.

"Oh, I'm sorry, I was lost in thought," he replied.

"Really, Bill. What are we going to do?" Holly asked.

Bill paused a few seconds before he answered, "That adds strength to our suspicion that Ned's accident wasn't an accident. If we can determine why Ned was killed, it would explain why someone would want to kill me. Does it have anything to do with the mysterious planes that only specific employees get to work on? Does it have something to do with someone who wants to buy the company, like Mr. Koto or Mr. Smith? On more than one occasion, I remember Ned found himself in dicey situations, usually of his own making, but what motive would make someone murder Ned and stage it to look like an accident, if in fact that's what happened?"

Holly snuggled in closer to him, linked her arm in his, and laid her head on his shoulder.

"That's nice; why don't we go in now? I think I'm feeling better."

He tipped his head toward hers and kissed her. "You don't feel better, you feel good," he said.

28

UNDER COVER—DESERT WELLS, CALIFORNIA

Gregg Newman, concealed in the shadows, watched as Bill and Holly left the club and walked toward their quarters. He keyed his microphone. "They just left and are walking back," Gregg whispered.

Hank Zellar answered, "Check; I'm going in." Dressed completely in black, including a ski mask, he pulled the screen from the window and pushed the window open. He then slipped into the ground floor apartment and dropped noiselessly to the floor. He surveyed the residence; it consisted of a bedroom, a living room–dining room combination, and a full kitchen. In the kitchen, he extinguished the stove's pilot light and turned on the gas to all four burners. The hiss of escaping gas made an eerie sound in the darkness as the gas began to fill the room with its pungent odor. He quickly taped a spark device to the door and to the doorjamb just above the lock. Once more he surveyed the apartment; all was ready. He climbed out the window and replaced the screen.

Hank rounded the end of the building and saw Bill and Holly pass under the streetlight at the driveway entrance. *There's going to be a hot time tonight,* he thought and smiled a sadistic smile. Crouched in the bushes across the street from the quarters, he waited. His elation grew as he watched Bill and Holly divert to the bench and sit down. *The longer you take, the better! We'll get more bang for the buck!* he thought.

Within minutes, the torrential gas flow from the four burners completely saturated the apartment. The bomb expanded its killing potential with each passing second. Fortunately for Bill and Holly, a hole existed in the dining room wall that adjoined the apartment next door. The contractor who had installed fiber-optic cable had created the hole, but had been unable to complete the installation because of the untimely arrival of the new boss and his wife.

The gas reached the saturation point and began to seep into the neighboring room.

Bill and Holly stood up and walked toward the building; suddenly, an explosion rocked the entire facility. It blew out the walls of the executive quarters and turned them into a flaming inferno. The explosion and fire completely gutted the building and left it a smoking ruin.

Newman did not see Bill and Holly get knocked to the ground by the blast, so he presumed the ignition had happened when they opened the door.

"Holly! Are you all right?" Bill asked as he rolled over.

"Uh, yeah . . . yes. I think I am," she replied.

"Come on!" he whispered coarsely. "Let's get out of here." Bill spied a Jeep across the street parked next to a hangar. It had the Litten Industries logo on the side. "Over there, keep down." Staying in the shadows, he led her to the Jeep. There were no keys, but it took little effort to hot-wire it.

"You're very good at that. Something else they teach at MIT?" she mused.

"Never know when the practical side of electronics will come in handy," he said as he pulled away from the curb. Bill kept the lights off and drove in the opposite direction from the wail of the approaching fire engines. The street ended at the runway. He slowed enough to pull over the curb and drove toward the runway.

"Uh, excuse me, Dr. Chandler," Holly said, "any reason you're not on the road anymore?"

"I hate traffic," he grunted. Bill crossed the end of the runway and slowly drove down a small incline into a dry river bed. There, he switched on the lights. He followed the river bottom for fifteen minutes. Finally, he turned off the lights, pulled up a small embankment, and spun the Jeep around to face Litten Industries. They could see the orange glow of the burning building punctuated by the strobe-like red lights of the emergency vehicles.

The local police chief walked up to the fire chief. "Think anyone's inside?" he asked.

"If they are, they're goners," the fire chief replied.

"Uh, Chief," a man in jeans and a black shirt said to the police chief.

"Yeah?" the chief replied, turning around. "Oh, hi, Hank."

"A little before the blast, I came out of the club and started down the street; I saw two people heading up the walk here." He motioned with his hand toward the front of the burning building.

"Yeah, who's staying there?" the chief asked.

"The new head of the company and his wife, Dr. and Mrs. Chandler, are the only ones as far as I know. I'd dropped them at the club earlier tonight. Gosh, I sure hope it wasn't them I saw going in . . ." He let his voice trail off.

Bill and Holly sat in the dark and looked back at the Litten Industries complex.

"Bill, I wonder if they think we were in there when it blew up," Holly said. "You think it was an accident?"

"Sure, the same kind of accident that's happened twice since we arrived on the West Coast. Holly, someone doesn't want us to take the helm of Litten Industries. They're trying very hard to get rid of us. The next time we may not be so fortunate," he answered.

"Okay, Doc. Just what do you have in mind?"

"Let's drop out of sight and see if we can turn up anything," he said.

"Certainly, want to disappear into the desert?" she asked.

"No; tomorrow morning, when they discover this Jeep is gone, I have a feeling that they will start an aerial search. Let's find a place to hide that no one will ever suspect and later head back to San Francisco." He turned the Jeep north and drove slowly over the flat desert toward Death Valley. About an hour later, they crossed an east-west highway. They turned west. Just before daylight, the road merged onto Highway 395. Bill turned north toward Carson City, Nevada. At Mammoth Lake, they pulled into a motel parking lot and stopped.

"I need some sleep," Bill said.

"Do you think it's safe to stop here?" Holly asked.

"We should be out of the search range. Let's stay here today, and tomorrow morning we'll head west through Tahoe."

29

FIRE'S AFTERMATH— DESERT WELLS, CALIFORNIA

Soot smudged the fire chief's clothes. He took off his gloves and banged them together as he walked back from the smoldering ruins. "Melted everything it couldn't burn," he said to the police chief. "My men are going to have to sift every damn bit of ash to find out if they were in there."

"Well, we know this for sure. People saw them leave the club and witnesses claim two folks walked up to the building a few minutes before the explosion. Now Dr. and Mrs. Chandler are nowhere to be found." The police chief shook his head. "My guess is when you're done sifting, you're going to find a couple scraps left of the former owners." He took a deep breath and let out a sigh. "That's a damn shame, Chief," said the police chief.

The fire chief then turned to Hank Zellar and said, "Looks like you've lost your second boss in a month. A feller might wonder if being the boss of this outfit is unhealthy."

"I can't believe it. Only a gas leak could cause that kind of explosion. We've had some renovations going on. I hope none of the workmen screwed something up," Hank said and shook his head. Hank then walked back to his office and shut the door. He picked up a phone and dialed an access number that switched his call into an encrypted circuit. The call rang into the console of Lee Koto.

"Hello," Koto said as he picked up the exclusive line.

"This is Hank Zellar down at Litten."

"Yes. You have news for me?"

"It would appear they are dead," he said.

"Define *appear,*" Koto said.

"The building burned to the ground; we have witnesses who watched them go in before the explosion. Now we can't find them anywhere. I have to presume they are dead," he answered.

"Have you seen the bodies?" Koto demanded.

"No, sir, but—" Hank was cut off abruptly.

"I want positive proof. I want body identification, and don't call until you have it!" Koto slammed the phone back into its cradle. Koto thought, *If they are now dead, I will proceed with the acquisition of Litten. If that is true, there will be no further use for Charlene. Pity.*

"Prick!" Hank said as he hung up the phone. He then punched a button on the intercom line.

"Howdy," Gregg Newman said into the phone.

"Koto wants proof the doc and his wife are dead," Zellar said.

"So, get a strainer. After that blast, there won't even be teeth, hair, or eyeballs!" he said sarcastically.

"Don't give me any lip, Newman!" Zellar shouted into the phone. "Get over there and find some proof!"

30

ESTABLISHING A NEW HEADQUARTERS—SAN FRANCISCO

Bill woke at first light. He tried to quietly slide out of bed, but the movement awakened Holly.

"Hmm . . ."

"Good morning, Mrs. C," he said.

She rolled over and smiled at him. "Good morning, Mr. C."

"That's Dr. C. What, did you forget so soon?" He laughed; that was an inside joke from the time they'd first met. They kissed and she pulled him close. After the terrifying night before, she felt secure and loved with him holding her.

The motel coffee shop provided a light breakfast. Afterward, they drove north on US 395 and then turned west on US 50. The route took them past Lake Tahoe and down the western slope toward San Francisco.

"So, exactly where are we going and what are we going to do?" Holly asked.

"That's an excellent question. I want to gather information and have a safe place to stay tonight. My bet is that they think we're dead, but they have a lot of debris to sift through to confirm it. We need to get to our command post and determine who is after us. Hopefully, we can eliminate them first."

As they drove toward Sacramento, she thought, *This wasn't supposed to happen.*

Several hours later, they arrived in San Francisco.

Bill used a newly acquired cell phone to call his associates from his Maryland company. "John?"

"Hi, Bill, I'm really glad to hear from you," John replied.

"Where are you?" Bill questioned.

"We found a place by the water and set up shop as you told us to," he answered.

"Does anyone from Litten know where you are?" Bill asked.

"No, Bill," John replied.

"Good. Give me directions to your location, and John, have one of our people contact a boat captain named Sam Barkley. He's on the payroll. Have him meet us as soon as possible."

Bill parked the Jeep alongside a warehouse not far from the Embarcadero. Holly and Bill walked to a small door and knocked. The door opened.

"Hi, Boss!" A young man with long blonde hair who wore a neon orange T-shirt, blue jeans, and hiking boots, greeted them. He tossed his head to throw the hair back from his face and stepped back. "Oh hi, Mrs. Boss."

"Hi, Randy," Holly said as she walked into the small office. An old desk and a desk chair with a torn seat and the springs showing were the only furniture in the room. The light came through the windows, but the accumulation of smoke and dirt over the years served as blinds and blocked any prying eyes. "Great interior decorator," Holly quipped.

"Hi, Randy, where's the rest of the crew?" Bill asked.

"Once we got the equipment unloaded and assembled, John went to find your boat captain. The rest went to get some cots and food. How long do you think we'll be here, Doc?" Randy asked.

"Honestly, I don't know for sure. That's why I need you guys to gather information." He looked around. "You don't happen to have a newspaper, do you?" Bill asked.

"Naw, but I can run out and get ya one, if you want," Randy said.

"No, not right now; why don't you show me what we have?" Bill asked.

They walked through another door into the main warehouse. Three tables were set against the wall. "We brought the Tel-Ray system." Randy motioned toward the first table. "We have a communications center on the second table. It can remotely access Tel-Ray and has satellite links with GEO tracking." He handed Holly and Bill each a small black plastic case about the size of a quarter. "Put this on the inside of your belt or wherever it's comfortable to wear. I can track you anywhere along a line from the north pole to the south pole."

Holly opened the case; a small medallion fell into the palm of her hand. "I'm impressed; could this hang on a chain?" she questioned.

"Sure, just slip a chain through this hole." He pointed to a small hole along the edge.

Bill looked at the third table and raised his eyebrows. "Did John know you brought that?" He pointed at the electronics placed on the table.

Randy looked at the floor to avoid Bill's gaze. "Well, Boss, I've been working on this for a while, and we do need to field test it." He shuffled nervously. "In any case, I thought you might need some firepower." His voice trailed off.

"Firepower?" Holly asked and looked at Bill.

"Just a little project we've had on the drawing board for a while. We're not even sure it works," Bill replied.

The door scraped as it swung open. John Goldstein, Bill's number one research assistant, walked in followed by Sam Barkley. "Bill, Holly, am I ever glad to see you. There's a story in the paper that says you two are presumed dead in a fire at the Litten Industries Desert Wells site," he said as he shook their hands. "I found your boat driver," John continued.

The comment brought a glare from Sam, who turned to Holly and put his finger on the bill of his cap; the gesture was a cross between a salute and a greeting.

They all shook hands, and then they sat down on wooden shipping boxes.

"Why's it so unhealthy to run Litten Industries? And just what the hell is Litten Industries anyway?" Randy asked.

"In a thumbnail sketch, Litten Industries is a company that overhauls and renovates airliners. It performs mechanical services, electrical services, engine overhauls, and interior and exterior decorating and painting. During the last three years, the company has worked on several hundred or more airliners and military aircraft," Holly replied.

"Why it cost Ned Litten his life and why Holly and I are now targets is another question. We don't have the vaguest idea. A Japanese businessman approached me the day before yesterday to buy Litten. He implied that Ned desired to sell Litten to him before Ned's untimely death. Additionally, a Mr. Smith also made a very generous offer for the company. That proposal included a heavy who wanted to beat me into signing the deal when I refused."

"Okay, Bill," John spoke up. "What's the plan?"

"First I want the commercial lines to Litten monitored. It won't be illegal, since I own the company. Also, I want background information on Lee Koto and Larry Cotting."

"Who are they?" Randy asked.

"Cotting is the legal counsel for Litten; technically, he's my lawyer. Koto is a Japanese businessman who I know less about; he is one of the people who wants to buy the company. There is also a Mr. Smith who is a complete unknown. In fact, I don't know how to contact him. We'll have to wait for surveillance on him when, or if, he contacts me again," Bill answered.

John looked at the assembled men. "Randy, set up Tel-Ray to monitor Litten Industries and Cotting. I'll find out where Koto hangs out and learn as much as I can without stirring the pot. Eventually we'll need Tel-Ray on him too. But first, we need to know as much about him as possible." He then looked at Sam Barkley. "Boss, what's your assignment for the captain?"

Sam smiled approvingly.

Bill turned to him and said, "Sam, Holly and I need a safe place to stay at night that's not obvious. Could you bring your boat here and let us live on it for a few days?"

"Sure, you're paying the bill. I'll have to arrange with the port authority for the dock space. And—" he stammered, "uh, are you paying the dock bill? I owe them a little—"

"Not a problem. Just tell John how much you need. Okay, we all have things to do, so let's get to it. I want a staff meeting here at seven tonight, and we'll see if we have uncovered anything. Any questions?" Bill looked around the room at each of his men and made certain he made eye contact so each could have a chance to say something. "Good. Just one more thing; whoever is behind this plays for keeps. Captain, can you get us some firepower?"

"Anyone that has any special requests, just let me know," Sam replied.

The men left the warehouse quietly. When the door closed, Holly looked at Bill. "So, Boss, what's my assignment?" she asked.

"Tomorrow, after we get some results from our Tel-Ray surveillance, you and I will return to Litten Industries. With the guys watching, I think we'll be reasonably safe there. I want you to start through any records we can get our hands on and see if we can determine if there's a problem with the company. You might see if you can get Phyllis, Ned's secretary, to open up." He pulled her close to him and kissed her. "I love you."

"I love you too. Please be careful, Bill," she said as she laid her head against his chest.

"As soon as Sam gets the boat here, we'll get some rest," Bill said.

The next morning, Phyllis, distracted by some papers on her desk, failed to notice when Bill and Holly stepped from the elevator and silently crossed the lobby. They stopped in front of her desk. She realized someone was standing there, and she slowly looked up.

"May I help—oh my God!" She sat straight up in her chair with a look of shock and surprise on her face. "I mean, Dr. Chandler and Mrs. Chandler. You're alive!"

"Phyllis, is there a problem?" Holly asked innocently.

"Well, yes," she stuttered again. "The newspaper carried a story and the notice of it spread throughout the office—" she stammered "—that you both were believed killed in a fire at the Desert Wells Facility."

"Now, Phyllis, we look very much alive, don't we? So how about getting us some coffee and then come in; I need you to find some things for us." Bill and Holly walked from her desk and into the president's office.

Word spread through the company like a wildfire that the Chandlers were still alive.

Larry Cotting heard the news in the men's room and rushed toward the executive suite. Almost at a run, he burst through the door into Bill's office. "Dr. Chandler!" he gasped as he stared at Bill. "You're alive!"

"Mr. Cotting, just what seems to be wrong with everyone here today?" Holly asked.

"The fire at the plant—you are presumed dead," he stammered. "What happened?" he blurted out.

"Was there a problem at the plant?" Bill questioned.

"Well, yes. The executive quarters blew up, some kind of gas leak. The entire structure burned down; everyone thought you two were inside. How did you get out?" His voice carried a little concern and a lot of suspicion.

"Well, you see," Holly began, "after we walked home from the club, it was such a beautiful night I persuaded Bill to take me for a ride in the desert. We got lost and ended up a long way from the plant, so we just drove back to San Francisco. We thought we'd call from the office today." She smiled sincerely at Cotting. "Do you suppose you could call them for us? And please let them know we had a great time and we're sorry we left like that." She gave him a commanding look and arched one eyebrow for emphasis. "Thank you, Mr. Cotting."

He turned toward the door to hide his look of anger and fear.

"Say, Larry," Bill said, "I would like to see the proposal that Japanese fellow made for the company; I believe his name is Lee Koto. And something else . . . now, what was it?" He turned around and looked out the window for a full thirty seconds of silence. The tension in the room rose faster than the stock market on a good day. "Oh yes, please get the work orders and supplies for the last one hundred planes overhauled and restored." It was an order, not a request. "Thanks, Larry; give those to Mrs. Chandler, please." Bill never turned around from the window, but he knew there was a degree of panic on Cotting's face.

Holly pushed the intercom button for Phyllis.

"Yes, Mr. Chandler," she answered.

"Phyllis," Holly said, "please have someone return the Jeep we borrowed back to the plant. It is in our parking place in the garage. Thank you."

Meanwhile John, Bill's research assistant, checked into the hotel across the street from Litten Industries. From his eighteenth-floor window, he directed a Tel-Ray unit at Bill's office. After checking and calibrating the equipment, he recorded Bill's conversation with Larry Cotting. Then he began a sweep of the floors to pinpoint Larry's office. He easily locked onto Cotting's office and started to listen to his conversations and capture his phone signals.

"Hello, this is Cotting. I need to talk to Zellar, NOW!"

"Security, Hank Zellar."

"Zellar, this is Cotting," Larry Cotting said into the phone.

"Yeah, Mr. Cotting. What's up?" Hank asked with an edge to his voice.

"I got a call this morning from Joe Turnball saying the Chandlers were killed in a fire at the Desert Wells plant. Well, Dr. Chandler and his wife are alive and here in San Francisco," he paused, "and they're asking for things."

After a moment of silence, Zellar replied, "Yeah, what things?"

"They want the proposal from Koto and the reports on the last hundred planes processed. They seem to be suspicious about something," Cotting said.

"Well, I'm no high-powered corporate lawyer, but if I was taking over a company this big, I'd probably ask for some records too. If you make too much of a big deal about it, they'll get suspicious. So, get a grip, Cotting." One part of his brain felt that what he said was true. The other part wondered if Cotting might be right. Zellar was certain Cotting knew nothing about the Special Projects, but even Cotting could sense something was wrong. Zellar knew that he and a few others on the team at the plant were the only people in the organization who really knew the significance of the Special Projects. He personally had invested too much time and effort to let it fall through now. Lee Koto had made Hank Zellar a rich man, but Koto demanded results. Zellar realized his plan for the elimination of the Chandlers had gone awry. That did concern him. The next time, he would handle it himself.

Cotting's voice brought him back to the present. "So that's what you think we should do?"

"Uh, what?" Hank asked.

"Hey, asshole, you listening or not? We may have a problem and you sound like you're on vacation!" Larry snarled.

"Watch your mouth, you legal slime. Just give the man what he wants. It's all covered. They can't possibly find anything in the regular company records, and there is only one disk they should not see, right?" Zellar inadvertently asked.

"A secret disk?" Larry asked. "I don't know anything about a secret disk," Larry said.

"Leave that to me!" Hank said as he realized his mistake. "You keep them busy with your legal mumbo jumbo, and I'll take care of the rest. I'm putting a man on the Chandlers to keep track of them. We want to know everything they're up to and everywhere they go. And, Cotting, if there's anything you think I need to know, call right away. We don't want to get behind the power curve now." He paused for emphasis. "GOT IT?"

"Yeah, Zellar," Larry Cotting answered. Then he thought, *What was he talking about, a secret disk the Chandlers should not see?*

"Just leave everything to me!" Zellar answered.

"Yeah, right. You know best," Cotting growled as he hung up the phone. *Zellar, you prick, sometimes I wonder if you work for us or if you work for Koto,* Larry Cotting thought.

Across the street, John had heard the entire conversation, as clear as if he were seated in Cotting's office. "Doc, this Tel-Ray is a gas!" John said out loud.

31

TOKI–TOKYO, JAPAN,

1969

Lee Koto enthusiastically followed the antiwar demonstrations in America almost nightly. One evening, while he watched the television news, Koto recalled the young girl he had saved at the event in Kamakura. For some time, he had wanted an agent to live in the United States who had the attributes of an intelligent, energetic, and committed rabble rouser. He thought, *I can use her.* The next morning, he ordered Han to locate her and to call on her personally.

As instructed, Han invited her to Koto's house outside Tokyo for the weekend.

Toki arrived late Friday afternoon on the Bullet Train from Yokohama. Koto's chauffeur and Han met her at the train station and drove her to the house. Han escorted Toki to a small guest house. Surrounded by trees on the other side of a small lake, it sat nestled in an exquisitely manicured garden. The main house occupied the ground between the road and the lake. A small island in the center of the lake was connected to both the main house and the guest house by arched bridges.

"Dinner will be at eight," Han announced before he closed her door.

As Toki entered the guest house, she noticed a traditional kimono placed on the futon bed; it was a silk garment trimmed in gold and deep scarlet. She ran her fingers across the fabric.

"Mr. Koto would like you to wear it to dinner tonight, if you would please."

Toki, startled by the sound of another voice in the small guest house, guardedly asked, "Who are you?"

"I am Mr. Koto's housekeeper; I am here to get you anything you might desire. Is there anything you need?"

"Why should I wear this emblem of Japanese repression of women just because Koto would like it?" Toki asked.

"Because you are a Japanese lady like I am. We all want to wear a beautiful kimono sometime in our lives. You don't know—you may never get another chance. Even a bridal dress is not so pretty, but if you want to go to dinner like you are, it's all right with Koto. He is a man of great generosity and great tolerance. I'm sure you know that already."

When the housekeeper returned, night had gently settled over the compound. Toki, dressed in the kimono, had accented her makeup in a traditional Japanese fashion. "You are most beautiful, Toki," the housekeeper said. "Dinner will be served shortly. You must cross the bridge at the edge of the garden. The path on the other side will lead you to the dining room. Mr. Koto will be pleased."

Toki walked on the small bridge; at the island, she stopped. A twisted pine tree shared the island with a single wooden bench and a small rock. She sat down. Japanese lanterns hung on wires across the bridges and around the shore of the lake. The lanterns cast moving shadows on the small island and the water below. Occasionally, a koi broke the surface with its dorsal fin. Toki thought of her ancestors, especially her mother. The wind gently blew through the leaves, and the water quietly lapped at the small island. Toki could feel her ancestors; they wanted to communicate with her.

"I can often hear my dead mother when I sit here at night," Koto said.

"Oh—uh," Toki said, startled.

"I'm sorry, I didn't mean to frighten you. I saw you sitting here in the starlight; you too feel the presence of your ancestors. Mine also talk to me here; especially those whose souls cannot rest until there is retribution for the evil done to them."

"Koto, it was as if . . ." she searched for the right words, "as if I could feel the presence of my mother and my father here; however, I do not understand their thoughts," she said disappointedly.

"The spirits know many things, but we get so busy in our lives we never take the time to listen to them." Silence prevailed between them for several minutes. Then he said, "This is where I hear them best. They talk about many things."

"What do they say? I want to hear them," Toki said.

"Come," he held out his hand to her and lifted her from the bench, "let's talk as we eat. The spirits know nourishment is essential if we are to listen and learn." They walked across the small bridge that led to the main house. Toki followed Koto.

Rays of candlelight radiated from a single room; the open rice-paper door welcomed them. A painting of flying storks graced the opposite wall. A little table and cushions were the only furniture. On the table sat two settings of rice, fish, and tea.

As Toki carefully sat down on the cushion with her legs crossed under her, she elegantly draped the kimono around her. Gracefully, she picked up the chopsticks; Toki's childhood training by her mother returned. These simple acts helped Toki immerse herself back into the traditional Japanese culture. At the university, professors and students scorned the old culture; now it felt good, warm, and safe.

After dinner, the servant brought Koto a glass of sake. Koto leaned back on the pillows. Toki stood and bowed; she then walked to his cushion, knelt at his feet, and bowed her head. He reached out and stroked her cheek with the back of his fingers; she pressed her cheek to them.

"You have a part of your being which has been dormant too long, Toki," Koto said.

"Koto, I—"

"Don't talk," he murmured, "You are a brilliant and beautiful woman. I want you to be a very special person for me." He took her face in his hands, drew her to him, and kissed her gently on the lips.

"As you wish, Koto," she cooed.

"I know," he said.

She reached up and took out the pin that held her hair in place. She then shook her head gently, like a young colt shakes its mane, and let her long black hair fall in waves around her shoulders. Next, she untied the belt that held her kimono together and let the front edges of the fabric part slightly. She took his hand and placed it inside the kimono. She had nothing on underneath. She then began to untie his belt. Inside she felt hollow of love, but not empty of lust; she knew her surrender to him meant a life of subservience. Her body and soul ached for true love; Koto would give her many things, but never that; however, tonight she did not care.

As she awoke, her head rested on his bare chest and her hair formed a blanket over him. She smiled. Toki knew students and a professor at the university, but no one had ever satisfied her like Lee Koto. Toki, the former radical communist student, now loved one of the top capitalists in Japan. She shared the weekend and stayed for another week. One afternoon, they sat on the island between the main house and the guest house. Silence dominated the intimate moment. Small white clouds, like drops of cotton, spread across the sky. In the distance, the snowcapped peak of Mount Fuji stood stately against the heavens. A gentle breeze created ripples on the lake that bent the sunlight into a full-color spectrum; it looked like a thousand stars glittered on the surface of the water.

"Toki, you said on the first night you were here that you could feel the presence of your mother. How and when did she die?" Koto asked.

"I was fifteen when my mother died of heart problems. Though I believe the grief of my father's death caused her heart to break. She never got over it. Mother spent many hours at the temple, where she burned prayer papers, threw coins, bowed and clapped; but the gods did nothing. At night, after she assumed I'd gone to sleep, I would hear her weep until she fell asleep."

"You sound angry with the gods?" Koto asked.

"If they were really gods they should have . . . could have done something. The communist party doesn't believe in god; I learned that at the university, so I joined immediately." Her jaw was set and her eyes were hardened. The beauty of the moment vanished for Toki. She never wanted the pain she saw her mother experience, so she had once vowed never to fall in love. Now it troubled her; she realized she had violated that vow.

"Well, whose fault was it that your father never came back from the war?" Koto asked.

"I don't know; I never thought about it like that," she answered.

"Where was he when he was killed?"

"Okinawa," she answered.

"My mother lived on Okinawa before the war," Koto said. "She told me stories about how beautiful and how peaceful it was there. Unfortunately, the Americans," he spat the word out, "destroyed everything that was wonderful, including your mother and mine." Silence punctuated the air for several seconds. Suddenly, a distant bird's screech seemed to add emphasis to Koto's words.

"My father was a doctor stationed at the underground Japanese Naval Headquarters at Naha. Of the four thousand soldiers attached to his unit, none survived. He was killed deep within the compound. We, my mother and I, went to Naha once to see where he died. It was a horrible place deep within the ground." A tear trickled down her cheek. Toki had never allowed herself to cry for her father. Somehow, as she sat in this serene setting with the man she loved, she felt comfortable and let her emotions flow freely.

"Have you ever wanted to extract some retribution from those who have made you suffer so?" Koto asked.

"How could I make a country like the United States pay for the pain they caused my family and me?" she responded.

"If there was a way, would you?"

"If it were possible, I'd do anything I had to . . . could do . . ." Her voice was as hard as the wooden bench they sat on.

Koto returned to Tokyo the next week; Toki followed him on the following Monday. He provided an apartment for her, and she began rigorous courses of psychology, economics, and English.

Lee frequented her apartment. Toki prepared his meal, bathed him, and afterward they made love. He used these emotional evenings to further inflame her passion against those responsible for the death of her father and her mother. Toki quickly developed a financial and an emotional dependence on Lee Koto. After six arduous months, Toki became a dedicated instrument for his vengeance. Koto then used his influence to obtain her admission to the University of California, Berkeley.

Toki quickly infiltrated herself into the antiwar movement. She easily passed for a second generation Japanese American due to her exceptional language skills. Koto channeled money through her to fund the movement's demonstrations. Within the first year, she traveled to other campuses, both within and outside California, to propagate the antiwar effort. Toki's ability to coordinate and to incite protests quickly impressed the local leaders of the antiwar movement. On more than one occasion, she personally committed acts of arson during riots which led to the burning of several blocks of stores.

Early in 1970, Toki sent a letter to Koto:

Dearest Lee,

It has been five long months since we parted. I miss you deeply and long to be with you and have you. The work you sent me to do is going well. As you can see from the newspaper accounts, the demonstrations are increasing. It is much easier to initiate one this year than last year. The violence is also increasing as you predicted. It is amazing to see the police and other government officials project their hatred onto their own people. You are right about my feelings. Every time I see a confrontation that turns bloody, I secretly say this is for my mother and my father. I love you so much for helping me understand that. I have a plan I intend to act on soon, and I'd like you to be here when it happens. It will be the culmination of our work in this awful country. My darling, please come to the States at the end of April, if you possibly can. I await your decision. I promise you, it will be the best work so far.

All my love,

Toki

Toki provided compulsive documentation of the newspaper accounts and mailed each one to Lee Koto in Tokyo. She also enclosed long letters of her loneliness and her desperate craving for him. Her emotional tension spurred her to undertake brasher and bolder actions.

Koto took each coveted newspaper article and created a book. He considered it a sacred document, and he secretly stored it at his country house. The book's cover showed the only picture he had of his mother. Page one revealed an artist's rendering of the bomb's explosion at Hiroshima. Page two, written in red conge script, contained the words: *Vengeance Is Mine*. The letters Toki wrote to him, he read and immediately burned. The only woman on earth worthy of his love was his mother Sinshee. He used women for his sexual gratification and for whatever else they could provide, but he would never love any of them, including Toki.

32

THE RECORDS—SAN FRANCISCO

The next morning, Holly and Bill returned to Litten Headquarters, where they found the boardroom table piled high with records and documentation of the last one hundred aircraft overhauls and renovations.

"Well, Holly, what do you think you'll do after lunch?" Bill laughed.

"Are you sure we want to look at all one hundred?" Holly said in amazement at the volume of paperwork ahead of her.

"Get started. If you see a trend develop, or something that doesn't look right, let me know and we'll go down that corridor together. Is there anything you need?"

"How about a computer and a database that I can easily use, and some clerical help, huh, Boss?" she quipped.

"Yes, ma'am, they're on their way." He smiled as he pushed the button for Phyllis.

"Yes, Dr. Chandler?" Phyllis said into the intercom.

"We need a couple computers with database software and some clerical help for Mrs. Chandler in the boardroom. Can you help us out?"

"Yes sir, I'll get right on it. By the way, Mr. Cotting left the Koto proposal on your desk this morning," she paused, "and, Dr. Chandler?"

"Yes, Phyllis?" he replied.

"May I see you sometime today about a personal matter?"

"Sure, what time's good for both of us?" he asked.

"Right after lunch would be the best for your schedule," she said.

Bill left Holly as soon as the computers and help arrived. He found Lee Koto's proposal for the acquisition of Litten Industries. Reading through it, he thought, *This looks very generous and aboveboard. Why don't I just sign this thing and walk away? Holly and I are set for life as it is now. No, even if this is a legitimate offer, something doesn't seem right. Since Ned's death, we've been shot at on the beach, we've met a sheriff who doesn't believe us, and we've driven off a ferry into the middle of San Francisco Bay, and on top of all of that, I don't know if the desert facility fire was accidental. I can't believe that Lee Koto has anything to do with what has happened, but there's no sense in taking chances. After the conversations John recorded from Cotting and Zellar yesterday . . . no, I can't just walk away.*

He spent the morning on routine matters and met Holly for lunch in the executive dining room. "How's it going?" Bill asked as she walked up to the table. He let his eyes drift slowly from her face down her body to her legs and smiled.

"Keep your mind on the job, fellow," she joked.

"Hard to keep my thoughts on business when you walk in like that," he said and winked at her.

"Well, we have a database created, but there is a lot of information to input. At the current rate, I think I'll be ready to draw a pension before we have anything to start looking at." She sat down as the waiter brought a bowl of French onion soup and a salad.

"I took the liberty of ordering for both of us before you got here," Bill said.

"Thanks; this looks good." She paused after she sampled the soup, looked at Bill, and said, "I've been thinking about the conversation between Larry Cotting and that security man, Hank Zellar."

"Yeah, I have too. But so far, I haven't come up with anything," Bill replied.

"What if, now remember I'm just saying *what if,* the file they mentioned and the Special Projects the lady referred to when we were in the desert have something in common?" Holly looked at Bill intently.

"I don't see what you're getting at," he replied.

"I'm not too sure either. We know that they have specialized crews, but what if they have unique parts they use only on certain planes?" She took another spoonful of soup and stopped with her spoon halfway to her mouth. "What if those Special Projects involve doing something to the planes? Something that, later on, will make the planes unsafe or worse?"

"Holly you have too much of an imagination," Bill replied. "You may be able to use that line of thought to cut down the volume of data points. It shouldn't be too hard to spot anomalies by a check of the employment records and the work crew assignments." Bill gave her a concerned stare, narrowed his eyes, and furrowed his brow. "We'll have to be very careful; at this point, I don't think we should trust anyone at Litten. So don't talk about what we're looking for with anybody."

"That should be easy. I don't know what I'm looking for." Then she added, "This soup's delicious."

"Yeah, well, so are you," he said and smiled at her.

After lunch, Holly met with her assistant and continued to enter the data from the last one hundred renovations and overhauls. She concentrated on the employees who worked on each of the units.

Bill met with Phyllis. She gave him a copy of her latest evaluation, which included a recommendation from Ned for a substantial raise.

"Since you just became the CEO, I was afraid you might want to wait some time before you approved this. If so, I completely understand," Phyllis said and let her gaze fall to the desk.

"Phyllis, it's true that I am new to this job; however, if Ned felt it was time to give you a raise, I won't stand in the way," Bill replied.

Phyllis let out a sigh of relief. "Oh, thank you, Dr. Chandler. That's just great. Thank you."

"Is there anything else?" Bill questioned.

"No, sir. Thank you again." She stood up and left the office.

Later in the day, Holly's assistant looked at her and said, "Mrs. Chandler, if we're going to work all night, I need to call home; is that okay?"

Holly looked at the clock; it was six thirty and was starting to get dark. "Oh, I'm sorry; I guess I got carried away." She stood up and walked around the room and stretched. "No, you can go ahead and leave. We'll pick it up here in the morning."

"Are ya sure? I can stay, and I can certainly use the overtime."

"No, that's okay. I'll see you in the morning," Holly said. At that moment, she heard a sound as if someone had bumped into the door. "Did you hear that?" she asked.

"Yes, I—"

"Quiet," Holly whispered as she softly walked to the door and pressed her ear against it. She could hear someone moving down the hall toward the elevator. Then she heard the elevator door close. Cautiously she opened the door slightly and peered out the small crack. The reception room was empty, but the fluorescent bulbs burned brightly. She opened the door further and surveyed the room.

Suddenly, her assistant let out a blood-curdling scream.

Holly jumped as if an electric current passed through her. She turned around and saw her assistant, who stood frozen in the center of the room with her hand protecting her throat. Slowly, she pointed with the other hand at the open door behind Holly. Holly turned and gasped; a bloody knife pinned a note to the door. Rivulets of blood ran down from each letter on the note.

"STOP OR DIE"

"Mrs. Chandler! Who did that? What do they mean?" A quiver in her voice, and tears about to overflow her eyes, attested that she understood the message.

"Stay here and keep the door locked! I'll be right back," Holly ordered. She closed the door and ran toward Bill's office. A single light illuminated his desk; he was not in the room. *Could the blood on the note be his?* she thought. Frantically, she looked in the other offices along the hallway and found no one. Everyone had gone home for the night. Holly and her assistant were alone. Holly thought, *Bill would never leave us alone. I just know he wouldn't.* Suddenly, the bell on the elevator sounded two rings. *That means it's stopping on its way down!* Holly knew she had to hide. Quickly she ducked behind Phyllis's desk as the door to the elevator opened. She peered around the corner of the desk. Bill stepped off. "Bill! Where have you been!" she screamed.

"Hey, whoa, what's the problem?" he asked as she ran to him and threw her arms around him. He hugged her back.

Holly led him back to the conference room. He read the note pinned to the door with the knife. "Well," he exclaimed, "guess we'll need maintenance to fix the door."

"Bill, how can you joke about something like this? It's serious!" She was irritated with his nonchalant attitude.

"You're right, Holly, I know it's serious." They called security to provide an escort for Holly's assistant. Bill gave her money for a cab. They did not tell security about the note; they decided, at present, to keep it to themselves.

Bill and Holly copied the database file to a disk and took the elevator to the lobby. At the front desk, Bill signed them out. He looked at the logbook. There were no records of entries or exits since the front door had been locked for the night. That meant the guards were involved or the messenger was still in the building, or the perpetrator could have entered and left the building unnoticed at another exit. He made a mental note to check the video security footage in the morning.

At the warehouse command post, they gave John the disk. He immediately started the analysis. The first pass of the data showed five of the last one hundred planes were grouped into the Special Projects. This assumption was based on the personnel employed who worked only on those projects. It appeared from Holly's data that Litten Industries had hired two separate workforces. The two groups had similar work qualifications. The first group had the average number of employee problems and firings expected for a large corporation; however, the second group revealed no employee problems or firings. Also, all members in the second group had Asian surnames.

33

MURDER AND MAYHEM—MIDWEST AMERICA

Lee Koto's private plane left Japan late in the evening. He arrived in the United States well rested and anxious to continue his journey to meet Toki. In Los Angeles, he had a first-class ticket on an American carrier flying nonstop to a large city in the Midwest. Koto chose not to use one of his own planes; he wanted this trip to be anonymous. The flight attendant brought him wine before dinner and a second glass with dinner. No one sat next to him.

The plane touched down in the late evening on the flat midwestern land. *It feels strange to see an area so large with no hills or mountains,* Koto thought as he emerged from the jetway. He saw Toki standing behind the gate.

Toki threw her arms around him and pressed herself tightly against him. "Lee, oh how I've missed you," she whispered.

He kissed her with feigned passion. *I hope her plans will make this trip worthwhile,* he thought.

They stepped outside the terminal building. The evening felt warm, the sky was overcast, and the breeze portended rain.

It was a short drive from the airport to Toki's apartment. Her suite occupied the top floor of a high-rise building and had a commanding view of the midwestern landscape. On the horizon, a massive storm cloud emerged. Bolts of lightning flashed in the advancing front. The spectacular light displays progressed toward them and mesmerized Lee Koto.

Toki shut the balcony sliding door and started to draw the draperies.

"No, Toki. Do not shut out the storm. I want to see its power."

"But, Lee, I want to see yours," she said.

"And you shall, but come—we can enjoy the storm." He pulled her close and kissed her. "How powerful will the storm be?" he questioned.

"The big ones are very terrible on this flat, godforsaken land," she murmured. "I close the blinds and go into my bedroom and play music loudly when one comes along." She trembled as he held her. "They scare me. They are dangerous." Suddenly, a flash of lightning illuminated the room and a distant clap of thunder reverberated the air. "Lee, keep me safe," she pleaded as she wrapped her arms around him and pressed her body against his.

Koto held her closely and moved away from the patio door.

Toki responded as if a volcano of caged emotion vented up from within her.

He pulled her down; the next bolt of lightning flashed; a torrential rain began to beat against the penthouse; Koto felt his passion intensify to a level he had never experienced.

Her fear of the savage tempest that raged from the sky encouraged her surrender. However, she had no doubt that Koto held a far greater and much deadlier storm within his soul.

The storm passed, and Toki quietly retrieved a bathrobe for herself and one for Koto. She then went into the kitchen and made some tea. No words were spoken for several minutes.

Finally, Koto said, "Now, what is the surprise you have promised me?"

"Was that not enough to make you journey to this foreign land?" Toki asked.

"We had that in Japan. I had no need to send you to America if all you were going to be was a Geisha." There was no love or feeling in his voice. "I believe I have made you an effective weapon to change the world, have I not?" he asked.

Toki, longing for a moment of tenderness after their intimacy, found only coldness. She suppressed her feelings and began to explain her plans for an antiwar demonstration at one of the major defense plants.

Three days later, she and Koto spent the night in a motel a few miles from the plant's location.

Early the next morning, a massive demonstration started; the State National Guard was activated to manage any disturbance. Angry anti-war protestors marched toward the plant. Toki, using her persuasive skills, stirred the crowd to a fever-pitched intensity. A large group of people marched to the front gate to block it. The National Guard took up its position. A stand-off developed across a four-lane road. However, neither side was aware that Toki had slipped away and lay concealed on the top of an adjacent building with a sniper's rifle. She watched the confrontation through her binoculars. The marchers started across the road.

Lee Koto positioned himself near a deserted building on the fringe of the demonstration. Shadowed by the building, he had a clear line of sight of the developing drama. There were shouts and taunts, all unintelligible from his vantage point.

Suddenly, the sound of small arms fire echoed above the demonstration. First, just one shot was heard; then, seconds later, a staccato of rifle fire. Screams were heard; he watched a guardsman drop to the ground in a twisted position. Koto smiled. More shouts and gunfire erupted across the battlefield. Smoke drifted across the road and spread like a blanket. Then sirens, wails, and screams all mixed together in a macabre symphony. He slowly began to retreat from his position toward their car. Confusion reigned as people ran in all directions. Police and emergency personnel moved in the direction of the battlefield. Minutes later, a semblance of order revealed several protestors and one guardsman dead. Nine other protesters were injured and transported to a hospital. When Koto found their car, Toki sat in the driver's seat. He climbed in and closed the door as she carefully drove away.

"Well?" she asked.

"Toki, it was more than I ever imagined," he said as he sat back in the seat and smiled an evil grin. "That was beautiful!" He leaned over and kissed her on the cheek. "You have exceeded my expectations. Whatever you want that I can provide is yours."

"Anything?" she asked, looking at him.

"Toki, for what I saw today and the anguish it will cause the great country of America, anything I can provide." He smiled. Once more, the thought surged through his head—*Vengeance is mine!*

That day Toki became a vice president in Lee Koto's organization. Her ruthlessness smoothly transitioned to the business world. It garnered her the nickname the Dragon Lady.

Over the next few months, Koto reveled as he watched the international news detail the conflict of the American people. He enjoyed reading about the committee hearings in Washington, DC, and the finger-pointing and the inability of anyone to conclude exactly what had caused the tragedy. Koto cherished the knowledge that no one knew that he was responsible for the heartbreak outside the defense plant.

34

GREGG NEWMAN AND TOKI—LAS VEGAS, NEVADA

Every time Koto read a news article about the hearings in Washington or read that the National Guard held the blame, his heart rejoiced. His companies profited from the Vietnam war; therefore, he sincerely hoped it would continue for quite a while. However, he knew that the end was inevitable, and he recognized that he must look elsewhere for his vengeance.

Toki and Koto returned to Japan after the incident at the defense plant. And for a time, she lived at his country house. Toki eventually realized that Koto was not interested in a permanent relationship that involved love and commitment, and she did not desire to be Koto's occasional sexual diversion.

"Koto, can we talk?" Toki asked.

"Talk?" He acted surprised. "Yes, we can talk if you would like to."

"I think it would be best if we—I mean if I—moved back to Tokyo and began to work in the company."

"And why would you want to do that?" Koto asked.

"You did promise me a company job at the end of my time in America." She gazed at him with resolve in her eyes. "I believe that's what you promised."

"Yes, it was, and I meant it." He wondered if he was too settled with their arrangement. He thought about the solitude he had enjoyed before Toki had come to his estate. *Yes, it would be best to have her move back to the city. I can still use her there when I feel the need anyway,* he thought. "I agree with you. Yes, I promised to make you a vice president in the company. You have rested enough; it is time for you to go to work."

"Thank you, Koto." She smiled at him.

Koto introduced Toki to the directors of his company. She assumed the position of vice president of advertising for products sold in North America.

Backroom comments were whispered concerning her relationship to Koto; however, no one dared say anything out in the open. The talk faded as it became evident to all that Toki understood the Western mind better than they did. She earned their respect for her abilities and for her shrewdness. In dealing with employees, she was ruthless. She had no tolerance for mistakes, and those under her were demoted or fired for relatively minor infractions. Her division's sales skyrocketed compared to the other divisions. In her approach to the business world, the Dragon Lady used the same strategies that she had earlier deployed when she incited antiwar demonstrations. She positioned strategic people in major market areas and used deception in the advertisement of competitors' products to win market share. Within two years, Toki became the head of sales for the entire organization.

By the late 1970s, money flowed into Japan faster than many companies had imagined or planned for. The insight Toki provided propelled Koto Industries to the head of the pack of successful Japanese firms.

Toki found an apartment on the eighty-fifth floor of a new high-rise building called Sunshine City. If the smog was not too thick, the view from her Tokyo living room extended to the ocean. Her apartment showcased the latest in Western architecture and design. The living room furniture was chrome and leather. A glass-topped dining room table, set on four carved granite pedestals, occupied a choice view in front of the window. Modern art sculptures and a few traditional Japanese paintings accessorized the apartment.

Koto stopped by Toki's apartment one evening; he sat on one of the chrome chairs as Toki served him sake. "Toki, one of the best decisions I've made in years is choosing you to work in the company. What you have accomplished in the sales division is exceptional."

"I'm pleased you like my work," she said.

"How would you like to have a new challenge?" he asked.

"A new challenge?" she answered with a question, her voice guarded.

"Yes, as you know, we are making so much money it's hard to know where to invest it for the most profit. And you know what I really seek." He sat back and took a long drink. "Do you mind if I smoke?" he asked as he pulled a cigarette from a sterling silver case.

"Of course not, Lee," she answered. Inwardly she hated cigarette smoke, but she knew she had to tolerate it from him.

He lighted the cigarette, inhaled deeply, and let the smoke exhale as he watched the blue cloud expand across the room. "Just as that smoke slowly and silently crosses from here to there," he pointed at an original Yoshida painting that hung on the far wall, "we will steal quietly into America and hurt it at every opportunity."

"I'm out of the terrorist business," Toki said flatly.

"Yes, I agree. You are much more useful in business, but I want you to hurt them financially!"

"I don't understand," Toki said. "How do you expect me to hurt them financially?"

"I have started to acquire American enterprises, and I plan to leave some of the other casinos in Las Vegas economically far behind. America won the shooting war, but our triumph is assured in the business war."

The prospects of this new venture excited Toki. She moved over to Koto, sat down at his feet, and looked up at him. "Lee, you took a schoolgirl and made me an executive. I have learned so much from you. You know I'd do whatever you want. If you want me to go to America again, you know I will. Do you have something in the near future?"

As she sat at his feet with her hands resting on his knee, he stroked her hair. "Yes, I plan to start with things thoroughly American. You will invade the tourist and entertainment capital, Las Vegas, Nevada. Negotiations are well underway with one of the largest casinos. It is in financial trouble due to a large hotel construction project that is not going well. I—that is, we—will bail them out, and in the process, we will become the owners. I want this to be your first venture."

Several months later, Toki arrived in Las Vegas and checked into the newly acquired hotel and casino. The manager met her at the door with a complete set of waiters and bellhops to escort her. As she quickly whisked through the lobby with the fanfare due a visiting dignitary, the staff and patrons watched and wondered if a Hollywood star had entered their presence.

"I know you will find the accommodations satisfactory," the manager said as he opened the elevator double doors to the apartment. A bellhop and maid stood inside the apartment to serve her.

Toki walked through without a comment and looked around the expansive living area. "You may leave," were Toki's only words to them.

Quickly, they all retreated as if dismissed by royalty and were happy to get out with their heads still intact. The manager left last; he closed the two giant doors and quietly bowed at the waist.

Toki looked at the lavish decor and felt somewhat revolted. She held a grudge against the ostentatious displays of wealth. Her apartment in Tokyo revealed that she was not against wealth or the things it could buy, but here she saw decadence. She thought, *They are barbarians with no appreciation of the beauty and the serenity of the world.* Her mind drifted back to the first few weeks at Koto's country home and the love she had thought they shared. She felt a longing in her heart to return there. She remembered sitting on the small island looking at the stars and feeling the closeness of her ancestors. She wanted to lay naked against Koto and feel the warmth after they made love. *Or was it love?* she thought. Maybe it was just more of Koto's ability to use people. *Did he use his love for me to accomplish his own purposes?* She walked to the sliding glass door leading to the balcony. She approached the glass and felt the intense desert sun burn through the glass. "This is a hard and harsh land. I will be as hard and harsh as this land to accomplish Koto's goals," she said out loud as she walked through the glass doors onto the balcony and felt the fierce heat.

Early the next morning, Toki strode into the administrative suite. She immediately fired several midlevel managers for no apparent reason. Then she replaced them with personnel outside of the gaming and entertainment industry. The notice was clear; she was in control.

At the same time, Gregg Newman waited in the reception area of Koto's Tokyo office. A soldier of fortune, he earnestly sought the most lucrative assignment. A business associate had recommended him to Koto. This man had used Newman to eliminate a Korean rival.

"You may go in now," the secretary said.

"Thank you," Newman replied in flawless Japanese. Entering the room, he bowed in front of Koto's desk.

"Please sit down." Koto motioned to a chair. "You come highly recommended by someone I trust. You have a reputation for results and discretion."

"Thank you," Newman replied.

"You are American?"

"No, South African," Greg said.

"Can you appear to be American?"

"I am a soldier and an actor. I can do what a soldier does and be whoever I need to be, within the limits of my appearance. And I can appear to be whatever I wish." His reply was not arrogant, but self-confident.

"Then I have an assignment. It will pay quite handsomely." Koto kept a stern face as he explained his plan.

Several weeks later, Toki walked through the casino. Stunning best described her. Her hair was draped over one bare shoulder. She wore a form-fitting floor-length Oriental silk dress that split up the side to midthigh. A wide strip of silk covered one shoulder and created a partial sleeve. She walked with a sensuous sway that attracted everyone's attention. Toki stopped at a blackjack table and watched the play for several minutes.

A man sat with several stacks of chips in front of him. He looked up and saw her watching him. Gregg flashed a small smile from the corner of his mouth and then looked down at his cards. A seven was showing. He signaled for a hit—a two. He signaled again; the next card was a five. He had fourteen showing. If his down card was above a seven, he would lose. Gregg now had four cards; three up, one down. Silence permeated the area around the table. His gaze met Toki's, and their eyes locked.

Toki saw his twenty thousand dollars' worth of chips on the table.

Each dared the other to turn away first.

Toki felt challenged and excited.

The silence lengthened, and several of the other players began to fidget uncomfortably.

"So, little lady, should I take another hit?" he asked Toki.

Startled, Toki hesitated and stuttered. "Ah . . . I . . . I'm sorry, I don't know what your down card is," she said recovering.

"I don't either. That makes it a gamble, doesn't it?" He smiled a challenging smile.

Toki felt his eyes look at her and begin to peel her clothes away. She felt vulnerable and at the same time stimulated. "You want me to call it?" she asked.

"Yes, ma'am—do I take my fifth card or not?" His smile became more intriguing to her.

"Yes," Toki said.

The dealer looked at her and then at Newman, not certain what to do.

"The lady said I need a hit," Newman replied.

Slowly, the dealer turned up the next card: a six. Newman had twenty showing.

"Is one your lucky number, little lady?" Newman asked.

"I think the more correct question is, is it yours?" she sensually answered back.

The other players folded their hands and slowly got up from the table, leaving only empty space between Toki and Gregg.

"Let's see if one is my lucky number," he said to the dealer. Newman looked at the dealer, then he turned over his down card. The ace of spades—his total was twenty-one with five cards.

The dealer turned his down card over; he had a five and a jack showing. "Fifteen to the dealer and the dealer takes a hit," he said. The dealer flipped the top card over: a seven. "House breaks. Congratulations!" He reached across the table to shake Gregg Newman's hand; then he began to count out twenty thousand dollars in chips.

"Pay him double," Toki said.

An audible gasp escaped from the dealer's throat. "Double? Ma'am?"

"I said double," she said firmly as she walked toward Gregg. She held out her hand. "I'm Toki, the manager here. You like to gamble."

He took her hand in his; instead of shaking it, he held it firmly, but gently, and stared into her black eyes. "You have the most beautiful face I've ever seen this side of Broken Bow," he said.

She wanted her hand free; his firm grip did not hurt, but it conveyed something that intrigued her. She had a fleeting image of that firm, calloused hand drawing her to him and him to her. She felt a chill of intense eroticism flash up her spine, and it frightened her. She pulled her hand from his.

"Ma'am, would you let me buy you a drink? You sure did bring this ol' cowboy luck tonight."

"Certainly, I have a table over there." She pointed toward the nightclub area of the casino. "Just ask for me after you've cashed out." Toki turned and walked in the direction she had indicated; she sensed the burning pleasure of his eyes on her hips.

Gregg cashed in his chips and walked toward the nightclub. Toki watched him. He stood at least six feet three and had broad shoulders and a narrow waist. He wore a western suit, a string tie, and reptile cowboy boots. He carried a cowboy hat. He dressed like hundreds of others who imagined they were cowboys, but Toki perceived a significant difference. He *was* a cowboy.

Gregg Newman approached Toki's table. With her legs crossed, the slit in the side of the dress exposed a generous portion of her thigh. "Ma'am, I appreciate the luck you brought me, and I appreciate your company more," he said as he sat down. "Please let me buy you a drink." He signaled to a waiter, who appeared almost immediately. "I'd like a bourbon on ice, and for the lady . . ." he hesitated.

"My usual wine," Toki replied. "So, what do they call you, cowboy?" she asked.

"I'm sorry, ma'am. Gregg, Gregg Newman." He started to rise from his chair.

"Relax, Gregg," Toki said. "What brings you to our casino tonight?"

"Aw, I was in town for some business, and it finished early. I thought, well, Gregg, you can get an early plane out, or you can spend the night and contribute to the economy of Las Vegas." He laughed a deep laugh that indicated he truly enjoyed life. "Well, as it turns out, Las Vegas contributed to my economy." He flashed a warm and sincere smile. "Thanks to you, ma'am."

"My name is Toki. Please stop calling me ma'am." She smiled. "It makes me feel like your elderly aunt."

"No, ma'am . . . er . . . I'm sorry. Yes, Toki." He leaned forward and brought his face within inches of hers. "Toki, your name is almost as beautiful as you are."

Toki blushed for the first time in many years. "Thank you," she said as she tipped her head demurely. Toki placed her hands in her lap to keep them from trembling. *He makes me feel like a teenage schoolgirl,* she thought.

"So, Mr. Newman, where are you from?"

"I have a little place over in the Sand Hills of Nebraska," he replied.

"And what do you do in that little place in Nebraska?" Toki asked.

"Well, I run a few cattle. You know, ranching," he said.

"What do you consider a little place and a few cattle? The way you put money down on the table, it looked like you might be made of it."

"Oh, I have about ninety thousand acres and run about ten thousand head of cattle, more or less," he answered. "It's a real nice place, lots of grass and hills, not like the desert you have around this part of the country." He smiled at her again. "Ya know, ma'am—Toki, it's kind of noisy in here for talking. How'd ya like to go somewhere quieter?"

"And where would that be?" she asked accusingly. "Your room?"

"Oh, no, ma'am. That's not what I meant at all. I hope you didn't get the wrong idea. I just wondered if you'd like to go for a walk. Have ya seen the back forty on this place? Right here in the middle of the desert there's a lake and trees and trails. I just thought that it might . . ." He started to ramble.

Toki smiled. She liked this real cowboy. "Sure, cowboy, let's go for a walk."

They walked out of the casino's back door and entered a surreal world of swaying palms, subdued lighting, exotic plants, cascading waterfalls, and a shimmering lake. A million stars and a quarter moon provided natural light from the night sky; soft elevator music played in the background. Gregg put his arm around Toki's small waist and held her close to him. For the first time in her life, she felt secure and safe with this big American cowboy. She nestled in closer to his side. She knew the desire she felt would lead her to his bed. She wondered if he would be as gracious and caring once they were alone as he was out in public, but at that moment she didn't care. She wanted him.

The next morning the sun shone through the massive glass sliding door and woke Toki from an exhausted sleep. She lay on a bed in shambles and thought, *What a fantastic night!* She could still feel his gentleness, yet dominance, as he lifted her into his arms, carried her to the bed, and placed her as if she were a piece of precious art. She reached over to touch him. Her hand didn't find what she expected, so she turned; the bed was empty. She sat up, pulled the sheet up over her breasts, and looked around the room. Empty. This cowboy had taken her as a one-night stand! She was furious! Toki jumped out of bed and stomped into the bathroom; every muscle in her body tightened. She felt used. She didn't mind using other people, but so far in life, the only one who had used her was Koto, and she tolerated that. She wasn't about to put up with it from some two-bit cowboy! Then she saw a note pinned to the shower curtain. Toki grabbed it and started to read. Her face softened.

Ma'am, you are the greatest woman I've ever met. I suppose I should say I'm sorry for what we did, but I'm not. I didn't think it would be good for your reputation at the casino if I was seen leaving your place in the morning. So I'm slipping out now, while it's still dark, to be sure no one sees me. If you want, I'd like to buy you breakfast in the dining room downstairs about nine this morning. If you don't show up, I'll understand. I'm just an old cowboy and I'll head on back to my place.

Hope ya slept well.
Gregg

Toki smiled again as she reread the note. "He is interesting!" she said. She looked at the clock on the nightstand. Eight forty-five!

At precisely nine o'clock, Toki walked up to Gregg Newman's table. "I think you invited me for breakfast?"

Later that day, Gregg went back to his hotel room across town. He sat down on the bed, picked up the phone, and dialed an international number. The phone rang several times before an Asian voice came on the line: "Hai!"

"Newman here."

"Hai." Then silence.

"Ah, Mr. Newman," a new voice said.

"I'm in. She offered me a job as head of security," he answered.

"Excellent, that's more than I expected. You must be even better than your reputation would indicate," Koto replied.

"She's predictable. Don't worry about her; I'll see she's well taken care of." He paused, but there was no answer from Koto. "Well, I'll be in touch, Mr. Koto," Gregg said and he then hung up the phone.

Koto considered the call from Newman. *I assume, from what he said, that he seduced Toki to get the job that quickly,* he thought with an uncharacteristic pang of jealousy and resentment. He tried unsuccessfully not to think about her small supple body responding to the large soldier of fortune. He clenched his jaw as the vision swept through his mind. "Someday, I'll make them both pay for that. I hope she got everything she wanted from him." It was not that Lee Koto loved Toki, but he thought of her as one of his possessions, and he hated the thought of anyone else having what was his. He resolved to send for her soon just to remind her that she belonged to him. *If she is traveling around the world letting any man between her legs, I will tell her who owns her.* Koto ground his teeth, visibly shaken from rage, as he finished his thoughts.

That day, Gregg Newman moved to an apartment near the hotel. He traveled light; he was at the casino by the time the sun went down to begin his duties as the new chief of security for Toki and for the High Desert Casino.

Koto relished the thought that each day he drew closer to what he had always wanted. These events set the trap for Ned Litten like a mouse drawn to cheese. *Ned Litten will soon be mine. Then, my conquest of Litten Industries assures my success for vengeance,* he thought.

Koto's assistant, Kim Long, had arranged for Liz's employment at Litten Industries six months earlier. Long had studied Ned Litten thoroughly and knew that Liz would be the perfect bait.

35

THE DISK—SAN FRANCISCO

"Hi, Boss, Mrs. Boss!" Randy said with a grin from ear to ear.

"Randy, is there ever a time when you don't smile?" Holly asked.

"Yes, ma'am," he replied grinning.

They all laughed. Bill and Holly had just arrived from Litten. Open boxes of pizza and bottles of soda and beer lay on a table. They walked over and helped themselves before sitting down.

"Okay, everybody, let's go over what we have," Bill said as he took charge. "John, you go first."

"It was a full day, and I haven't been over all of the recordings yet . . ." he quit talking as he rummaged through a notebook. "Here it is, but I can tell you, Doc, that Mr. Cotting works hard, but not always for you. I'm not sure he's a company man. Or, he's working for a different company."

"So, John, give us the condensed version," Bill said.

"This morning, just after you and Mrs. Chandler reported in, he went to his office and called a Mr. Hank Zellar, who I believe is head of security at your desert facility."

"Interesting, what did they have to talk about?" Holly asked.

"Just a minute," John said as he fiddled with a computer, "ah, here it is. You need to listen to this."

"Hello, this is Cotting. I need to talk to Zellar, NOW!"

"Security, Hank Zellar."

"Zellar, this is Cotting."

"Yeah, Mr. Cotting. What's up?"

"I got a call this morning from Joe Turnball saying the Chandlers were killed in a fire at the Desert Wells plant. Dr. Chandler and his wife are alive. They are here in San Francisco and they're asking for things."

"Yeah, what things?"

"They want the proposal from Koto and the reports on the last hundred planes processed. They seem to be suspicious about something."

"Well, I'm no high-powered corporate lawyer, but if I was taking over a company this big, I'd probably ask for some records too. If you make too much of a deal about it, then they will get suspicious. So, get a grip, Cotting."

"So that's what you think we should do?"

"Uh, what?"

"Hey, asshole, you listening or not? We have a problem, and you sound like you're on vacation!"

"Watch your mouth, you legal slime. Just give the man what he wants. It's all covered. They can't possibly find anything in the regular company records, and there is only one disk they should not see, right?"

"A secret disk? I don't know anything about a secret disk."

"Leave that to me! You keep them busy with your legal mumbo jumbo, and I'll take care of the rest. I'm putting a man on the Chandlers to keep track of them. We want to know everything they're up to and everywhere they go. And, Cotting, if there's anything you think I need to know, call right away. We don't want to get behind the power curve now. GOT IT?"

John stopped the playback. "Does any of this make sense to you?"

"There's a picture developing here, but it is very fuzzy," Bill answered.

"Well, maybe you need to hear the rest of it." John started the audio again.

"Yeah, Zellar."

"Just leave everything to me!"

"Yeah, right. You know best."

After listening to the conversation, Randy was the first to speak. "So, Boss, why don't we just snare the disk, blow the whole thing open, and beat it back to the Beltway?"

"Great idea," John said. "But there are two problems: first, where is the disk and second, what is on it?"

"Say, guys," Holly said. "We obviously don't know the answers to those questions, though I'm sure with the brain power in this room you will figure it out once the disk is located. Let's not focus on what is on the disk. Cotting stated that they thought they knew where the disk was, but they couldn't get it. Let's work backward. If Ned wanted to hide something, where would he put it so that he could get it, but no one else would find it?"

"I'm the only one who really knew Ned," Bill said. "And I don't have the vaguest idea where he would hide something like that."

"Then it's simple; we must turn Ned's life upside down until we know," Holly said.

Sam Barkley sat in the corner and listened to the conversation. "There might be an easier way," he said.

"Oh, what might that be?" Bill asked.

"Let me take that Cotting guy out fishing for a day; when we get back, he'll tell us that and more."

Randy spoke up enthusiastically, "Fishing . . . you mean deep sea fishing?"

Sam nodded.

"What would you be fishing for?"

"Sharks."

"What would you use for bait?" he asked.

"Him," Sam said with a straight face.

The conversation began again after a brief embarrassing pause. No one was sure if Sam was serious or not. They decided on tomorrow's first order of business: research the backgrounds of Larry Cotting, Hank Zellar, and Ned Litten, a task that fell to John and Randy.

Randy, John, and Sam then took a short walk to a bar Sam mentioned earlier.

The evening's work concluded, Bill and Holly retired to Sam's boat for the night. They were pleasantly surprised to find the captain's quarters cleaned, with new bedding and towels provided.

"Can we afford all this luxury?" Holly asked as she squeezed through the door of the small head.

"I think, at the moment, if we keep out of sight at night it might be safer," Bill replied. "Anyway, I think it's kind of romantic."

"Yeah, well, when you get into this bathroom you'll feel more like a sardine," Holly quipped.

The next morning when Bill arrived at the office, Koto's proposal still lay on Bill's desk.

Holly's research assistant called in sick. Holly guessed the frightened girl probably quit or would do so within the week because of the threatening note the night before. Holly sat down at the computer and started entering data. *I haven't done this since I started at Neustyle Imports with Jarvis,* she thought; a chill ran down her spine at the thought of him. Suddenly, Holly's thoughts turned to two import firms. *My former employer, Sidney Jarvis, used his import company to sell hardware, software, and national secrets to the highest bidder. Cotting mentioned that Ned's import company, Rogers and Bailey, was involved with the Special Projects. Why not run their records instead of the records for Litten?* she thought.

She rushed into Bill's office. Bill was engrossed in Koto's proposal as she slammed the door and ran in. "I have an idea!" she almost shouted.

Bill looked up startled. "What?"

"Let's go through the records of Rogers and Bailey and look for anything unusual." She leaned on the desk and looked down at Bill. "Maybe that's where the money is!"

"Okay, Holly, I'll have Phyllis put someone on the records, and we'll take a drive to Rogers and Bailey Imports." He told Phyllis what they wanted to do.

"Dr. Chandler, I'll call for the car and have Sara start on the records in the conference room," Phyllis said.

"No thanks, we want to get some fresh air, so I think we'll grab a cab."

"Well, sir, you're the president, you can't ride in a cab," Phyllis said indignantly.

"Yes, Phyllis, I am the president, so yes, I can do whatever I want," Bill said sarcastically as he and Holly walked toward the elevator.

The elevator door had just closed when Phyllis dialed Larry Cotting's extension. "Mr. Cotting, this is Phyllis. They just left to catch a cab to Rogers and Bailey Imports. I tried to tell them they should have the limousine take them, but he insisted."

"Phyllis, I am very glad you let me know. It's important for us to take care of the company. I know that you have the welfare of Litten at heart, and I do appreciate it. You are a vital member of the team."

"Why thank you, Mr. Cotting."

"As the company's legal counsel, it would be very helpful if you kept me informed of the Chandlers' movements," Larry continued.

"Certainly, I'll keep you informed." She hung up the phone and smiled. *Larry really noticed me today. I didn't think he knew I existed,* she thought to herself.

Cotting picked up the phone. "Zellar? They're going to take a cab to Rogers and Bailey. Have your man get on them and stay on them, but don't let them know they're being followed." He paused. "Keep your distance, but don't lose them."

"Don't worry, I have someone from outside the company on them," Zellar said.

Holly and Bill left the Litten Building. A beautiful San Francisco day greeted them. "Let's walk to the cable car and take it to the wharf. We can get a cab from there," Bill suggested.

"That sounds like fun," Holly agreed.

They caught the cable car as it slowly climbed the steep grade. Holly sat on one of the outside seats; Bill stood on the footboard and faced her. Greg Newman boarded the rear of the car at the next block. He looked like one of the tourists and went unnoticed by Bill or Holly.

The cable car crested the hill, then it descended the long grade toward Fisherman's Wharf.

The breeze coming through the car and the rhythmic ringing of the bell lifted their spirits. "This is great. We should travel like this more often," Holly said.

Bill felt the cell phone on his belt begin to vibrate. "Uh oh, got a message," he said. He saw a corner grocery ahead. "Let's get off." He grabbed Holly by the hand and they jumped off the car.

Newman saw them leave and waited a block before he left the car and crossed the street.

Bill dialed the number.

"Hi, Boss," Randy said.

"Randy, what's up?" Bill asked.

"Do you know you're being followed?" he asked.

"No, you're kidding."

"No, Boss, I wouldn't kid about something like that. John picked it up on a phone con as you left the office. I watched the guy. He jumped off about a block down from where you are now."

Bill wanted to look, but thought that might give it away. "What can you do to distract him?" Bill asked.

"Just a minute . . ." there was silence on the other end of the phone. "Sure . . . let's do it."

"What?" Bill asked.

"Oh, just talking to someone else. Tell ya what, you and Mrs. Boss get on the next car coming down the hill; we'll take care of the rest." The line went dead.

"What was that all about?" Holly asked.

"Just act like it was routine; we're going to catch the next car coming along," Bill said.

At the corner, they waited a few minutes; another cable car crested the hill and descended toward them. "Okay, let's get this one," Bill said as the tension in his voice mounted.

They easily stepped onto the car as it slowed and grabbed the railings as the clutch engaged and propelled the car faster down the street toward Fisherman's Wharf. Bill saw a man in khaki slacks and a turtleneck sweater quickly cross the street toward their vehicle. At that moment, a small pickup truck rounded the corner and started up the hill toward them. It slowed as it neared the man; suddenly someone rose from the truck bed, grabbed the man by the shoulders, and lifted him into the back of the truck. The truck sped up the hill. It occurred so quickly that no one on the cable car except Bill noticed it happened.

When a very surprised Newman landed in the truck, he had the wind knocked out of him. As he regained his breath, he noticed the barrel of a nine-millimeter pistol aimed at him.

"Laddie, I'd lay real quiet," Sam Barkley said as he held Newman in one hand, the gun in the other. They drove quickly to the warehouse.

Randy got out and opened the door, then drove the truck in. Sam and Newman didn't move until the door was completely closed and locked.

"End of the line," Sam grinned. "Oh, maybe that wasn't a good term to use," he said as he jerked Newman to a sitting position.

"Just what do ya think you're doing, kidnapping me off the street in broad daylight?" Greg Newman demanded.

Sam patted him down and removed a 44-caliber revolver from Newman's jacket. "My, what an upstanding citizen we have here. Hey, my boy," he hollered at Randy, "why do ya suppose he's packing heat?"

"Well, I heard San Fran's a rough town," Randy replied.

At the cable car turntable, Holly and Bill hailed a cab for the ride to Rogers and Bailey. As Bill anticipated, they were expected.

"Dr. Chandler, what a welcome treat to have you visit so soon. I didn't expect you to pay much attention to this piece of Litten. We're so small," the office manager, a man named Willis, said as Bill and Holly came through the door.

"We want to have a good overall view of the entire organization as soon as possible," Bill answered. "This is my wife, Holly. She used to work for an import firm, and she was anxious to see your operation."

"As I said, we're not very big, but we do have a good volume of imports from Asia." His manner was decidedly effeminate in nature.

"Oh, I used to deal with that area quite often," Holly said. "What products do you specialize in?"

"Well," Willis said taking her by the arm, "fabrics mostly. Our large volume orders are for the interior of the airplanes; however, for some of our dress designers and interior decorators, we import some of the most beautiful and expensive cloth in the world. Would you like to see a few samples?" He walked her through a door that led to the attached warehouse. "Japan and China are sending us some of the most exquisite fabrics. You just have to see them."

"Uh, Holly, I have a few calls to answer," Bill said. "I'll use the phone in here." He motioned to an office.

"Oh, Dr. Chandler!" Willis exclaimed as he put his hand to his face. "Please use this room; it's mine." He pointed to a closed door.

Bill smiled. "Thank you."

In the warehouse, Willis and Holly walked along a corridor created by shipping crates. About midway in the long building, Willis stopped. "Mrs. Chandler, you must . . ."

"Please call me Holly," she said.

"Oh, thank you, Holly," Willis said with too much emotion. "You're just going to *love* these." He opened a box and began to extract exotic woven fabrics in every color and design imaginable.

"Why, Willis, these are beautiful," Holly said.

For the next hour, he showed Holly fabric samples for dresses, for suits, for draperies, and finally, for upholstery. This sparked Holly's interest.

"What market do you sell most of the upholstery fabric to?" she asked Willis.

"We do an excellent business with some of the smaller local companies, but honestly, most of it is sent to the airplane renovation plant. For the airplanes, you know."

"Please show me some that would be used there," Holly requested.

"Oh, Holly, most of it is such dreary stuff. I'm honestly surprised they buy it, but I guess they must put in what the customer wants. If you ask me, as depressing as most of it is, if a plane crashed, the passengers would probably die from boredom." Willis tried to make a joke that fell flat.

Holly laughed politely; however, something clicked in the back of her mind. She had a thought she wanted to pursue, though she was not completely sure how. Willis was obviously comfortable with her and she was sure that if he knew anything, she would be able to get him to open up. They concluded their tour and returned to the office.

Bill was still on the phone. He looked up. "Hi, you two finished?"

"Yes," Holly exclaimed. "It was an incredible tour. Willis is so knowledgeable about the fabrics. He is a veritable encyclopedia of information," Holly said as she patted his arm.

By the look on Willis's face, Bill knew Holly had Willis eating out of her hand.

"Bill?" Holly asked.

"Yes," he said as he hung up the phone.

"Don't you have to get back to that meeting?"

"Meeting?" He appeared puzzled, and then he realized she wanted to be left alone with Willis. "Oh yes, I do need to catch a cab back to Litten," he said.

"I'd like to stay and talk with Willis more. Being here brings back so many memories of working at Nustyle. Would you mind terribly if I came back later?" she asked Bill.

"I don't know," Bill said.

Willis said. "Don't worry about a thing, Dr. Chandler. I'll personally drive her so she doesn't have to take one of those awful cabs."

After Bill left, Holly asked, "Do you have any tea?"

"Yes, I could have guessed you drink tea." Willis scurried around the room; he put water into an electric pot and then placed several exotic teas on a tray. "I'll bet you're a Capricorn," he said.

"Uh, no," Holly answered. She wasn't sure what sign her birthday fell under, but she didn't want to say so. "No, I'm a Gemini." It was the only sign she could recall.

"Oh well, never mind," Willis answered as he poured the tea. He sat down across from her. They drank in silence for several minutes. "Now, what more can I tell you about Rogers and Bailey?"

She didn't want to scare him off, but she wanted to see the upholstery fabric invoices for the desert plant. "Willis, you and I are probably the only ones who really understand the complexities of importing large quantities of goods, especially from Asia. And it's obvious to me that you are a real expert."

He nodded in complete agreement and took a sip from his cup. "Oh, my, yes, Holly." He took a deep breath for emphasis, "Those Litten bozos that order and receive our fabrics have no idea what we have to go through for them," he said, over-accentuating each word for impact.

"Are there problems?" Holly asked.

"Problems, oh my, yes; there certainly are problems, particularly with some of their Special Projects, Holly." He raised his arm and let his wrist go limp. "Dear, you have no idea!"

"Why would anyone want to make problems for you? They must be aware that you know more about fabric and importing than any of them," she said sympathetically. "Why don't you show me what kinds of problems you are having; maybe I can do something to help so you don't have to put up with that any longer." Holly thought, *Willis really is a dear, and I feel that I can trust him. I hope he'll trust me and maybe as a team we can find some information that will solve this mystery. I certainly don't want to hurt him or cause him trouble; I really like him.*

"My dear, that would be wonderful." Willis practically jumped out of his chair and darted over to the file cabinet in his office. He rummaged through the top drawer and finally produced several large folders. He carefully carried them to a table and began to look through them. "Well, just look at this; this is just what I'm talking about!" he said indignantly.

Holly leaned over the table and allowed him to show her several of the files.

"The invoice numbers don't match; they haven't been signed for appropriately, and what is even worse, we're prohibited from inspecting the containers. How am I to know if another order is inside? They just tell me that if there's something in there that they don't need, they'll send it back to us." He looked up at her to stress his displeasure. "But between you and me, I'm sure they don't."

"Why do you think that?" she asked.

"Well, if you look at the shipping weights, they're much too heavy for just fabric, but do we ever get anything back? NO!"

"That's curious," she agreed.

"Well, my dear Holly, I'll bet every lost order we have is in those containers! But do the people at Litten care? No. When Mr. Bailey was still alive, God rest his soul, things like that never happened."

Holly wanted to copy a few of the invoices, but she didn't want Willis to know. "Willis?" she asked.

"Yes, my dear," he answered.

"Could I ask you a favor?"

"My dear, anything you want," he answered.

"Do you remember that royal blue silk with the gold pheasants?"

"Isn't that just dreamy?" Willis replied.

"Do you suppose I could have a sample of it? I want to consider it for an evening dress."

"That would be absolutely ravishing on you. I'll get you some. Just wait here. I don't want you in that dreary warehouse again."

When he left the room, Holly quickly searched through several of the files and pulled the appropriate invoices and bills of lading along with the customs' certificates. A photocopy machine sat in the corner of his office. It was off. She turned it on and waited. Finally, the machine flashed READY. She quickly copied each document and put them in her purse. Holly had just slipped the last paper back into a file when she heard the door open behind her. Willis walked in as she turned from the table.

"Oh, it's even more beautiful in the daylight. Bring it over to the window, Willis. I just love it!" Holly exclaimed as she ran her fingers over the smooth silk.

He carefully folded it and placed it into a small box. "Now, let me run you back to Litten before the traffic gets too bad." He scooped up the package from the desk. "I'm going to bring the whole bolt in here and keep it just for you, dear," he said.

36

DEATH IN THE SKY—SOUTH CHINA SEA

A United States government jumbo jet sat on the tarmac at Andrews Air Force Base and awaited the arrival of a trade mission delegation. President Randolph R. Drexel, the First Lady, and Secretary of Commerce Allen Thorp, had agreed it would be advantageous to include the First Lady on the trip. An airplane from the presidential fleet, which had recently undergone extensive renovation, provided transportation. Invited businesspeople, from all parts of the country, eagerly awaited the journey. The administration hoped to increase the United States export base to the Asian markets. The leaders of government and industry in Tokyo, Hong Kong, Taipei, and Bangkok received extensive publicity of the trade mission and of the First Lady's presence. The secret service took no chances; they X-rayed and hand inspected each piece of luggage and equipment loaded onto the plane.

Earlier in the morning, President Drexel had said, "I don't know, I feel uncomfortable about you taking this trip without me."

"There's nothing to be concerned about," his wife answered. In many ways, she handled personal politics better than he. Historically, she had bailed him out on more than one occasion by the right conversation with members of the opposition party, or even within their own party. Her personality displayed sincerity and kindness; she wasn't overbearing or pretentious as some in her position have been. Known as a gracious lady who knew how to make anyone she met comfortable, she could win consensus on any issue if given enough time. She smiled and kissed him lightly on the cheek as she walked to the dresser for one more item.

"Well, I want to talk to you every night," he said as he smiled at her.

The fully loaded plane waited for the Marine helicopter from the White House. The rhythmic whomp vibrated throughout the jumbo jet airliner, and everyone on that side of the aircraft craned their necks to see the First Lady arrive.

"Is President Drexel coming to see us off?" one excited visitor asked.

"Probably not," Allen Thorp said.

The helicopter landed, and the First Lady alighted with the assistance of the Marine flight chief. He escorted her to the government plane and up the stairs. Then he remained atop the ramp and secured the door.

The airliner taxied out and received clearance. It rolled down the runway, took off, and turned north from the Washington air traffic control area. The flight plan took the polar route toward Tokyo, their first stop.

After several hours, the status and the excitement of travel in one of the government planes subsided. The pattern of extended overseas flights took over: reading, sleeping, and eating. Travel on the executive jet did provide more comfort, but it still carried a certain boredom.

The plane arrived in Tokyo late in the evening. A motorcade took them to a large hotel in Tokyo, where they efficiently checked into their rooms. Though most wanted to sleep, their minds would not cooperate. The change of the time zones confused everyone's circadian rhythm.

Security carefully screened the First Lady's suite, and they felt confident that no problems existed. She felt almost overwhelmed by fatigue as well. Immediately, she opened her suitcase and took out her nightgown. In the bathroom, she turned on the shower to let the steam fill the small room while she disrobed. After a hot shower, she placed a call to her husband, who anxiously awaited her call.

"Hello," the president answered on the first ring of their private line.

"Hi, it's me," his wife said.

"Did you just get there?" he asked. "How was the flight?"

"We got in about an hour ago; I had to take a shower first. That's really a long trip," she answered. "How was your day?"

They made small talk like normal married couples who have shared most of a lifetime together, and then finally and reluctantly, they hung up the phones.

The leaders of the trade mission had scheduled three days in Tokyo with meetings of government officials and industrial leaders.

Lee Koto gave the First Lady a personal tour of his production facilities at Yokohama; then he served a gourmet dinner to her and to Secretary of Commerce Thorp that evening. The talks went well, with promises of new import markets for American goods. Everyone agreed the First Lady's presence represented a stroke of political genius.

The phone rang beside her bed; she fumbled for it. She did not want to open her eyes because of the pounding in her head. Nausea and a headache told her this was a migraine. Since the last one, several years ago, a new medication had kept her headache free.

This can't happen now! she thought. The phone persisted and it seemed to her that it was increasing in intensity. Finally, her hand found the receiver. "Uh, yes," she mumbled.

"Begging your pardon, ma'am," the Secret Service agent murmured, "but we're due to leave in ten minutes, and I wondered if your bags were ready?"

"Oh, we can't!" she said. "My head . . . I have a migraine."

The accompanying White House physician arrived, confirmed her migraine, and gave her medication.

"Doctor," she said.

"Yes, ma'am," he answered.

"Please don't call my husband. It's late in Washington, and I don't want to worry him. I'll call him when I feel better."

"As you wish. I'll let Secretary Thorp know, and I'll stay in Tokyo until you're able to travel. Now go back to sleep." He turned out the light as he left the room.

The physician placed a call to Secretary Thorp. After they consulted for several minutes, they decided the rest of the mission would continue as scheduled. The availability of a US Air Force military aircraft at Yokota Air Force Base guaranteed that the First Lady would be able to quickly rejoin the mission when she was ready. An hour later, as the First Lady slept soundly, the trade mission boarded the plane for its flight to Taipei, Taiwan.

The trade mission jet left Haneda Airport and climbed to twenty-seven thousand feet; Mt. Fuji appeared in the righthand windows. Industrial executives acted like typical tourists as they snapped pictures of the famous mountain.

Simultaneously, a meditating Lee Koto sat contemplating the beauty of Mt. Fuji. He was momentarily disturbed by the distant noise of a jet airplane that flew overhead.

The plane crossed the west coast of Japan and turned south toward Taiwan. The air force pilot radioed the control tower for clearance into their air space.

"Ladies and gentlemen," the pilot said into the intercom, "we will be starting our descent into Taipei International Airport shortly. I recommend you finish whatever you're doing and return to your seats. I'm turning the seat belt sign on and should have you on the ground in about thirty minutes."

Lee Koto looked at his watch; he counted down the seconds to the appointed time.

Several miles from the coast of Japan, a small fishing trawler sailed through mildly choppy seas, due to a storm the night before. The captain had received new orders earlier that day. Initially his course had taken him north toward Korea, but at the last minute, the home office had instructed him to go south to Nagasaki. There he picked up a Mr. Kim Long and proceeded to Kagoshima. *Why couldn't he have taken the train?* the captain wondered.

Kim Long stood on the starboard side of the trawler with a small electronic box, about the size of a pack of cigarettes, in his hand. He too looked at his watch as the second hand moved steadily toward the twelve. At precisely ten forty-five, Kim Long pushed a small red button on the black box. For Kim and the crew of the trawler, nothing changed in their world. The ship encountered another four-foot swell.

Dick Wallins, the president and CEO of a major midwestern firm that manufactured tractors and other heavy equipment stepped from the airplane's lavatory. He closed the door, turned to his right, and headed toward the seats he and his wife occupied. He was walking past the divider when it exploded; it blew him almost intact through the gaping hole of the aircraft.

The pilot felt the explosion and the loss of all control; he screamed, "Explosion!" He knew the black box would survive even though he would not. He hoped it would give the investigators direction. The government jumbo jet broke apart and fell twenty-five thousand feet into the East China Sea, approximately sixty nautical miles north of Taiwan. Pieces of luggage, plane parts, and body parts rained down from the cloudless sky. Some sank, some floated, but all the pieces would prove instrumental in solving the mystery of the airliner's crash.

"Mr. President," the chief of staff quietly said as he softly closed the door of the oval office.

"Yes?" he said and looked up from the security report on his desk.

"Sir, there's been an accident."

Randolph Drexel saw the look of pain on the face of his chief of staff and the tears that welled up in his eyes. "What accident?" he asked, concerned.

"The trade mission plane has crashed near the coast of Taiwan." The tears spilled over and ran down his cheeks.

"Survivors?" the president asked.

"We don't know yet," he answered.

"My wife?"

"We don't know yet, sir." He took a deep breath and dabbed at his tears. "We've dispatched everything in the area. If there is anyone . . ." his voice trailed off. They both knew the odds of surviving a catastrophic plane crash.

Meanwhile, in Tokyo, the First Lady slept for several hours after the medication the doctor had given her. When she awoke, the headache was gone, but her heartache began.

Koto's watch reached ten forty-five. He smiled. He whispered to the wind, "Now, America, you will know what it is like to lose someone special." His voice became louder, "Sinshee, vengeance is mine." He stood surrounded by water, ducks, and Koi—the perfect scene of tranquility. "Vengeance is mine!" he screamed at the top of his lungs. It so startled one of the ducks that swam nearby that the duck frantically flapped its wings, propelled itself across the water, and flew into the air to get away from the screaming human.

37

SEARCHING FOR ANSWERS—SAN FRANCISCO

After the evening warehouse brief, Bill and Holly drove back to Ned's house in Pacific Heights, accompanied by Randy and John. They hoped to find the disk; however, a thorough search of the house brought no results.

Randy and John then returned to the warehouse. Randy muttered, "The brass always has the best accomodations."

"Look, Randy," John said, "if it wasn't for Bill, the way you spend money, you'd never get the chance to visit San Francisco. So, don't complain."

Bill and Holly bought a carry-out dinner from a deli on the way to the house. They sat at the ornate dining room banquet table and ate the deli sandwiches on paper plates and drank wine from Ned's Waterford crystal wine glasses.

"Our dinner would never pass with the town's elite," Holly remarked.

"Yeah, but think of the time it saves doing dishes," Bill retorted.

"Men—all you ever think of is getting out of housework," she teased.

They ate in silence for several minutes, then Bill said, "I've been thinking about the disk."

"Oh, great, the elusive disk, the one we don't know what's on it or where it is." She smiled at him. "That's a great thing to think about; here we have this beautiful house to ourselves," she coyly remarked.

"No, seriously, I've been thinking about Ned and where he might hide it." Bill stood up and took his wine glass as he began to walk the length of the dining room. "You know Ned had a pretty rough childhood. He never told me all of the details, but over the years I picked up bits and pieces."

"Oh, like what?" Holly asked.

"Well, for openers, his mother killed his father when he was young. Ned's father was an alcoholic and an abuser. It seems one night when he was beating her, she killed him. She was never prosecuted. Shortly after that, they moved in next door. That's when we met." He wandered aimlessly around the room in silence, staring into the distance.

Bill's mind searched into the past and tried to pull from then what he couldn't see in the present.

Holly didn't know his thoughts, but she knew his mood, so she sat quietly.

"They lived in a trailer, but after his father's death, they always lived in rental properties. They never had a house of their own. Ned's mother died before he could buy her her own home. He once told me that was one of his regrets. He didn't regret much in life, but he did regret that."

"You think, if he had something valuable, he'd hide it here because he never had a house before this?" Holly asked.

"No, that's too logical for Ned. He'd try to imagine what people would think he would do, and then he'd do the opposite. No, I don't believe he hid it here, but he may have left a clue to its location. If Ned thought I had to follow up, where would he put the clue?" Bill was lost in the past again.

Young Bill and Ned

"Hey, Bill!" Ned shouted as he barreled his bicycle straight at Bill. He applied the brakes at the last minute and turned the wheel, causing the bike to slide sideways.

It stopped inches from Bill.

"Ned, you're an idiot!" Bill yelled. "One of these days you're going to run over me. You ride that bike like a maniac."

"Right on. You know me, Bill, ol' die young Ned Litten," he teased.

"Ned, someday people are going to believe that, if you keep on," Bill replied.

"Let's go to the racetrack. I heard they're running the time trials for the race this weekend. We can slip in and watch them." He jumped on his bike before Bill could reply and rode toward the dirt stock-car track at the edge of town. Bill pedaled hard and finally caught him. The two boys were evenly matched physically, but Ned clearly had the head start that day. When they arrived at the back fence of the racetrack, they got off and walked their bikes down the ravine that ran along the far turn. They laid their bikes down in some brush and covered them. The new nine-foot hurricane chain-linked fence, at first glance, seemed impenetrable, but Ned and Bill had earlier discovered a place in the ravine where they could lift the bottom of the fence and wiggle through on their bellies. Bill held the fence for Ned, and when he was safely inside, Ned held it for Bill. They stealthily climbed the hill and hid themselves under a small bush near the far turn. From this hidden vantage point, the boys watched many a stock-car race on a hot Saturday or Sunday afternoon. In the distance, they heard an engine rev and saw the dust as the car began to accelerate down the track. Bill and Ned considered themselves experts on this track. They knew the driver would take the first lap carefully, to check the traction of the car and to get a feel for the track. The real excitement came on the second lap when the driver would try for the fastest time to gain the pole position in the race. The car accelerated as it came into the turn, and then it rocketed away on the back stretch. Ned's eyes appeared as large as silver dollars as he watched the receding car. They anxiously awaited its return. The whine of the engine grew louder and louder as it bore down on the turn again. The car had nearly negotiated the turn when the right front tire blew out. It immediately went into a skid. As the leading wheel dug into the soft dirt berm atop the bank, the car rolled and became airborne. The mass of steel hurtled toward the boys. Mesmerized by the unfolding spectacle, Ned and Bill never thought about moving, even if they had time. The hood of the car impacted the ground and dug into it. This changed the general direction of the spinning metal coffin the hapless driver rode in. It missed the bush and the boys by inches and bounced end over end down the hill toward the fence. Suddenly, it hit on all four wheels and exploded into a giant yellow-orange fireball that killed the driver instantly. The boys jumped up, ran down the hill, climbed through the broken fence, and ran past the burning car. They retrieved their bicycles and sped toward home. As the sound of sirens in the background rapidly approached, they rode as fast as they could back to Bill's house. After parking their bikes behind his house, they retreated to his basement. They were frightened and excited beyond belief.

"When I go, that's how I want to do it!" Ned whispered loudly in Bill's ear.

"Not me; that looked awful," Bill replied.

"Someday I'm going to have a car that goes fast," Ned said.

"Hum . . ." Holly's noise brought Bill back to the present.

"Yes?" he asked.

"You look like you were a long way away. Where did you go?" she asked.

Bill told her about the story. "You know, other than his mother, fast cars were about the only thing that was really important to Ned."

"Well, he's got a stable full of them out back," Holly said.

"I thought the same thing as I told you the story, but that would be too simple," Bill answered.

"Simple or not, why don't we look?"

Bill unlocked the door to the old carriage house, stepped through, and turned on the light. Everything looked the same as it had the first night they'd ventured to the house.

Holly walked past him, "You take one, I'll take one," she said. "By the way, using your infinite knowledge of Mr. Ned Litten, do you have any idea what we should be looking for?"

"My knowledge is woefully inadequate in that department, so the answer is no. I don't have the foggiest idea," Bill replied.

They searched for over an hour, carefully inspecting the automobiles, the motorcycle saddlebags, and the many tool chests and storage cabinets Ned accumulated. The storage cabinets held parts he used to restore his vintage fleet.

Bill walked to the '57 Chevrolet, opened the door, and slid in behind the wheel; Holly opened the passenger door and got in. "Well, what now? Go through them again?" she asked.

"I don't know; it was probably a crazy idea." Bill leaned his head back and closed his eyes. She moved over and began to massage his temples. "Oh yeah, don't stop," he said.

"Did you ever do it in the back of a fifty-seven?" she teased.

"Like that's a question I should answer?" he asked.

"If you don't answer, then I'll have my answer." Holly playfully punched him in the stomach.

He grabbed her, kissed her, and pulled her close to him. "What if I answer no, not yet?" He whispered at the end of their kiss. "Have you?"

"Of course not!" she said sharply. "But I might be persuaded . . ."

He interrupted her thought with another kiss and placed his hand on her thigh. "Let's do it," Bill said. He flipped down the visor and caught the keys. Bill slipped in the ignition key, turned it to accessory, and flipped on the radio. "You find the oldies station while I kill the lights in the garage and lock the door." He opened his door and got out. *I feel like a teenager trying to score the first time,* he thought, *almost feel like I need a condom,* he laughed to himself.

Holly waited for the radio to warm up; then she turned the knob and looked for the inevitable radio station that made a fortune from nostalgia and the songs from the fifties and the sixties. Neither she nor Bill had actually been teenagers during that time, but it seemed like the right kind of music to listen to if you were going to make love in the back seat of a '57 Chevy.

"Please stay tuned for the details on a breaking story from Japan. A White House spokesman has just confirmed the crash of a US government airliner in the East China Sea near the island of Taiwan. Details are sketchy at this time, but it is believed there were no survivors. President Drexel was not on the plane. It carried a group of American industrial leaders and Secretary of Commerce Thorp on a long-awaited trade mission to Asia. The first stop was Tokyo. They were flying to Taiwan for their second stop. There are unconfirmed reports that the First Lady was on the plane. That has not been confirmed. I repeat . . ."

Bill opened the car door; the dome light shone on Holly's face and Bill could instantly see something was wrong. "Holly?" he asked.

"Bill, there's been another plane crash; this one is a government aircraft."

"When, where?" he asked.

"Near Taiwan, they think possibly the First Lady was on it."

Just then his satellite phone rang. "Chandler."

"Boss, got a call that I need to put through to you; he's quite insistent," Randy said nervously.

"Okay, Randy, settle down. Who is it?"

"He won't say, just told me to tell you he has information on the government plane. Do you have any idea what he's talking about?" Randy asked.

"Unfortunately, I do. Go ahead and put it through," Bill said soberly.

The phone uttered a click, followed by a moment of silence, then, "Dr. Chandler?"

"Chandler here."

"This is Useph."

"What can I do for you?" Bill questioned guardedly.

"We believe that an onboard explosion took down the American plane," Useph said solemnly.

"Who are you and why are you telling me? Why not tell the CIA, FBI, or someone like that?" Bill asked.

"Our organization knows for certain that the two recent airplane accidents can be tied directly to Litten Industries. There is only one common ground for those accidents. They both obtained service or overhaul by Litten Industries. Since our sources tell me that you control Litten Industries, I thought you might like to know."

Bill was silent for a long time.

"Are you still there, Dr. Chandler?" Useph asked.

"Ah, yes. Yes, I'm still here. Just thinking," Bill answered. "Do you have anything else that might help? By the way, who do you work for?"

"At the moment, I am not at liberty to say, but we do want to help. Right now, that's about the extent of our information. If I get anything more, I'll let you know right away."

"Thanks," Bill paused. He terminated the connection. Bill turned and looked at Holly. The only light in the car came from the radio dial. Bill gazed intently at Holly's face; shadows obscured her eyes. "Holly, I think I know what the Special Projects were," Bill said with a grave tone in his voice. "And I have a hunch I know what's on the disk." He took a deep breath as if to clear his brain from the revelation. Then, with a resolute tone filled with fear and anger, he said, "We *must* find that disk, as soon as possible, and no one else can beat us to it."

38

GONE FISHING—SAN FRANCISCO

Bill called John at the warehouse. "I assume you still have our guest?" he asked.

"Yes, sir. He's resting in the back room," John said.

"Get Sam to warm up his boat. I want to go fishing," Bill said into the phone.

"Bill, I don't know what you're thinking about, but don't stoop to their level. You're better than that," Holly pleaded.

"Holly, someone is out there killing hundreds of innocent people. They don't give a damn about the rules or what's right. They don't even care about who they're killing. It's not a war. They're worse than animals, and they don't deserve to be treated any better than animals!" he shouted.

"Bill," she cried, "don't become like them."

He got out of the car, took the keys with him out of reflex, and walked around to Holly's door. He opened it and helped her out. Without a word, he walked across the garage and onto the brick drive. "Go in the house. I'm going to the dock."

"When will you be back?" she asked.

"Later," he replied as he got into their rental car. He started the engine, and without looking back at Holly, drove out of the drive and accelerated toward the warehouse and Gregg Newman.

When Bill arrived at the warehouse, Sam's boat idled beside the pier. He walked through the door and said, "Where is he?"

"Got him occupied in the back," John answered.

"Get his ass on your boat!" Bill said to Sam.

"Now this is more like it. All you guys' high-tech stuff was givin' me the willies." Sam displayed an enthusiastic attitude as he headed back through the warehouse to get Newman. "Out on the water, we won't use any high-tech stuff. Just hook a line on him and troll for sharks!"

Sam dragged Gregg Newman out of the makeshift jail. Newman's hands were tied behind him. He glared at Bill as he stumbled past, but said nothing.

"So, Boss, what's the deal?" Randy asked.

"Not here; I'll tell you on the boat."

They boarded Sam's boat and walked into the wheelhouse.

"Git out there and untie the bow," Sam said to Randy.

"Okay, then what?" Born and raised in the Midwest, Randy had never actually set foot on any kind of boat.

"Then push the bow away from the dock," Sam said.

"So how do I get on?" Randy asked.

"Jump, you land-lovin'—"

"What if I miss?"

"Then not all the fish will go hungry tonight," Sam said as he shoved Randy out the door.

They cleared the dock and started for the channel that led toward the Golden Gate Bridge. Bill related what he knew about the newest plane crash. He told them he was suspicious that Litten Industries somehow rigged airplanes to blow up. He didn't know how it was done, where it was done, or how they were triggered, but he was confident that the explosion must be from a signal sent from somewhere else. The person or persons behind this terrorism were the greatest threat.

"That sounds like a mighty tall tale," Sam said.

"So, Bill," John said, "do you think this fellow down in the hold knows the answer to some of your questions?"

"Well, I think so. And if he does, I want to find out."

They motored in silence under the bridge and entered the open water of the Pacific.

It was much rougher than the bay, and in no time at all, Randy was seasick. "I have to go lie down," he gasped.

"You jus' better not throw up all over my boat!" Sam yelled after him. A few minutes later he said, "Mr. Chandler, we're nearin' the fog bank. That's far enough out you can do whatever you want with the fellow. No one will see, and no one will ever know what happened to him. Even if he falls overboard, the sharks will have him for lunch before anybody finds his body."

"Bring him up!" Bill said to John.

John opened the bait locker and motioned for Newman to come.

Gregg Newman stumbled on the ladder; the pungent smell of the fish bait nearly made him pass out. The cold fresh ocean air started to clear his head quickly as John shoved him into the wheelhouse. "You know the penalty for kidnapping is life in prison," Newman said defiantly.

"Is that so?" Bill answered. "What's the penalty for mass murder?"

"I don't have any idea what you're talking about," he answered.

"I'm talking about airplanes that blow up in the air with hundreds of innocent people on board. That's what I'm talking about."

"Sorry, partner, I don't have any idea what you're talking about," he said.

Sam stood behind the wheel and steered a steady course to the northwest. In the dim light of early morning, nothing lay ahead except a retreating fog bank. "Well, do you think a little swim in the ol' Pacific might help his memory jus' a bit?" Sam asked.

Gregg Newman looked at the old sea captain, who looked more like a skid row rummy, then looked back at Bill. "You ain't thinking of doing anything stupid out here, are you?" he asked with real concern in his voice. His voice changed from the drawl of a cowboy. Suddenly, a South African English accent appeared.

"I can assure you, if we do anything, it won't be stupid," Bill answered.

"Here, let me put this on autopilot; we can git out of these cramped quarters," Sam said. Sam took Gregg to the boat's flattened fantail. A small crane projected from the upper deck. Sam used it for hauling in the nets when he could afford fishing nets. The last several years, he'd used it for loading extra drums of diesel fuel if he went for an extended trip. Occasionally, he used it to unload contraband when he returned. Sam took a rope and tied a bowline knot around Newman. He then pulled the cleat from the crane and fastened the line to the hook. He looked up at John. "Okay, crank 'im up!" he shouted.

John began to crank the winch; after the third turn, Gregg Newman swung free above the deck. "You can't do this!" he shouted over the sound of the boat chugging through the gentle swells.

"Now swing 'im over the side!" Sam barked at John. "What's that?" Sam yelled.

"What? Where?" John answered.

"That thing over there—I can't tell, is it a dorsal fin?" Sam yelled back at John.

"Oh, you mean that," John pointed to the water. "Yeah, ya know, it might be. I've never seen a shark for real, but I saw a bunch on the National Geographic channel. Sure, looks like one." He looked at Newman, who swung over the water ten feet in the air. "I sure wish I'd brought my camera along. I've never seen a real shark before."

"Oh, god! Please!" Newman pleaded.

Bill noticed tears streaming down Newman's face.

"Please, don't do this!"

Sam looked at John and said, "Lower away!"

John turned the bolt on the winch and started to unwind the cable. Newman began a slow descent toward the cold Pacific Ocean.

"The good thing is, even if the sharks don't git ya, you'll only last about ten minutes in this cold water." He laughed a rummy's belly laugh and added, "So it won't last too long."

Newman's feet were within three feet of the water. The spray from the wake of the boat soaked through his pants and boots. "Okay! I'll tell you!" Newman shouted.

John stopped the winch.

"Tell us what?" Bill asked coldly.

"I'll tell you about the planes. How they're rigged to blow up!" His voice whimpered just audibly above the wind and the waves.

Bill looked at John and gave him a signal to bring Newman up. John began to crank Newman up and swing him toward the deck below. At that moment, a wave struck the port side of the trawler and threw John off balance; his hand slipped from the winch crank and it dropped Newman like a rock into the water.

"Help!" Newman shouted as he disappeared under the surface. The rope went slack as the port screw sliced it. Gregg Newman slowly sank into the Pacific Ocean trench, fifty miles from the mouth of San Francisco Bay.

John regained his footing and looked panic-stricken at his boss. "Bill, I'm sorry, it was an accident . . ." He held his hands out helplessly.

Bill stared at the receding wake of the boat. "It's not your fault, it's mine," Bill said as he shook his head in disbelief. He'd killed again. *Damn it!* Holly had begged him not to go. *She was right,* he thought.

Sam turned lazy eights in the ocean while they searched for Newman's body. It was nowhere to be found.

"Might as well head in, Dr. Chandler," Sam said. "Shame he didn't tell us what he knew. From the sound of it, he was aware of the operation. Well, hope the sharks don't git heartburn trying to stomach him." Sam, at least, had no second thoughts; he felt that the incident was for the best.

39

BILL AND SAM—SAN FRANCISCO

It was subdued on the return trip to the warehouse dock. John felt terrible; he had let the winch get away from him. Randy stayed in the bowels of the boat and heaved his guts out. Bill sat on the fantail and watched the receding wake from the trawler. He did not realize they were back until the boat bumped against the side of the pier and the noise of the engines quieted.

Sam walked back to Bill. "Well, didn't go just like we figured, but what the hell. You know the saying, 'Shit happens.'"

"That man died because of my ego," Bill said.

"Mr. Chandler, I'm not a very smart guy, okay? I mean, I've spent most of my life just on this side of starvin'. In the ways of the world, I ain't turned out to be much, but I've learned a thing or two sitting out there on the ocean," said Sam as he sat down beside Bill. The usual seagulls swooped and hovered around the back of the boat, as they glided and flapped and hoped for a free meal. "Ya see them birds? Each of them is capable of flying over the bay and finding its own fish and doin' what them birds is supposed to. But these here, well, they'd rather take the easy way out. They learned that boats like this, with people on them, usually is good for a handout. They're takin' birds, not givin' birds." He stopped talking and looked at the birds again.

"So, Captain, I don't see what that has to do with losing Newman out there," Bill said. "What makes me any different than him?"

"Well, he was just like most of them birds. Sometime in his life, he decided it was easier to hang around and eat the scraps rather than tryin' to fish for himself." Sam stood up and looked at Bill. "What I'm trying to say is, he chose to be a scavenger in the world . . . not fish for himself, not do somethin' that's right, somethin' that helps and not hurts." Sam walked to the stern and looked into the water. "Now, you," he turned and faced Bill, "you've spent a lot of time tryin' to do things that help people, tryin' to do things that make the world a better place for everyone. That feller out there, he worked for the scum, and the only reason he was ready to talk was to save his own hide. Do ya think he'da given ya a thought if the tables were turned?" Sam turned away from Bill and watched a freighter pass the pier. "The difference between you and him is this: maybe ya played some part in his death. It bothers ya, so you'll have to learn to live with it. But I'll guarantee that if he coulda thrown *you* overboard, he wouldn't have given it a second thought. And the other difference is, ya have to keep on until ya find out who's making them planes crash and how they're doin' it. Ya got to make them stop, 'cause ya know it ain't right!" Sam turned and walked toward the bow of the boat.

Bill sat on the trawler for a long time; he watched the birds and thought. *In a way, what Sam said made sense.* However, he still felt responsible. Sam was right; it was something he'd have to live with, but Sam was also right about the planes. Some airplanes, which had passed through the Litten facility, blew up and killed people for no apparent reason. He had to do something about it—not because he was any hero or even wanted to be involved, but because his friend Ned had left him this legacy. Right now, he didn't care about Ned or Litten Industries or wealth. He just wanted the killing to stop.

The walk back to his car was a slow and painful one. It was a night he just wanted to forget. He thought, *I might as well go home.* Then he said aloud. "Home, no this isn't home; the mansion in Pacific Heights might as well be a haunted house!"

Holly slept as he crept into the bedroom. He went to the bath, closed the door, and turned on the shower. Soon hot steam blocked the mirror and created a fog in the room that reflected the fog of death that hung over his soul. He stepped into the shower's hot spray and let the water run over his head. Bill did not hear the door open.

Holly slipped in quietly and sat down on a dressing stool in front of a makeup mirror.

When Bill stepped from the shower, she knew things had not gone well. "Rough night?" she asked.

"That's saying it mildly," he muttered.

"What did you learn?"

"I'm not God," he replied.

"That bad?"

"I killed a man," he responded in a monotone voice.

"Oh, Bill!" she said as she arose from the stool and put her arms around him to comfort him.

His tears cascaded onto her back and soaked through her thin nightgown. They stood silently in the mist-shrouded bathroom and held each other. Bill wondered about the direction of their lives.

"I'll go make some coffee; you need a shave," Holly said as she headed for the kitchen.

People in love know when the emotion of the moment is spent, whether it's sex or sorrow.

Bill wiped the haze from the mirror. "You'll have to forgive yourself if you're going to go on," he said to the haggard reflection that looked back at him. With that, he began to lather the soap in his shaving mug.

When he entered the kitchen, Bill saw a hot cup of coffee and a bagel on the table. He walked over to Holly, gave her a kiss, and said, "Thanks, darling."

Holly slowly sipped her coffee; her bagel lay half eaten. Her attention was focused on a small TV set that hung under a cupboard.

"There are confirmed reports that everyone onboard the US trade mission airplane died when it crashed into the ocean sixty nautical miles north of Taiwan. An American carrier group is steaming to the area to assist in recovery operations. All the US Navy's deep-sea submersibles are on their way by air to begin the salvage work. Earlier reports that the First Lady was on board have now been corrected. She stayed over in Tokyo and planned to catch up with the trade mission later. We are expecting the president to hold a live news conference within the hour. Stay tuned and see it live on this station. Please stay tuned for further developments on this breaking story."

"Bill, it's just awful. Everyone on board—"

"Have they said what happened?"

"No," Holly answered. "They're waiting for the black box, although there is an unconfirmed report that a satellite registered a footprint of an explosion. The military is on full alert, and there is a lot of talk about a missile from China. Some groups blame China, Iran, Iraq, or North Korea. Other groups blame the government's failure to maintain the aircraft."

"Holly, I just can't believe Ned is ultimately behind all of this," Bill said as he sat down. He found the blare of the television irritating. "Would you turn that off?" he asked.

She got up and walked to the set. An X on a map indicated the location of the wreck. She shook her head and shuddered as she thought about a giant airliner plunging toward the ocean. She hesitated, then switched off the television.

After breakfast, Bill told her about the last night's events on the trawler and about Newman's death. "Well, that's what happened."

"Okay, Bill, you're right, in the vernacular of the street, you screwed up!" Her crudeness shocked Bill away from his self-pity. "But the captain was right too. You may be one of the few people capable of putting this whole nightmare together. Learn what you can from what you did and get moving!" She picked up the keys to the car and threw them at him.

He caught them just before they would have hit him in the face."You know what I love about you?" he asked with a tone of irritation in his voice. He wanted sympathy and got a lecture.

"No, what?" Holly asked guardedly.

His face softened to a smile."Everything," he answered as he headed for the back door.

Holly looked at his back as he opened the door.

He turned,"Well, come on, lady. We've got the world to save!"

"You are impossible!" she said as she walked through the door that he held for her.

"Yes, that's what you find attractive," Bill replied.

40

KOTO'S PLAN—BERKELEY, CALIFORNIA

"Han!" Koto shouted.

"Hai!" he said as he ran into the library.

"I sent for Toki last night. When will she arrive?" he questioned.

"She said she would be here before evening," Han replied. "She told me to tell you there was a meeting with the owners of one of the other major resorts which she couldn't reschedule. They would be in Las Vegas only a short time. She is very certain she can add the resort to your inventory."

"Very well, would you see if you can get an appointment with Dr. Chandler this afternoon? I'd like to see him again." Koto talked with his back to Han the entire time.

Nevertheless, Han bowed in respect as he left the room. He then immediately placed a call to Litten Industries.

Lee Koto stood at his Berkeley Hills window and looked at San Francisco Bay. The fog started to lift from the bay; the distant bridge's pillars could be seen, but the rest of the bridge was shrouded.

Two days after the crash of the trade mission airplane, the recovery effort had produced a lot of debris, but only a few bodies. The black boxes remained elusive. The debris retrieved so far gave no immediate clue as to the cause of the catastrophe.

Koto silently gloated. He obtained every major newspaper that carried the story and had his staff continually videotape WNN (World News Network) and the major networks in the United States, Europe, and Asia. As each day dragged on, he enjoyed the rhetoric from the fringe groups in America, both right and left. The very fabric of that nation appeared to be unraveling.

Han placed a call to Litten Industries.

"Yes, Phyllis," Bill said into the intercom.

"Lee Koto would like an appointment today," Phyllis said.

Bill grimaced. "Yes, that would be fine." Bill stood up and walked to the couch, where Holly was studying the files she had previously copied at Rogers and Bailey. "Now, what do you suppose he wants?" Bill said out loud more to himself than to her.

"Huh?" she asked. "I wasn't paying attention."

"Oh, nothing really; Lee Koto wants to meet with me today," Bill said. "I believe I told him I'd get back to him after I read the proposed contract."

Outside Bill's office, Phyllis dialed another number. "Mr. Cotting, I thought you might want to know that Lee Koto called and asked for an appointment with Dr. Chandler."

"Phyllis," his voice was playfully familiar, "remember, call me Larry."

She paused to listen. "Yes, Mr. Cotting . . . I'm sorry, yes, Larry," she blushed and continued, "he'll be here at two this afternoon."

"Phyllis, are you going out for lunch?" Larry asked, though he knew the answer.

"Why no, I usually bring my lunch." She smiled.

"Would you go to lunch with me today? Say about twelve fifteen, and meet me at the Chatelet Benoit?" he asked.

"Why sure, er yes, I'd love to have lunch with you." She hung up the phone and thought, *Thank goodness, I wore this dress today. Imagine, having lunch with Larry Cotting.* Phyllis had developed a schoolgirl crush on him when he had been named legal counsel four years earlier.

At noon, Phyllis took the elevator to the ground floor and left the building. She walked the two short blocks to Chatelet Benoit, an upscale restaurant that catered to business lunches at noon and rendezvous at night. She walked past it frequently but always considered it too expensive for a secretary's salary. Besides, you did not eat alone at Chatelet Benoit, and Phyllis usually ate lunch alone. She walked through the revolving door. Several men and women, dressed in business attire, stood in a small group and talked quietly while they waited for their table.

The maître d', dressed in a black tuxedo, looked up from his podium. "Yes. May I help you?"

"I'm to meet someone here," she answered timidly.

"Is she," he patronizingly smiled and continued, "or is he expecting you?"

"Cotting, Mr. Larry Cotting, is expecting me," she said proudly.

"Yes, ma'am. Right this way!" He snatched a menu from the podium and walked toward a corner table.

The secluded table was shunned at noon. However, that was all right with Larry; his business deal required an intimate setting. Phyllis approached the table; Larry looked up and smiled. He stood and held her chair; his hand intentionally touched her shoulder. Two glasses of fragrant white wine sat on the table. Larry's was half empty.

"Phyllis, I'm glad you didn't have other plans today," he said, though he knew she never had other plans.

"Why thank you, Mr. Cotting. It's not even National Secretaries' Week," she said as she tried to take the edge from her excitement.

"First, Phyllis, call me Larry. Mr. Cotting sounds like we're at work. I just wanted to have lunch with you," he said.

"Thank you, Larry." Every defense she'd developed after her divorce began to crumble like the walls of Jericho.

On Phyllis's return to the office, the memories of lunch lingered in her head.

The door opened to Bill's office. "Mr. Koto to see you, sir," Phyllis said as she escorted Lee Koto through the door.

Bill walked from his desk, stopped a few feet from Koto, and bowed slightly. Koto returned the bow, then put his right hand out and shook Bill's. Bill guided him to one of the couches; they sat down across from each other.

"May I get you anything?" Phyllis asked.

"Mr. Koto? Tea?" Bill asked.

"Thank you, no," he replied.

"Well, to what do I owe the honor of your visit today?" Bill questioned.

"I was curious, Dr. Chandler, have you considered my offer?" Lee asked.

"I read the proposal; it looks very sound on the surface. In fact, I'd go so far as to say it seems generous," Bill replied.

"Thank you. There is an old Japanese expression, 'If all prosper, the world will live at peace,'" he said.

Bill smiled. "I suppose when our country is as old as yours, we may also have wise sayings." Bill's defenses were on high alert. Holly had researched Lee Koto's background; she had informed Bill that Koto was a ruthless businessman who would never cut a rival an even break if he could help it. His reputation was the antithesis of his appearance at the moment. "I've always admired the men of your generation, Mr. Koto."

"And why would that be, Dr. Chandler?"

"I assume you were a child during World War II."

Lee nodded his head in agreement.

"I'm certain to live in Japan at the close of the war brought terrible struggles; however, you and your contemporaries forged a new and powerful nation and actually taught the rest of the world how to not only survive, but to move forward in the face of adversity." Bill paused to get a reaction.

Lee sat silent for a few moments as he contemplated the answer. He looked at Bill. "We children saw our fathers give their lives in a cause of selfishness and dedication to an emperor they believed was God. What they really did made many children orphans and many women widows. Some of us who survived realized that we must build a new kind of country . . . not one based on our national pride, but one that would make the world a better place."

"Where did you live then? Tokyo?" Bill asked.

"Hiroshima," Koto whispered. For an instant, his face flashed a story of hate, then it was gone.

Their discussion then centered on the proposal's details. A diplomatic impasse developed. Both men knew that Bill was not ready to seriously consider the offer, and Koto was not about to withdraw it.

They parted with a customary handshake and bow.

"So how did it go?" Holly asked, as she walked back into his office.

"A civil meeting, as meetings go," Bill answered.

"What did he want?"

"I'm not sure, maybe to feel me out about selling the company. Who knows? It was interesting at one point."

"Oh, what was that?" Holly asked.

"We talked a little philosophy at first, and then I asked him where he was raised. There was something strange in his look when he said Hiroshima."

"Well, if you were his age and raised in Hiroshima, you'd probably have a strange expression when you said it too." Her face brightened. "I may have found something interesting."

"What's that?"

"Do you remember I told you that Willis showed me invoices of containers that cleared customs and went directly to the Desert Wells Plant without going to the Rogers and Bailey warehouse first? Willis wondered why they bypassed his warehouse," she said.

Bill nodded his answer.

"Well, some of the shipments that went to Desert Wells were much heavier than expected for textile supplies."

"So, what's that mean?" Bill asked.

"I don't know for sure, but if we could find out what was in those containers, then maybe it would give us another lead."

Bill saw her discouragement since she had found nothing concrete. "Hey, this is one heck of a puzzle; that's another piece. Don't let it get you down."

When Koto returned home, Han met him at the door.

"How did the meeting go, Koto? Is he ready to sell?" Han asked.

"No!" he answered Han.

It was a sharp one-word answer that Han learned over the years meant "I don't want to talk and get out of my sight."

Koto hoped a handsome profit for Litten Industries would encourage Chandler to sell. But his intuition or wisdom from the gods, he wasn't sure which, told him Chandler had no intention of selling. He could have bought it from Ned Litten at any time. He owned Litten. If anything had gone wrong, Ned Litten would have taken the fall. Now, with a whole new set of players, he needed a new plan. *Maybe it will involve the beautiful Mrs. Chandler,* he thought.

An hour later, Han returned to Koto. "Toki will be here within the half hour," he said submissively.

Koto looked up and said nothing.

Han bowed and retreated backward out the door.

41

LARRY COTTING—SAN FRANCISCO

The grandeur of San Francisco Bay and the downtown skyline looked like an elaborate painting when viewed from the living room and balcony of Larry Cotting's apartment. Matching L-shaped low white leather sofas gave comfortable seating without obstructing the magnificent views. A large glass and chrome coffee table separated the sofas and gave easy accessibility for a drink and hors d'oeuvres, but still allowed for easy conversation. Tasteful modern art invited inspection and admiration. Larry enjoyed entertaining, whether it was a party of his friends or just one person. The apartment reflected his desires: money, power, and sex. He knew many ladies, married and otherwise, who enjoyed his company, prestige, and money, and he felt no need to marry. The social page of the newspaper considered him one of the most eligible bachelors in the bay area, and his private reputation far outweighed his public one.

As he sat on his balcony and enjoyed the unusually warm evening, the phone rang. "Cotting here."

"Mr. Cotting, this is Phyllis . . ." she said timidly.

Now what could she want? I hope she's not a buy you lunch and I own you type, he thought. "Yes, Phyllis. I was just thinking about you," he said smoothly. "And please call me Larry; we're not at work, you know."

"Larry, I left the office late today, and I discovered something you might be interested in." She left a long silence without revealing what the item might be. *There's always going to be a certain amount of gamesmanship in every relationship,* Phyllis thought.

"What might that be?" Larry asked.

"I think it would be best if I showed you," she answered.

What is this lady up to? Larry knew he needed someone close to Chandler; however, he didn't know how much the Chandlers trusted Phyllis. The up side was that Phyllis did have access to Chandler's office anytime. He had started to push her for information at lunch earlier. Now she thought she had something for him. He might as well look at it. Larry glanced around his apartment; he always enjoyed showing it off. Inviting her over might even make her more ardent in supplying him information. "I hate to ask, but could you bring it to my apartment? I have some work I need to finish. I could come to you, but it would be late tonight," he lied. "I hate to inconvenience you."

"That wouldn't be any inconvenience. I would be happy to bring it over," she answered.

"In about an hour?"

"That would be perfect," she answered. *I'll have time to get ready!* she thought excitedly. "Oh, Larry, I don't know your address," her voice tingled with anticipation. She wrote it down and placed three hearts on the paper.

The cab stopped at the front of Larry's building; a doorman opened the door for Phyllis and directed her to the elevator. As she stepped in, she pressed the button for the twenty-eighth floor and waited for the door to close. Mirrors covered three walls of the elevator. She looked right, then left; her hem appeared straight. Her calves were enhanced by the three-inch heels she wore, not the mousy one-inch heels she normally wore at work. Smiling, she surveyed her blouse; she opened two buttons to expose a slight hint of her breast and a touch of lace from her bra. The elevator stopped and her heart began to race. *Do I really want to do this?* she thought. "Yes," she said out loud to herself as the door of the elevator opened.

Larry opened the door seconds after she rang the doorbell. "Phyllis!" he said as he stepped back. "I had no idea—you must have plans tonight; I hope I didn't inconvenience you too much," he apologized. *This doesn't look like Phyllis at the office!* he thought. His face also conveyed the thought.

Good! she thought. *He's interested.* "Oh, not at all, Larry. A friend and I planned dinner. Unfortunately his boy became ill and he canceled at the last minute. It was no problem to drop this off." She motioned to the leather case that she carried.

"Would you like a drink?" he asked.

"Are you having anything?" she responded.

"I usually have a glass of wine to relax before bed," he laughed politely.

"That would be nice. What a lovely apartment. Is this an original Dali?" she asked as she walked over and looked at a picture on the wall.

It's probably as close as I'll ever get to one. It's a signed print," he responded.

"It's beautiful," she said as he handed her a glass of wine.

He took the leather briefcase from her and they walked to a glass dining room table. The lights of the Golden Gate Bridge sparkled in the distance. "May I?"

"Yes, certainly; I don't know if they mean anything, but after our discussion at lunch, I thought you might want to see them." She sat down beside him, crossed her legs, and exposed enough thigh to be alluring without being brash. He noticed, and she noticed he noticed. Neither spoke as he thumbed through copies of the papers Holly had copied at Rogers and Bailey.

"You say Mrs. Chandler got these from Rogers and Bailey?" he asked.

"Yes, and I don't think Mr. Willis knows she took them," Phyllis answered.

"What makes you think that?" Larry asked.

"I saw her take them from her purse and show them to Dr. Chandler when she got back that day. I didn't know what they were until this evening. I called Willis and asked him if he had given any papers to Mrs. Chandler. He said no." She shifted slightly on her chair and straightened the edge of her skirt when she was sure Larry was looking at her legs.

He smiled and added, "Well, they do seem quite secretive about everything they do, don't they?"

"The office is so different since poor Mr. Litten's accident." She turned her face toward the window and looked sad.

Larry stood up and offered Phyllis his hand. She took it. He led her to the couch; she sat down and leaned against a pillow that allowed her blouse to fall open more. He walked to the table, picked up their wine glasses, stopped by the wall, turned up the music, and turned down the lights. Neither said a word as he sat down and bent toward her. He handed her a glass. "Oh, I don't remember which was which," he said.

"It doesn't make any difference. I'm sure I won't catch anything from you or vice versa." She laughed a demure laugh. "This is excellent wine."

He bent forward from the waist and kissed her lightly on the lips, not a threatening, passionate kiss, but a light and easily repelled kiss if she felt intimidated. She kissed him back. He took the wine glass from her hand and set it on the chrome and glass coffee table. "That was nice," he said.

Phyllis modestly gazed downward.

He followed her eyes, but his eyes stopped at her opened blouse. The roundness of her breasts revealed a cleavage that drew him in as the nectar of a Venus flytrap draws the insect. He kissed her again, this time more assertively.

She allowed him to press her onto the couch.

"Phyllis, come with me," Larry whispered in her ear.

She remembered how wonderful it was to bask in the afterglow with a man. How she had longed to feel her body against a man. Her ex-husband was a louse, but he was an excellent lover and had taught her well.

However, she caught him teaching other women, so she had divorced him five years earlier.

"Is there anything else I can do for you?" She gazed immodestly at him while snuggled into his arm.

"I could ask the same," he responded and kissed her ear.

"I'm referring to work, silly." She smiled.

"It would be helpful if I knew anything unusual that either Dr. or Mrs. did." He paused and kissed her. "It's really up to us to make sure Litten Industries survives this period of change. We are the leadership. A lot of people depend on us." He hoped she would not only feel a sensual loyalty toward him, but a global responsibility to the employees of the company. He thought, *Taking her to lunch was brilliant.*

42

COTTING AND KOTO—MARIN COUNTY

"Hello, Mr. Koto," Larry Cotting said softly into the phone. He did not want his secretary, or anyone passing by, to hear. "It's Larry Cotting, at Litten." He paused as Koto cleared his throat. "I need to see you, sir."

"Is it important?" Koto asked.

"Yes, sir, I think it's crucial."

"Where would you suggest we meet?" Koto asked.

"There's a tourist viewpoint, on the other side of the Golden Gate Bridge. Could you meet me there, at say, eleven thirty?"

"I will be there," Koto answered.

"Thank you, sir; I'll see you then." Larry hung up the phone and sat back in his chair. He smiled with the knowledge that he could talk with the movers and shakers in the world. Larry's ego swelled with pride.

The Tel-Ray unit's voice-activated recording system copied only part of Cotting's and Koto's conversation to a disk because the disk was full. No one had actively monitored the listening post, and it was over twenty-four hours before Randy transferred the information from the disk.

A deserted viewpoint greeted Larry Cotting. That morning, the fog never completely lifted. The city remained shrouded in a gray haze. Only the tops of the towers that held the gargantuan cables of the Golden Gate Bridge loomed visible in the distance. Tourists who hoped to get the perfect picture of the skyline or bridge ignored the viewpoint, oblivious to the fact that some of the best pictures were obtained on a day like this.

Larry could hear the forlorn wailing of a foghorn that warned passing ships of danger. *This is going to be even better than I expected,* he thought as a long black limousine rolled to a stop near his car. The back door opened as he walked toward it. Koto was not alone. Larry bent over and stepped in. He sat on a small seat that faced Koto and smiled. A stunning Asian woman sat at Koto's side; she sat closer than a business associate.

"So, Mr. Cotting, what is the necessity for this meeting?" Lee Koto asked.

Larry looked at the woman, then back at Koto, and raised his head to indicate he questioned her presence.

Koto ignored the gesture and stared emotionless at Cotting.

This made Larry very uncomfortable. He had assumed he and Koto would have one-on-one face time, and this would be an opportunity to further his career with Koto. Larry entertained visions of running Litten Industries when Koto controlled them. "Err, well, sir, I received some information that Mrs. Chandler acquired some documents from Rogers and Bailey associated with some Special Projects. I've seen this information; I wonder if it could lead the Chandlers toward the real purpose of those projects."

"Is that so?" Koto said slowly. "And you are aware of the use of these Special Projects?"

Larry stammered slightly, "No, not exactly. However, I am mindful of the fact that some planes are renovated outside the normal channels. What their purpose is, I have no idea."

The answer satisfied Koto. He thought a moment. "And what are these documents?"

"Invoices, customs receipts, bills of lading, the weight of the shipping containers, and data that might make them wonder if someone outside the company is directly involved with these projects."

"How do you know this?"

"I have copies of what she has." Larry smiled smugly.

"I see, and do you have any idea how we should proceed?" Koto asked.

"No, sir. You might want to talk with her," Larry said. "As a lawyer, it would be best if I didn't know what you chose to do with that information unless—" Larry's heart began to pound within his chest as he thought, *It was time to plant the seed.* He wondered if it would take root.

"Unless what?" Koto asked.

"Unless I have a lawyer-client relationship with you," Larry answered.

"That is something we may want to pursue in the future. I will keep that in mind," Koto said as he took the envelope Larry offered. "In the meantime, I do appreciate all of your thoughtfulness in this matter." Then with a slight nod of his head, he dismissed Larry, who promptly exited the limousine.

Larry walked to the retaining wall. The fog lifted from the top of the bridge and the sun started to peek through the mist. *Yes!* he thought as he leaned down on the wall and gazed out at the bay.

"Don't you feel dirty since you have to work with people like that?" Toki asked as the limousine slowly drove away.

"To accomplish our goals, I'd collaborate with the devil himself," Koto muttered. "Now, let me look at these documents." He opened the envelope. After inspecting them, he turned to Toki. "So what do you think we should do now?" he asked her.

"Do you think Chandler will sell soon?"

"No, I don't believe he will."

"Why not?" Toki asked.

"Dr. Chandler is a builder, whether he knows it or not. He does not do something to turn a quick profit. And I believe he suspects that something is wrong with the company. He is a man who likes to solve problems, and he speculates there is a problem with Litten Industries."

"Is his wife like him?"

"I don't know. She is very observant and stays in the background. I think she gives him insights that he doesn't have as an engineer," Koto said.

"Then maybe you need to talk with her alone," Toki suggested. "If she understands that it would be best for her husband to rid himself of the company, she might become your ally." Toki watched the city flash by through the darkened window. "By the way, Lee," she said.

"Yes?" he answered raising one eyebrow in surprise. He knew whatever she had to say next was important and personal to her.

"You sent for the head of my hotel security a week ago." She tried to keep all emotion from her voice by concentrating on her breathing. "Do you have any idea when you'll be finished with his services?"

"Do you miss him?" Koto asked with a hint of edge in his voice.

"Miss him?" She laughed. "No, Lee, I don't miss him, I need him. I've never had a better man to direct the security of the casino. I know he's doing something important for you, but he also does important things for the hotel." She tried to keep this on a business basis.

However, Koto felt troubled. He had told Hank Este to use Newman to keep close surveillance on Dr. Chandler. Este had informed him that Newman disappeared several days ago. Koto presumed that Newman had slipped back to Las Vegas to see Toki. Apparently, that was not the case.

"I will return him to you shortly," he said. "And you are right, he is superb at what he does. I had a project that required a man of his talents. I'm certain he will contact you shortly."

He lifted his arm which indicated he wanted Toki to move closer to him. "I like your idea. I think I will arrange a meeting with Mrs. Chandler." He felt Toki stiffen as he laid his hand on her.

South China Sea

When the US trade mission plane disappeared from the radar screen, the CNO dispatched every United States Naval ship in the area. Search planes filled the air. AWACS handled air traffic control and communications. An Arleigh Burke-class destroyer left Taiwan earlier in the day and was less than thirty nautical miles from the last reported position of the plane. At flank speed, it reached the impact area in under an hour. Crew members saw debris, suitcases, clothing, and airplane parts scattered to the horizon.

"Now hear this, now hear this," the ship's overhead address system sounded, "all hands man the rails for retrieval of debris; all hands man the rails for retrieval of debris."

The command was unnecessary; word of mouth raced through the ship when it changed course and advanced to flank speed. Silence prevailed as each sailor tried to grasp the immensity of the disaster. The silence on deck was shattered when a sailor yelled, "A BODY! I see a body!"

"Where away?" the chief boatswain mate on the forward deck shouted.

"There, four points off the starboard bow," the young sailor yelled and pointed.

"Bridge," the chief boatswain said into the microphone.

"Bridge, aye," the communication petty officer said.

"A body spotted four points off the starboard bow, fifty yards' distance," the chief boatswain answered.

"Bridge, wait one," the third-class petty officer who handled communications said. "Captain, a body spotted four points off the starboard bow, sir."

"All stop!" the captain ordered.

"All stop," came the reply from the helmsman.

"Lieutenant Jamison, lower a boat and retrieve the body," the captain ordered.

"Aye, aye, Captain," Lieutenant Jamison answered.

They quickly recovered the body of Dick Wallins, proceeded back to the ship, and immediately placed him in cold storage. The captain then reported this find up the chain of command.

The ship remained on station and picked up debris from the ocean's surface until another ship arrived. It then set a course at flank speed toward the aircraft carrier group. When the ship reached helicopter range, they loaded the body aboard the chopper for transport to the carrier.

Wallins's body arrived at the aircraft carrier and was transferred to a C-2A Greyhound twin engine fixed wing airplane and flown to Kadena Air Force Base, Okinawa, Japan. From Kadena, a C-141 Star-lifter took his body to Dover, Delaware. Within seventeen hours of the explosion, Dick Wallins lay in the US Army forensic pathology laboratory.

Twelve hours later, they confirmed the cause of the crash.

The oval office door opened slowly. The president's chief of staff entered quietly and spoke softly, "Pardon me, Mr. President. FBI Director Hawkins needs to speak with you."

The president, while reading a report about the lobbying efforts for a new farm bill, did not hear his chief of staff arrive.

"What?" He looked up. "I'm sorry, who did you say?"

"FBI Director Hawkins. He needs to talk with you. He said it was urgent."

"What line is he on?" None were illuminated.

"He's here, sir."

"Here must be significant. Send him in."

"Mr. President, I'm sorry to barge in like this, but I was afraid to call. Somehow the news people always know when I've called ahead."

"Henry, don't worry about it. I wish more people would drop in from time to time." He arose from his desk and walked over to the facing sofas. They each sat down. "I need some coffee, how about you?" the president asked. A coffee service sat on the coffee table between the men.

"That'd be nice," Director Hawkins said and immediately poured one for the president and one for himself.

"Now, Henry, what's the crisis?" President Drexel asked.

"It's not a crisis, it's the reason the trade mission plane crashed," Hawkins said.

The president raised his eyebrows and looked intently at his FBI director.

"It was blown up."

"Blown up?" he questioned. "How? A missile? Who?" the president stammered.

"A bomb planted on board." Hawkins let his voice fall almost to a whisper. As director of the FBI, he knew he shared part of the responsibility for the safety of that airplane. The Secret Service, Homeland Security, and the Air Force also shared responsibility. He could imagine this incident might cause political disaster at home as well as destabilization in Asia. When it became known that an onboard bomb had brought the plane down, it might fuel the current speculation by the country's extremist groups, who would blame North Korea, China, Iran, Iraq, or one of the Muslim fundamentalist groups for the disaster. He knew that demands for retaliation would soon reverberate throughout Washington.

"A bomb." The president took a long drink of his coffee before setting the cup down. He looked through the window; the lights twinkled in the darkness. "Okay, Henry, a bomb brought down the trade mission plane. Who put it there? Was there a demand made? Did someone claim responsibility?" He rubbed his chin with his hand, a habit he did when he was in deep thought. "I'm certain that security around that plane couldn't have been tighter. And I imagine the preflight security of baggage, food, and passengers was second to none. So, Henry, what happened?"

"We don't know. The first ship on the scene found a body almost intact. They flew it to the carrier group, then to Kadena, and finally to Dover. The pathologists and other scientists found residue from an explosion, most likely C-4 or something like that."

Randolph Drexel sat back and closed his eyes. He tried to imagine the plane flying along and then suddenly exploding. He felt ill for the people on board, but he secretly felt elated that his wife had had a migraine that morning. "We have to find out who did this and string them up by their—"

Director Hawkins cut him off. "Yes, sir."

43

USEPH—SAN FRANCISCO

Bill and Holly parked in the Litten Industries building underground parking lot and walked toward the elevator. A car rounded the corner and slowly rolled up beside them; three doors opened, and men jumped out of each door. Holly gasped; Bill immediately pulled her behind him.

"Dr. Chandler?" the man closest to him questioned.

"Who wants to know?"

"Useph," he said and extended his hand.

"Useph?" Bill said warily; he still stood poised for trouble.

Useph smiled. "You did an outstanding job of saving that France International Airline flight."

Bill took Useph's hand and shook it.

"Too bad the United States didn't hire you to protect their airplane."

"Why do you say that?" Bill asked.

"Can we go somewhere private and talk?" Useph asked. "I am aware you don't know me." He took out a leather case that had a counterfeit ID card with his picture and the word Interpol printed on it.

"I have a whole building above us, but I'm not sure that we can find anywhere in it that is private," Bill said.

"The warehouse?" Holly suggested.

Bill nodded in agreement. "Let me give you directions, Useph. We'll check in upstairs and meet you there later. Holly, call John and tell him these gentlemen are on their way."

Bill and Holly proceeded to the elevator to begin their day at Litten Industries.

"Good morning, Dr. Chandler and Mrs. Chandler," Phyllis said.

"Good morning, Phyllis. What's on the books today?" Bill asked.

"Mr. Cotting said he wanted to see you as soon as you came in, and there was a call from a man who only gave his name as Randy. He said he wanted you to call." She glanced up from the appointment book and added, "Truthfully, Dr. Chandler, he seemed kind of weird."

"Eccentric would be a better word. By the way, Phyllis, I like your new look." As Bill walked into his office he said, "Tell Larry Cotting to come in, and could you bring us some coffee, please?"

Cotting said that Koto wanted to discuss some minor changes in the proposal to buy Litten.

"Larry, what do you really think about Koto's offer?"

"Well, sir, it is a generous offer. And honestly, I believe that you are more interested in your electronics business than you are in doing make-overs on aging aircraft." Larry thought he might have a real chance to move Bill in the direction of acceptance of Koto's offer. "You know Litten would mesh well with Koto's other enterprises. His organization has a wider financial base; it would give us economic stability, should the economy start to falter, and it would take us international." He didn't want to push too hard. "However, the decision is really yours."

Very politically correct, Bill thought. "Well, I'm looking it over, and I do appreciate your thoughts about it."

Phyllis came into Bill's office as Larry left. She avoided looking at Larry. "Mrs. Chandler, I'm glad you're here. These just came for you." She handed an envelope to Holly.

Holly laid the papers on the coffee table and scanned them.

"Good news or bad?" Bill asked.

"It depends on how you look at it. The French plane and the government plane were both worked on at Desert Wells," she said sadly.

Later that morning, Bill and Holly left Litten and drove to the warehouse, where John, Randy, Sam, Useph, and two other men waited for them. They arrived as John was explaining how the Tel-Ray unit used a satellite and cloaked the French plane suspected of having the bomb on board.

"Well, I still don't understand it, but it actually worked," Useph said.

"Useph, did you ever figure out how they got the bomb on board?" Bill asked.

"That is a big mystery." He looked at Bill. "Do you have any ideas?"

Holly looked at Bill for a silent signal to indicate it was acceptable to tell what they knew. He gave an acknowledgment with his head.

"The most likely scenario involves a bomb installed at the factory," Holly said.

"What?" Useph responded.

"We know for certain the plane that exploded on its way to Japan several weeks ago received an extensive overhaul and renovation at the Litten Desert Wells facility. I asked for documentation about the France International Airline plane and the recent government plane. I hoped to find out if Litten worked on them. But so far, no luck with paperwork on the French plane or the government plane that recently crashed," Holly said.

Bill looked at her questioningly but said nothing.

"Let me see if I can help you," Useph said to Holly. "My sources say that since the crashes, Northern Pacific Airways and France International Airline inspected every one of their remaining planes and found nothing. For the present, we must assume that bombs were planted on the planes before they took off. As you can guess, the security details from both airlines received reviews without finding anything suspicious." Useph paused and then continued, "Don't you have company records on all of the planes which pass through your facility?"

"Yes, we do," Holly responded. "I'm still waiting for some paperwork."

"Useph, who do you work for?" Bill asked.

"I showed you my identification. Interpol," he answered.

"Then that's how you know so much about the investigations," Bill replied.

Useph motioned for the two men who stood in the background to come forward. Dr. and Mrs. Chandler, I'd like to introduce Pierre Sardon, a former French intelligence agent, and Walt Jackson, a former CIA agent. I am a former Mossad agent." They all shook hands. "We work for a suborganization of Interpol specifically dedicated to world peace and the elimination of terrorism," Useph stated. "Dr. Chandler, you and your lovely wife appear to have some insight into what is going on."

"That's scary," Bill said, "because we just have a lot of pieces that don't fit together to make anything concrete."

"Well, let's sit down, look at the parts, and see if we can start to form a puzzle."

Over the next hour, they talked and asked questions of each other. Analysis of the France International Airline plane revealed C-4 explosive residue; the experts determined the explosion occurred in or around the middle cargo bay. However, the exact location remained elusive. "We know the French authorities are still examining the wreckage, but there's little hope of pinpointing the location any closer," Pierre said.

"Obviously, they've just started to work on the pieces of the Air Force plane, but they haven't even located the black box yet," Walt Jackson announced.

"Do you know a Mr. Smith who talks with an English accent?" Holly asked.

The three ex-spies glanced at each other. "That's a very common name," Useph said.

Holly detected the unspoken communication among the men; she decided to press her point. "Mr. Smith is maybe sixty or sixty-five; gray hair, what there is of it; and has at least one thug working for him, a man named Emmet."

"Where did you meet Mr. Smith?" Walt asked.

"In the woods," she replied. "He wanted to buy Litten Industries and was very insistent. Do you know him?" She slowly surveyed the men; her eyes looked deeply at them until she knew they all held back something.

They all shook their heads no.

"Just thought I'd ask."

After they agreed to keep in touch, they left.

Bill turned to Holly, "So what do you make of it?" He looked into the distance and then he continued, "At least we're not alone now."

"I'm not so sure," she replied.

"What?" Bill, aware Holly read subtleties of people much better than he, questioned her, "Why do you say that?"

"There was some silent communication between them when I mentioned Mr. Smith," she said. "Also, as we talked about the planes that exploded, I felt they knew more about them than they let on."

"I didn't see anything," Bill said. "I assume the information you held back was because you're not certain about them."

"Yes, especially when I mentioned Mr. Smith, I noticed their reaction; they tried to mask it, but it triggered something that they were unwilling to share. I didn't like it."

Bill and Holly left the warehouse and returned to Litten.

44

CHARLENE DOMINIC—SAN FRANCISCO

"Did you have a nice lunch?" Phyllis asked as they entered the reception area.

"Very nice. Anything happen while I was gone?" Bill asked.

"There was a call for Mrs. Chandler," she said as she consulted her appointment book. "A woman named Charlene Dominic asked if she could see you. I gave her a tentative appointment for three this afternoon. If that's not good, I have a number I can call and reschedule," she concluded.

Bill and Holly looked at each other and tried to determine if either recognized the name. Their silent communication confirmed that they didn't. "No, that should be all right," Holly answered. "Did she say what she wanted?"

"No, she said it was a private matter and that it was important," Phyllis replied.

At 2:55, the Litten Headquarters' elevator door opened and a tall woman, who wore a dark blue slenderizing double knit suit, emerged. She walked toward Phyllis.

"May I help you?" Phyllis asked.

"I'm here to see Mrs. Chandler. My name is Charlene Dominic," she replied.

Phyllis escorted her into Bill's office.

Holly stood, walked across the room, and extended her hand. "Hello, I'm Holly Chandler. How may I help you?"

Charlene took off her white glove and they shook hands. "I'm Charlene Dominic," she said with a warm smile. "This is difficult for me. You see, Ned Litten and I were friends." A tear formed at the corner of her eye. She repeatedly blinked to prevent it from spilling.

Holly took her arm and led her to a couch. She then handed Charlene a tissue. They sat down and turned toward each other; their knees almost touched. "You were a friend of Ned's? We didn't see you at the funeral."

"I've been out of town, a trip to Europe," she said as she looked down at the floor. "A mutual friend told me about it when I arrived in London, so I returned to the States yesterday. It was unbelievable. I mean, he was so much alive; we were so in lo—" She took a small handkerchief from her purse and began to cry almost silently as she held the handkerchief to her lips. "The newspaper said he was with a woman when the accident occurred."

"I'm so sorry," Holly gently replied as she took Charlene's hand. "Would you like to talk about it?"

"Ned and I met at a charity art auction about six months ago. We saw each other occasionally for two months. Then we began to date," she replied and sobbed quietly. "Oh, I hate myself when I do this." She paused and wiped her eyes. "You don't want to hear this."

"Yes, I do, Charlene. And I think you need to talk about it," Holly consoled her.

"Well, Ned and I just found that special thing. I'm a widow; my late husband died from cancer. After that, I was content to only date socially until I met Ned. He was so gregarious and so alive, and he brought me out of the past. He inspired me to start living again. Ned knew I loved Paris, so he insisted I go for a short visit. 'Let the wind of the Champs-Elysees blow the past away,' he told me. The month in Paris was wonderful. In London, I tried to reach Ned for two days, but there was no answer." She broke down again.

Holly and Charlene talked for nearly an hour. Then Charlene said, "Would you like to go for some coffee or something?" Holly agreed, and they left the building.

They walked to the Chatelet Benoit restaurant, where they ordered a glass of wine. Their friendship grew as they talked. While in San Francisco, Holly had missed female companionship; it felt good to have a new friend. Holly looked at her watch; it was almost five o'clock.

"I really need to get back. I'm certain Bill's ready to leave the office soon; I didn't tell him where I was going," Holly said.

"Oh, my goodness; I have to go too. Holly, it was great to meet you and it really helped to talk about Ned." She paused, then added with sadness, "I still can't believe it."

"Can we get together again?" Holly asked.

"I hope so. Here's my phone number. I have yours. Are you staying at Ned's house in Pacific Heights?" she asked with a blush.

Holly nodded.

"I have that number too," Charlene replied.

They parted outside the restaurant. Holly returned to Litten Industries and Charlene headed straight to Lee Koto's house.

Over the next two days, Holly kept looking through the files and Bill made another trip to Desert Wells to review the operation. He wanted more first-hand information about the planes undergoing restoration. While there, he talked with the work crews and became familiar with the remainder of the company. *Strange, all the workers who work on the Special Projects are on vacation,* he thought.

Holly didn't find anything else that seemed meaningful in the files from Rogers and Bailey. Discouragement set in as no new leads developed.

Bill and Holly sat in large rocking chairs on the master bedroom's balcony and enjoyed an unseasonably warm evening.

The phone rang. "Hello?" Holly said.

"Hi, Holly, I didn't catch you at a bad time, did I?" Charlene questioned.

"Oh, hi Charlene."

"I wondered if we could have lunch tomorrow?" Charlene asked.

"Lunch tomorrow?" Holly looked at Bill. He nodded his head yes. "That would be fine. Maybe we could do something afterward."

"Let's meet at Ghirardelli Square at noon; there's a great seafood restaurant on the third floor," Charlene suggested. "Do you need directions?"

"Sure, that sounds like fun. I'll see you at twelve. No, I don't need directions; I'm certain I can find it." She hung up the phone.

"So, you have a new friend?" Bill asked.

"She seemed to really care for Ned, the way she talked about him," Holly answered. "Charlene suggested they were getting serious."

"It's a little strange, though," Bill replied.

"Oh, and why is that, Mr. *I know everything*?" Holly teased.

"Well, Ned, at least in our earlier days, liked his women a little less sophisticated, sort of like Chris Wall's lyrics to the country song, 'I like my women just a little on the trashy side,'" Bill said. "Charlene didn't fit that description."

"That's awful to talk about your friend that way." Holly threw a pillow from her chair at him. "I can guarantee you, Charlene is not on the 'trashy' side at all," Holly answered, "or else she really knows how to hide it."

The next morning, Holly left Litten Industries at eleven thirty for the taxi ride to Ghirardelli Square. At precisely twelve o'clock, she stepped from the elevator and entered the restaurant. It was early for lunch, so very few tables were occupied. She easily spied Charlene seated by the window. As she approached the table, Charlene stood up; the women hugged a friendly greeting before they sat down.

"I am so glad you could make it," Charlene said.

"Me too; I skipped breakfast so I'm starved. I heard the tuna here is magnificent," Holly said.

They had a great view of the boat traffic on the bay as they dined on grilled tuna, steamed vegetables, and a Caesar salad. The conversation centered on travel and places they'd both traveled to.

"May I get you ladies anything else?" the waiter asked as he cleared the table. "Did you save room for dessert?"

"No, I couldn't eat another bite," Charlene said.

"No, thank you," Holly replied.

Charlene paid the check, and both women walked out of the restaurant toward the elevator.

"You said you had somewhere special you wanted to take me?" Holly questioned.

"I'd like it to be a surprise, if that's okay?" Charlene asked.

Holly smiled an approval.

They took the elevator to the parking garage and walked to Charlene's car. It was a BMW convertible.

With the top down, the sun warmed them as they drove from the garage, across town, and onto the Oakland Bay Bridge. They drove around UC Berkeley and then up a steep winding mountain road on the east side of the bay. Charlene then turned into a driveway. A splendid black iron gate with gold trim slid noiselessly backward to allow them to pass. After Charlene negotiated the curve in the driveway, a large mansion came into view.

The Georgian architecture is stunning, but it is somewhat out of place on this mountain top, Holly thought as she gazed at the large fountain encased by the circular driveway.

"Do you live here?" Holly asked as she looked at the pristine gardens that surrounded the front of the house.

"No, a friend of mine does. I needed to pick up something from him. When I told him about you, he insisted on meeting you," Charlene said.

"Oh, what's his name?" Holly asked.

"Koto, Lee Koto."

"Lee Koto!" Holly exclaimed. "We've met. Didn't he tell you that?"

"No, he said he knew your husband and he wished to talk with you privately. So he asked me to bring you by." She turned to face Holly after she shut off the car. "I hope that's all right. I've known Lee for several years. He's really a doll and a fascinating man."

Holly was skeptical and felt somewhat betrayed as they walked to the front door. Han opened the door before they rang the bell. "Ms. Dominic, how nice to see you again. Mr. Koto told me to expect you today. Please come in." Han showed them into the library. "Mr. Koto will be with you shortly. May I get you anything?"

"No thank you, Han. We just ate," Charlene said.

The library shelves revealed many leather-bound first edition books. The heavy sofa gave the room a decidedly male atmosphere. Since the room faced west, the afternoon sun bathed that side of the house. Han intentionally angled the louvered shutters to let just enough light into the room. This gave the room a particularly gloomy appearance.

The women sat silently as they waited for Lee Koto. Suddenly the door opened.

"Charlene, so good of you to come by and see an old Japanese shopkeeper," Koto said.

"Lee Koto, you are not old, and you are not a shopkeeper." Charlene bowed, then gave him a friendly hug. "I brought my new friend, Holly Chandler, to meet you, but Lee, she tells me you have already met." Charlene scolded him playfully.

"Alas, it is true, and I deceived you, but it was the only way I could think of to have the beautiful Mrs. Chandler call on me."

"And just why would you want me to call on you?" Holly asked cautiously.

Lee walked over to the desk, sat down in the leather executive chair, and faced the women. Backlighted by the sun that filtered through the shutters, Lee's facial features were difficult to distinguish.

Holly thought it a purposeful move to place her in a more difficult position. A chair sat to the left of the desk; she moved over to it and sat down. This placed them both on an equal visual footing. Each could only see half of the other's face.

Charlene, on cue, said, "Lee, I want to pick up that print I left here after the auction. It is in the carriage house. Do you two mind if I take Han to help me put it in the car?"

"By all means, Han will assist you," Koto replied.

Charlene quietly left the room, walked toward the back door, and entered the carriage house.

Koto and Holly stared at each other in silence for several seconds.

"Well, you seem to have orchestrated my coming here, Mr. Koto. Might I be so bold as to ask why?" Holly challenged.

"Mrs. Chandler, you are as perceptive as you are beautiful!" Koto exclaimed. "I used my dear friend Charlene; I misled her and, consequently, you also. For that, I must offer you my humble apology." He paused and hoped she would let her intellectual guard down.

Holly sat quietly and looked at him. He wanted to fidget. She made him uncomfortable, not the other way around.

"Nevertheless, Mrs. Chandler, I felt compelled to talk with you about the proposition I've submitted to your husband for acquiring Litten Industries."

"And you thought going behind his back would be a useful tactic?" She glared at him. "The key word, Mr. Koto, is *husband*. In our culture, and in our mind, that makes us one. We don't try to one-up each other, nor do we go behind each other's back. So I'm afraid your maneuver is not only wasted, but could prove counterproductive." Holly was nervous; she realized that she may have pushed it a little too far and decided not to be as forceful on the next response.

"Again, please accept the repentance of an old Asian businessman who is somewhat desperate to obtain Litten Industries. You see, many years of work have gone into building an international corporate organization, and Litten would fit perfectly. I have studied your husband's electronics firm in Maryland. Litten does not fit well with that company, and I can assure you, there would be a very generous financial arrangement which would allow unlimited expansion of his electronics business."

"I will convey that to my husband, but whether he sells or not is up to him." Holly wanted to leave and wondered when Charlene would get back. "Now, if there is nothing else, I need to be going," Holly said.

Koto leaned forward; his forearms rested on the highly polished cherry wood desk. "There is one more thing you might want to think about—and not share with your husband, Mrs. Chandler. I want that company and will eventually get it. Dr. Chandler has received the best financial offer he will ever have. Try to encourage him to sell now."

Holly perceived his venomous fangs as he spoke.

He continued, "And I can also assure both of you that you would be much healthier if you left California soon and returned to your business in the east. I am not a man to lose when I have invested as much time and energy as I have on this project!"

Holly stood up. "Mr. Koto, if that was a threat, it wasn't veiled, and I understood it well." She glared at him. "Now, if you don't mind, I'll wait for Charlene by her car." Holly turned and walked toward the library door.

"Mrs. Chandler."

Holly stopped with her hand on the doorknob. "Yes?"

"Do not trifle with something the gods have determined!" he threatened with a menacing voice.

Holly's pulse pounded in her ears as she closed the door and walked across the Italian marble foyer to the front door.

Charlene came around the side of the house as Holly quickly walked up to the car.

"Why, dear, what's wrong?" she asked.

"Please take me back to the city, now!" Holly demanded as she opened the car door and sat down.

45

THE DIVERSION—SAN FRANCISCO

Charlene stopped the car in front of Litten Headquarters. "I'm sorry for whatever happened with Koto," Charlene said. "He didn't tell me what he wanted to see you about. I feel he used me unfairly, and I am sorry he upset you. I . . ." She paused pensively.

"I know you didn't have anything to do with it," Holly said as she opened the car door. "Let's just chalk it up to one of those days." She exited the car and waved goodbye.

On the way home, Holly could see Bill's anger fester as she summarized her encounter with Koto.

"Okay, so he wants to get to me and thought he might do it through you." Bill stopped talking long enough to concentrate on traffic for a few seconds. "What part do you think your new friend Charlene played in the whole thing?"

"I don't believe she had anything to do with it," Holly replied. "She seemed honestly sincere that she didn't know why Koto wanted to see me."

That evening John, Randy, and Sam came to the house with the latest surveillance information. Dull described most of the information on Tel-Ray until they heard the recording of Cotting's conversation with Koto.

"Hello, Mr. Koto. It's Larry Cotting, at Litten. I need to see you, sir."

"Is it important?"

"Yes, sir, I think it's crucial."

"Where would you suggest we meet?"

"There's a tourist viewpoint, on the other side of the Golden Gate Bridge. Could you meet me there, at say, eleven thirty?"

"I will be there."

"Thank you, sir; I'll see you then."

"So what do you think that Lawyer Cotting has to talk to Koto about?" John questioned.

"You might think he'd have a conflict of interest, wouldn't you?" Randy asked.

Bill sat and stared into the distance. A picture started to develop in his mind, but it was blurry; there seemed to be a great deal of haze like a thick fog in San Francisco. However, he was certain about two things. One, it involved Litten Industries' renovation facilities. And two, it caused Ned Litten's death. The sharp sound of the telephone interrupted the tension in the silent room.

"Chandler," he said.

"Dr. Chandler, this is Useph."

"Hello, Useph, you're working late tonight, aren't you?" Bill asked.

"We tracked the girl who was killed along with Mr. Litten," Useph said.

"The sheriff told me she was a secretary who worked in San Francisco and that she had no living relatives," Bill answered.

"Well, she was a working girl, but not the secretary kind. She was a hooker from Las Vegas, and it is true, she had no living relatives. There are a few more interesting things about her," Useph added.

"Oh?"

"For openers, she worked in Tokyo six months before the accident; then she moved to the States. Someone set her up in Las Vegas, but she didn't work for any of the established pimps. She worked mostly in a casino run by a Japanese company. A man named Lee Koto seems to be the principle stockholder."

"Koto?"

"Yes, Mr. Lee Koto. The casino is just one of many holdings he has in the United States. Does that name mean anything to you?" Useph asked.

"Yes, Lee Koto is obsessed with buying Litten Industries."

"We probably better not talk too much about this on the phone," Useph said. "Can we meet somewhere?"

"Tonight?" Bill asked.

"It might be best," he replied.

"All right, thirty minutes at the warehouse?" Bill questioned.

"That sounds fine. By the way, the fewer people that know about this, the better," Useph said.

"Thirty minutes." Bill hung up the phone.

"Let's go to the warehouse. Useph wants to meet," Bill said.

"I'm tired," Holly said. Still upset about the day's events with Koto, the thought of another meeting depressed her. "Do you mind if I stay here? I want to go to bed early."

"No, that's fine," Bill said. "Randy, double check the security of the house and meet us at the car in ten minutes." Bill took Holly in his arms and kissed her. "Don't wait up; I don't know how long I'll be."

After Useph hung up the phone, he turned to his associate. "Let's see what happens now." They crouched hidden in the trees next to Bill's house and watched the back door.

"Okay, I'm exhausted anyway," Holly said as Bill walked toward the door.

Bill got into his car and pulled out of the drive, followed by John, Randy, and Sam in their car.

"Great! It looks like the wife stayed home," Useph said and then turned to the other man. "You know what to do." Useph then returned to his car and drove off.

Useph's companion stealthily entered the backyard and slipped unseen to the back door. There he quickly bypassed the house alarm, picked the lock, and entered the kitchen.

The room was filled with steam when Holly opened the door to the bathroom. She earlier had turned on the shower, closed the bathroom door, and stepped back into the bedroom. Holly undressed, hung up her dress, and removed her slip. She sat down at a dressing table and slowly took off her jewelry, laying the pieces in a small Waterford crystal dish. Holly stood up, removed her bra and panties, and donned a terry-cloth robe. The steamy bathroom's air was a welcome relief from the cool damp foggy night. She hung her robe on a porcelain hook and stepped into the tile and glass shower. The hot water began to ebb the fatigue and the fear she felt from the meeting with Lee Koto. His thinly disguised threat against her husband continued to give her a feeling of trepidation. The noise from the shower obscured the sound as her bedroom door opened.

Silently, the lone figure crossed the carpeted room. The black gloved hand grasped the doorknob and noiselessly turned the handle. The white painted door swung into the fog-shrouded room. A pale ghost moved through the gray, mist-filled air.

Holly stood with her back to the shower door as she rinsed her hair. Suddenly she realized she was not alone, but it was only a microsecond before her world turned black.

46

HOLLY—SAN FRANCISCO

Useph met Emmet near the warehouse a few minutes after Bill and his friends arrived. "Okay, Emmet, hit me and leave a mark. We have to make it look good," Useph said.

"This will hurt you more than me," Emmet joked. He hit Useph in the mouth and split his lip. Blood trickled down Useph's chin.

"Now rub dirt on my clothes," Useph ordered as he tore his own shirt and ripped some of the buttons off. "After you leave, I'll lie beside the door."

Bill, Randy, John, and Sam sat around the warehouse's makeshift table and waited for Useph. Sam and Randy each opened a beer. Sam drank his in several rapid swallows while Randy sipped his and absent-mindedly drew lines in the frosty water on the side of the can. John occupied himself by running data on a laptop computer while Bill stared into space. All activity stopped when they heard a noise at the door.

"Useph?" Bill called.

No answer came.

Each person glanced from one to the other and hoped that one of them knew the caller. It was evident to all that no one was certain.

"John, Randy," Bill whispered. They looked at him; he motioned with his head to a second story office that sat above the warehouse floor. They immediately moved in that direction.

"Sam," Bill murmured. Sam looked at him as Bill pointed to a back door. Sam took his beer can and quickly moved toward the portal. The noise increased outside the door. It sounded like someone wanted to pick the lock. Bill heard the tumblers fall. He sat at the table. John's laptop computer, now in a screen saver mode, cast a bluish reflection onto Bill's face. The door came open and a man hesitantly stepped through the door. The light above the open door revealed the glint of a gun. Bill saw a revolver in the man's hand.

"Useph? Is that you?" Bill asked.

"Chandler?" the voice answered.

"Who wants to know?"

"Well, partner, I guess you don't remember me." He stepped farther into the room. "Last time we saw each other, you and your missus left in kind of a hurry."

"Emmet, now what brings you to San Francisco?" Bill asked with a whimsical tone in his voice. "Are you tired of living by yourself in the woods?"

"Mr. Smith wanted me to stop in and say hi," he replied.

"You've said hi. So leave!" Bill said, no longer patronizing Emmet.

"Well, partner, that ain't no way to act when a man's bringing ya a business proposition," Emmet said.

"I don't think I'm interested in doing business with you or your boss," Bill replied.

"You ain't heard the offer yet."

"It better be good," Bill answered.

"That's a mighty pretty wife you got there, ain't she?" Emmet said in a threatening tone. "Would be a shame if you didn't get to see her anymore, wouldn't it?"

The hair on Bill's neck stood up and his arms crawled with goosebumps at the implication of harm to Holly. "What are you saying?" Bill demanded.

"Oh, nothing really, cause she's okay for now." He paused to let the phrase sink into Bill's mind. He enjoyed the resignation of the truth in Bill's face. He sneered by elevating his right lip like a lion that had just brought down a wildebeest. "But if you don't want to do business with Mr. Smith, well . . ." Another prolonged hush swept throughout the cavernous hall.

Bill's stomach turned rancid; he felt it churn. His muscles tensed. "Are you saying Holly's not at home?" Bill asked.

Emmet pushed up his sleeve, in an exaggerated motion, and revealed his watch. "About now she will be waking up and wondering where she is. Now, do you want to talk or not? Makes no difference to me; I get paid either way," he snapped.

Bill trembled; he dug his fingers into his legs to keep from showing his emotion, and in a very soft and controlled voice, he said, "So what's the deal?"

"What?" Emmet said as he leaned down toward Bill. "I couldn't hear ya."

"I said, so what's the deal?"

Emmet reached into his inside coat pocket, pulled out a small packet of papers, and laid them on the table beside the laptop. "You read these. They explain everything." He turned around to leave.

"Wait!" Bill shouted.

Emmet slowly turned back toward Bill and brought the barrel of the revolver up within inches of Bill's face. "I said, read the papers; everything you need is there." He then turned and quickly walked outside into the dark fog-shrouded San Francisco night.

Bill pulled the cell phone out of his pocket and quickly dialed the house number. The phone rang unanswered.

John and Randy rushed to his side.

"I have to get to the house!" Bill said as he rushed toward the door.

"What about Useph?" John asked.

"When he gets here, reschedule the meeting for tomorrow."

Bill opened the door and almost stumbled over Useph. "John! Useph's out here and needs help. Take care of it!" Bill shouted.

Bill drove with reckless abandon; he wove in and out of traffic, ran traffic lights, and made illegal turns to reach Ned's house in record time. The lights in the master bedroom and in the bathroom burned brightly. The back door stood open. He leaped from the car as it skidded to a stop on the brick driveway. He didn't bother to shut off the engine or lights. Bill sprinted up the stairs, two at a time, and burst through the bedroom door. Holly lay on the bed dressed in a white nightgown. Her arms were folded across her chest, and her eyes were closed. She didn't move. Bill couldn't see her breathing as he rushed to her side. He bent over the bed and leaned closely to her. Her respirations were faint. He shook her—no response. He shook her harder—still no response, but she did appear to take a deeper breath. Bill grabbed the phone and dialed 911.

"Emergency response," the voice said.

"I need an ambulance quickly!" he said.

"What is the problem?"

"My wife, I can't wake her up!" Bill said.

"Is she having difficulty breathing?"

"She's not breathing very deeply," he said as he shook Holly again. "When I shake her, there's no response. Hurry!"

"I dispatched an ambulance and paramedics; they should be there shortly. Can you check her pulse and count her respirations for me?"

"Ah, sure, sure—" he stammered, "wait a minute."

Bill felt for her pulse; it was hard to find. "I can't find her pulse!" he screamed into the phone.

"Feel her neck; go straight in from the corner of her jaw," the operator said. The line was quiet for several seconds. "Sir, are you still there?"

"Yes, I found it, but it feels weak," Bill responded. "Her pulse is sixty; she's breathing eight times a minute. Please hurry!" In the distance he thought he could hear the sound of a siren. Two minutes later, two paramedics and a uniformed patrolman rushed through the door.

Bill stood back as they opened their emergency boxes and began to work on Holly. He retreated from the scene until his back was against the bathroom door. He looked down; steam rolled from under the door. He opened it. Hot water still flowed from the shower head. Bill stepped into the cloudy room and turned off the shower. As he spun around, he saw the bathroom mirror. It contained a message scrawled on the fog-cloaked mirror. "It was so easy; we could have killed her. Sell!" He stood and looked at it in stunned silence.

"Sir!" the patrolman said as he pushed the door slightly open.

Bill quickly turned and rushed back into the bedroom, blocking the man's view of the bathroom mirror.

"Yes?" Bill answered.

"Does your wife have a drug problem?" the patrolman asked.

"Of course not!"

One of the paramedics looked up at Bill and the officer and then raised his eyebrows. He turned over her right arm and showed a needle track in the crease of her elbow. "You don't have any idea what she might have mainlined, do you, sir?" he asked.

"My wife is not a drug user," Bill protested.

The other paramedic started an intravenous line in her other arm; they placed an oxygen mask and a monitor device on Holly. The paramedic who had shown Holly's arm to Bill dialed the phone. "Hi, Doc, looks like an OD," he said. "Okay, one dose of Naloxone hydrochloride IV."

"No!" Bill shouted; he started to rush forward.

The patrolman stepped in front of him and said, "Sir, why don't you let them do their job? They're good at it, and they will take good care of her." He eased Bill back into a chair. "I need some information; do you think you could answer some questions for me?"

Bill watched the activity around Holly. *So this is what Emmet meant!* he thought. *Mr. Smith seems to have unlimited power. I might as well sell!*

"Sir," the patrolman repeated, "can you answer some routine questions for me?"

"Uh, oh—sure, I—I was just watching them," Bill said.

"Sure, I understand. What is your name?"

"Chandler, William Chandler."

"Your wife?"

"Her name is Holly."

"Where do you work, Mr. Chandler?"

"Uh, Chandler Electronics in Maryland."

"Maryland? What are you doing in San Francisco?" the patrolman asked. He started to eye Bill with suspicion as he looked around the lavish surroundings.

"I'm the executor for a friend of mine. We're here to settle his estate."

"Who would that be, sir?"

"Ned Litten, Litten Industries," Bill answered.

"Oh yeah. I read about him. Killed up north; a car wreck, as I recall. Ran his car off a cliff or something like that. Huh?" the patrolman asked.

"We're ready to transport. Going to take her to General, it's the closest and they do great work with drug ODs," the paramedic said. They loaded Holly onto a gurney and rolled it out of the room.

Bill and the patrolman followed. "Are you driving yourself to the hospital?"

"Yes, I am," Bill answered.

"Do you know how to get there?" the officer asked. Bill shook his head no. "Why don't you follow me? I can get the rest of the information I need there," the patrolman said.

The ambulance left with lights flashing and sirens blaring.

Bill followed the black and white squad car to the hospital at legal speeds. He did not notice the dark car that sat on the side street.

The driver of that car watched the vehicles leave the compound. When they were gone, he turned on the ignition and slowly wheeled around the corner. He punched the pre-programmed button on his cell phone. "The message has been delivered. She's on her way to the hospital."

He clicked off the phone and drove back to his hotel's bar and ordered a whiskey and soda.

They admitted Holly to the intensive care unit; then they drew blood for a stat drug screen, a complete blood count, an electrolyte series, and a liver and kidney profile. While they awaited the results from the laboratory, the ICU team administered supportive therapy.

Bill was sitting in the waiting area of the third floor, lost in his own thoughts, when his cell phone rang. "Chandler."

"Hi, Boss," Randy said into the phone. "Where did ya go? We're at the house, but obviously, you aren't."

"I'm at General Hospital," Bill said. "Holly got some kind of overdose. She's in intensive care in a coma."

"Gosh, Boss, I'm sorry. Is there anything we can do?" Randy asked.

"Not at the moment. We're waiting for the lab results," Bill said. "If you want, spend the night there; I may be home later. How is Useph?" Bill questioned.

"He seems to be okay, just got roughed up a little. He wouldn't even go to the emergency room and get looked at," Randy answered.

Several hours later, Holly started to stir. Before the laboratory identified the drug, she regained consciousness. "Bill!" she called.

The nurse found Bill asleep in a waiting room chair. It was still dark. "Mr. Chandler, your wife is awake now; you can go in and see her."

Bill cautiously walked up to Holly's bed. She looked pale, almost the color of the sheets. An intravenous line snaked into the back of her left hand; the red LED readout on the intravenous pump showed a small hash mark which spun in a circle and indicated the flow-rate was set correctly. The soft beep of the cardiac monitor provided background white noise in the aseptic setting.

Bill looked down at Holly and smiled. "Decided to wake up?"

"Where? What?" Try as she might, Holly couldn't form a sentence.

"Don't try to talk. You were drugged. Do you remember anything?" Bill asked.

She stared up at the acoustic tile ceiling. Holly's eyes appeared dilated. Her eyes were open, but her brain slipped back to sleep again. She blinked her eyes and closed them.

Bill held her right hand in his. He looked at her; a tear ran down his cheek and splattered as it hit the back of his hand.

The nurse put her hand on his shoulder. "Why don't you go home and try to get some rest? We'll call you when she's really awake."

Reluctantly, Bill laid Holly's hand down carefully on the sheet; then he bent down and kissed her gently on the lips. "I'm the handsome prince, and you're supposed to wake up," he whispered to her. She didn't move.

47

CHARLENE AND BILL—SAN FRANCISCO

"She's in the hospital," Charlene told Lee Koto. "Someone who answered the phone at her house told me she was admitted with a drug overdose."

"Are you going to see her?" Koto questioned.

"Yes, I'm going to go there and I will try to see her."

"And, my dear, remember to keep the pressure on. I want Litten Industries," Koto stated emphatically.

Charlene walked to the nurses' station and said, "I'm a friend of Mrs. Chandler's. Can she have visitors?"

"I'm sorry, it's family only. She's in intensive care," the nurse replied.

Charlene turned toward the elevator and saw Bill. He sat in a chair in the waiting area, his legs sprawled out and his arms draped over the armrests. Bill's head lay back and rested on the wall. His eyes were closed and his mouth was slightly open; he snored softly. Bill's clothes were wrinkled and askew. A dark shadow of whiskers completed his exhausted look.

She walked up and sat down next to him. "Dr. Chandler," she said.

"Ah, yes." Bill snapped awake. As he sat up, his neck muscles protested when he moved from the awkward position. He grabbed his neck and stretched. "I'm sorry, I must have dropped off." He looked at her. Although he had only seen her from a distance when she first came to Litten, he recognized her. Today she wore a dark blue pantsuit trimmed in red. A red turtleneck sweater, tight at the throat, accentuated her statuesque profile and highlighted her dark eyes.

"I'm sorry; I didn't mean to wake you," Charlene said. "I'm Charlene Dominic, Holly's new friend. When I heard she was in the hospital, I came right down. I wanted to see how she was doing, but they wouldn't let me in."

"How did you know she was here?" Bill asked.

"I called your house. Someone answered the phone, kind of a crazy sounding guy."

"Randy," Bill said.

"Anyway, he told me an ambulance rushed her to the hospital last night," Charlene said.

Bill rubbed his neck and stretched again.

"Let me buy you a cup of coffee and you can tell me what happened," Charlene said.

Bill checked with the nurse, who told him there was no change in Holly's condition.

He and Charlene walked to the hospital cafeteria and poured coffee into paper cups.

Bill carefully sipped the steaming contents silently for a few minutes. Finally, he told her about the previous evening's events. He left out the attempted meeting with Useph and the conversation with Emmet.

"I know that I just met Holly, but really Bill, I can't believe she is a druggie."

"Holly has never used drugs in her life. This was not an accidental overdose. Someone did this to her." After he had said it, he was sorry he'd divulged so much information.

"You look terrible," Charlene said with a friendly smile.

Bill went back to the ward; there was still no change in Holly's condition, and she had not wakened again. He reminded the ward clerk of his cell phone number and asked to be called immediately if there was any news.

Bill and Charlene were on their way out of the hospital when they met Randy and John. The four decided on breakfast at a small diner nearby. Randy, John, and Charlene made small talk. Bill picked at his food while he continued to ponder Charlene and Ned's relationship. What Holly had told him seemed plausible enough on the surface, but something underneath bothered Bill. Charlene had too much class for Ned. After they ate, Charlene suggested he lie down and get some rest at her house, since he had slept in a chair all night.

Bill declined and opted for his own house.

John and Randy volunteered to go to the hospital, promising to stay in the waiting room until he got back.

Bill went to his bedroom and lay down on the bed. In no time, he was fast asleep.

48

LARRY AND PHYLLIS—SAN FRANCISCO

On Saturday morning, Larry Cotting pondered his weekend activities. *I think I'll take a run to the Embarcadero, come back, and work out down in the gym. Then maybe I'll take a spin to Monterey. I haven't had the Corvette out for a while.* As he laid there and contemplated the weekend, he felt lonely. He thought about Phyllis and her deep throaty voice and her sensual moaning. Just thinking about her aroused him. Larry dialed Phyllis's number.

A somewhat sleepy voice answered, "Hello."

"Did I wake you?" Larry asked. "I'm sorry."

"Larry!" The voice suddenly came alert and purred. "No, I was just lying here thinking," she lied.

"Oh, where are you lying and what are you thinking?" he asked.

"I'm lying in my bed, silly. And I was thinking about you . . . about us," she whispered with a provocative accent on the word us. "What are you doing?"

"The same."

"It's a shame," she said.

"What's a shame?" he asked.

"We're both thinking the same thing in two different beds." She paused. "What are you wearing?"

"Pajamas," he replied. "But I'd rather have something else on," he said.

"Oh," she purred, "and what would that be?"

"I think you can guess."

"Umm . . ." she said in a way that would make you believe she had just bitten into a piece of cheesecake. "Is that why you called?"

"Yes and no." He needed to be a little honest with her even if she aroused him. "But lying here talking to you makes me wish it was the only reason." He paused. "Are you busy today?" he questioned.

"Just the usual." Her voice changed to a more conversational tone. "I need to do some grocery shopping, cleaning, you know, the usual. Why?"

"Oh, I thought we might do something. I have to stop by the office and look for something."

"Could I help you find it?" Phyllis asked.

"If you don't mind—it probably won't take long. I was thinking of driving to Monterey after that. How does that sound?" he asked.

"I love it!" she responded.

"Great, I'll pick you up in, say, an hour and a half?" Larry asked.

"I'll be waiting." She hung up the phone and smiled. "It's going to be a beautiful day for me!" she sang to herself.

Larry and Phyllis parked in the underground parking garage and rode the executive elevator to Litten Industries' twenty-third floor. Larry let them in with his pass key. It felt odd to be at the office on a Saturday; it was so quiet, it seemed eerie.

"Certainly is quiet," she said to relieve some of her own tension. She wished they had started for Monterey immediately. She almost felt like a burglar. Something felt wrong, but she had agreed to help him. "What is it we're looking for?" she asked.

"You know that Koto wants to buy Litten from the Chandlers, don't you?" Larry asked.

She nodded her head in acknowledgment.

"Well, I think it'd be best if that happened. Chandler doesn't know anything about our business, and Mr. Koto does. Plus, there'd probably be promotions in it for anyone who could facilitate the transaction," Larry replied.

"Promotions for lawyers?" Phyllis questioned.

Larry turned, grasped her arm, pulled her close, and kissed her passionately on the lips. "The promotions would be for *anyone* who helped," he whispered at the end of the kiss.

She pressed her body tightly to his. "Then let's see what we can find," she purred.

They entered Bill's office. Larry went to the desk. Phyllis started on the file cabinet built into the credenza. After forty-five minutes, they came up empty. "I don't find anything here that would help us one way or the other," Phyllis said.

"No, it looks pretty clean," Larry agreed. He was about to get up from the desk when he spotted a small piece of paper that stuck out from the edge of a drawer's track. It apparently had gotten wedged there. Carefully he pulled out the crumpled paper. "Hello, what's this?" he asked.

Phyllis hurried over to the desk and peered over his shoulder as he pressed the paper flat on the blotter. The paper read:

1 plane down
1 plane saved
1 plane down
Ned—dead
Newman—dead
Explosion

"What's it mean?" Phyllis asked.

"I'm not sure, but isn't that Chandler's handwriting?" Larry asked.

"It certainly looks like it," Phyllis replied. She felt her heart beat faster. She imagined Larry and her moving into top management positions if Koto bought the company. She was certain, if the Chandlers owned Litten Industries, the best she would ever do would be executive secretary. "But, Larry, what does it mean? One plane down, one plane saved?"

"We'll just have to put our heads together and figure it out," he replied. "I think the best when I'm relaxed. Why don't we head for Monterey and see if we can find some way to unwind?" He spun his chair toward her.

Phyllis laid her head on his shoulder and looked at him through her bangs.

"Can you think of *anything* that might help you relax?" she purred.

"HERE?" he whispered.

Phyllis smiled.

49

AT THE WAREHOUSE—SAN FRANCISCO

When Bill returned to the hospital, Holly still lay comatose. After her condition stabilized, the doctor transferred her from the ICU to a private room. The CAT scan and the MRI showed some swelling of the brain; the doctor called it cerebral edema, but so far, no brain damage was evident. Privately, her team of doctors questioned her continued lack of responsiveness and feared the drugs she was given had permanently damaged her brain. The neurologist told Bill, "Only time will tell." The drug screen showed a combination of barbiturates and heroin in doses that were usually fatal. The intensive care unit physician relayed to Bill that his prompt action was the only thing that saved Holly's life. Now she rested in a private room as Bill sat by her bedside.

The door opened and Useph entered. "How is she?" he asked.

"About the same; she's only awakened once, said two words, and lost consciousness again," Bill replied.

"I talked to our friends in Mossad." Useph pulled up one of the chairs beside Bill. "They told me something about the trade mission plane that went down." Useph stopped and looked around the room again just to be certain there was no one else within hearing distance. "It was a bomb on board."

Just then the door opened. "Dr. Chandler?" A young man in a dark blue suit stepped through the door. "I'm officer Simmons, San Francisco Police." He showed Bill his credentials. "Since you told the investigating officer you thought someone gave your wife the drugs, the chief has assigned security until she's awake. We'll have a twenty-four-hour guard outside her door."

"Thank you very much," Bill replied. "That will make me feel much better."

Bill took Useph by the arm and led him toward the door. He stopped and looked back at Holly for several seconds. They walked to the stairwell at the end of the corridor. Bill pushed the door open and pulled Useph inside. "But now, I want to know what you know. Who were the terrorists that blew up the France International Airline plane?"

"We're still working on that."

"No offense, Useph, but we have helped you one hell of a lot more than you have helped us. In fact, it appears you haven't given us a thing. So unless we have something meaningful to talk about, you and your buddies, and anyone else connected with your organization, can hit the road," Bill said and turned away from him. "I've sent an inquiry to Interpol. I haven't heard back yet. I wonder why."

"Chandler, I won't leave until I get the codes!" Useph demanded.

Bill pulled a 38-caliber revolver from inside his coat.

"Now, Useph, the hammer is back, and the safety is off. A good friend of mine taught me how to use this. I'm going to ask you one more time about your dirty little business." Bill's steady hand, his low voice, and his cold stare told Useph all he needed to know. "Here's the way I figure it, Useph, I think you arranged for the meeting with Emmet. In fact, you may have been the one to arrange Holly's OD while I cooled my heels in the warehouse."

"Dr. Chandler, I can assure you that I had nothing to do with that."

"Useph," the softness of Bill's voice carried no less a threat, "am I supposed to believe that? Like I'm expected to believe you have never heard of a guy named Mr. Smith with an English accent?" Bill lowered the barrel of the revolver and aimed at Useph's crotch. "You see, when I mentioned Mr. Smith, something passed between you and your buddies. I didn't catch it, but Holly did. And I can tell you, she's good at that. Do yourself, and any offspring you may hope to have in the future, a favor and tell me the truth about Mr. Smith and the planes, and about the drugs that someone gave to Holly." Bill stared at Useph with an unflinching stare.

Sweat appeared on Useph's forehead as he looked at Bill. "Do you really think this is the time and place for a discussion like this?" Useph asked as he stalled for time.

Bill reached into his coat pocket and pulled out a cell phone. He punched a speed-dial key on the pad and waited. "Randy?" Bill hesitated. "Good." He looked at Useph and smiled. "Randy, I want you and Sam." He paused. "Sam's not back yet? Okay. You and John bring a car to the back of the hospital near the emergency room. Useph and I need a ride to the docks." He listened again. "Good, ten minutes. We'll be downstairs. And, Randy, should anything happen to me, Useph is not one of the good guys." Bill clicked off and slipped the phone into his pocket.

"Do you really think you can get me out of here?" Useph asked. "Remember, I used to work for Mossad."

"Well, let's look at it this way: if we don't make it to Randy's car, you won't work anywhere again." Bill motioned for Useph to walk down the steps. "And, Useph, I can't miss at this range." Bill grasped Useph's shirt and shoved Useph down the first step. At the ground floor, they came to another door and waited for a few minutes to give Randy time to arrive at the hospital. "Open it," Bill finally whispered.

Randy was waiting outside when they emerged.

In the car, Bill turned to Useph and said, "Well, Useph, I guess you weren't ready to take the chance, were you?"

At the warehouse, Bill tied Useph into a chair and then relaxed. He walked over to their makeshift kitchen and poured a very old cup of coffee. "Still no word from Sam?" Bill asked.

Suddenly the door burst open; two men stumbled into the room and the door slammed shut behind them.

Sam stood with his back to the closed door.

The figure on the floor rolled into a ball and moaned in agony.

"Uh, Mr. Chandler, this feller that stopped by . . . well, he decided he wanted to come back and talk some more." He pointed at the man on the floor.

"Emmet?" Bill asked as he used his foot to roll Emmet over. "You decided to come back and see us? Don't tell me, Mr. Smith has another message for me." Bill then glared at Useph.

Useph looked down at the man writhing on the floor.

Bill helped Emmet into a chair. "From the looks of him, I'd say he didn't want to come back and see us. Is that right, Sam?" Bill asked.

"Well, Mr. Chandler, after what he said 'fore, I thought we might like to talk to him again. So, I sorta went after him an' asked him if'n he'd like to come back." Sam grinned. "Ya know, at first, he didn't seem to want to. But, well, us ol' fishermen have our ways." Sam looked pleased with himself. "Did I do okay?"

"Sam, you did great. You see, Sam, Useph here and Emmet are old friends. My guess is they haven't seen each other for gee, three or four hours. I'm betting they work for the same man. A man named Mr. Smith. So it's good to get old friends together again, right, Useph?" Bill looked at Randy and John. "One of you get Emmet something to drink and an aspirin, if he wants one. I think he has some more talking to do. Right Emmet?"

"Don't you say a word!" Useph said in Yiddish.

"Why, Useph, you speak very good Yiddish," John said to him in the same language. "I guess you didn't know my last name is Goldstein." He smiled.

Useph closed his eyes.

Bill walked up, grabbed Emmet's hair, and yanked his head up so he could look him in the face. "Now, Emmet, let's start out with who you are, who you and Useph work for, and who Mr. Smith is. Then we'll get to the harder questions."

"I can't tell you," Emmet said.

"That's a shame, Emmet," Bill said. "Because, you see, if you're no use to us, I'll be forced to give you to Sam. It looks like you know what Sam can do."

Sam walked up and smiled at Emmet.

Emmet's eyes darted back and forth between Useph and Sam. Neither option looked good.

"Emmet, are you shy around your boss? Useph, I think you're making Emmet nervous." Bill looked at Sam and Randy. "Take Useph into the back room and tie him up."

Sam and Randy returned a few minutes later.

Bill said, "Okay, Emmet, I want it all, or I swear, I'll give you to Sam and he can do whatever he wants with you. You guys tried to kill my wife, and if she is permanently damaged . . ." He paused to regain emotional control. He leaned closer and whispered into Emmet's ear, "You'd better hope Holly wakes up, and you'd better tell me everything you know."

"All right, I didn't want to go after your wife. I told them if we went after anyone, it should be you." He looked up. "You have to believe that, Chandler."

"Maybe I will believe it, if everything else you say makes sense. Let's hear it," Bill snarled.

"There really is a Mr. Smith; he's the one you saw on the computer screen. He runs our organization. He was very high in British Intelligence. The group is made of former agents in most of the intelligence communities in the Western world. Useph is from Israeli Mossad, I'm CIA, there are others. We . . . uh, it's kind of hard to define what we do."

"You mean you don't have a mission and vision statement? What kind of a modern organization is it?" Bill asked sarcastically.

"There's not a lot of money working for the government, not anybody's government. So, we formed a group. To be candid, we are arms dealers who sell to the highest bidder."

They heard the sound of breaking glass. Emmet slumped forward; a small round hole appeared in the middle of his forehead. The low velocity hollow point bullet pureed Emmet's brain.

"Lights!" Bill shouted.

John, nearest the circuit breaker, plunged the warehouse into darkness.

"Sam! Check on Useph!" Bill yelled.

A moment later Sam's voice echoed through the cavernous room, "Useph's gone!"

50

LARRY, PHYLLIS, AND KOTO—BERKELEY, CALIFORNIA

"Do you think we should drive up unannounced?" Phyllis questioned nervously.

"This is just the kind of aggressiveness that Lee Koto will appreciate, and you and I will be at the top of Litten soon," Larry answered confidently. He then pulled up to the closed iron gate and stopped at its speaker.

The speaker squawked, "May I help you?"

"Larry Cotting, legal counsel for Litten Industries, to see Mr. Koto."

"Do you have an appointment?"

"No, but if he is available, I'm sure he would like to see us," Larry said confidently.

Phyllis liked his self-confidence.

A few minutes later, the iron gate opened. The speaker squawked again, "Drive to the front door."

Larry stopped his car, then quickly walked around to Phyllis's door. Together they strolled to the front door. It opened as they approached. "Good evening, Mr. Cotting," Han said.

"Good evening, Han. This is Phyllis Monroe," Larry said as he introduced her to Han.

"Mr. Cotting, Miss Monroe, would you please come with me?" He led them into a large sitting room. A fireplace, flanked by matching Danish modern couches, dominated the end of the chamber. A separate seating area in front of a bay window held a panoramic view of the Oakland Bay Bridge. Italian marble floors and deep rich paneled walls tastefully completed the room. Larry and Phyllis sat on one of the couches. Fifteen minutes later, the door opened. Han entered; he carried a silver tray with tea cups and a pot of tea. "If you please?" he asked.

"Thank you very much," Phyllis replied.

Han poured three cups and left.

Lee Koto entered the room wearing a Japanese dressing gown and slippers. "Good evening, Mr. Cotting, Miss Monroe." He bowed.

Larry and Phyllis stood up and bowed toward Koto. "Thank you for letting us see you on such short notice, Mr. Koto," Larry said.

"Not at all, Mr. Cotting; you said it was important. I assume it has to do with the acquisition of Litten Industries." It was a statement, not a question.

"Yes, sir, it does."

Koto took his tea cup, looked into its steamy contents, and then sipped from it. "What can I do for you?" Koto asked.

"It may be more of what I can do for you," Cotting said as he took a small sip of tea. *I hate this lukewarm water!* he thought. "I don't believe that Dr. Chandler is contemplating a sale of Litten Industries at the moment." In a jury trial, an appropriate pause hooks the listeners. Larry assumed it would work here.

"But . . ." Koto quickly filled in the silence and paused.

What a negotiator, Larry thought. "I, or rather we, discovered some information that might influence him. Dr. Chandler might sell quickly and for far less than Litten is worth. The information is very powerful." Larry was on a roll and he knew it.

"And what would that be?" Koto asked.

"Well, sir, before we get to that," he leaned forward for emphasis, "some might consider it irregular for the company's current legal counselor and the company's Eexecutive Ssecretary to talk to the prospective buyer. You know, insider knowledge and all that." Cotting sat back silently.

"Well, Mr. Cotting, Miss Monroe, how can we make it so there, as you say, isn't a conflict of interest?"

"Honestly, we probably can't, but if the transaction is successful, and if Miss Monroe and I were very highly placed in the organization, then no one would ever have to know about this meeting, would they, Mr. Koto?" Larry stated smugly.

"Ah, yes. You may have a point. I am just a poor Asian businessman. I don't always understand the American way, but in Japan, it is customary to reward anyone who has played a significant part in any transaction. I am sure that some positions will need the kind of cunning leadership you and Miss Monroe demonstrate." Koto took another sip of tea and smiled.

Larry nodded his head in agreement.

Phyllis began to feel scared; something about Koto reminded her of her ex-husband.

"So what kind of news do you have for me?" Koto asked.

"Do you know a man named Newman?" Larry asked. He thought, *I know the words* Newman—dead *on that note mean something. I'm going to play that card.*

"Newman, is that a common name in the United States?" Koto asked.

"Probably not, but he's dead. I am confident that Dr. Chandler had something to do with it," Larry replied.

"Dr. Chandler a killer?" Koto asked with no emotion. *So that's why we haven't heard from Newman for several days,* Koto thought. *I find it difficult to believe that Chandler's a killer.*

"I'm very sure he was involved. If we find any way to prove it," again the pause, "I'm sure it could be leveraged and could encourage Chandler to sell."

Lee Koto stood and walked to the window. The sun had set and the night quickly fell. *It was predictable they came at this hour. Their moral fiber is as dark as the night. What they say must be true. I will enjoy it when Toki finds out.* Lee Koto's mind sifted the new facts and wondered how he would use them.

"An old friend and I are dining shortly. Would you two like to stay and join us?" Koto asked and commanded at the same time. He then left the room without waiting for their reply.

Larry and Phyllis looked at each other in silence. They then followed him to the dining room.

Koto's dining room mesmerized Larry and Phyllis by its simple elegance. The noise of a fountain's soft splash drifted through the large French doors that opened onto a brick patio. A hand-polished cherry table sat sixteen; it dwarfed the four place settings. Hung on the wall opposite the French doors, a large royal blue kimono trimmed in gold drew Phyllis's attention. Larry walked to the credenza. There sat a lacquered stand that held both an antique Samurai sword and a helmet.

Koto took his place at the head of the table. Toki sat on his right and Larry and Phyllis sat on his left. During dinner, Koto entertained them with stories of his childhood in post-war Japan.

The tenacity and the cunning of this slightly built elderly Japanese businessman captivated Larry and Phyllis's interest.

After dinner, they adjourned to the sitting room for sake.

"If you will excuse me, Koto, I have something to attend to," Toki said.

"I don't know when I've had such an enjoyable evening. And the meal was delicious, Mr. Koto," Phyllis said.

"I'm pleased you are delighted with my humble offerings," Koto said patronizingly.

Larry said, "Mr. Koto, may I call you Lee?"

The look in Koto's eyes said it all.

Larry blushed when he realized his mistake and he retreated. "Err . . . Mr. Koto, if there is anything that comes up that I can help you with, you know I'm in your corner to expedite the transfer of Litten to you."

Koto nodded his head in the affirmative. His eyes drifted to the door, a signal the time had come for them to leave.

"Well, Mr. Koto, thanks for a great evening. Phyllis and I need to get back to the city." He stood and offered Phyllis his hand. "Remember, if there's anything . . ." He bowed and walked toward the door.

"Would you kill Dr. Chandler for me?" Koto interrupted.

Larry froze in his tracks. His stomach began to sour and his heart began to pound. He turned to face Koto. Larry's face turned ashen. "Sir?"

Koto smiled at him. "Just an Asian joke," he said with no emotion in his voice.

Larry and Phyllis left without another word. In the car, they were both silent for several minutes.

"That wasn't funny," Phyllis said.

"I don't understand Asian humor," Larry agreed. Overall he thought the day went very well. Now he looked at Phyllis and began to wonder what the night held.

Lee Koto watched their car depart. The door behind him opened. "Ah, Toki, what do you think about our visitors tonight?" he asked without turning around.

"Lee, do you always know who comes through the door behind you?" she asked.

"When a lotus blossom is blown by the evening breeze, its fragrance fills the air."

"Koto, you sound like a man who has been away from Japan too long," she replied. "How long will you stay here and pursue Litten Industries and Dr. Chandler?"

"I hope it won't take too much longer." He smiled. "Our guests brought me some news that may expedite the transaction."

Toki and Koto walked to one of the couches and sat down. He continued, "It seems that Dr. Chandler has a little secret he may wish to hide, one that might encourage him to sell Litten and go back to his previous life." He let the sentence fall into a chasm of silence.

"And what might that be?" Toki asked.

"It appears Mr. Newman met an untimely death, and Dr. Chandler probably had something to do with it." At these words, he turned to face Toki. He wanted to see her expression. *I'll see if the Dragon Lady is as tough as everyone thinks,* he thought.

The news hit Toki with the force of a tsunami. Her emotions crumbled as if a blade had pierced her heart and let her blood drain out. The shock and disbelief were clear on her face as tears began to well up in her eyes. Somehow, she knew instantly it was true. "NO!" she screamed and wailed at the same time. "It can't be true!" She stared at Koto as her eyes pleaded for something to soften the news.

"Toki," he said smoothly, "does this Mr. Newman mean something to you?" He enjoyed the pain he saw in her eyes. "I thought he was just one of your employees."

"You son-of-a...—" she yelled. Toki jumped from the couch and started to slap Koto's face.

His reflexes were quicker than her intent. He grabbed her wrist, spun her around, and brought her arm up behind her back. "My beautiful little Toki," he hissed, "you are what you are and who you are because I made you. You will only have those emotions and tears for me," he murmured into her ear as he pulled her arm higher and forced her to stand on her tip-toes. "I let you indulge yourself with that Western pig because you spent so much time in this godforsaken country, but I did not expect you to do more than amuse yourself. You are mine. I made you, and I will use you for as long as I wish," he snarled. Koto pushed her forward and down onto the Italian marble floor.

She slid on the slick surface several feet from him. Slowly she raised up on one arm and looked back over her shoulder at Koto. Hate burned in her eyes.

"Now, my dear Toki, go to your room and prepare yourself. I will be up shortly."

Toki gradually lifted herself from the floor. She rubbed her aching shoulder. Tears streamed down her face. She walked with almost a shuffling step, which broadcast her despair and grief. Later, when Koto entered her room, she submitted as one who was owned physically, emotionally, and spiritually by her mentor. A vast emptiness enveloped her.

Koto left her room without a word. He went to his room and summoned Han. "I wish to see Kim Long as soon as possible."

"Hai!" Han said. He bowed and left the room.

Koto took off his robe and went into the bath. He lay in the steamy water for twenty minutes and contemplated the events of the day. When he felt fatigue, induced by the hot water, he got out, dried off, and went to bed. *Yes, it was an enjoyable day,* he thought just before he dropped off to sleep.

51

THE HOSPITAL—SAN FRANCISCO

Bill, Randy, and John returned to the hospital after dark. The hospital was as quiet as a big city trauma hospital ever gets. The emergency room had an overflow crowd, some sick, some wounded, and some just looking for another person to talk to. Several black and white squad cars sat in the patient parking areas, and blue uniformed officers milled about in the waiting room. Bill and his friends entered unnoticed and followed the signs to the radiology department. It took only a few minutes in the deserted halls to locate some green scrub tops and to steal two white laboratory coats.

Bill took the stairs and ran to the third floor.

Patrolman Simmons still sat outside of Holly's door. "Good evening, Dr. Chandler," he said as Bill approached.

"Evening," Bill responded. "Have the nurses said anything about her lately?"

"No, sir, they go in every twenty minutes or so and check; I usually go in with them. She seems to be sleeping all the time," Simmons answered.

"Have you had a break?" Bill asked.

"No, but don't worry about it. I'll be relieved in another half hour."

"I appreciate everything," Bill said. "I really do." He shook the policeman's hand and went quietly into Holly's room. She lay on her back with the intravenous drip running slowly into her arm. The pump purred softly.

John and Randy rolled the gurney onto the elevator and punched the button for the third floor. The door closed quietly, and the elevator started to rise after a short pause.

"Do ya really think we can pull this off?" Randy asked.

"Bill is counting on us. Just keep quiet and let me handle it. I was an orderly at Mass General when I was in school. I took hundreds of patients to X-ray. No one will think anything of it," John answered.

The elevator stopped on the third floor. The door opened. John pulled the gurney out of the elevator and headed directly for the nurses' station. "What room's, ah . . ." he hesitated and pretended to look at a small notepad he carried, "Chandler, Mrs. Holly Chandler, in?" he asked the ward clerk who sat there with her head buried in a chart.

The middle-aged lady looked up with a disinterested expression, "Who?"

"Chandler," John said.

"Three fourteen," she answered.

Randy started off in the wrong direction.

"Hey! Are you new here or something?" She looked at them suspiciously. "Three fourteen is that way." She raised her arm and pointed with a pen in the correct direction. "What are you guys doing up here? I don't remember any order for Mrs. Chandler to be moved."

Randy began to sweat.

"We're from X-ray. And yeah, I'm new here; and dufus there," he pointed at Randy, "would get lost finding the bathroom in a one-room apartment," John responded.

She laughed.

They pushed the gurney around the corner. The policeman came into view as they approached three fourteen.

John's stomach began to churn. He feared it was audible.

They rolled the gurney up to the room and started to open the door.

"What's this?" Patrolman Simmons asked.

"Here to take Mrs. Chandler down for a CAT scan," John said.

"I'm not aware that she's supposed to get a CAT scan now," Patrolman Simmons said.

"You her doctor?" John asked the officer. "If you are, then ya better cancel the order. We have an order for a CAT scan. If I don't take her down now, there will be ten add-ons ahead of her and it won't happen until tomorrow afternoon. Now, if you want to explain that to the doctor, okay, but I just started this job, and I don't want to lose it on the first day." John sounded believable. "So, if you don't mind ..." He shoved past the policeman, wheeled the gurney into the room, and closed the door behind them.

John looked at Randy.

Randy mouthed the words, "I'm about to piss my pants!"

John smiled.

With Bill's help, they moved Holly onto the gurney and covered her with a sheet and blanket. John then put the safety strap on and moved the IV onto the portable stand attached to the stretcher. After he pulled the safety rails up, they all took a deep breath and opened the door.

Policeman Simmons stood up. "Guess she's going down to X-ray. Are you going with her, Dr. Chandler?" he asked.

"I think I will. I'll probably get a cup of coffee while she has the test. Would you like me to bring anything back for you?" Bill asked.

"No thank you, sir," Simmons said and sat down in the chair. "If it takes longer than twenty minutes, I'll be gone, but another policeman will be here."

"Good night then," Bill said. "And again, thanks."

"Good evening, sir," Simmons said.

They wheeled Holly past the nurses' station and into the elevator. As the door closed, they heard an alarmed female voice say, "Hey! Hold that elevator! Where do you think you're taking her?" The floor's head nurse, who had just realized that someone removed Holly Chandler from the floor without an order, yelled at them, "STOP!"

The elevator started down. To all on board it seemed to move slower than it had on the way up.

The nurse ran around the corner.

Policeman Simmons bounded out of his chair when he heard the nurse yell. He ran toward the nurses' station. "What?" he demanded.

"Mrs. Chandler!" the nurse blurted out. "Someone just took Mrs. Chandler out of three fourteen and they shouldn't have!"

Simmons looked around and spied the stairwell door marked with an EXIT sign.

He bolted toward it; he hit the door handle and descended the stairs two at a time. He reasoned that if they were trying to take her out of the building, they would go directly to the ground floor. He did not bother to stop at any other level.

The elevator door opened. John, Randy, and Bill wheeled the gurney off and turned right toward the emergency department so fast that they almost ran into a food cart parked at the intersection. They slowed only when another gurney rounded the corner and started down the corridor toward them. They all tried to look tired and disinterested as they passed the other gurney. They then proceeded into the chaotic patient care area. There was enough confusion that no one paid any attention to them as they maneuvered toward the exit.

Simmons burst through the door on the ground floor. He stopped and looked both ways. He saw a gurney turn the corner with two people in attendance. He ran after it, drew his service revolver from his shoulder holster, and pulled back the hammer. "Hold it right there!" he shouted as he approached. "Don't move and get your hands in the air so I can see them!" He rushed up and pushed the person at the back of the gurney out of his way. "Up against the wall!" The two men immediately complied and pressed their backs against the wall with their hands and arms extended as high into the air as they could get them. He looked down at the gurney; there lay an elderly gentleman fast asleep. Policeman Simmons realized he had turned the wrong direction. Immediately, he turned and ran in the opposite direction.

Bill carefully lifted Holly from the gurney, laid her on the back seat of the car, and crawled in beside her. "Let's go!" he whispered coarsely.

John slid in behind the wheel; Randy closed the rear door and jumped into the front seat. They drove out of the parking lot just as Simmons burst through the door of the emergency room exit. All he saw were the car's taillights.

"Crap!" he shouted as he slowly returned his revolver to his holster.

52

BILL AND USEPH—SAN FRANCISCO

Holly lay quietly as the car pulled into the warehouse. John cut the engine. Randy jumped out and closed the warehouse door before he turned on the lights. Bill had carefully cradled Holly's head on the ride from the hospital. He continually watched her breath. It was regular, and she appeared to be sleeping naturally. She looked healthy, except she wouldn't wake up. He didn't relish the idea of taking her out of the hospital, but he knew he couldn't leave her there. Useph and his gang had already used her to get to him once. He knew the warehouse was no place to leave her. His logical engineer's mind searched for an alternative. Suddenly he had an idea. He grabbed his cell phone and dialed.

"Hello," Charlene said on the second ring.

Bill paused a few seconds. He felt some hesitation whether this was a good idea or not. A sixth sense said caution. However, he knew he had very few choices at the moment.

"Hello, who is this?" Her voice conveyed irritation.

"Charlene, sorry; this is Bill. Bill Chandler."

"Oh, Bill!" Her voice sweetened. "Are you all right?" she asked.

"Yes, I am. But—" he paused and thought. *Should I really be doing this?* An alarm sounded again in the far recesses of his brain. There was something familiar about Charlene. Like he had seen her somewhere before, but he continued, "I need your help with Holly."

"Well, Bill, you know you just have to ask, because I'd do anything for her or for you." She didn't have any idea where this conversation was headed, but she felt somehow it would be to her advantage. "Even though we just met, I feel like she is an old friend. Do you need me to come to the hospital and sit with her?"

"No, she's no longer in the hospital," Bill answered.

"Oh! Then she woke up! That's great! Where is she, at home?" Charlene questioned.

"No, not exactly, you see, well, I didn't think she was safe there, so I sort of . . . moved her," Bill answered.

"Oh, I see," Charlene let her voice drop at the end of the statement.

"No, I doubt if you do; however, will you help me?" Bill asked.

"What can I do?" she queried.

"I need a safe place that I can keep her and have her cared for. I'd like a doctor and a special duty nurse. Can you find one that will take care of her with no questions asked? Expense is no problem."

"I can probably arrange everything you're asking for," Charlene answered and without hesitation added, "I have some contacts. Bring her to my apartment; I know exactly what to do."

Within the hour, Holly was in the guest room of Charlene's apartment.

A special duty nurse arrived. She evaluated Holly in anticipation of the physician's arrival.

Meanwhile, Bill, Randy, John, and Charlene sat at her dining room table. Charlene poured coffee for each of them. Although it was the middle of the night, none of them appeared sleepy.

"Okay, Boss, now what?" Randy asked.

"Now that Holly's safe, the next thing is to find Ned's disk. That's the key to this whole mess," Bill said as he looked at John. "What I need from you, Randy, and Sam . . . by the way, does anyone know where Sam is?" Bill looked around the table; his question produced blank stares. "That's what I thought. When you get back to the warehouse, see if you can find him."

John nodded that he understood.

"In the meantime, I need you to keep the electronic surveillance on the appropriate parties. Ever since this started, we've been a few steps behind the power curve. Somehow, we must take the initiative and make them play our game. I'm through playing catch-up. You get started, and I'll be in touch."

John stood up. "Bill, may I go in and see Holly?" he asked.

Bill shook his head in the affirmative.

As John approached the bed, the nurse stood and adjusted the flow rate on the intravenous drip in Holly's arm.

A few minutes later, Randy and John left without a word.

The chiming of a clock prompted Bill to look at his watch. It was 1:45 a.m. The adrenaline produced when they had pirated Holly from the hospital had his brain wired. He knew that if he tried to sleep now, it would be an exercise in futility.

"Why don't you take my bed and get some rest?" Charlene asked. "You look exhausted."

"Thanks, but I couldn't sleep right now if I had to," Bill replied. "I want to check on something. Will you be okay if I leave for a bit? I'll be back in an hour or so; maybe then I'll sleep."

Charlene smiled, "We're safe here. Just let me take care of her."

Bill quietly entered Holly's room. She still slept peacefully. The private duty nurse sat by her side and monitored Holly's vitals.

The nurse looked at Bill and shook her head to signal there was no change in Holly's condition.

Bill acknowledged the silent message with a nod of his head and exited the room. He left the apartment and drove the deserted streets to Litten Industries' headquarters. He parked in the underground garage, boarded the elevator, and leaned against its wall with his eyes closed during the ascent. The elevator door opened into the eerie quietness of an office building that, at this hour, looked more like a desert island.

In the background, the sound of numerous desktop computers provided the only indication that people worked there. He plodded across the foyer into Ned's private office. The lights sprang to life, automatically triggered by floor sensors under the carpet. He sat down at the desk and began to look around the room.

"Okay, Ned, you designed this office. You know where you hid the disk, and although I'm your friend, I am not a mind reader. I need to find it." Bill spoke out loud more to provide himself with a touch of reality than to commune with Ned's dead spirit. "So, Ned ol' boy, let's have some help."

Placed on an angle, the desk provided the best views of the city, the Golden Gate Bridge, and the bay. The city lights compelled Bill to gaze at the vista. Then he systematically surveyed the room again. The desk held a pen set, a matching letter opener, a computer terminal, and a model of a 1957 Chevrolet. This car was identical to the actual car in Ned's garage. Pictures and display shelves covered the wall to his left. Celebrity photographs and letters of appreciation from CEOs of companies with whom Litten Industries did business, hung on the wall. A credenza sat below the pictures. Display shelves, on the wall to his right, held models of a Jaguar XKE convertible, a 1960 Triumph, and a 1950 Ford Coupe; these also represented the real cars in Ned's garage. The Dali prints hung on each side of the models. *Holly pointed out the paintings when she first walked into the room. When we first walked in ...* Bill thought. *That was only about ten days ago, but with her in a coma, it feels more like an eternity.* He leaned back in the chair and stared at the ceiling. Slowly, his eyes closed and he lapsed into a deep, but troubled, sleep.

In his dream, Bill felt the boat rock and saw Newman tied up like a pig ready for slaughter as Newman swung over the railing of Sam's boat. He watched the bravado on Newman's face turn to fear when Newman viewed the black swirling water. The fear turned to panic when he slid to a watery grave. Bill felt like a man paralyzed. He wanted to pull Newman back into the boat, but he was unable to move. Bill awoke; his heart pounded and his sweat stained his shirt. He hit the desk with his fist and silently cursed himself for causing Newman's death. He remembered that afterward, when he returned to the house, Holly said nothing, but her silence said everything. Bill knew that he'd tried to play God, and when he did, he caused Newman's death. He laid his head down on his arms and wept. He sobbed for Holly, for Ned, for the woman killed with Ned, for the people on the planes, for Newman, for Emmet, and most of all, for himself. His guilt engulfed him.

"Now isn't that something? The hero of the hour crying himself to sleep on his desk!" Useph mocked. "That was a neat trick, getting your wife out of the hospital. There's a policeman who is going to spend a lot of time trying to explain what happened."

At the sound of Useph's voice, Bill sprang from his chair. The door had opened so quietly that he was oblivious to Useph's presence. He wondered if Useph had arrived before he fell asleep. "What the hell are you doing here?" Bill challenged.

"Wasn't nice, Bill," Useph said. "That wasn't nice at all, taking Holly out of the hospital the way you did. Now, where is she?" he demanded.

"Screw you," Bill growled through his clenched jaw. "Get out of my office!"

"Bill, you know you've gone from a public hero to a lawbreaker in a rather short period of time," Useph said.

"ME?" he shrieked. "Me? What about you and your associates, Useph? What about that?" Bill pushed his chair back, moved around the desk, and faced Useph. "You and your arms dealers don't seem to mind what laws you break to sell your wares to the terrorists of the world. You probably incite murder and mayhem just to stay in business."

Useph looked somewhat surprised at the challenge. He involuntarily raised his eyebrows.

"Oh, so you didn't know I knew, did you?" Bill taunted. "Yeah, you killed Emmet, but unfortunately not quite soon enough. He told us about the little business you and your friends from the other countries started. He detailed your group's efforts to supply terrorists." Bill advanced a few steps toward Useph. "One question I have to ask: what was your interest in the France International Airline incident?"

Useph recovered his composure and steadily moved across the room toward Bill. "It's really quite simple. We purchased two codes from Koto: one was used for the Northern Pacific plane and the other was used on the France International Airline plane. We sold them for a handsome profit," he stated matter-of-factly.

"You bunch of jackals! Who do you think you are? You kill for money! Innocent people die to line your pockets!" Bill bordered on losing all control. "Do you people think you are the world's rulers or do you think you are God? What kind of sick personalities get together and decide to make money at the expense of innocent peoples' lives?" Suddenly Bill's voice changed. A confident resolve took control. "You are the vermin of the world, and you need to be exterminated!" He moved closer to Useph.

"It's irrelevant what you think," Useph said. "You have something we need, and that *is* relevant. So turn it over now, and we'll forget you ever had a part of it. Who knows, you might just get some lucrative contracts later."

"And just what is it that I have?" Bill asked.

"A computer disk that Ned Litten created with codes on it."

"Ned's disk?" Bill questioned. "You've already gone after my wife. Why should I give it to you now?"

"Don't you want to be alive if your wife wakes up? Or would you rather make her a widow? Give it to me, and if your wife wakes up, you can go back to your life of plenty before this started. Like I said, who knows, you may even get more business. The way you handled the France International Airline incident impressed everyone. It's a shame you couldn't have done the same for the government plane. Then again, we didn't know it also was rigged."

"Rigged?" Bill questioned. "What do you mean *rigged?*"

"Think about it, Dr. Chandler." Useph smiled a demonic smile. "What is the common bond among all of the blown-up planes?" He paused for effect and delighted when the recognition registered on Bill's face. "That's right; Litten Industries renovated them all. Litten Industries called them Special Projects. We know Ned Litten kept the records of those planes on a disk. That disk contains the encryption codes for arming and detonating the devices. You see, Ned Litten turned individual planes into flying bombs. A simple principle: detonate them by a satellite-transmitted frequency from anywhere in the world. You have the key to the rest of the fleet. We need it for its commercial value."

Bill backed up in disbelief; then he sat on the edge of the desk and stared blankly at Useph.

"You really didn't know, did you?" Useph laughed.

Bill struggled to regain some advantage. "Tell me exactly what information is on the disk," Bill demanded.

Still smiling, Useph said, "The disk contains the identification of the planes, what the explosives are and where they are located, the transmission frequencies, and the codes for the detonation."

Bill shook his head and desperately wanted to believe Ned was not a part of such an evil scheme.

"I want the disk. There may be other arms dealers out there who might also want the same information to sell to the highest bidder." Useph walked around the room. He stopped and picked up the model of the Jaguar from its perch on the credenza. He noted it was quite heavy. He continued his odyssey around the room and inspected the intricate detail of the model as he walked. The leather heels of his shoes clicked on the marble tiles and added emphasis to his gait. "So, Dr. Chandler, it's time to stop playing around. You are into something that is much too big for you. Consequently, the only real solution is to turn the disk over to me."

"You people are nothing more than savages in pinstriped suits!" Bill clenched and unclenched his fist as he spoke.

Suddenly, Useph hurled the model car toward Bill's head. Bill ducked just enough that the car missed him by a fraction of an inch. It impacted the window with the force of a baseball hit out of the park. "I'm going to kill you!" Useph screamed.

With unexpected swiftness, Bill dove toward Useph's upper abdomen and knocked the wind out of Useph. They rolled across the floor. Useph, though struggling to breathe, reached into his shoulder holster for his gun. Bill grabbed Useph's wrist and slammed the back of Useph's hand against the coffee table. The gun flew out of Useph's hand and skidded toward the credenza. Useph clutched Bill by the throat. Gasping for breath, Bill fought to tear Useph's hand away. The two men spun apart and struggled to their feet. For a moment, they stood and panted, bent at the waist like two sumo wrestlers. They each gazed intently into the other's eyes. Useph's eyes deviated for an instant toward the gun that lay on the floor.

"I know what you're thinking. You think you can make it to the gun before me," Bill growled. "If I were you, I wouldn't try it. You aren't that quick," Bill warned ominously.

"So, you think you can get to it first?" Useph challenged.

Bill knew Useph did not think beyond the obvious. "I didn't say that," Bill countered.

Useph wanted to stall until his hand quit throbbing. He slowly worked his fingers to restore their mobility. He knew that when he went for the gun, he must grab it, aim it, and fire it in a split second.

Bill, a highly skilled soccer player in college, stood poised.

A split second before he dove for the gun, Useph's eyes flinched.

Bill side-stepped and kicked Useph's forehead. The force instantly broke Useph's neck. Bill saw the stunned look of surprise on Useph's face as Bill watched Useph's body twitch one last time. "I told you," he paused, shook his head, and quietly muttered, "you weren't that fast."

53

HOLLY'S CAPTIVITY—KOTO'S PLANE

Koto's plane lifted off, circled over the city, and passed by the Golden Gate Bridge on its flight to Tokyo. Ten people were on board: six passengers, the pilot, the copilot, and two flight attendants. The six passengers included: Koto, Toki, Charlene, Han, a private duty nurse, and Holly. Strapped onto a stretcher, Holly slept quietly. The private duty nurse monitored her vitals and checked her intravenous drip. Koto, Toki, and Charlene, comfortably secured in the plane's large leather recliners, relaxed after the plane was airborne.

With the fasten seatbelt light out, Koto unbuckled his seatbelt and walked forward to the stretcher. "How is Mrs. Chandler?" he asked the nurse.

"Her vitals are stable, but she shows no sign of waking up. She does react slightly to deep pain, so maybe there is less brain swelling. I have one more steroid dose to give her. The doctor thought it should be enough to help the swelling in her brain go down."

"It is imperative that nothing happen to her," Koto said sternly. Then he thought, *For now.*

Charlene glared at Toki as the women sat quietly together.

The flight attendant gave her a glass of wine. Charlene took a sip and looked over the rim of the goblet at Koto and Toki.

"Would you like something to eat?" the flight attendant asked Charlene.

"Yes," she answered. "Do you have a cheese plate?"

The flight attendant, in a traditional Japanese kimono, bowed and moved toward the galley.

"I still don't understand, Lee," Toki said. "Why did you think it necessary to bring Dr. Chandler's wife with us?"

"Chandler is a very stubborn man and will not sell Litten Industries quickly. I learned through the years that every man places a price on everything. I am sure the price he sets on his wife is far more than the price he puts on Litten Industries," Koto smugly answered.

"Every man has a price, Koto?" Toki asked. "Even you?"

"Yes, my Toki. Even I have a price," he answered.

"And what is your price, Koto?"

"Vengeance," he replied quietly.

Koto stood up and took Toki by the hand. "Come," he said emotionlessly.

Koto and Toki walked toward the sleeping compartment.

54

THE AFTERMATH—SAN FRANCISCO

Bill's breath came in deep gasps after his fight with Useph. He heard the door open. Bill dropped onto one knee, grabbed Useph's revolver, and assumed the firing position. He pulled the hammer back with his thumb.

When Sam stepped through the door, he looked down the cavernous barrel of the weapon. "Hey, Doc! Don't shoot! Okay?" Sam yelled.

"Sam, where in the hell did you come from?" Bill asked hoarsely, his voice still affected by Useph's attempt to strangle him.

"Doc, you sound awful."

"I'll get over it," Bill replied.

"Well, ya sure look better than he does." Sam motioned toward the lifeless body of Useph.

"Anyway, what are you doing here?" Bill asked again.

"After he shot that Emmet feller," Sam motioned toward Useph, "I decided to follow him and see where he was goin'. He ended up here. He had a key to git in and he took the elevator. I had ta' walk the damn stairs. Do you have any idea what floor this is?" Sam retorted.

"Remind me to give you a key," Bill responded.

"Hey, Doc, can I give ya a hand gittin' him outta here?"

Together they moved Useph's body to Useph's car. "Sam, you sure you don't need any help from here?" Bill asked as Sam slid into the driver's seat of Useph's Explorer.

"Nah, not a problem. I can take care of him. From what you said, he won't be missed. I'll see ya back at the warehouse." With that, Sam drove from the underground parking garage.

Bill returned to his office in the Litten Building and began to straighten the room. The model of the Jag was beyond repair. Bill held it in his hand and noted the weight. He thought, *Useph, I'd be the dead one if you had thrown better.* Next, he straightened the furniture knocked over during their struggle. Finally, he stepped back to view the room. He wanted it to appear completely normal for the employees when they returned to the building.

As his eyes swept the room for the final time, he noticed the '57 Chevy lying on the floor. Knocked from the desk during the fight, it lay under the coffee table. He picked it up; a front wheel fell off, so he started to pitch the car into the trashcan. Bill turned it over, and the turquoise top fell into his hand. He examined the top and saw a thumb drive fastened to the underside. *The disk! The disk! It was sitting on the desk, right in front of me, the whole time!* he thought. "Ned, you are one sneaky son-of-a-gun!" Bill said out loud, laughing. After he straightened the rest of the office, he left the building and headed back to Charlene's apartment.

55

ARMAGEDDON—PAKISTAN

On August 6, Koto sat on the island at his Tokyo estate and meditated about his life. He knew that soon his life would end. It was inevitable with age. He remembered his mother's death and it weighed heavily on his soul. This day, he realized that he had limited time to extract the full measure of vengeance for the death of his beloved mother, Sinshee.

The quietness around him starkly contrasted with the rage that boiled within him. Koto no longer wanted to just wreak chaos; he now wanted to cause complete destruction. He remembered his acts of violence against his hated enemy, the United States. He recalled his efforts during the Viet Nam War and the chaos he and Toki had caused in the United States. He celebrated his plan for planting bombs on airliners. He gloated about the chaos created throughout the world from these airplane crashes. He remembered his plan to kill Ned Litten to gain control of Litten Industries and to give him an unlimited supply of planes. Suddenly, the piercing shriek of an owl disturbed his thoughts and interrupted his plans for retribution.

That night, Koto relived his final plan for vengeance hatched two years earlier. Since his beloved Sinshee had died in Hiroshima's nuclear holocaust, he decided that Washington, DC, should experience the same devastation. *I will start construction of a facility to build my weapon. When it is ready, I will acquire the nuclear material for my weapon,* Koto thought.

Two years later, he was ready to leave on his trip to the United States. He planned to kill Ned Litten, acquire Litten Industries, and secure the codes. Before his trip, Koto sent Kim Long on a mission to find and to purchase bomb-making material.

When the Cold War had ended, several new sources of enriched uranium became available on the black market. Pakistan, in its arms race against India, provided a logical source of enriched U-238 and plutonium. But after the fall of the USSR, new sovereign states, such as Kazakhstan and Uzbekistan, also might provide bomb-making material.

Koto's plane, with Holly Chandler aboard, was still in the air on its way from Los Angeles to Tokyo when Kim Long placed an encrypted satellite call to Koto.

The plane's overhead intercom crackled to life. "Mr. Koto, forgive the intrusion, but I have an urgent call for you from Kim Long," the pilot said.

Lee Koto lay asleep on the compartment's king-sized bed. He reached for the phone and pushed the speaker button.

"Yes!" Koto said abruptly.

"Mr. Koto," Long's high-pitched, nasally voice echoed throughout the compartment. "I signed a contract with a man who can supply the merchandise you seek."

"Excellent; that is indeed splendid, Long. You accomplish much in so short a period of time." Koto smiled inwardly. "Please accept my admiration. You will be well-rewarded."

"Mr. Koto, it is always a pleasure to serve you. If you like, I am ready to give you the details."

Koto cut him off. "That would not be wise now. Please meet me on the Island of Hinua as soon as you can. I will hear the details there," Koto said.

"Yes, sir. I will be there in two days." Long hung up the phone.

Toki looked at Koto as he hung up the phone. He smiled and said, "We will soon have the entire world at our doorstep. And you, my most trusted and lovely work of art, will grace my throne." Koto reached up and pushed a button beside the phone.

Quickly, the door opened and Han appeared. "Mr. Koto?" he said.

"Inform the pilot that we will refuel in Tokyo and then fly on to Hinua."

"Yes!" he replied and silently closed the door.

56

HINUA ISLAND

With very little headwind, they made the flight to Tokyo in near record time. Koto's plane touched down at Tokyo's Narita Airport and taxied to the company hangar. The plane sat quietly on the tarmac as the service personnel, dressed in white jumpsuits, white rubber boots, and white helmets, scurried around and through the plane like a small army of ants. Customs officials approached the plane and talked with the pilots. Once they learned that Mr. Koto was aboard, they stamped the paperwork without entering the aircraft. A fresh crew boarded to replace the pilots and the flight attendants.

To assure an untraceable flight to Hinua Island, the pilot filed a new and erroneous flight plan. The flight termination listed a private airport, owned by Koto International, in southern Japan. Koto's airport would falsely and intentionally report his on-time arrival in southern Japan.

As the plane sat on the ground in Tokyo, Holly began to stir and to move against the restraining straps of the stretcher. Although she was not yet conscious, the nurse suspected that she would soon awaken.

"How is she?" Koto asked.

"She has started to move some. In several more hours, she may awaken. The question is whether she will have brain damage or not," the nurse stated.

Holly could hear the conversation. However, it sounded a long way off. The voices seemed to come from the distant twilight. Who was talking? She was not certain. Who were they talking about? She was not sure. Where was she? She did not know. Then she heard more voices and her mind strained to understand. Her mind did not comprehend completely what had happened to her.

"Lee," Toki said, "may I remain in Tokyo?"

"I'd prefer that you come with me to the island," he answered.

"It's been a very long time since I've been home. There are some things I need to do. If I could remain for just a few days, then I could join you there." In a very polite manner, Toki pleaded her case.

Holly slowly reached a higher level of consciousness. She realized the arm restraints made protesting useless. Holly quit fighting her straps and appeared to sleep peacefully. However, she listened intently.

"I suppose you do need a few days," Koto replied to Toki.

Holly recognized Koto's voice.

"But you must join us on the island by Friday. One of my planes will fly you to Hinua Friday morning," Koto concluded.

"You are too kind. Your servant, Toki, will be there on Friday."

"Charlene," Koto called.

Holly heard Koto's voice again.

"Yes, Koto," Charlene answered.

"You will assume Toki's duties until Toki returns from Tokyo."

"Yes, Mr. Koto," she answered, "as you wish."

Holly thought, *Charlene! That sounds like her, but ... her voice seems different ... detached.* Holly's comprehension was confused. It was Charlene's voice, but something had happened. Charlene's voice appeared much more submissive. *I must remember,* she thought. *But what do I remember?* Her mind desperately tried to make sense of her surroundings. *The noises—maybe I am in a factory. The smell—was it the smell of kerosene? Yes! It smells like jet fuel. What am I doing at an airport and strapped down? What's the last thing I remember? Try! Think!*

Suddenly, the door closed and the engines started. The plane began to taxi from the hangar.

Holly's stretcher began to vibrate. She was on an airplane; she knew that with certainty. Holly's mind struggled to remember. Disjointed thoughts swirled in her head. Maryland . . . the phone call . . . a funeral . . . San Francisco . . . Bill! Where is Bill? Panic seized her.

"Mr. Koto, I think she's waking up," the nurse said.

He unbuckled his seatbelt and walked forward to look at Holly lying on the stretcher. She appeared to be unconscious as before.

"Well, maybe not, but soon," the nurse said.

Koto returned to his seat and buckled his seatbelt.

Holly lay quietly. Slowly, thoughts from the last few weeks worked their way to her conscious brain. *Ned Litten, of Litten Industries, died, and Bill inherited his business. The last thing I remember, I disrobed in the bathroom at the Pacific Heights mansion in San Francisco. I heard a sound or something, then all went black. Now I'm strapped down in an airplane. Why? Why do I hear Charlene's voice and who is Toki? Why is someone saying something about brain damage? I think I'll feign amnesia and pretend that I can't speak. That's going to be my plan, not much of a plan, but a plan.* Holly felt the plane accelerate, lift off, and climb. *Now where are we going? And Bill, where is Bill?* Holly fell asleep before the aircraft reached cruising altitude and headed toward Hinua, a small island near Hainan, China.

When Holly awoke, she lay in a bed surrounded by white mosquito netting. As she looked about the room, she saw the windows encased by plantation shutters. Through their open blades she saw tropical tree leaves and gigantic Bird of Paradise plants. A gentle breeze moved the mosquito netting above her. Pungent air of mold and of decomposed vegetation contrasted with the fragrance of tropical flowers and of salt air. The small bruises on her arms hurt from the intravenous needles. She knew she had lost weight. *What a way to diet!* she thought, as she patted her flat stomach. She felt sore, weak, and stiff as she slowly swung her legs over the edge of the bed and sat up. The room twisted like a merry-go-round, and she felt nauseated. Holly tried to orient herself to time and to place. She saw the sun through the window. *Okay,* she thought, *it's daytime. But where am I?* Like a movie playing in slow motion, she recalled the conversations she'd heard on the airplane. With great effort, she stood on wobbly legs and hesitantly took a step; she fell backward onto the bed, and let out an, "Ugh."

The door opened and Charlene entered. "Holly! Oh, thank goodness, you're awake!" Charlene said.

"Who? What—?" Holly stammered. "Who are you? Where am I?"

"Holly, dear," Charlene said soothingly, "you've been sick. You're in a place to rest and to recuperate."

"Sit . . . chair . . ." Holly uttered.

"Yes, let me help you." A white rattan chair sat near an open window. Charlene practically carried her across the room and eased her into it.

Holly settled into the chair and gripped the arms tightly with her hands. She gazed out the window, expressionless and emotionless. The house sat on the side of a mountain surrounded by jungle. Below the window, she could see a bay or lagoon and the azure sea beyond. The vegetation left no doubt that this house was in the tropics. She heard chatter and observed dark forms moving through the trees. *Possibly monkeys,* she wondered. Suddenly, a small green lizard scurried along the window ledge and then sat perfectly still. She recognized it. *A gecko. Am I in the South Pacific or in Asia? If so, then how did I get here? Maybe I'm dreaming . . . no, the needle tracks in my arms, the way my head feels, my weight loss, and my weakness, no, Holly Chandler, you're not dreaming.* Holly looked at the hospital bracelet on her right wrist. A second bracelet encircled her wrist just below it. It did not look familiar. She touched it. It was real. All of this convinced her, this was not a dream. Her plan, to fake amnesia, presented one obstacle. She wanted answers. "Who are you?" she asked Charlene, hoping to keep up the charade.

Charlene put her arms around Holly's neck, hugged her, and said, "Oh, Holly, darling." Then she held Holly's hand, "Oh, my poor Holly. I'm Charlene, your friend Charlene. Don't you recognize me?"

Holly felt uncomfortable with the closeness and tenderness Charlene displayed.

She pushed her away. "Where am I?" she demanded.

"You're at a peaceful island to recuperate from your horrible experience and your terrible illness," Charlene said. "I'm going to get you something to eat." Charlene left the room.

Holly heard her close the door and lock it. She pulled herself out of the chair and leaned on the windowsill. She walked unsteadily around the room. She knew she had to regain her strength. It was important to eat well and exercise if she hoped to survive or to escape.

"Mr. Koto! She's awake!" Charlene yelled and then descended the stairs to the large open foyer.

Koto sat on the porch that surrounded three sides of the mountain villa. Large French doors gave easy exit to the veranda.

Charlene approached Koto and knelt at the side of his chair. Her metamorphosis, from dominatrix to servant, had completed itself on the flight from the United States. Pleasing Koto became her desire.

"Excellent, I'm glad that she is awake. I can now make plans to contact her husband," Koto said as he absentmindedly stroked Charlene's long hair. "Kim Long should be here later today," he said aloud. *This rare beauty is valuable both as my sexual entertainer and as my private assassin,* he thought. *However, she is not an intellectual giant.* Still, Koto had to admit that after her sexual inhibitions were released, he had never seen any other woman with her sexual appetite and enthusiasm. He decided to keep her around longer than he had initially planned.

Koto walked to the edge of the veranda. He leaned on the rail and surveyed the cove below. The time to play his hand had arrived. He called San Francisco and reached Larry Cotting.

"Cotting here."

"Mr. Cotting," Koto said, "Mrs. Chandler is missing, and I know where she is."

"Missing?" Cotting questioned. Larry raised his eyebrows, glanced at the phone, and signaled for Phyllis to pick it up and monitor the call.

She took her notepad out and began to write.

"I wasn't aware Mrs. Chandler had disappeared. I know it's been several days since they've been to the office. We, I mean, I just assumed they wanted a long weekend," Cotting said.

"Her disappearance is of little consequence to you. I want you to understand that I am preparing to acquire Litten Industries. I expect your cooperation and your support." He stopped and looked at the ocean again. "May I count on that, Mr. Cotting?"

"Mr. Koto, you know that Phyllis and I are ready to do anything that you need." Larry smiled at Phyllis, who returned the smile and gave him a high five sign.

"I appreciate that, Mr. Cotting. I need you to find the computer disk with Mr. Litten's private files. That is the most important thing you can do now. Do you think you and Phyllis can do that for me?"

"We'll do our best, Mr. Koto," Larry promised.

"I'm certain you will, Mr. Cotting. You understand how vital that information is, don't you?" Without waiting for an answer, Koto ended the call. He then turned to Charlene. "Come here."

She rose from the floor and walked to Koto.

He looked into her cat-like green eyes.

"You will leave for San Francisco in a few days. I have a crucial job for you."

"Will you and Toki come too?" Charlene asked.

"No, this is something you do exceptionally well," Koto said.

"What would you like from me that I haven't given, Mr. Koto?" she questioned.

"I want you to kill Mr. Cotting and his girlfriend."

"As you wish," she answered and then bowed in reverence to her master.

57

BILL'S SEARCH—SAN FRANCISCO

Unknown to Bill, as he and Useph fought to the death, Koto's plane, with Holly aboard, left US air space and headed for Japan. Bill cleaned the office and hurried back to Charlene's apartment. He rang the bell. He looked at his watch as he rang the bell a second time. *Strange, six thirty in the morning and no answer,* he thought. He rang a third time and waited; only silence filled the hallway. Fear descended on him like an avalanche. He kicked the door. It shuddered, but held. He stepped back and kicked again. This time, the bolt gave way and the double-door entrance to the apartment swung open. The silence of the empty apartment coldly greeted him. Bill raced through every room and threw open the doors to the bathroom and to the closets. There were no clothes and no linens in the closets and there was no food in the kitchen. Even the well-stocked bar sat empty. A bitter hollow feeling flooded over him as if some unseen hand had pierced his heart with an arrow. Holly was gone. He rushed down the stairs and drove back to the warehouse.

While John and Randy drank coffee and reviewed Holly's research database, Bill burst through the door.

"She's gone!" Bill screamed.

"Gone? Who's gone?" John asked.

"Holly. Holly's gone, Charlene's gone. Someone scrubbed Charlene's apartment. It's like no one ever lived there," Bill exclaimed.

Randy and John looked at each other questioningly, but said nothing.

Bill slumped into a chair and buried his face in his hands. He felt utter and complete exhaustion as he rocked back in the chair and stared at the ceiling. He tried to formulate a plan. He now possessed the disk. Besides ownership of Litten Industries, it was the item that both Mr. Smith and Lee Koto wanted. All he could do now was pray that whoever kidnapped Holly would keep her safe and would want to negotiate.

"Gentlemen, I found the disk," Bill announced.

John looked at him, handed him a cup of coffee, and said, "What can we do, Bill?"

Bill took the thumb drive from his pocket and handed it to Randy. "Tell me what's on this and make me a copy."

"Right, Boss." Randy took the drive and walked to a computer on another table. "Can we use this to get Mrs. Boss back?" he questioned.

"I sure hope so," Bill answered quietly.

For the next two days Bill, John, Randy, and Sam looked for Holly throughout San Francisco. They replayed all the Tel-Ray communications that had been recorded earlier. They checked all of the hospitals in the San Francisco area. Bill filed a missing person's report with the police department, which sent out a bulletin, but they did not suspect foul play because she now had a history of a drug overdose with an admission to General Hospital and a record of checking out AMA.

They had reached a point of desperation when Bill's satellite phone rang. "Chandler!" he barked.

"Dr. Chandler, how very nice to talk to you again," Lee Koto said. "We haven't spoken for several days. Have you considered my offer?"

"I'm a little busy at the moment, Mr. Koto. Maybe later," Bill replied cryptically.

"I understand; maybe I'll have an offer modification for you shortly. May I call you on this number later?"

"I'm a little busy," Bill reiterated. He had expected a ransom demand, not a call from Koto. He wanted to get Koto off the phone. His objective was to find Holly, not to sell Litten Industries.

"Until later then," Koto said with a mocking intonation in his voice. *He has no idea I have his wife!* Koto thought with elation.

Bill hung up the phone and stared at his friends hopelessly.

A small light on one of the computer monitors started to blink. The screen went from power-save mode to active mode.

"John!" Randy called. "Window-peeper-one just came to life."

John shook his head; he disliked the child-like names Randy gave to his Tel-Ray monitoring stations. John looked back at Bill and said, "Randy decided to take Tel-Ray a step further. Each unit now operates remotely. The unit activates when it senses conversation or movement of data. It turns on and captures the signal. Then the information is encrypted and is automatically downloaded to us here." He looked at Bill. "So we don't have to babysit the equipment, and there is much less chance of being discovered."

Randy rushed up and said, "Activity in Cotting's place." His fingers flew across the keyboard; an audio icon appeared on the screen. "We have telephone contact." Randy punched a few more keys. The conversation began:

"Cotting here."

"Mr. Cotting, I have news for you that might help with the acquisition of Litten Industries. I know that Mrs. Chandler is missing and I know where she is."

"Missing? I wasn't aware Mrs. Chandler disappeared. I know it's been several days since they came to the office. We, I mean, I just assumed they wanted a long weekend."

"Her disappearance is of little consequence to you. I want you to understand, I am preparing to acquire Litten Industries. I expect your cooperation and support. May I count on that, Mr. Cotting?"

"Mr. Koto, you know that Phyllis and I are ready to do anything that you need."

"I appreciate that, Mr. Cotting. Finding the computer disk with Mr. Litten's private files is the most important thing you can do now. Do you think you and Phyllis can do that for me?"

"We'll do our best, Mr. Koto."

"I'm certain you will, Mr. Cotting. You understand how vital that information is, don't you?"

The line went dead.

Bill, Randy, and John looked at each other in shocked silence.

"Well, at least we know someone who knows where she is," John said with an upbeat tone in his voice.

"Sure, we do. Koto has her. He could have her anywhere in the world!" Bill looked crushed. "I guess he won."

"Why's that?" John asked.

"I have the disk. I have the company. But he's got Holly."

"So, Boss," Randy said, "why don't we just go and get her?"

"Randy, you may not know it, but Koto owns property all over the world. She's been gone long enough to be halfway around the globe by now. How in the hell do you suppose we'll just go and get her?" Bill asked sarcastically.

"Uh, John, you didn't tell him?" Randy looked at John accusingly.

Embarrassment spread across John's face and he shook his head no.

"Didn't tell me? Didn't tell me what?" Bill asked.

"We can pinpoint her now, if you want us to," John said as he talked faster and faster. "Gosh, I'm sorry, Bill. I didn't even think about tracking her bracelet when you said she was missing. It didn't even occur to me. I'm really sorry."

"Randy, get the tracking started," John ordered. "I'll work on the disk."

Randy pulled a small laptop from a briefcase which sat beside the table.

John continued, "Bill, when I went to see Holly just before we left Charlene's apartment, I slipped a tracking bracelet on her wrist. I didn't ask you. I'm sorry. I don't know why I did it. I gave her a necklace with a tracking chip when we first arrived, but she wasn't wearing it. I thought they took it from her in the hospital, so I slipped the bracelet on her before I left Charlene's apartment."

Bill grabbed John by the shoulders and gave him a bear hug. "John, I love you!" he shouted as he squeezed him.

Embarrassed, but happy, John smiled.

They both moved behind Randy as he initiated the program. "This will take some time and money. I'll have to buy time and work from multiple satellites." Randy looked at Bill and asked, "If you were to bet, do you think he has her on the West Coast? If not, which way do you think he went?"

"You have the authority to buy as much satellite time as needed. Use the standard account from Chandler Electronics. I can reimburse it from my personal account later," Bill said. Then he added, "If she isn't in the United States, I'd bet on Asia. Try West," Bill replied.

"Well, like I said, this will take a while. So why don't you get me something to eat? I'm starved. Hopefully, I'll have something by the time you get back." Randy went to work in earnest.

58

KOTO'S PRIZE—HINUA ISLAND

Kim Long flew commercially from Pakistan to Hanoi, Vietnam, and arrived late in the evening. One of Koto's helicopters then transported him to Hinua Island.

Charlene entered Holly's room and said, "I have to leave for a few days on business. Don't worry; you'll be well taken care of."

Holly feigned amnesia and pretended to fall asleep as Charlene spoke. She heard Charlene mumble to herself as she left the room, "Damn, what if we gave Holly too many drugs and she's permanently brain damaged?"

A Japanese steward dressed in a white waiter's jacket walked to Holly's room and served her dinner on gold-rimmed china. He left and relocked the door.

Holly, famished, ate everything on the plate. Night was descending over the island when Holly heard a helicopter arrive outside her window. The rotor blades of the helicopter gradually spun down and the sounds of the jungle returned to her bedroom. Holly hurried to her window and strained to see the machine that sat on its pad below. Thoughts of escape surged in her head. Then, aloud, she said, "Escape? I don't even know where in the world I am. Even if I could escape from this room, where would that get me?" Suddenly she saw Charlene in the landing lights that surrounded the helicopter. Charlene carried a small suitcase as she stepped into the craft. Holly watched as the chopper lifted off. *Well, Charlene, you obviously weren't my friend, but you are really the only person who knows I'm here. I think I'm sorry to see you go,* she thought to herself. Holly softly walked across the room and lay down on the bed. Still exhausted from her ordeal, she quickly fell asleep.

Meanwhile, Kim Long entered the living room, escorted by one of the house servants.

Koto sat at his desk reading a book. A small desk lamp cast an eerie glow over the upper part of his chest and face.

Kim Long loved and respected his employer and master, but he also feared him.

"You have news for me?" Koto asked without looking up.

"Yes!" Kim answered. "I concluded the business in Pakistan for the items you requested. The price they asked was within a few dollars of your estimate."

"That's excellent. If the price was too far off, I would conclude that they did not know their product or it was of inferior grade." Koto paused and looked at Kim; the triangular beam of light shone only on Koto's chest. This gave Koto the appearance of having no head. "When may I expect shipment?" his disembodied voice asked.

"The material is being loaded in northern Pakistan as we speak. It will to arrive in Karachi in two days. One of your planes is standing by in Karachi. The money transfer will take place as soon as the plane is airborne."

Koto cut him off in midsentence. "I'm confident your arrangements are sound. When can I expect its arrival here?"

"Is this where the device will be assembled?" Kim asked.

"Yes; does that bother you?" Koto questioned.

"No; I assumed it would be safer to do it here than anywhere else. You will have it in two and a half days."

"You have done well, Kim Long." Koto stood, took Kim by the arm, and escorted him to the veranda. "I consider you my most trusted aid."

He paused long enough to let Kim's ego process that information. Then he continued, "Now, I have something new that I need you to do."

"I am ready to do whatever you ask," Long answered.

"Mrs. Chandler, Dr. Chandler's wife, is our guest. I want you to meet Dr. Chandler in America. He will have a computer disk, and you will take a contract for him to sign. I must have the disk and the contract regardless of the difficulty."

"Consider it done," Kim replied. "But, sir, it does not sound like a difficult task. Why do you believe it will be a challenge?"

"Dr. Chandler is a resourceful man and a dangerous man. I suspect he desires to obtain his wife's release without giving up the company or the information. I must have the data that is on the computer disk. He claims he does not know where it is. I do not believe him."

"Mr. Koto, I will leave immediately," Kim replied. "I will come back with what you want."

"First, we will dine together. Afterward, you will have your picture taken with Mrs. Chandler so Dr. Chandler is convinced she is well and is still alive."

Together they walked around the veranda to the dining room, where the evening meal awaited.

"By the time you get back, my project will be finished and will be ready for Washington," he said with veiled anticipation in his voice.

The plans for Koto's ultimate vengeance gained strength daily. He felt a warm sensation of satisfaction churn throughout his body. *Toki will be here in two days. I want her!* he thought.

59

THE CALL—SAN FRANCISCO

By the time Bill and John returned with food, Randy's disposition had sunk to near despair. He worked frantically on the keyboard, clearly frustrated.

"Have you gotten the location yet?" Bill asked hopefully.

"Trouble, Boss," Randy muttered while he continued to work.

"What's the problem?" John demanded like a disappointed father. "I thought this was your baby. You claimed it could find a gnat in a hurricane. Why can't you find Holly?"

"LOOK, JOHN!" Randy countered back, "Locating the signal is hard enough, but I get no response from two of the satellites, and I don't even know if you turned the bracelet on when you put it on her wrist. For that matter, how in the hell do we know that she still has it on?"

"Yeah, you're the computer expert! Go ahead and say it's everyone else's fault because you can't get the signal right."

"Hey, guys. Cool down!" Bill snapped. "Randy, I know this isn't easy. I know that you'll do your best work and find her. Okay? Just take your time and do it like any other project. You know, when we're in a research project, if we get in a hurry, we screw up. Do it like it was a regular project. You know how to debug a program. Use your expertise, not your emotion! Here, take a break and have something to eat."

They sat down at the table and began to pick at the burgers and fries. Their thoughts focused on finding Holly's location.

Bill jumped as his cell phone rang.

"Chandler."

"Dr. Chandler," Koto said smoothly. "It's so nice to talk to you again."

"Cut the bull," Bill tersely answered.

"Don't get tense, Dr. Chandler. By now I am certain you suspect she is my guest. Mrs. Chandler is doing fine. In fact, I can assure you, she awoke yesterday. She is resting and eating well."

"I want to talk to her," Bill demanded. He pointed at some electronic equipment on one of the tables.

John rushed to the equipment and started a trace on the call.

"What you want is not important. Maybe you can speak with her at another time. However, she is asleep at this hour anyway. I'm certain you'd not want to awaken her."

Sleeping now? Either she's still sick or she's not in this time zone, Bill thought. "So, if I can't talk to her, why the call?" Bill asked.

"My emissary, Kim Long, is on his way to you. Give him the disk and sign the papers he will have, for the sale of Litten Industries. Mr. Long will arrive in San Francisco the day after tomorrow."

It'll take until the day after tomorrow? They must be coming from a long way off. Japan? Is that where she is? Bill thought. "I told you the last time, the sale of the company is no problem, but so far, we've found no disk that would be of any use to you or anyone else."

"Well, Dr. Chandler, you have two days to find it. The company without the disk is of no use to me. Either I get both," he paused for effect, "or Mrs. Chandler will simply disappear from the face of the earth."

"How do I know she is alive right now?" Bill demanded.

"I will send my emissary, Mr. Long, with a picture of Mrs. Chandler and himself holding today's newspaper. That proves she is alive." Koto's voice became cold and metallic in quality. "Whether she stays alive is entirely up to you." The line went dead.

"The call was scrambled and rerouted so many times there is no way to track it," John said. "Sorry."

"Nice try," Bill's anguished voice replied.

Randy encouraged him. "Hey, Boss, I feel a lot better after eating. I'll find her. It's just a matter of time."

"Thanks, Randy," Bill said. "Let's stay concentrated on a line either side of Japan, north pole to south pole."

The door opened and Sam walked in. He looked around the room and said, "Now this looks like a wake."

"Yeah, we just missed finding Mrs. Chandler," John answered.

60

LARRY AND PHYLLIS—SAN FRANCISCO

Two hours after she left the island, Charlene boarded a plane from Singapore bound for San Francisco.

Charlene's plane was still two hours out of San Francisco when the workday ended for Larry and Phyllis.

"It seems kind of strange," Phyllis remarked as they rode the elevator down from the executive suite.

"What seems strange?" Larry responded.

"Chandler called and canceled his entire day. You'd think his wife would come in and check on things if he didn't feel well."

"Maybe she stayed home to take care of him," Larry remarked.

At that comment, Larry pulled Phyllis close and kissed her.

"Hmm," she moaned softly into his ear at the end of the kiss. "Want to stop by my place on your way home?"

"What did you have in mind?" he asked.

"I don't know, lawyer Cotting, what do you have in mind?" she teased.

"Oh, I thought I might have some dinner." The elevator car stopped; Larry dropped his hand to his side as the elevator door opened at the executive parking level.

"Let's have dessert first, then go out," she cooed.

"I have a better idea," Larry replied. "I know an excellent Italian restaurant. Let's stop there and then go to your apartment."

Phyllis smiled approvingly and said, "That sounds fantastic."

On the drive to the restaurant, she let her hair down and it draped onto her shoulders. She then unbuttoned the top two buttons of her dress and exposed a single small diamond on a chain, which she knew would draw his eyes to her cleavage.

Located in the waterfront section of the city, the Italian mom and pop restaurant held only eight tables, each with a red and white checkered tablecloth and a wine bottle for a candle. The cracked and faded plaster on the walls displayed a few faded pictures of Italy.

Larry, fidgeting with his cappuccino, concentrated his attention on Phyllis. No longer the matronly executive secretary, she looked entirely different to him tonight. "You're beautiful," he whispered to her.

"Thank you," she said and bent her head demurely.

"No, I really mean it. I don't know how I walked past you all those years and did not realize how beautiful you are." He looked into her eyes and he wanted her. "Phyllis, you have made me come alive," he said.

"Larry, you were so busy you never stopped to look or to smell the roses." She smiled and continued, "But I wasn't really in the mood for a relationship. After my divorce, I never thought I'd want to be with another man, except for social reasons. I wanted no emotional entanglements; I liked my job, and it provided more income than I needed. I didn't want to become dependent on anyone. I found the prospect of relying on a man again frightening." Then she whispered, "Until I met you."

Larry took her hand gently into his and they sat quietly.

Later, they walked out of the restaurant arm in arm. Larry said, "Spend the night at my place?"

"Oh, I can't," she minimally protested. "I don't have anything with me: clothes, nightgown, makeup—you know, girl stuff."

"I don't care; you won't need a nightgown anyway," he replied.

"Now that sounds enticing," she said and laughed an intriguing laugh.

"I have a better idea. We'll go by your apartment and you can pick up what you need, within reason of course."

"Of course," she parroted. "And then?"

"We'll spend an incredible night." He squeezed her hand.

After they stopped at Phyllis's apartment, they drove toward Larry's place; at the same time, Charlene's plane entered its final approach to San Francisco International Airport.

At the airport, Charlene quickly cleared Immigration and Customs. She traveled with only a carry-on, and with nothing to declare at customs, she headed for the rental car counter and rented a nondescript two-door sedan. *It's time to get back to basics. Don't stand out. Search out the target, know the target, get the target,* she thought. Charlene was back in her element. Her thoughts were no longer focused on Toki or Koto. Her total concentration was on her job. She drove to a rented locker. This familiar drop-site held the tools of her trade. She selected the appropriate weapon, then drove toward Phyllis's apartment.

At Phyllis's apartment building, Charlene pushed the buzzer. No answer. She tried again. Still no answer. Next, she pushed several buzzers. No one answered, but the electric gate clicked and swung open. She walked in and closed it.

Phyllis's apartment faced the street on the third floor. Charlene took the stairs. She decided to make it simple. Get the woman to answer the door, snuff her with a small caliber silenced revolver, then slip back down the stairs. After that, move on to Cotting, and then leave town. She planned to drive to Los Angeles International Airport, dispose of the gun along the way, drop the car, and fly back to Japan. A quick and easy hit. If all went well, tomorrow afternoon she would board a plane for Japan. Another job well done.

Charlene approached the door. First, she listened for noise in the apartment. Everything was quiet. She knocked on the door; silence from the apartment greeted her. Charlene wore a coat with large sleeves that allowed easy, uncomplicated concealment of the gun in her hand. She knocked again.

A door opened, but it was the one next door. "She ain't home," a slightly overweight woman in her forties or fifties said. The woman wore a stained housecoat and scruffy slippers. She appeared disheveled and spoke with an alcohol slurred voice.

"Oh, do you know where I could find her?" Charlene asked, cursing the fact that someone had seen her at Phyllis's door.

"Why, are you a bill collector?"

"Oh, goodness no; I'm her cousin from San Diego. I came to San Francisco unexpectedly; I wanted to surprise her."

"Well, you'd sure have surprised her a couple hours ago," she replied with a smirk. "That's for sure."

"Oh?" Charlene asked innocently.

"Yeah, her and that new boyfriend of hers were in there. They were makin' noise like no one else in the world existed. Don't get me wrong. I don't mind folks having a good time, mind you, but you'd think they'd have some sort of decency. I mean, what if some young kids heard all that carrying on."

Charlene tried to smile and act somewhat embarrassed at the reference to their sexual frolicking. "You don't know where they might have gone, do you?"

"They probably went over to his place." She slammed the door, which indicated the conversation was over.

"You're just jealous," Charlene said aloud as she headed for the elevator. *Phyllis obviously has a nosy neighbor. I wonder if the woman used a glass against the wall to listen, or did she have a physician's stethoscope?.* Charlene no longer had a reason for secrecy; that had disappeared with the nosy neighbor. *It's best to kill them somewhere else,* Charlene thought.

Charlene drove to Larry Cotting's building. She parked a block down the hill, then walked. She approached the doorman outside. *I've been seen twice since leaving the airport. Nothing is going well tonight,* she thought.

"Good evening," he said as he opened the door for her.

A concierge sat behind a stainless steel and glass desk. "May I help you?" he asked.

"Uh, I'm going to Larry Cotting's," she answered.

He looked at her. "Take the elevator to the twenty-eighth floor, turn right, and it's the last door on the hallway. Would you like me to announce you?"

"No, thank you; I'm expected. Thank you, though," she answered.

An alarm went off in her head. *I should do this later, but if they're together, I can get it over all at once,* she thought.

Charlene entered the elevator and pressed the button for the twenty-eighth floor. Before she stepped from the car, she took her weapon from her handbag and again concealed it in the sleeve of her coat. The thick hallway carpet muffled her footsteps. She stopped at the door and pressed the buzzer.

Inside the apartment, Larry was in the bathroom. Phyllis stood on the patio and enjoyed the night air. She wore only a short robe tied at the waist and held a glass of wine in her hand.

The doorbell rang again.

"Can you get that? I'm shaving," Larry called.

Phyllis walked to the door and looked through the peephole. She saw a tall woman with blonde hair standing in the hallway. She opened the door. "Yes?" Phyllis asked.

There were two high-pitched metallic pings as Charlene fired the silenced semiautomatic twice.

The first bullet went straight through Phyllis's heart and lodged in her spine. The second bullet ripped the aortic arch. She died before she fell onto the marbled floor. The wine glass shattered and the red wine mixed with her blood.

Charlene stepped through the door and closed it.

"Who is it?" Larry called as he walked into the bedroom. "Did you drop something?"

Charlene moved toward the sound of his voice.

Larry opened the bedroom door and saw Charlene approaching him with a gun in her outstretched hand. He slammed the door, locked it, took two steps, and dove beside the bed. From under the bed, he pulled a twenty-two caliber semiautomatic pistol concealed in a hidden compartment.

Charlene stood beside the door and tried to turn the knob: LOCKED! She aimed at the knob and fired. The door lock exploded. Quickly, she kicked the door and it swung open. Silhouetted in the doorway, she entered the room.

Larry fired; the first bullet entered her upper chest and splintered her left collarbone. His second shot missed her.

Charlene fired; however, the wound to her shoulder threw off her usual deadly aim. The bullet hit Larry in the upper right chest. Although his lung collapsed, it was not a fatal shot.

Larry fired again and hit her in the neck; the bullet tore Charlene's jugular vein.

Blood flowed down her neck and chest as she put the final round into Larry's brain just above his right eye. She pressed her hand to her neck wound to try to stop the blood flow. Charlene staggered across the living room. At the patio door, she left a bloody handprint on the glass before she fell forward to the patio railing. Her vision narrowed; she felt dizzy and cold. She held the railing with a bloodied hand. Charlene leaned forward to get more air into her lungs. Suddenly, her body went limp and she tumbled over the railing. She fell twenty-eight floors onto the top of a delivery truck.

The doorman rushed into the building and screamed, "Call the police!"

61

BILL CHANDLER AND KIM LONG—SAN FRANCISCO

Bill watched Randy work on the program and on the satellite communications. After a few minutes, he found it too tedious and turned away.

John tried to open the disk that Bill had found in the office after the fight with Useph. The directory revealed several files, all password-protected. His computer ran a program to identify passwords, but so far this had been unsuccessful.

Bill's knowledge that Koto held Holly captive weighed heavily on his mind. "I have to get out of here," he told the others. "I'm going to the house. When anything breaks, give me a call." He slipped on a leather jacket. To Bill, it felt like an eternity, even though it was now only three days since she had disappeared. He stopped at the door. "Hey, guys," he said. They all looked up. "Thanks." He then stepped through the door into the cool evening air.

Bill drove to Ned's house and stopped in front of the garage. He opened the garage door and surveyed Ned's collection of cars and motorcycles. In the back corner sat an old black Harley-Davidson motorcycle. It looked like one James Dean rode in his movies in the fifties. He checked the gas and oil and climbed aboard. "I haven't ridden a Harley for years," he said aloud. "I'll bet I can't get Holly on one of these when she gets back." Bill then clenched his jaw and added, "When she gets back, and you're dead, KOTO!"

After several attempts with the kick starter, the engine roared to life but quickly sputtered and died. Bill dismounted and began to tinker with the engine. Soon, the mechanics of the classic Harley-Davidson motorcycle occupied his mind. Three hours later, he had just put the last bolt back into the machine when his phone beeped.

"Chandler!"

"Dr. Chandler, I am Kim Long. I believe Mr. Koto mentioned me."

"Yeah, he mentioned you." There was no formality or diplomatic tone in his voice.

"My plane lands in San Francisco in two hours."

Bill checked his watch; it was nine thirty. "So?"

"I would like to meet you as soon as possible. Is there somewhere you would suggest?" Long asked.

"Why don't you stop by the house when you get into town?" Bill figured the sarcasm was probably lost on Koto's stooge, but what the hell?

"I was thinking of something more public. It's not that I don't trust you, but . . ."

"Okay," Bill replied and thought, *maybe the sarcasm was not lost on him.* "I get the picture. There is an all-night restaurant down by Fisherman's Wharf. The name of the place is Tony's Bar. I'll wait for you there."

"That sounds fine, Dr. Chandler. Tony's, near Fisherman's Wharf, in about three hours." The line went dead.

Bill immediately called Randy. "Any luck?" he asked hopefully.

"I can tell you about a million square miles where she isn't. That's the bad news, but the good news is the program is debugging itself as we go along. That means it will run faster and faster the longer we use it," Randy answered.

"Good work, Randy. Please put John on the phone."

"John here, what can I do for you?" he asked.

"John, I just had a call from Kim Long. He's about two hours from landing in San Francisco. Tell Sam I'm to meet Kim Long at Tony's Bar about twelve thirty. He can follow him from there."

"Right, I'll get Sam on it. He's getting grumpy as he watches us byte-heads at work. I'm afraid he's going to shoot one of our computers," John answered.

Sam scowled at him.

John laughed.

When Bill hung up the phone, he threw his leg over the seat of the Harley and kicked the starter. The machine rumbled to life. He let the clutch out slowly, and the machine eased into motion. Once outside, he closed the garage door and dropped the Harley into low gear. Bill roared down the brick drive and onto the glistening black asphalt heavy with dew. The cold wind in his face and the power beneath him put life back into his spirit. He coursed through the deserted streets toward the Golden Gate Bridge. *Just enough time to really road test this thing before Long gets here,* Bill thought.

He crossed the bridge and entered Marin County. His mind started to rev like the high-performance camshaft in the engine. Two items became cemented in his brain: one, the meeting with Long would be pivotal. And two, he would give Koto the disk, but he would never give him the codes. However, the problem of Holly's return remained unsolved.

Bill returned to San Francisco and settled into a booth at Tony's twenty minutes before Kim Long was scheduled to arrive. Bill chose the back booth after he ordered a cup of coffee. Only two other men sat at the counter. Sam was one of them. The other man looked like a fisherman. When Kim Long walked through the door, the men at the counter looked up and then looked back down at the flat counter surface pitted with cigarette burns and years of spilled coffee.

Kim walked to Bill's booth. "Good evening, Dr. Chandler."

Bill nodded his head and motioned to the seat with his hand.

"I hope the hour is not too late for you. Since I changed so many time zones, it makes little difference to me," Long stated.

"You came through so many time zones?" Bill asked.

"Yes, I just flew in from Japan. However, you are an intelligent man; you knew that already, didn't you?" Kim quipped.

Bill said nothing.

Kim slid into the booth.

Bill noticed Kim's briefcase. "I believe you have something for me." Bill made it a statement, not a question.

Long reached inside his jacket pocket. As his hand entered the coat, Bill tensed and wondered if a gun would appear instead of a picture. Slowly Kim pulled out a picture and slid it across the table toward Bill. The picture showed Holly and Long holding yesterday's Singapore newspaper. The lighting in the photo was bright, most likely due to the flash. Holly wore a white bathrobe that accentuated her colorless complexion.

It took all of Bill's resolve to keep his hands from shaking as he picked up the picture.

"As you can see, she is alive and well," Kim said.

"That's only a picture; I want to talk to her."

"That was not what Mr. Koto said to you on the phone."

Bill bent forward, "Look, you little slime-ball, I don't give a damn about you or Koto. I want my wife back, and you are here to negotiate. Now, we can do it one of two ways, hard or easy. Statements like you just made will make the negotiations hard. Do you get the gist of what I'm saying?"

Kim exercised control of his voice, but he was unaccustomed to threats, and his face revealed his anger. "Dr. Chandler, I am simply an employee of Mr. Koto. I am certain he would have no problem trading my life for your wife's life. Do you know what I'm saying?" he asked. "I believe Mr. Koto wants a particular computer disk, and he wants you to sign the contract for the sale of Litten Industries. Mr. Koto is certain that you have the disk; I have the contract."

"Give me the papers, and I will sign the agreement," Bill acknowledged. "However, I don't have the disk. We've looked everywhere and have not located it, if it even exists," Bill stated, then sat quietly.

Kim had not been expecting Bill to deny that he had the disk. He reasoned that this American would never gamble his wife's life, so he must not yet have found it. "Then I guess we have no further business to discuss now. When you locate the disk, I'll be at the Waterfront Towers Hotel. You may contact me there." He slid out of the booth, handed the briefcase containing the contract to Bill, and headed for the door.

While Bill and Kim talked, Sam finished his coffee and left the diner. When Long left, he was not alone. Sam shadowed him all the way to the hotel.

Bill returned to the warehouse. "How's it going, Randy?" Bill questioned.

Randy remained completely engrossed in his computer. "All systems are up, and I don't think there's any more debugging to do."

"Why don't you search in Japan and work your way west?" Bill suggested.

"Right, Boss," Randy answered. "Ya got an idea?"

"This picture looks tropical. I suppose it could be Florida or South America, but knowing Koto, I doubt it."

Fifteen minutes later Randy shouted, "Bingo! I got her, Boss!"

Bill and John ran over to the computer terminal. A small red dot blinked. Randy did a split screen and brought up a Mercator Map of the world. He magnified it repeatedly until the dot corresponded to the Island of Hinua.

"China?" Bill asked.

"Yep, she's in China," Randy answered. "Near the border of Viet Nam."

The phone rang and interrupted the moment. "Chandler here."

"Mr. Chandler," Sam said, "that Japanese feller checked into the hotel over by the Sausalito ferry landing. Went up to his room an' he ain't come out. Do you want me to stay here or what?"

"No, I think he's settled in, so get back here. I need you for something special," Bill said. He began to formulate a plan.

"John, set a remote Tel-Ray unit on Kim Long as soon as possible," Bill said.

62

THE ISLAND OF HINUA

Perched precariously on the edge of a volcanic cliff, Holly's prison had panoramic views of the jungle, the beach, and the ocean. From her window, she could see a path that sloped to the water's edge, where a substantial pier extended into a protected bay. The cliff, below her window, dropped several hundred feet to the beach. In many ways, the scene reminded her of the cliff Ned Litten had driven over the night he died. Holly began a regimen of exercise in her room and ate everything they brought. Holly knew she could not escape on her own, but she wanted to be as strong as possible if rescue came. She vowed never to lose hope. *Bill will find a way to save me,* she thought.

The sound of a key inserted into the door lock brought her back to her present reality. The door opened and an attractive Asian woman walked into the room. "How are you feeling?" she questioned.

Holly stared at her with a noncommittal gaze.

"Mr. Koto would like to know if you are well enough to have dinner with him tonight."

"I'd prefer to eat with roaches," Holly answered.

"Then you must be feeling better," Toki replied as she threw some clothes onto the bed.

Holly said nothing.

"I believe you'll find these fit. Someone will come for you in an hour. Be ready. Mr. Koto does not like to be kept waiting."

"I don't like being kidnapped. So I guess there are things in this world people don't like," Holly answered with contempt.

Toki turned, walked back to the threshold, and said, "An hour." She then closed and locked the door.

Holly looked at the clothes and then looked at the hospital gown she wore. "Well, it'll be a change of wardrobe," she said aloud as she picked up the clothes and walked into the bathroom.

Precisely an hour later, her door again opened. A Chinese man, wearing jungle camouflage clothing and a holster, entered the room. He said nothing but pointed to the doorway. When Holly did not respond quickly, he unsnapped his holster and drew the gun. He pointed at the door with the barrel of the weapon, and then at Holly.

She obediently walked to the door.

Using the gun as a pointer, the guard then directed her down a flight of stairs, along the main hall, and into the dining room.

If this were a five-star hotel and Bill and I were here together, it'd be a perfect setting, Holly thought to herself as she looked through the open French doors and saw a full moon cast its light across the bay.

"Good evening, Mrs. Chandler," Lee Koto said as she entered the room.

Holly glared at him and said nothing.

"I'm glad you are well enough to join us for dinner." He gestured to Toki. "You have met my assistant, Toki, I presume."

"We've met," Holly answered.

"Please have a seat," Koto said as he sat down at the head of the table.

The guard took a step toward Holly.

Holly quickly turned on her heel, walked to the table, and sat to the left of Koto.

Toki took the chair to the right.

They ate in silence throughout most of the meal. As coffee was served, Koto spoke, "I hope you don't find your stay with us too uncomfortable. I am, as we speak, transacting business with your husband that will secure your return to the United States and to him."

"Mr. Koto, I am acutely aware that you want to buy Litten Industries from Bill. However, don't you think kidnapping is a little severe in the negotiating process? As I clearly remember, about a week ago, you made a not so veiled threat to harm him," Holly replied. "Your negotiating skills seem primitive for a successful businessman."

"It is true; most of the time I don't find this a very useful tool. However, in any business negotiation, one must occasionally use special opportunities that arise. I did not drug you or try to kill you. I trust you are aware, there is another group trying to get control of Litten Industries. However, when you were presented to me," he paused, "well, let's just say, I took advantage of the situation. I do hope you understand."

Holly did not understand. The last thing she remembered before waking up in the tropics was the bathroom at Ned's San Francisco house. "I don't have any idea what you are talking about."

"It doesn't really matter as long as you are my guest on Hinua. I sincerely hope that you will be comfortable here. If there is anything you need, please request it. Since we are the only people on this island, I will unlock your door as a gesture of my sincerity. You may come and go as you wish. I assure you, there is no way of escape. You see, a particularly nasty species of shark inhabits these waters, so I doubt that you will want to swim in the ocean. However, I have an Olympic-sized swimming pool in the back that you may use whenever you like. If there is any clothing you need, please ask Toki." With that, he and Toki stood up and left the room.

Holly sat alone at the long dining room table for several minutes. Then she went to a phone in the foyer and picked it up. There was no dial tone. She returned to her room.

Koto and Toki walked into his bedroom. He sat in a chair; she stood beside him and looked out the door. "I think it was a mistake to bring her here, Lee," Toki said.

"In business, sometimes you must take chances; and sometimes you must seize an opportunity that presents itself," Koto answered.

Later that night, Toki lay tormented on her bed. The ache in her heart for Gregg Newman overpowered her. She felt she must do something. She did not blame the Chandlers for Gregg's death. She blamed Koto. She rose from her bed and prepared herself. In a ceremonial manner, Toki applied traditional Japanese makeup and styled her hair. She then selected the most elaborate kimono from her closet. The wide belt around her waist concealed her intended surprise for Koto. When she completed her preparations, she lighted incense and said a prayer to the gods. Silently, she glided down the hallway toward Koto's room. Toki slipped into Koto's room without his knowledge. The room was dark. The ceiling fan's blades gently stirred the air. She could hear him breathe softly as he slept. With the carefulness and the gracefulness of a ballet dancer, she advanced across the room toward Koto's bed.

Suddenly, the light on his nightstand sprang to life.

Toki froze in the middle of the room.

"You wanted to see me?" Koto asked as he questioningly looked at her formal attire.

For several seconds, Toki said nothing. Then she replied, "I hoped you were not asleep, Lee. I want to talk to you. I am truly sorry if I awakened you." She took several more steps toward his bed. Toki could feel the cold steel of the hidden knife.

"Stop right there!" Koto said. "Let me look at you." He studied her for several seconds. "My Toki, you become more beautiful every year. What a change from the young girl I rescued in Kamakura so many years ago. I wonder," he continued, "have you become more lethal also?"

"Mr. Koto, you are most generous with your words, but I only know what you taught me. You instructed me in business and you instructed me in vengeance."

"Are you here for business? If so, then come to my bed," he answered.

She stood still. "I wanted to talk to you about the Chandler woman," Toki finally said.

"Yes, what about the Chandler woman?" Koto questioned.

"Do you really intend to give her back to her husband?"

"That depends on him. If he gives me what I want, then yes, I will give her back to him. If he does not, then no. He will never know what happened to her."

"He should never see her again," Toki hissed.

"Why not?"

Toki's eyes riveted on Koto. "I believe you know the answer to that," she said.

"You wouldn't be referring to the man you toyed with in Las Vegas. I believe his name was Gregg Newman, wasn't it?" Koto replied.

"Yes, it was Gregg Newman, and I did not toy with him. I loved him! Chandler killed him, and so I intend to kill Chandler's wife." The words flowed out like venom from a serpent. "He deserves to know the pain I live with every day. I want him to live a long life without her."

"At this point in time, Toki, that would not be a good business decision. After I have obtained the codes from Dr. Chandler, then, if you still feel that way, you may kill Mrs. Chandler. However, I don't think you will."

"Koto, you are the one who taught me vengeance. You will not be the one to keep me from it." She advanced a few more paces toward Koto. "I demand—"

"You will demand nothing." Koto's words cut her off sharply. "You will do as you are told and obey me. You see, Toki, I own you, just like I own all my possessions. I knew you had fallen for that soldier of fortune. I sent him to you. He was to seduce you and to keep track of you in the United States. I had not planned to use him against the Chandlers; someone else did that. When I realized that you had fallen in love with him, I was not unhappy that he met his demise. You see, I did not like his use of *my* property." Koto lay back on the bed and stretched his arm over his head.

At that moment, Toki wrapped her fingers around the dagger and pulled it out. The light on the nightstand caused the razor-sharp blade to gleam. She lunged at Koto.

Koto's fingers encircled the hilt of a samurai sword which hung on the wall above his bed. Before Toki could reach him, Koto swung the sword. The tip of the blade neatly sliced her neck and cut the carotid artery and the jugular vein. Blood spurted over her face and dress. She dropped to the floor at the side of Koto's bed.

Koto looked down at the dying woman and said, "You had one fault, Toki. You cared."

63

THE BOMB—HINUA ISLAND

Holly, awakened by a sudden flash of light, jumped from her bed. The whap, whap, whap sound of a helicopter's blades echoed in her head. She crossed the room and pushed the shutters open. A helicopter was landing.

Two men carefully slid the craft's cargo door open and pulled something to the opening. A small forklift approached, then gently lifted a metallic case from the chopper. The forklift then disappeared into the darkness. As quickly as it arrived, the helicopter lifted off and left the island.

The forklift slowly drove up an asphalt path through the jungle. At the hillside, a set of steel doors blocked the road. The lead man stopped and entered a code into the keypad. The doors quietly slid open and revealed a large tunnel that penetrated the mountain. Fifteen feet inside lay a set of narrow gauge rails where a small flat-car waited. As it neared the flat-car, the forklift stopped. Two men carefully lifted the box, placed it on the flat-car, and secured it. An electric engine pulled the car several hundred feet into the volcanic mountain to a large laboratory. The enriched U-238 arrived safely at Koto's bomb assembly plant.

Koto had invested more than $100 million erecting the laboratory. Initially, he had considered the use of either nerve gas or a biological agent for his final act of vengeance, but the memory of his mother's fate in Hiroshima drove him like a tsunami toward the use of a nuclear weapon.

The scientists and technicians conversed among themselves in Russian. As Lee Koto approached, they drew silent.

"Professor Rostinoff, I have delivered the enriched U-238," Koto said.

"Yes, Mr. Koto. It arrived much more quickly than I expected," Rostinoff answered.

"How long will it take to assemble the device?" Koto asked.

"We must machine the chamber, manufacture the firing mechanism, and shape the core. That will produce the maximum efficiency for the device. If all goes well and we have everything we need, I would estimate it should be ready within two to three days at the most," Rostinoff stated confidently.

"That is good," Koto answered.

"You provided a laboratory superior to anything we ever saw in the Soviet—in Russia. It will not take long." He paused for a moment. "Mr. Koto, may I ask you a question?"

Koto looked at him and nodded his head.

"How and where do you plan to use the bomb?"

"The answers to those questions, Professor, are my secrets alone," Koto replied as he exited the laboratory.

64

THE DISK—SAN FRANCISCO

John worked for seven hours without a break and without success. The program, securely protected by a password program, seemed to be unbeatable. Looking at the computer screen, John shook his head in frustration.

Bill walked up behind him. "No luck?" he asked.

"Nothing. I've tried everything I can think of, and I've run every hacking program I know. I even tried some of the old ones I used when I was a teenager. Nothing seems to work." He looked at Bill and said, "Sorry."

"Why not take a break and let your brain cool off?" Bill suggested.

"There's a signal from that Kim guy's place," Randy said.

"Let's hear it," Bill answered.

They moved to the system that monitored the Tel-Ray.

Koto's voice said, "Kim?"

"Yes!" Kim said.

"Ah, Kim. How are things in San Francisco?" Koto asked.

"I met Dr. Chandler as soon as I landed. He is ready to deal and says he has the papers signed for the sale of Litten to you, but—" Kim paused.

"But what?" Koto demanded.

"He said to tell you he hasn't yet found the disk. He doesn't know where Mr. Litten hid it."

"Do you believe him?"

"Yes, I believe him," Kim answered.

"And why would you believe him?"

"I don't think he cares about the company. He would sell it quickly, but I do not believe he would risk his wife's life on a lie," Kim answered.

"I believe you are right. I had dinner with Mrs. Chandler. She is a woman most men would cherish. However, we must have the disk. The item you obtained in Pakistan arrived and is nearly complete as we speak. I need the information on the disk. My surprise must be aboard the correct airplane.

"I understand, Mr. Koto. I will not let you down," Kim answered. "I have other news for you also," Kim Long said.

"What is that?" Koto asked.

"There is a story in the news of a triple killing. Larry Cotting, Phyllis Monroe, and Charlene Dominic were all killed at Mr. Cotting's apartment last night."

"That is excellent news," Koto answered.

"I will talk to Dr. Chandler immediately," Kim Long responded.

"I will call you later," Koto replied and broke the connection.

"Well, just what do you make of that?" John asked.

Bill looked at his friends and wondered what they thought of him. Kim Long did not think Bill would risk Holly's life. Unfortunately, that was exactly his plan. However, he knew the stakes in this game were too high to do otherwise. He felt the vice grip of guilt squeeze his chest. Bill wondered whether he had developed a heart as hard as Koto's. Now he had placed Holly's life in the balance. "John! We don't have much time left! You have to crack that disk's code. Please John," Bill pleaded and walked toward the door of the warehouse. Outside, he headed along the pier to Sam's boat.

John looked at the computer. "Damn it! What's the code?" he said out loud.

"Have you tried that?" Randy asked.

"What?" John growled.

"Damn it," Randy answered trying to break the tension.

"Unless you have a good idea, keep it to yourself!"

"Hey, John, I'm just saying, maybe you're getting too complicated. Bill grew up with Ned and told us that Ned was somewhat of a free spirit."

John turned to the computer. The screen showed **********, and he tapped the enter key. The screen blinked and suddenly began to display the file names. He clicked on the first one, and it began to open. "GOT IT!" he shouted.

"You're kidding!" Randy rushed to his side and looked at the screen. "What was it?"

"You're not going to believe it—HICHANDLER," John answered.

Sam worked on the crane that accidentally dropped Gregg Newman into the Pacific Ocean as Bill walked toward the boat. Bill stepped onto the boat and looked up at Sam. "Hi, Sam," he said.

Sam gave up on the rusted bolt and looked down at Bill. "How are the whiz kids doing in there?"

"No luck yet," Bill answered.

"Do you really think this disk is the key to solvin' the plane crashes?"

"I hope so; it is the only link I can find. If it isn't, we've wasted a lot of time," Bill said as he looked past Sam and saw a freighter slowly wind its way toward the Golden Gate and the mouth of the San Francisco Bay. "Whether we get the disk opened or not, I'm going after Holly. I could use you, if you want to come along," Bill said.

"This Koto guy, he's pretty smart?" Sam queried.

Bill nodded.

"An' near as we can tell, he's holdin' her on some island he owns?"

Bill nodded again.

"An' most likely, he has a small army of some kind there?"

"I'd bet on it," Bill answered.

"Sure, why the hell not?" Sam replied with a grin.

"Sam, I don't want you to think I'd lie to you. The chance of success is slim, and the chance of getting killed is high," Bill said.

"Ah, hell, Doc; them guys there don't have any idea what they're up against. We'll git her back." He smiled at Bill. "There are worse things than bein' killed doing somethin' ya believe in." He stood up and looked Bill squarely in the eyes. "We're goin' to git her back. You can make book on that." He paused. "Do ya have a plan or do we just storm the beach?"

"I have satellite photos of Hinua, along with maps and charts. They show a bay with a deep-water dock on the island's northwest corner; it's just below a house that sits on a cliff. I suspect there's not much of a tide in the area. It's not a floating dock. The south end of the island has a beach surrounded by a coral reef."

"Doc, I'm the sailor; why don't ya give me those pictures and I'll git us on that piece of rock, if that's what ya want. After that, it's just a matter of takin' the hill and gettin' the lady back. A piece of cake," Sam said.

"HEY, BOSS! HEY, BOSS!" Randy yelled as he ran down the pier. "WE GOT IN! WE GOT IN!"

All four men sat in silence as John brought up page after page of information about the Special Project planes. The disk contained the identification of the aircraft by company, nationality, and registration number. It also had the airframe serial number. Each file gave the bomb's location on the plane. Highlighted in red were the transmission frequencies and an alternate frequency for each unit. The file also included information about booby traps, in case someone discovered the bomb. Without that information, it would be impossible to disarm any of the planes.

Bill let out a long whistle and said, "I don't think anyone had any idea about the destruction possible with these planes. Technically, Ned really did a good job on these planes. I'm sorry he was my friend!"

"Now that we have decoded the disk, what do we do with it?" John asked.

"First, copy that damn disk, then change each of the transmission codes!" Bill emphatically said.

"Consider it done," John answered.

"Next, we set up the trade. There's absolutely nothing we can do until Holly's safe," Bill said resolutely.

Sam raised his eyebrows and said, "Yer not goin' to give that Koto feller all this, are ya?"

"I'm going to give him the information, but not in a way that will do him any good," Bill answered.

"Where are we going to make the trade?" John asked.

Bill smiled. "Let's do it right here—San Francisco in broad daylight on the cable car."

65

THE TRADE—SAN FRANCISCO

Bill had John take the original disk and change the transmission frequency codes. A few minutes later, he contacted Long.

Kim Long answered the phone, "Hello."

"Long, this is Bill Chandler. I found the disk," Bill said. "I want the trade in forty-eight hours. That should give you time to bring Holly back to the States." Bill laid out his requirements for the exchange.

He wanted Holly, Koto, and Kim Long to ride the cable car from the downtown terminal toward Fisherman's Wharf. He set the time for eleven thirty in the morning. Bill said he would simultaneously take a cable car coming from the opposite direction. When the cars passed each other, Bill would disembark and step onto the car Koto and Kim Long rode on. At that time, Holly and Long would disembark and cross to the car Bill just departed from. Then Bill would give the briefcase that contained the disk and the signed contract for the sale of Litten Industries directly to Koto. The only two conditions were: first, Lee Koto must accompany Holly; and second, Bill would step off his cable car only when Holly was away from Koto. They transmitted the terms to Koto.

"Mr. Long, as usual, you have done an excellent job," Koto said. "The only change I will request is that it be done in seventy-two hours. I must have the transmission code of the aircraft that will carry my bomb to

Washington. It will take that long to have the bomb ready. While I sit with Dr. Chandler, I will load the disk into a computer to transmit the signal. It will be a source of great joy for me to do it in his presence."

The automated Tel-Ray transferred the conversation directly to the warehouse. Unfortunately, it was encrypted; they could not immediately decipher it.

The phone rang. "Chandler here."

"Dr. Chandler," Long's voice sounded as if it were dipped in honey, "Mr. Koto accepts most of the conditions for the exchange, with only a couple minor changes. He requests seventy-two hours, and he wants the frequency of a specific plane that belongs to World Wide Air Rentals. Please copy down the airframe number and the detonation code on a sheet of paper. It must accompany the disk."

Koto wants that? Bill wondered what scheme Koto planned.

"Dr. Chandler? Are you still there?" Long asked.

"Yes. Why does he want a code?" Bill questioned.

"If he sees the correct airframe number, then he will know the disk is authentic," Lee explained.

"Uh . . . yes . . ." Bill stalled for time. He had to think. "Forty-eight hours here in San Francisco—what's the problem with that schedule?"

"Unfortunately, there is a storm that will delay their departure from the island. I can assure you that your wife is in good spirits and is in no immediate danger."

"I want to talk to her," Bill demanded.

"That can be arranged, if you will agree to Mr. Koto's terms," Kim answered. "She will call you at this number in two hours, after I talk to Mr. Koto." The line went dead.

"What's the deal?" John asked.

"They agreed, but they want seventy-two hours and a specific plane's airframe number and its detonation frequencies. It's an airliner that belongs to a rental firm."

"If we could decipher that last phone call, we'd have our answer," Randy said.

Bill and John looked at him and nodded.

"Okay," Randy replied. "I'll get right on it."

The call from Holly was very short, but not sweet. She told him she was alive and she did not know where she was. Then the line went dead.

The next few days passed sluggishly.

In a small Greek restaurant the night before the trade, Bill, John, Randy, and Sam gathered around a table. They shared a pitcher of beer before ordering food. Bill looked at his friends who had stood with Holly and him during the last month. "Let's go over the plan one more time." He took a drink of the cold beer.

"Sam, you will be on the cable car with me coming from Fisherman's Wharf. At the exchange, wait for Holly to get on. You will then take her and make tracks for the warehouse."

"And if Koto has someone come with her?" Sam asked.

The steel-hardened-look in Bill's eyes gave Sam his answer.

Bill then looked at John. "You'll get on the cable car at the downtown terminal with Holly, Koto, and Long. If Koto has anyone else along, you will have to take care of him. Do you think that will be a problem?"

"Maybe for that person; not for me," John replied.

He then turned to Randy.

"I know, I'll be waiting in the warehouse; and as soon as Holly and Sam arrive, I'll signal you. Right?" Randy preempted Bill's instruction. "Don't worry, Boss, we'll get her back."

"After the exchange, I will ride with Koto until I hear from Randy," Bill said.

"Got it," John answered.

That night, Bill hardly slept. Now it was only two hours until the trade. Bill signed the papers for the sale of Litten Industries to Lee Koto for one hundred seventy-five million dollars, payable over ten years. The paperwork seemed very simple. With Larry Cotting dead, he decided to ignore the terms of the contract. He wanted Holly back and did not care about money or Litten Industries. He knew that John had sufficiently altered the disk and rendered the transmission codes useless; however, he also knew that production on new planes for future bombings was inevitable once Koto controlled Litten Industries. Therefore, he assumed that while he and Holly would be happily reunited, their life spans following the reunion would be sadly short.

66

VENGEANCE IS MINE—SAN FRANCISCO

Intermittent rain pelted San Francisco the morning of the exchange. A low fog and a cold drizzle hung over the bay and completely obscured the bridge, Marin County, and Alcatraz. Few tourists, and only the hardiest of natives, took the cable car that day. A black stretch limousine coasted to a stop near the cable car turnaround. The occupants looked through the window at the cable car as the cable car driver dismounted and began to push it around for the return trip. There were three people in the queue waiting to board.

Koto nodded at his driver; he immediately got out and opened the back door. The driver held an umbrella as Lee Koto stepped from the automobile. Kim Long pushed Holly's shoulder and urged her out of the car. Koto walked under the umbrella and did not offer it to Holly. The people in the queue boarded the cable car as they approached. Koto went into the interior and sat on one of the seats that faced forward. Long seated Holly on one of the side seats that faced the street; he then sat down beside her.

Kim leaned toward her. "When we see the car coming from the wharf, you and I will get off and cross to it. Dr. Chandler will get on this car," Kim whispered into her ear. "You will not acknowledge him or try to reach him. When Mr. Koto is satisfied that he has what he wants, he will call me and I will let you off the cable car. Do you understand?" Kim asked.

"Yes." Holly gave him a one-word answer.

"If you try to do otherwise, I'm afraid I will have to kill you." He pushed the barrel of a small semiautomatic pistol into her side. Though he kept it hidden in his pocket, Holly had no doubt that it was real and that Kim would use it.

The bell clanged twice, and the car jerked into motion. Holly felt the tension mount and she shivered. *Would they trade? Would they let her and Bill live after the trade? If so, how long would their lifespan be?* Finally, the car crested the hill and started down the steep slope toward Fisherman's Wharf. The rain increased. Holly's shoes and feet were wet and cold. She looked beyond the front of the cable car. Streaks of rainwater on the glass blurred the view and made it look like a surrealistic painting. Then she saw the cable car coming up the hill in the opposite direction. *That must be the one Bill's on!* she thought excitedly.

Lee Koto looked out the window and saw Bill standing on the cable car's side running board. Bill held on by one hand. In the other hand, he held a briefcase. Koto smiled.

Kim Long turned and looked at Koto and saw him nod. He took hold of Holly's arm and forced her to stand up.

The rain pelted her face and her hair. The water ran down her neck; she shivered again. Now she could see Bill. The cars were within one hundred feet of each other. Bill, Kim, and Holly each stepped from the cars at almost the same instant. Koto was so engrossed in the exchange that he did not see John move from the back of the car to the seat behind him.

Koto's car arrived first; Bill grabbed the leading rail and stepped onto the running board. He watched Holly and Kim board the opposite cable car. Holly now traveled back toward the downtown terminal. Bill slowly walked to the seat in front of Koto and sat down.

"Dr. Chandler, delighted to see you again," Koto sneered.

"Cut the crap, Koto. What you want is in here." Bill handed him the briefcase.

Koto almost shook as he took it. He had won the valued prize. He opened the case and looked at the documents that lay in the bottom. Bill's signature appeared on the appropriate line. A thumb drive, in a small plastic container, lay in the corner.

Koto smiled and fingered the thumb drive. "You've done well, Dr. Chandler."

"Call your man and tell him to let Holly off at the next corner," Bill demanded.

They reached the bottom of the hill at Ghirardelli Square; the car stopped abruptly with a screech of the metallic breaks. Neither Bill nor Koto stood. John remained seated behind Koto.

The driver walked up the aisle. "Usually you must get off while I turn the car, but if you're going back to town, just sit still since it's raining so hard." He dismounted and started to turn the cable car around.

"Just what are your plans?" Bill questioned.

"Not that it really matters, but I intend to continue to sell the transmission codes to whoever might have a use for them," Koto said. "And I may use one or two myself." He leaned forward to whisper into Bill's ear. "You see; I have already used one. It was the United States trade mission airplane." He opened a computer and typed in the code he had requested. He would touch the enter key when he knew the plane was in the Washington, DC, airspace.

Bill clenched his jaw. "Why would you do that?"

"Well, it was an attempt to kill the president's wife, but I guess she was sick that morning and couldn't make the flight."

"What's the purpose?" Bill asked.

"I'll tell you, though I don't think you'll ever use the information. I wanted vengeance for my mother who was killed at Hiroshima," Koto answered. "But I'll have real vengeance in a few minutes. I'm going to use another code to detonate a nuclear device over Washington, DC."

Bill smiled inwardly; he knew the code he had written down wouldn't work. "Are you going to call and tell your man to let Holly go?" Bill questioned.

"No, I'm not, Dr. Chandler."

They each instinctively grabbed the seat back as the car lurched into motion again on its return trip.

"I didn't think so." Bill looked past Koto at John.

"Mr. Koto," John said.

Koto straightened up, attentive to the strange voice behind him.

"I don't know how to tell you this, but I have a gun and it's pointed right at your spine. If there's a call the Doc wants you to make, I think I'd do it," John said.

"I kind of wondered about that," Bill said. "So, your stooge, Kim Long, just found out that he has a gun pointed at his back. I wonder if he would take a bullet for you."

"I imagine he would," Koto answered smugly.

John pushed the gun barrel harder against the seatback.

"Well, what do you suggest?" Bill questioned.

Koto answered, "Call your man off. I will release your wife," Koto said.

"And where will you release her?"

"Somewhere in the world," Koto replied, "but don't worry, I'll give her a ticket home."

At that same moment, Sam walked up the center aisle of the now nearly deserted cable car Holly was on.

Holly and Kim sat on one of the open seats that faced out. Sam sat down beside Kim. "We can do this the easy way, or we can do this the hard way," Sam said to Kim.

"What?" Kim answered.

"The hard way then," Sam said as he brought the barrel of his .357 magnum down on Kim's head. Kim slumped immediately to the side. "Shall we go, Mrs. Chandler?" Sam asked as he took hold of Holly's arm and pulled her from the cable car.

"SAM!" Holly shouted as they raced toward the curb to avoid traffic. "You always seem to be there when I need to be rescued."

The cable car continued down the hill as the driver never realized one of his passengers was unconscious.

Sam looked at Holly. "Let's not stand around and answer questions." He hurried her around the corner and into his car. In seconds, they were out of sight as they disappeared into the mist and the rain.

Bill felt the vibration of the phone in his pocket. It signaled Holly's safe rescue from the other cable car. He turned to Koto. "I'll expect your call soon." He tried to keep his voice even, without emotion.

Three blocks away, a man walked along the street with his head down. He did this not to keep the rain from his face, but to hide his identity. He wore baggy pants, high top shoes, and a football jacket. He walked close to the street and looked into each car that he came to. No opportunity presented itself yet. He thought, *Rainy days are especially good, because some folks, especially wealthy women, leave their keys in their cars while they run into one of the shops along the street.* This block was one of his favorite places to steal cars. Then he saw his prize. Just ahead was a Mercedes sedan with the motor still running and the emergency lights flashing. He opened the door and slipped into the driver's seat. The smell of leather flooded his senses as he dropped it into drive, eased out of the parking space, and onto the deserted street. He looked into the rearview mirror; a flashing red light moved up quickly.

For several days, the police had been conducting a stakeout along this street because of the many cars stolen in this part of the city. They had been watching the man from the time he had stepped around the corner.

The thief pushed the gas pedal to the floor. The sudden acceleration on the wet pavement caused the car to fishtail. However, driving fast cars was his thing, and he easily had it under control as the lights of the pursuing police car dropped back. He turned the corner and noted a cable car ahead. If he could time it right, he would slip around the cable car on the right and disappear down a side street. He accelerated. There was excitement and fear in his stomach as the speedometer shot past sixty miles an hour. The tires lost traction and caused the car to swerve erratically as it rocketed up the street. He was within a few feet of the cable car when he veered to the right.

Lee Koto stood up as the stolen car turned the corner. He walked to the edge of the cable car and stepped onto its running board. The rhythmic ringing of the cable car's bell provided a backdrop to his final words to Bill. "You should have your wife back within two days, if all of our arrangements are in order."

Koto stepped off the running board and down onto the wet San Francisco street just as the Mercedes sped to the right of the cable car. The front bumper hit Koto and lifted him onto the hood. His shoulder hit the windshield. He slid across the car's top, onto the trunk, and then bounced off. He landed on the blacktop between the cable car rails. The trauma broke his ribs, collapsed his lungs, and punctured his heart. Lee Koto, in extreme agony, had about thirty seconds to live.

When the Mercedes impacted Koto, Bill swung down from the cable car. He walked to the curb. There lay the briefcase. Bill picked it up, walked to Koto's broken body, and knelt down.

Koto's right arm and right leg lay at a twisted angle, with white bone exposed through his torn clothes. Koto gasped for breath.

Bill could hear the wailing of the approaching police car.

Koto tried to talk, but all that came out were frothy red bubbles.

Bill looked intently into Koto's eyes and whispered, "Vengeance is mine; I will repay, saith the Lord."[1]

1 Romans 12:19, King James Version

EPILOGUE

The patrol car that chased the Mercedes slid to a stop ten feet from where Bill knelt beside Koto. The police officer stepped from his car and approached Bill.

Bill stood up. "I'm Bill Chandler." He extended his hand.

"Officer Stevens." He took Bill's hand and the men shook hands. The officer looked at Koto, then he looked at Bill and said, "Is he dead?"

Bill nodded his head yes.

"Stay here, please, I need to check on that one," the officer said as he pointed at the wrecked Mercedes that had slammed into a parked car. He walked toward the crumpled machine.

The car thief sat pinned behind the steering wheel. He did not move and was partially covered by the deflated air bag.

An ambulance was the next to arrive. The police officer waved the vehicle toward the Mercedes. The paramedics sprang from the ambulance with their emergency equipment.

The officer then returned to Bill, looked down at Koto's mangled body, and asked, "Can you tell me what happened?"

"Yes, I can, but I need to make a call to Homeland Security first. Is that okay?"

"Homeland Security?" the officer questioned.

"I know it sounds strange, but it really is important. There's a possible terrorist bombing that may happen shortly. Please," Bill pleaded.

"See something, say something," the officer said. "Go ahead, but you can't leave."

Bill pulled out his cell phone and dialed David Strong at Homeland Security.

"David Strong, Homeland Security, how may I help you?"

"David, Bill Chandler here," Bill said.

"Dr. Chandler, what can I do for you?" he asked.

"There's not much time; a commercial airliner is en route to Washington, DC. It is owned by World Wide Air Rentals and has a nuclear weapon on board. You have to stop it!" Bill said emphatically.

"Dr. Chandler, can you give me any details?" David questioned.

"The aircraft number is NC51426. I don't know which direction it is coming from, but it probably originated in Japan or somewhere in Asia. So I'd guess it's coming from the west or possibly from the north. It will not blow up like the French plane or the trade mission plane. Even though the plane is rigged with an onboard bomb, the codes have been changed. However, it does have a nuclear bomb on board. The man who sent it is dead. You have to stop that airplane," Bill replied. "There are also other assets involved which you will need to deal with later."

"I understand. I'll call you back." David broke the connection.

John walked up as Bill put his phone away. "Bill, are you okay?"

"Yes, get Holly and the others and I'll meet you at the Pacific Heights house." He handed John the briefcase. "Take care of this."

John walked away as other police cars arrived.

A police sergeant approached Bill and asked, "What can you tell me?"

"I can tell you about the wreck," Bill answered solemnly. "This man stepped down from the cable car, I assume without looking, and didn't see the car."

"I'll need a statement," the officer answered. "If you will wait a minute, I'll get something for you to write on." It was not a question.

Five minutes later, Bill handed the officer a short- written statement. "Here is my information," he said and handed the sergeant a business card.

"Thank you," he looked at the card, "Dr. Chandler. If we need anything else, we'll call you later." He then walked toward the Mercedes.

Bill hailed a passing cab for a quiet, but reflective, ride to the Pacific Heights mansion. He arrived before the others, so he opened the garage, walked over to the '57 Chevy, opened the door, and sat down. "Ned, it's over. I don't know how you got into this mess, but it is over." Suddenly he heard a car drive into the driveway. He slipped out of the Chevy and ran outside.

As the car stopped, Holly opened the door. She jumped out of the car and into Bill's arms. "Don't ever let go of me," she whispered, rested her head against his chest, and cried.

ABOUT THE AUTHOR

Walter B. Goff II, D.O., FACR lives with his wife in San Diego, California. He is a retired United States Navy Captain. His medical career includes several years as a small-town Family Practice physician and nearly twenty-two years in the United States Navy, first as a General Medical Officer, United States Marines 1st FSSG, then as a Diagnostic Radiologist. His awards include: the Meritorious Service Medal, three Navy Commendation medals, and the National Defense medal. He was Chairman of the Radiology Department, Naval Medical Center, San Diego, California, and Specialty Advisor to the Naval Surgeon General. He recently retired from the Scripps Clinic Medical Group in San Diego, California, where he worked for nearly eighteen years.

He and his wife, Sandra, have two children. Their daughter, Tiara Kruse, is married to Major G. Allen Kruse III USMC (RET.). They have two children, Savannah and Wendy. Walter and Sandra's son, Wayne Hamilton Goff, was killed in 2001.

Walter's hobbies are reading, road trips, gardening, and riding his Harley-Davidson Heritage Softail Classic motorcycle.

You may contact him by his Facebook page or wg0538@gmail.com.

CPSIA information can be obtained
at www.ICGtesting.com
Printed in the USA
LVHW03s2232050618
579730LV00003B/5/P

9 781936 487370